IMPERIAL

WOMAN

Pearl S. Buck

MOYER BELL
Wakefield, Rhode Island & London

Published by Moyer Bell

Third Printing, 1999

LIBRARY OF CONGRESS
CATALOGING-IN-PUBLICATION DATA

Buck, Pearl S. (Pearl Sydenstricker), 1892-1973,
Imperial woman / Pearl S. Buck.
       p.   cm.
1. Tz'u-hsi, Empress dowager of China, 1853-
1908—Fiction. 2. China—History—19th century—Fiction.
     I. Title.
PS3503.U19815   1991
813'.52-dc20   CIP
ISBN 0-55921-035-4 pb.   90-20531

Cover illustration is from a hanging scroll
depiction a palace, late Yuan Dynasty

Printed in the United States of America.
Printed in the United States of America.
Distributed in North America by Publishers Group
West, 1700 Fourth Street, Berkeley, CA 94710,
800-788-3123 (in California 510-528-1444); in
Europe by Gazelle Book Service, Falcon House,
Queen Square, Lancaster LA1 1RN, England.

Pearl S. Buck

Pearl Sydenstricker Buck was born in West Virginia and taken to China as an infant before the turn of the century. The daughter of Presbyterian missionaries, she lived with her family in a town in the interior instead of the traditional missionary compound. Buck grew up speaking Chinese as well as English, and received most of her education from, her mother. She received an M.A. from Cornell, and taught English Literature in several Chinese universities before she was forced to leave the country in 1932 because of the revolution.

She wrote eighty-five books and is the most widely translated American author to this day. She has been awarded the Pulitzer Prize, the William Dean Howells Award, and the Nobel Prize for Literature. She died in 1973.

A long, richly woven and to me, quite absorbing novel.
—The Nation

. . .The details of the secluded life in the Forbidden City, then political juggling of the court, and the increasing pressure from Western powers as the Manchu Dynasty breaks up—these contribute to the novels movement.
—The New York Times

A long novel with a holding and compelling interest.
—Kirkus

Mrs. Buck is a skillful advocate of Tzu Hsi's point of view and she makes out quite a case for her. *Imperial Woman* will probably rank among the best of Mrs. Buck's work for its memorable portrait of a woman in whom, says the author, good and evil mingle, "always in heroic dimension."
—Catholic World

Other Novels by Pearl S. Buck

Foreword

TZU HSI, the last ruling Empress of China, was a woman so diverse in her gifts, so contradictory in her behavior, so rich in the many aspects of her personality, that it is difficult to comprehend and convey her whole self. She lived in a crucial period of history, when China was struggling against encroachment while at the same time the need for modern reform was obvious. In this period Tzu Hsi was conservative and independent. She was ruthless when necessary. Those who opposed her feared and hated her and they were more articulate than those who loved her. Western writers, with few exceptions, describe her unfavorably and even vindictively.

I have tried in this book to portray Tzu Hsi as accurately as possible from available resources and my own memories of how the Chinese whom I knew in my childhood felt about her. To them she was the imperial woman. Good and evil mingled in her, but always in heroic dimension. She resisted modern change as long as she could, for she believed that the old was better than the new. When she saw change was inevitable, she accepted it with grace but an unchanged heart.

Her people loved her—not all her people, for the revolutionary, the impatient, hated her heartily and she hated them. But the peasants and the small-town people revered her. Decades after she was dead I came upon villages in the inlands of China where the people thought she still lived and were frightened when they heard she was dead. "Who will care for us now?" they cried.

This, perhaps, is the final judgment of a ruler.

I

Yehonala

I T WAS April in the city of Peking, the fourth month of the solar year of
1852, the third month of the moon year, the two hundred and
eighth year of the Manchu, the great Ch'ing dynasty. Spring was
late and the northern winds, carrying their load of fine yellow sand from
the Gobi desert, blew cold as winter over the housetops. Sand drifted
down into the streets, sand whirled in eddies and filtered through doors
and windows. It silted into corners and lay upon tables and chairs and in
the crevices of garments, it dried upon the faces of children when they
wept, and in the wrinkles of old people.

In the house of the Manchu Bannerman, Muyanga, in Pewter Lane,
the sand was more than usually tiresome, for the windows did not fit
tightly and the doors hung loose upon their wooden hinges. On this
particular morning Orchid, his niece and the eldest child of his dead
brother, was wakened by the noise of wind and creaking wood. She sat
up in the large Chinese bed she shared with her younger sister and
frowned when she saw the sand lying upon the red quilt like tinted
snow. In a moment she crept out softly from the bedclothes, so that she
might not awaken the sleeper. Under her bare feet she felt the sand on
the floor and sighed. Only yesterday she had swept the house clean, and
all was to be swept again as soon as the wind died.

She was a handsome girl, this Orchid, seeming taller than she was because she was slender and held herself erect. Her features were strong
but not coarse, her nose straight, her eyebrows clear, her mouth well
shaped and not too small. Her great beauty lay in her eyes. They were
long and large and exceedingly clear, the black and the white pure and
separate. Yet such beauty might have been meaningless except for the

I

natural spirit and intelligence that informed her entire being, although she still was very young. She was self-controlled, her strength apparent in the smoothness of her movements and the calm of her manner.

In the sand-gray light of the morning she dressed herself swiftly and noiselessly, and putting aside the blue cotton curtains that served as a door, she went into the main room and from that into the small kitchen adjoining it. Steam rose from the large iron cauldron set into the earthen stove.

"Lu Ma," so she greeted the serving woman. "You are early this morning." Self-control was in the extreme gentleness of her pretty voice, held resolutely low.

From behind the stove a cracked voice replied. "I could not sleep, Young Mistress. What shall we do when you leave us?"

Orchid smiled. "The Emperor's Dowager Mother may not choose me —my cousin Sakota is far more beautiful than I am." She looked behind the stove. Lu Ma was crouched there, feeding wisps of dried grass into the fire, making the most of every blade of the scanty fuel.

"You will be chosen." The old woman's tone was definite and sad, and emerging at this moment from behind the stove, she looked desolate, a small hunchbacked Chinese, her blue cotton garments faded and patched, her bound feet stumps, her face shrunken into a net of brown wrinkles outlined with pale sand. Sand lay on her gray hair and frosted her eyebrows and the edge of her upper lip.

"This house cannot do without you," she moaned. "Second Sister will not so much as sew a seam because you have always done everything for her. Those two boys, your brothers, wear out a pair of shoes apiece in every moon month. And what of your kinsman Jung Lu? Are you not as good as betrothed to him since your childhood?"

"In a manner we are betrothed," Orchid replied in the same pretty voice. She took a basin from the table and an iron ladle from the platform of the stove and dipped the hot water from the cauldron. Then, reaching for a small gray towel that hung on the wall, she put it in the water and, wringing it steaming dry, she wiped her face and neck, her wrists and hands. Her smooth oval face grew pink with the damp heat and she looked into the few inches of mirror that hung above the table. There she saw only her extraordinary eyes, lively and dark. She was proud of her eyes although she never allowed a sign of pride to escape her. When neighbor women spoke of her moth eyebrows and the leaf-shaped eyes beneath them she seemed not to hear. But she heard.

"Aie," the old woman said, staring at her. "I did always say that you have a destiny. It is in your eyes. We must obey the Emperor, the Son of Heaven. And when you are Empress, my precious, you will remember us and send down help."

Orchid laughed soft controlled laughter. "I shall be only a concubine, one of hundreds!"

"You will be what Heaven ordains," the old woman declared. She wrung the towel out of the water and hung it on its nail. Then she lifted the basin and went to the door and poured the water carefully on the earth outside.

"Comb your hair, Young Mistress," she said. "Jung Lu will come early this morning. He said that today he might be the bearer of the golden summons."

Orchid did not reply, but she walked with her usual grace into her bedroom. She glanced toward the bed. Her sister was still sleeping, the slight form scarcely rounded under the quilt. Quietly she unwound her long black hair and combed it through with a Chinese wooden comb, perfumed with the fragrant oil of a cassia tree. Then she wound her hair in two coils over her ears, and into each coil she put a small flower of seed pearls surrounded with leaves of thin green jade.

Before she had finished she heard the footsteps of her kinsman Jung Lu in the next room and then his voice, deep even for a man's voice, asking for her. For the first time in her life she did not go to him at once. They were Manchu, and the ancient Chinese law and custom, forbidding the meeting of male and female beyond the age of seven, had not kept them apart. She and Jung Lu had been playmates in childhood and cousin-friends when childhood was past. He was now a guardsman at the gates of the Forbidden City and because of his duty there he could not come often to Muyanga's house. Yet he was always here on feast days and birthdays, and at the Chinese feast of the Crack of Spring two months ago he had spoken to her of marriage.

On that day she had neither refused him nor accepted him. She had smiled her brilliant smile and she had said, "You must not speak to me instead of to my uncle."

"We are cousins," he had reminded her.

"Thrice removed," she had rejoined.

Thus she had replied without yes or no and, remembering now what had passed on that day, and indeed she thought of it always whatever she did, she put aside the curtain. There in the main room he stood, tall and sturdy, his feet planted well apart. On another day he would have taken off his guardsman's round cap of red fox fur and even perhaps his outer tunic, but today he stood as though he were a stranger, holding in his hand a packet wrapped in yellow silk.

3

She saw it at once and he knew she saw it. They caught each other's thought, as always.

He said, "You recognize the imperial summons."

"It would be foolish not to know it," she replied.

They had never spoken with formal address, nor used the courtesies and small talk of man and woman. They knew each other too well.

He said, his eyes not moving from hers, "Is Muyanga, my kinsman, awake?"

She said, not moving her eyes from his, "You know that he does not rise before noon."

"Today he must rise," Jung Lu retorted. "I need his signature of receipt as guardian in your father's place."

She turned her head and called. "Lu Ma, wake my uncle! Jung Lu is here and must have his signature before he returns to the palace."

"Aie-ya," the old woman sighed.

Orchid put out her hand. "Let me see the packet."

Jung Lu shook his head. "It is for Muyanga."

She let her hand fall. "Yet I know what it says. I am to go to the palace with my cousin Sakota nine days from now."

His black eyes glowered under heavy brows. "Who has told you before me?"

She looked away from him, her long eyes half hidden under the straight black lashes. "The Chinese know everything. I stopped yesterday on the street to watch their wandering actors. They played *The Emperor's Concubine*—that old play, but they made it new. In the sixth moon, on the twentieth day, the play said, the Manchu virgins must appear before the Dowager Mother of the Son of Heaven. How many of us are there this year?"

"Sixty," he said.

She lifted her straight long lashes, black above her onyx eyes. "I am one of sixty?"

"I have no doubt that in the end you will be first," he said.

His voice, so deep, so quiet, went to her heart with prophetic force.

"Where I am," she said, "you will be near me. That I shall insist upon. Are you not my kinsman?"

They were gazing at each other again, forgetful for the moment of all except themselves. He said sternly, as though she had not spoken, "I came here purposing to ask your guardian to give you to me for my wife. Now I do not know what he will do."

"Can he refuse the imperial summons?" she asked.

She looked away from him and then, her smooth grace accentuated, she walked to the long blackwood table which stood against the inner wall of the room. Between two high brass candlesticks, under the painting of the sacred mountain of Wu T'ai, a pot of yellow orchids bloomed.

"They opened this morning—the imperial color. It is an omen," she murmured.

"Everything is an omen now, in your mind," he said.

She turned to him, her black eyes bright and angry. "Is it not my duty to serve the Emperor if I am chosen?" She looked away from him and her voice lowered to its usual gentleness. "If I am not chosen, certainly I will be your wife."

Lu Ma came in, peering at one young face and the other. "Your uncle is awake now, Young Mistress. He says he will take his food in bed. Meanwhile your kinsman is to enter."

She went away and they heard her clattering in the kitchen. The house was beginning to stir. The two boys were quarreling in the outer courtyard by the street gate. In the bedroom Orchid heard her sister's plaintive call.

"Orchid—Elder Sister! I am not well! My head aches—"

"Orchid," Jung Lu repeated. "It is too childish a name for you now."

She stamped her foot. "It is still my name! And why do you stay? Do your duty and I will do mine."

She left him impetuously and he stood watching her as she put the curtain aside and let it fall again behind her.

But in that brief anger her will was set. She would go to the imperial city of the Emperor and she would, she must, be chosen. Thus in an instant she decided the long argument of her days. To be Jung Lu's wife, the mother of his children—many children there would be, for they were passionate, he and she—or to be an imperial concubine? But he loved her only and she loved him and something more. What more? On the day of the imperial summons she would know.

On the twenty-first day of the sixth moon month she woke in the Winter Palace in the imperial city. Her first thought was the one upon which she had fallen asleep the night before.

"I am within the four walls of the City of the Emperor!"

The night was over. The day had arrived, the great and momentous day for which she had secretly waited since she was a small child, when she had watched Sakota's elder sister leave home forever to become the Imperial Concubine. That sister had died before she could become the Empress, and none of the family had ever seen her again. But she, Orchid, would live—

5

"Keep yourself apart," her mother had said yesterday. "Among the virgins you are only one. Sakota is small and delicate in beauty and since she is the younger sister of the dead Consort certainly she must be favored above you. Whatever place is given you, it is possible for you to rise beyond it."

Instead of farewell her mother, always stern, gave her these plain words and they were alive in her mind. She had not wept when in the night she heard others weeping, fearful lest they be chosen on this day of the Emperor's choosing. For if she were chosen, and this her mother told her plainly, then might she never see again her home and her family. Nor could she so much as visit her home until she was twenty-one years old. Between seventeen and twenty-one there stretched four lonely years. Yet must they be lonely? When she thought of Jung Lu they were lonely. But she thought also of the Emperor.

That last night at home she had been sleepless with excitement. Sakota, too, was wakeful. Somewhere in the silent hours she had heard footsteps and recognized them.

"Sakota!" she had cried.

In the darkness her cousin's soft hand felt her face.

"Orchid, I am frightened! Let me come into your bed."

She pushed aside her younger sister, lumpish in sleep, and made room for her cousin. Sakota crept in. Her hands and feet were cold and she was trembling.

"Are you not afraid?" she whispered, cowering under the quilts against her cousin's warm body.

"No," Orchid said. "What can harm me? And why should you be afraid when your own elder sister was the Emperor's chosen one?"

"She died in the palace," Sakota whispered. "She was unhappy there—she was sick for home. I, too, may die."

"I shall be there with you," Orchid said. She wrapped her strong arms about the slender body. Sakota was always too thin, too soft, never hungry, never strong.

"What if we are not chosen into the same class?" Sakota asked.

So it had happened. They were separated. Yesterday when the virgins appeared first before the Dowager Mother of the Son of Heaven, she chose twenty-eight from the sixty. Sakota, because she was the sister of the dead princess was placed in F'ei, the first class, and Orchid in Kuei Jen, the third.

"She has a temper," the shrewd old Dowager said, staring at Orchid. "Otherwise I would put her in the second class of P'in, for it is not fitting to put her with the first class with her cousin and the sister of my

6

daughter-in-law, who has passed to the Yellow Springs. Let her be in the third class, for it is better if my son, the Emperor, does not notice her."

Orchid had listened in seeming modesty and obedience. Now, a virgin only of the third class, she remembered her mother's parting words. Her mother was a strong woman.

A voice called through the sleeping hall, the voice of the chief tiring woman, whose task it was to prepare the virgins.

"Young ladies, it is time to rise! It is time to make yourselves beautiful! This is your day of good fortune."

The others rose at once upon this summons, but Orchid did not. Whatever the others did she would not do. She would be separate, she would be alone. She lay motionless, all but concealed beneath the silken quilt, and watched the young girls shivering under the hands of the women servants who came to attend them. The early air was cool, the northern summer was still new, and from the shallow wooden tubs of hot water the steam rose in a mist.

"All must bathe," the chief tiring woman commanded. She sat in a wide bamboo chair, fat and severe, accustomed to obedience.

The young girls, now naked, stepped into the tubs and serving women rubbed their bodies with perfumed soap and washed them with soft cloths while the chief tiring woman stared at each in turn. Suddenly she spoke.

"Twenty-eight were chosen from the sixty. I count only twenty-seven." She examined the paper in her hand and called the names of the virgins. Each virgin answered from where she stood. But the last one did not answer.

"Yehonala!" the old woman called again.

It was Orchid's clan name. Yesterday, before she left his house, Muyanga, her uncle-guardian, had summoned her into his library to give her a father's counsel.

She had stood before him, and he, not rising, his large body clad in sky-blue satin and overflowing the seat of his easy chair, gave his advice. She felt an easy humor toward him, for he was negligently kind, but she did not love him, for he loved no one, being too lazy for love or hate.

"Now that you are about to enter into the City of the Emperor," he said in his oily voice, "you must leave behind your little name, Orchid. From this day you will be called Yehonala."

"Yehonala!" Again the chief tiring woman shouted and still she did not answer. She closed her eyes and pretended to be asleep.

"Has Yehonala escaped?" the old woman called.

7

A serving woman answered. "Mistress, she lies in bed."

The chief tiring woman was shocked. "Still abed? And can she sleep?"

The servant went to the bed and looked. "She is sleeping."

"What hard heart is this?" the old woman cried. "Waken her! Pull away the quilts, pinch her arms!"

The servant obeyed, and Yehonala, feigning to wake, opened her eyes. "What is it?" she asked drowsily. She sat up, her hands flying to her cheeks. "Oh—oh—" she stammered, her voice as soft as that of a mourning dove. "How could I forget?"

"How indeed!" the chief tiring woman said, indignant. "Do you not know the Emperor's command? In two hours from now you must all be ready in the Audience Hall, every virgin at her best—two hours, I tell you, in which you must be bathed and perfumed and robed, your hair coiled, your breakfast eaten."

Yehonala yawned behind her hand. "How I slept! The mattress is much softer here than on my bed at home."

The old woman snorted. "It can scarcely be imagined that a mattress in the palace of the Son of Heaven would be as hard as your bed."

"So much softer than I imagined," Yehonala said.

She stepped upon the tiled floor, her feet bare and strong. The virgins were all Manchu and not Chinese, and their feet were unbound and free.

"Come, come," the chief tiring woman said. "Hasten yourself, Yehonala! The others are nearly dressed."

"Yes, Venerable," she said.

But she did not hurry herself. She allowed a woman to undress her, putting forth no effort to help her, and when she was naked she stepped into the shallow tub of hot water and would not lift her hand to wash her own body.

"You!" the woman said under her breath. "Will you not help me to get you ready?"

Yehonala opened her large eyes, black and brilliant. "What shall I do?" she asked helplessly.

No one should guess that in her home there was no servant except Lu Ma in the kitchen. She had always bathed not only herself but her younger sister and brothers. She had washed their clothes with her own and she had carried them as babies on her back, strapped there with broad bands of cloth, while she went hither and thither helping her mother about the house and running often to the oil shop and the vegetable market. Her only pleasure was to stop on the streets and watch a

8

troupe of wandering Chinese actors. Yet her uncle Muyanga, always kind, allowed her to be taught with his own children by the family tutor, although the sum of money he gave her mother went for food and clothing and provided little luxury.

Here all was luxury. She glanced about the vast room. The early sunlight was creeping over the walls and brightened the opaque shell-latticed windows. The blue and the red of the painted beams overhead sprang into life, and the reds and greens of the long Manchu robes of the virgins responded. Scarlet satin curtains hung in the doorways and the cushions of the carved wooden chairs were covered with scarlet wool. Upon the walls the picture scrolls showed landscapes or wise sayings brushed in black ink upon white silk. The air was sweet with perfume of soaps and oils. She discovered of a sudden that she loved luxury.

The serving woman had not answered Yehonala's question. There was no time. The chief tiring woman was pressing them to hurry.

"They had better eat first," she was saying. "Then what time is left can be spent on their hair. A full hour is needed for their hair."

Food was brought in by kitchen maids but the virgins could not eat. Their hearts were beating too fast in their bosoms, and some were weeping again.

The chief tiring woman grew angry. Her fat face swelled. "How dare you weep?" she bellowed. "Can there be a better fortune than to be chosen by the Son of Heaven?"

But the weeping virgins wept on. "I had rather live in my home," one sobbed. "I do not wish to be chosen," another sighed.

"Shame, shame," the old woman cried, gnashing her teeth at the craven girls.

Seeing such distress, Yehonala was the more calm. She moved with accurate grace from one step to another and when food was brought in she sat down at a table and ate heartily and with pleasure. Even the chief tiring woman was surprised, not knowing whether to be shocked or pleased.

"I swear I have not seen so hard a heart," she said in a loud voice.

Yehonala smiled, her chopsticks in her right hand. "I like this good food," she said as sweetly as a child. "It is better than any I have eaten at home."

The chief tiring woman decided to be pleased. "You are a sensible female creature," she announced. Nevertheless after a moment she turned her head to whisper to one of the serving women. "Look at her great eyes! She has a fierce heart, this one—"

9

The woman grimaced. "A tiger heart," she agreed. "Truly a tiger heart—"

At noon the eunuchs came for them, led by the Chief Eunuch, An Teh-hai. He was a handsome, still youthful figure, wrapped in a long pale-blue satin robe, girdled at the waist with a length of red silk. His face was smooth, the features large, the nose curved downward, the eyes black and proud.

He gave orders half carelessly for the virgins to pass before him and like a petty emperor he sat in a great carved chair of blackwood and stared at each one as she passed, seeming at the same time to be only contemptuous. Beside him was a blackwood table upon which were placed his tally book, his ink brush and box.

From under her long eyelids Yehonala watched him. She stood apart from the other virgins, half hiding herself behind a curtain of scarlet satin hung in a door way. The Chief Eunuch marked with a brush and ink the name of each virgin as she passed.

"There is one not here," he announced.

"Here am I," Yehonala said. She moved forward shyly, her head bent, her face turned away, her voice so soft it could scarcely be heard.

"That one has been late all day," the chief tiring woman said in her loud voice. "She slept when the others rose. She would not wash or dress herself and she has eaten enough food for a peasant woman—three bowls of millet she swallowed down! Now she stands there stupid. I do not know whether she is a fool."

"Yehonala," the Chief Eunuch read in a high harsh voice, "eldest daughter of the dead Bannerman Chao. Guardian, the Bannerman Mu-yanga. She was registered at the Northern Palace two years ago, aged fifteen. She is now seventeen."

He lifted his head and stared at Yehonala standing before him, her head drooping modestly, her eyes fixed on the floor.

"Are you this very one?" he inquired.

"I am she," Yehonala said.

"Pass on," the Chief Eunuch commanded. But his eyes followed her. Then he rose and commanded the lower eunuchs. "Let the virgins be led into the Hall of Waiting. When the Son of Heaven is ready to receive them, I will announce them myself, one by one, before the Dragon Throne."

Four hours the virgins waited. The serving women sat with them, scolding if a satin coat were wrinkled, or if a lock of hair were loosened. Now and again a woman touched a virgin's face with powder, or painted her lips again. Twice the virgins were allowed to drink tea.

At noon a stir in distant courtyards roused them. Horns sounded, drums beat and a gong was struck to the rhythm of footsteps coming nearer. An Teh-hai, the Chief Eunuch, came again into the Hall of Waiting and with him were the lesser eunuchs, among whom was one young and tall and lean, and though his face was ugly, it was so dark and so like an eagle's in its look that Yehonala's eyes were fixed upon him involuntarily. In the same instant this eunuch caught her look and returned it with insolence. She turned her head away.

But the Chief Eunuch had seen. "Li Lien-ying," he cried sharply, "why are you here? I bade you wait with the virgins of the fourth class, the Ch'ang Ts'ai!"

Without a word the tall young eunuch left the hall.

The Chief Eunuch then said, "Young ladies, you will wait here until your class is called. First the F'ei must be presented to the Emperor by the Dowager Mother, then the P'in. Only when these are reviewed and the Emperor's choice is made may you of the third class, who are only Kuei Jen, approach the Throne. You are not to look upon the imperial face. It is he who looks at you."

None answered. The virgins stood silent, their heads drooping while he spoke. Yehonala had placed herself last, as though she were the most modest of them all, but her heart beat against her breast. Within the next few hours, within an hour or less, depending on the Emperor's mood, she might reach the supreme moment of her life. He would look at her, appraise her, weigh her shape and color, and in that little moment she must make him feel her powerful charm.

She thought of her cousin Sakota, even now passing before the Emperor's eyes. Sakota was sweetly simple, gentle and childlike. Because she was the sister of the dead princess, whom the Emperor had loved when he was prince, it was all but sure that she would be among the chosen. That was good. She and Sakota had lived together since she was three years old, when, her father dead, her mother had returned to the ancestral home, and Sakota had always yielded to her and leaned upon her and trusted her. Sakota might even say to the Emperor, "My cousin Yehonala is beautiful and clever." It had been upon her tongue, that last night they slept together, to say to her, "Speak for me—" and then she had been too proud. Sakota, though gentle and childish, had a child's pure dignity, which forbade advance.

A murmur fluttered over the group of waiting virgins. Someone had caught a whisper from the Audience Hall. The F'ei were already dismissed. Sakota had been chosen from among them to be the first Imperial concubine. The P'in were few in number. Another hour—

Before the hour was ended the Chief Eunuch returned. "It is now the time for the Kuei Jen," he announced. "Arrange yourselves, young ladies. The Emperor grows weary."

The virgins arranged themselves in procession and the tiring women put the last touches on hair and lips and eyebrows. Silence fell upon all and laughter ceased. One girl leaned fainting upon a serving woman, who pinched her arms and the lobes of her ears to restore her. Inside the Audience Hall, the Chief Eunuch was already calling their names and ages, and each must enter at the sound of her name and her age. One by one they passed before the Emperor and the Dowager Mother. But Yehonala, the last, drifted away from her place, as though forgetfully, to pet a small palace dog who had come running through an open door. The creature was a sleeve dog, one of those minute beasts that Court ladies keep half starved in puppyhood and dwarfed enough to hide within a wide embroidered sleeve. At the door the Chief Eunuch waited.

"Yehonala!" he called.

The tiring women had already scattered and she was left alone, playing with the dog. She had almost deceived herself that indeed she had forgotten where she was and why. She held back the dog's long ears and laughed into the wrinkled face no larger than the palm of her own hand. She had heard of these little dogs that looked like lions, but no commoner was allowed to keep them, and she had never seen one until now.

"Yehonala!" An Teh-hai's voice roared into her ears and she stood up quickly.

He rushed at her and seized her arm. "Have you forgotten? Are you mad? The Emperor waits! He waits, I tell you—why, you deserve to die for this—"

She wrenched herself loose and he hurried to the door and shouted out her name again. "Yehonala, daughter of the Bannerman Chao, now deceased, niece of Muyanga, of Pewter Lane! Her age, seventeen years, three months and two days—"

She entered without noise or affectation, and walked slowly down the length of the immense hall, her long Manchu coat of rose-red satin touching the tip of her embroidered Manchu shoes, set high on white soles and center heels. Her narrow beautiful hands she held folded at her waist, and she did not turn her head toward the Throne as she passed slowly by.

12

"Let her pass again," the Emperor said.

The Dowager Mother stared at Yehonala with unwilling admiration. "I warn you," she said, "this girl has a fierce temper. I see it in her face. She is too strong for a woman."

"She is beautiful," the Emperor said.

Still Yehonala did not turn her head. The voices fell disembodied upon her ears.

"What does it matter if she has a temper?" the Emperor now inquired. "She can scarcely be angry with me."

He had a youthful petulant voice, thin and boyish in its quality. His mother's voice answering him was full and slow, wise with age.

"It is better not to choose a strong woman who is also beautiful," she reasoned. "There is that other one, P'ou Yu, whom you have seen, in the class of P'in. A sensible face, good looks, but—"

"A coarse skin," the Emperor said rebelliously. "Doubtless she had smallpox as a child. In spite of the powder on her face, I saw its marks."

Yehonala was now directly in front of him. "Stay," he commanded her. She stopped, her face and body in profile, her head lifted, her eyes gazing into distance as though her heart were somewhere else.

"Turn your face to me," he commanded.

Slowly, as though indifferent, she obeyed. In decency, in modesty, in all that she had been taught, a virgin does not fix her eyes higher than a man's breast. Upon the Emperor she should not look higher than his knees. But Yehonala looked full into his face and with such concentration that she saw the Emperor's eyes, shallowly set beneath youthful scanty eyebrows, and through her own eyes she poured into his the power of her will. He sat immobile for a long instant. Then he spoke.

"This one I choose."

"If you are chosen by the Son of Heaven," her mother had said, "serve first his mother, the Dowager Mother. Let her believe that you think of her day and night. Learn what she enjoys, seek out her comfort, never try to escape her. She has not many years to live. There will be plenty of years left for you."

Yehonala remembered these words. On that first night after she had been chosen she lay in her own small bedroom, within the three rooms given her to use. An old tiring woman was appointed by the Chief Eunuch to be her servant. Here she must live alone except when the Emperor sent for her. That might be often or never. Sometimes a concubine lived within the four walls of this imperial city, virgin until she died, forgotten by the Emperor unless she had means to bribe the eunuchs to mention her name before him. But she, Yehonala, would not be forgotten. When he was weary of Sakota, to whom indeed he owed a duty, he might, he must, think of her. Yet would he remember? He was accustomed to beauty, and even though their eyes had met, could she be sure that the Son of Heaven would remember?

She lay upon the brick bed, made soft by three mattresses, and considered. Day by day she must now plan her life and not one day could be wasted, else she might live solitary, a virgin forgotten. She must be clever, she must be careful, and the Imperial Mother must be her means. She would be useful to the Dowager Empress, affectionate, unfailing in small and constant attentions. And now beyond this she would ask to be taught by tutors. She knew already how to read and write, thanks to her uncle's goodness, but her thirst for real learning was never satisfied. Books of history and poetry, music and painting, the arts of eye and ear, these she would ask to be taught. For the first time since she could remember she had time to possess for her own, leisure in which to train her mind. She would care for her body, too, eat the best meats, rub her hands soft with mutton fat, perfume herself with dried oranges and musk, bid her serving woman brush her hair twice daily after her bath. These she would do for her body, that the Emperor might be pleased. But her mind she would shape to please herself, and to please herself she would learn how to brush characters as scholars do and to paint landscapes as artists do, and she would read many books.

The satin of her bedquilt caught on the roughened skin of her hands and she thought, "I shall never wash clothes again, or fetch hot water, or grind meal. Is this not happiness?"

Two nights she had not slept. In the last night in their home, when she and Sakota had lain awake talking and dreaming and she comforting the gentle one, and again in the last night with the waiting virgins, who could sleep? But tonight all fears were over. She was chosen and here in these three rooms was her little home. They were small but luxurious, the walls hung with scrolls, the chair seats covered with red satin cushions, the tables made of blackwood and the beams overhead painted in bright design. The floors were smoothly tiled and the latticed windows opened into a court and upon a round pool where goldfish shone under the sun. Her woman servant slept on a bamboo couch outside her door. She had no one to fear.

No one? The narrow evil face of the young eunuch Li Lien-ying appeared suddenly against the darkness. Ah, the eunuchs, her wise mother had warned her of the eunuchs—

"They are neither men nor women. They destroy themselves as men

14

before they are allowed to enter into the Forbidden City. Their male-
ness, stemmed and denied, turns evil in them. It becomes malice and
bitterness and cruelty and all things vile. Avoid the eunuchs from the
highest to the lowest. Pay them money when you must. Never let them
see that you fear them."

"I will not fear you," she said to the dark face of Li Lien-ying.

And suddenly, because she was afraid, she thought of her kinsman, Jung Lu. She had not seen him since she entered the palace. Then,
always bold, she had moved aside the curtain of her sedan chair an inch
or two as it approached the great vermilion gates. Before them the imperial guardsmen stood in yellow tunics, their broad swords drawn and
held upright before them. At the right, next to the central gate, Jung Lu
stood tallest among them all. He gazed straight ahead into the swarming crowds of the street and not by the slightest sign did he let her
know that to him one sedan was different from another. Nor could she
make a sign. Half wounded, she had put him out of mind. No, and she
would not think of him, even now. Neither she nor he could know when
they might meet again. Within the walls of this Forbidden City a man
and a woman might live out their lives and never meet.

Yet why had she thought of him suddenly when she remembered the
dark face of the eunuch? She sighed and wept a few tears, surprised
that she did, and she would not inquire into herself to know the cause
of her tears. Then being young and very weary, she slept.

The vast old palace library was cool even in midsummer. At noon the
doors were closed against the outdoor heat and the glittering sun shone
dimly through the shell lattices. No sound disturbed the stillness except
the low murmur of Yehonala's voice as she read aloud to the aged
eunuch who was her tutor.

She was reading from *The Book of Changes,* and absorbed in the
cadences of its poetry, she did not notice that her tutor was silent too
long. Then, glancing upward as she turned a page, she saw the old
scholar asleep, his head sunk upon his breast, his fan slipping from the
loosened fingers of his right hand. The corner of her mouth twitched in
a half smile, and she read on steadily to herself. At her feet a little dog
slept. It was her own, given her by the Imperial Keeper, when she sent
her serving woman to beg for a pet to mend her loneliness.

Two months now she had been in the palace and she had received no
summons from the Emperor. She had not seen her family, not even
Sakota, nor had Jung Lu come near. Since she had not left the gates she
had not passed him as he stood on duty. In this strange isolation she

might have been unhappy except for her busy dreams of the days to come. Some day, some day, she might be Empress! And when she was Empress she would do as she liked. If she wished, she could summon her kinsman into her presence, for a purpose, any purpose, such as the bearing of a letter to her mother.

"I put this letter into your hands myself," she would say, "and you are to bring back a letter from her in reply."

And none but they two would know whether the letter was for her mother. But her dreams waited upon the Emperor and meanwhile she could only prepare herself. Here in the library she studied each day for five hours with her tutor, the eunuch who held the highest degrees of scholarship. In the years when he was still a man, he had been a famous writer of eight-legged essays and poems in the T'ang style. Then, because of his fame, he had been commanded to become a eunuch in order that he might teach the young prince, now the Emperor, and after him the ladies who were to become his concubines. Among these some would learn and some would not, and none, the old tutor declared, learned as Yehonala did. He boasted of her among the eunuchs and gave good reports of her to the Dowager Mother, so that one day, when Yehonala waited upon her, the Dowager Mother even commended her for industry.

"You do well to learn the books," she said. "My son, the Emperor, wearies easily and when he is weak or restless you must be able to amuse him with poetry and with your painting."

And Yehonala had inclined her head in obedience.

At this moment, while she mused upon a page, she felt a touch upon her shoulder, and turning her head she saw the end of a folded fan and a hand that she had come to know at sight, a large smooth powerful hand. It belonged to the young eunuch, Li Lien-ying. She was aware and had been aware for weeks that he was determined to be her servant. It was not his duty to be near her, he was only one among many of the lesser eunuchs, but he had become useful to her in many small ways. When she longed for fruits or sweets it was he who brought them to her and through him she heard the gossip of the many halls and passageways, the hundreds of courts of the Forbidden City. Gossip she must hear, for it was not enough for her to read books, she must know also every detail of intrigue and mishap and love within these walls. To know was to acquire power.

She lifted her head, her finger on her lips, her eyebrows raised in question. He motioned with his fan that she was to follow him into the pavilion outside the library. Silently, his cloth-soled shoes noiseless upon the tiles, he led the way and she followed until they were beyond danger of rousing the sleeping tutor. The little dog, waking, followed her without barking.

"I have news for you," Li Lien-ying said. He towered above her, his shoulders immense, his head square and large, his features roughly shaped and coarse, a figure powerful and crude. She might have been afraid of him still except that now she allowed herself to be afraid of no one.

"What news?" she inquired.

"The young Empress has conceived!"

Sakota! She had not once seen her cousin since they entered the gates together. Sakota was Consort in her dead sister's place, while she, Yehonala, was only a concubine. Sakota had been summoned to the Emperor's bed, and she had fulfilled her duty. If Sakota bore a son, he would be heir to the Dragon Throne, and Sakota would be raised to the place of Empress Mother. And she, Yehonala, would still be only a concubine. For such small price would she have cast away her lover and her life? Her heart swelled and all but burst against her ribs.

"Is there proof of the conception?" she demanded.

"There is," he replied. "Her waiting woman is in my pay. This month, for the second time, there was no show of blood."

"Well?" she asked. Then her lifelong control took hold. No one could save her except herself. Upon herself alone she must now depend. But fate might be her savior. Sakota might give birth to a girl. There would still be no heir, until a son was born, whose mother would then be raised to Empress.

And I might be that mother, she thought. Upon the glimpse of sudden hope her brain grew calm, her heart grew still.

"The Emperor's duty to his dead lady is done," the eunuch went on. "Now his fancy will wander."

She was silent. It might fall upon her!

"You must be ready," he went on. "My reckoning is that within six or seven days he will think of a concubine."

"How do you know everything?" she asked, half fearful in spite of her will not to fear.

"Eunuchs know such things," he said, leering down into her face.

She spoke with dignity. "You forget yourself before me."

"I offend you," he said quickly. "I am wrong. You are always right. I am your servant, your slave."

She was so solitary that even though he was frightening, she compelled herself to accept his assurance. "Yet why," she now inquired, "do you wish to serve me? I have no money with which to reward you."

It was true that she had not a penny of money. Daily she ate of the most delicate dishes, for whatever the Dowager Mother left was given to the concubines and there was abundance of every variety of food. The chests in her bedchamber were filled with beautiful robes. She slept between silken quilts and she was waited upon day and night by her woman. Yet she could not buy so much as a handkerchief or a packet of sweets for herself. And she had not seen a play since she entered the Forbidden City. The Dowager Mother was still in mourning for the dead Emperor, T'ao Kuang, her son's father, and she would not allow even the concubines to enjoy themselves in a play, and this lack made Yehonala more lonely than the loss of her family. All her life, whenever her tasks were heavy, her mother scolding, her days without joy, she had escaped to watch the actors playing on the streets or in the courtyard of a temple. If she had a penny by chance, she saved it for the play, and if she had none, then she slipped away before the basket was passed among the crowd.

"Do you think I ask for gifts?" Li Lien-ying said. "Then you misjudge me. I know what your destiny is. You have a power in you that is in none of the others. Did I not perceive it as soon as my eyes fell upon you? I have told you. When you rise toward the Dragon Throne I will rise with you, always your servant and your slave."

She was shrewd enough to know how skillfully he used her beauty and her ambition for his own ends while he knit the ties of obligation between himself and her. If ever she reached the throne, and surely she would some day, he would be there to remind her that she had helped her.

"Why should you serve me for nothing?" she asked, indifferently. "No one gives without thought of return."

"We understand each other," he said, and smiled.

She looked away. "Then we can only wait," she said.

"We wait," he agreed, and bowed and went away.

She returned to the library very thoughtful, the little dog padding after her. The old tutor still slept and she sat down in the chair she had left, and began once more to read. And everything was as it had been before, except that her heart, in this short space of time, was no more the soft heart of a virgin. She had become a woman, bent upon her destiny.

How could she now consider the meaning of ancient poetry? Her whole mind was playing about the moment when she would be summoned. And how would the summons come? Who would bring the message? Would she have time to bathe and perfume her body, or must she hasten as she was? The imperial concubines gossiped among themselves often, and when one had gone and come back again, the others questioned to the last shred of memory to know what had passed between her and the Emperor. Yehonala had not questioned but she had listened. Better to know!

"The Emperor does not wish you to talk," a concubine had said. Once she had been the favorite, but now she lived forgotten, in the Palace of Forgotten Concubines with others whom the Emperor had not loved for long, or else who were the aging concubines of his dead father. Though she was not yet twenty-four years of age this concubine had been chosen and embraced and rejected. For the rest of her life she would live neither wife nor widow, and since she did not conceive she had not even the solace of a child. She was a pretty woman, idle and empty, talking only of the one day when she had lived in the private palace of the Emperor. That brief story she told again and again as the new concubines waited to be chosen.

But Yehonala listened and said nothing. She would divert the Emperor. She would amuse him and tease him and sing to him and tell him stories, weaving every bond between them of mind as well as flesh. She closed the *Book of Changes* and put it aside. There were other books, forbidden books, *Dream of the Red Chamber, Plum Flower in a Golden Vase, White Snake*—she would read them all, commanding Li Lien-ying to bring them to her from bookshops outside the walls if she could not find them here.

The tutor waked suddenly and quietly as the old do waken, the difference for them between sleep and awakening being so slight. He watched her without moving.

"How now?" he asked. "Have you finished your portion?"

"It is finished," she said. "And I wish for other books, story books, tales of magic, something to amuse me."

He looked stern and he stroked his hairless chin with a hand as dry and withered as a dead palm leaf. "Such books poison the thoughts, especially of females," he declared. "You will not find them here in the Imperial Library, no, there is not one among all the thirty-six thousand upon these shelves. Such books ought not even to be mentioned by a virtuous lady."

"Then I will not mention them," she said playfully.

And stooping she gathered the little dog into her sleeve and went away to her own chamber.

What she had known in the afternoon of one day was by the next day known everywhere. Mouth to ear, the gossip flew from courtyard to courtyard and excitement rose like wind. In spite of his Consort and his many concubines, the Emperor had never had a child, and the great Manchu clans were restless. If there were no heir, then an heir must be chosen from among them, and princes watched each other closely, guarding themselves and their sons, jealous of where the choice might fall. Now, since Sakota, the new Consort, had conceived, they could only wait. If she had a daughter instead of a son the strife would begin again.

Yehonala herself belonged to the most powerful of these clans, and from her clan three Empresses had already risen. Should she not be a fourth? Ah, if she were chosen, if she could conceive immediately, if she had a son, and Sakota but a daughter, the path of destiny would be clear indeed—too clear, perhaps, for who had such good fortune that one step could lead so swiftly to another? Yet all was possible.

In preparation she began from that day on to read the memorials that came from the Throne, studying every word of the edicts the Emperor sent forth. Thus she might inform herself concerning the realm and so be ready if ever the gods willed to send her forward. And slowly she began to comprehend the vastness of the country and its people. Her world had been the city of Peking, wherein she grew from child to maiden. She knew her ruling race, the Manchu clans who from their invading ancestors had seized and held the power over a mighty people who were Chinese. Two hundred years the northern dynasty had built its heart here in the imperial city, its red walls four square inside the capital. The Emperor's City, it was called, or the Forbidden City, for he was its king, its solitary male, and he alone could sleep here at night. At twilight the drums beat in every lane and cranny to warn all men to depart. The Emperor remained alone among his women and his eunuchs.

But this capital, this inner city, so she now comprehended, was but the ruling center of a country eternal in its mountains, rivers, lakes and seashores, in the endless numbers of its cities and villages, in the hundreds of millions of its various people, its merchants, farmers, scholars, its weavers, artisans, smiths and innkeepers, men and women of every sort, craft and art. Her bright imagination flew from the gates of her royal prison and traveled everywhere that her eyes led upon the printed pages of her books. From the imperial edicts she learned yet more. She learned that a mighty rebellion was rising in the south, the hateful fruit of a foreign religion. These Chinese rebels called themselves T'ai P'ing and they were led by a fanatic Christian, surnamed Hung, who imagined himself an incarnated brother of the one called Christ, son of a foreign god by a peasant woman. This birth was not strange, for in the ancient books were many such stories. A farm wife could tell of a god who came before her in a cloud while she was tilling the field, and by magic he impregnated her so that in ten moon months she bore a godly son. Or a fisherman's daughter, though still a virgin, would tell how a god came up out of the river while she tended her father's fishing nets, and by his magic she was impregnated. But under the Christian banner of T'ai P'ing rebels the restless and the discontents were gathering themselves, and unless they were quelled, these men might even overthrow the Manchu dynasty. T'ao Kuang had been a weak emperor and so now was his son, Hsien Feng, whom the Dowager Mother commanded as though he were a child.

Through the Dowager Mother, then, Yehonala must find her access, and she made it her daily duty to wait upon the elder lady, appearing with a choice flower or a ripe fruit plucked from the imperial gardens.

It was now nearly the season of summer melons, and the Dowager Mother loved very well the small yellow-fleshed sweet melons that grow on dung heaps, where in the spring the seeds are sown. Yehonala walked daily in the melon rows and searched for the first sweet melons, hidden under the leaves. Upon those most nearly ripe she pasted bits of yellow paper brushed with the name of the Dowager Mother, so that no greedy eunuch or woman servant would steal them. Every day she tested the melons with her thumb and forefinger and one day, seven days after Li Lien-ying had told her of the news concerning Sakota, she heard a melon sound as empty as a drum. It was ripe, and she twisted it from its stem and, carrying it in both hands, she went to the courtyards of the Dowager Mother.

"Our Venerable Mother is asleep," a serving woman said. She was jealous of Yehonala because the Dowager Mother favored her.

Yehonala raised her voice. "Is the Dowager Mother sleeping at this hour? Then she must be ill. It is long past the hour when she wakes—"

She had, when she wished, a thrush-clear voice that carried through several rooms. Now it reached the ears of the Dowager Mother, who was not sleeping but sat in her bedroom embroidering a gold dragon upon a black girdle which she wished to present to her son. There was no need for her to do such work but she could not read and she liked to embroider. She heard Yehonala's voice and since she was growing weary of her needle, which she soon did, she put it down and called.

"Yehonala, come here! Who says I am sleeping is a liar!"

Yehonala made a coaxing smile for the serving woman who frowned. "No one says you sleep, Venerable," she called, in reply. "It is I who heard it wrong."

With this courteous lie she tripped through the rooms holding her melon until she reached the bedchamber of the Dowager Mother, where the old lady sat in her undergarments because of the heat, and to her she presented the melon with both hands.

"Ah," the Dowager Mother cried, "and I sat here thinking of sweet melons and wishing for one, and you come at the very moment!"

"Let me bid a eunuch hang it in one of the northern wells to cool it," Yehonala said.

But the Dowager Mother would not allow this. "No, no," she argued, "if this melon falls into the hands of a eunuch he will eat it secretly and then when I send for it, he will bring me a green one or he will say the rats have gnawed it or it has fallen into the well and he cannot get it up. I know those eunuchs! I will eat it here and now and have it safely in my belly."

She turned her head and shouted to any serving woman who was near. "Fetch me a large knife!"

Three or four women ran for knives and in a moment they were back and Yehonala took a knife and sliced the melon delicately and neatly and the Dowager Mother seized a piece of it and began to eat it as greedily as a child, the sweet water dripping from her chin.

"A towel," Yehonala said to a serving woman and when it was put in her hand she tied it about the old lady's neck to keep her silken undervest from soiling.

"Save half of it," the Dowager Mother commanded, when she had eaten as much as she could. "When my son comes to present himself this evening as he always does before I sleep, I will give it to him. But it is to stay here beside me or one of those eunuchs will snatch it."

"Let me—" Yehonala said.

And she would not allow a serving woman to touch the melon. She called for a dish and placed the melon into it, and then she called for a porcelain bowl and this she placed over the melon and the dish was set into a basin of cold water. All this trouble she took that the Dowager Mother might mention it to the Emperor when he came and so her name would fall somewhere into the Emperor's hearing.

While she worked in such ways, Li Lien-ying worked in his, also.

22

He bribed the menservants in the Emperor's private courts to watch their lord and when the monarch appeared restless, his eyes moving this way and that after a woman, the eunuch bade them speak the name of Yehonala.

Thus in one way and another it was done, and the very day after the presentation of the melon Yehonala found in the pages of her book when she opened it in the library a sheet of paper folded small. Upon it were written two lines in rude handwriting. They said:

"The Dragon awakes again,
The day of the Phoenix has come."

She knew who had written the words. Yet how did Li Lien-ying know? She would not ask him. What he did to fulfill her purposes must be secret even from herself, and quietly she read her books while the old tutor eunuch slept and woke and slept again until hours passed. But this was the day when she received her usual painting lesson in midafternoon and she was glad, for her mind darted here and there and she could not keep her thoughts upon the calm words of a dead sage. Upon painting she must keep her mind fixed, for her teacher was a woman, not yet old, and very exacting. She was Lady Miao, a widow, a Chinese, whose husband had died in youth. Since it was not usual for Chinese ladies to appear in the Manchu Court, this lady was allowed to unbind her feet, to comb her hair high as Manchu ladies do, and to put on Manchu robes, so that at least she looked a Manchu, and she was thus permitted because she was perfect in her art. She came of a family of Chinese artists, for her father and her brothers were artists, too, but she excelled them all, especially in the painting of cocks and chrysanthemums, and she was employed to teach the concubines her art. Yet she was so skilled and impatient that she would not teach a concubine who had no will to learn, or no talent. Both will and talent Yehonala had, and when Lady Miao discovered this to be so, she devoted herself to the proud young girl, although she continued insistent and severe as a teacher. Thus she had not as yet let Yehonala paint anything from life. Instead she compelled her to study ancient woodcuts and the prints of dead masters, so that she might engrave upon her mind the strokes they made, the lines they drew, the colors they mixed. After such study she allowed Yehonala to begin to copy and still forbade her to work alone.

This day Lady Miao arrived as usual upon the exact hour of four. There were many clocks in the Imperial Library, gifts of foreign envoys in past centuries, and so many in the palace that it was the entire duty of three eunuchs to keep them wound. This Lady Miao, however, looked not at the foreign clocks but at the water clock at one end of the hall. She did not like foreign objects, for she said they disturbed the calm needful for painting.

She was a slight and almost beautiful woman, the smallness of her eyes being her defect. Today she wore a plum-colored robe and upon her hair, combed high, the beaded headdress of the Manchu. A eunuch followed her and he opened a high chest and took from it brushes and colors and water bowls. Meanwhile Yehonala rose and remained standing in the presence of her teacher.

"Be seated, be seated," Lady Miao commanded.

She seated herself so that Yehonala could also sit. Now Yehonala saw from yet another window the vast country and its people at whose center she lived and the art of centuries stretched out before her as her teacher spoke, from the most famous of Chinese artists, Ku K'ai-chih, living fifteen centuries before this day. Especially did she love the paintings of the early artist, for he painted goddesses riding above clouds, their chariots drawn by dragons. And he made pictures of imperial palaces, painted on a long hand roll of silk, upon which the Imperial Ancestor Ch'ien Lung had set his private seal, a hundred years ago, and had written with his own hand these words, "The picture has not lost its freshness." The scroll was eleven feet long, nine inches wide, the color brown, and of the nine royal scenes it portrayed Yehonala's favorite was the one wherein a bear, breaking free from gamers to amuse the Court, rushed toward the Emperor, and a lady threw herself across its path to save the Son of Heaven. This lady Yehonala thought was like herself. Tall, beautiful and bold, she stood with folded arms and fearless looks before the beast, while guardsmen ran forward with their outthrust spears. And yet there was another scene she pondered on, the Emperor and his Empress and their two sons. Nurses and tutors stood beside these boys, and all was family warmth and life, the younger boy so mischievous, grimacing and rebellious while a barber shaved his crown, that Yehonala laughed to see him. Such a son she would have, too, if Heaven willed.

But today's lesson was of Wang Wei, a physician born thirteen centuries ago, who gave up his ancestral skills and turned poet and artist.

"Today," Lady Miao was saying in her sharp silvery voice, "you will study these sketches by Wang Wei. Observe the bamboo leaves so delicately drawn against the dark rocks. Observe the plum blossoms mingled with chrysanthemums."

She allowed no conversation that had not to do with painting, and

Yehonala, always docile in the presence of her teachers, listened and observed. Now she spoke.

"Is it not strange that plum blossoms and chrysanthemums are upon the same page? Is this not to confuse the seasons?"

Lady Miao was not pleased. "It is wise not to mention confusion when speaking of Wang Wei," she said. "If the master wishes to place plum blossoms among chrysanthemums, this is to convey a meaning. It is not a mistake. Consider that among his most famous paintings is the one of banana leaves under snow. Can it be possible that snow lies upon banana leaves? If Wang Wei paints it, then it is possible. Pray meditate upon its poetry. Some declare Wang Wei more poet than painter. I say his poems are paintings, his paintings poems, and this is art. To portray a mood and not a fact—this is ideal art."

While she talked she mixed the colors, choosing brushes while Yehonala watched. "You will inquire why I ask you to copy the work of Wang Wei," the lady said. "I wish you to learn precision and delicacy. You have power. But power must be informed and controlled from within. Then only may it be genius."

"I would ask my teacher a question," Yehonala said.

"Ask," Lady Miao replied. She was brushing fine quick strokes upon a large sheet of paper spread upon a square table which the eunuch had brought to her side.

"When may I paint a picture of my own?" Yehonala asked.

Her teacher held her hand poised for an instant and cast a sidelong look from her narrowed eyes. "When I can no longer command you."

Yehonala did not reply. The meaning was clear. When she was chosen by the Emperor then Lady Miao could not command her, for then no one could command her save the Emperor himself. She would be raised too high for any other to be above her. She took up her brush and began carefully to copy plum blossoms among chrysanthemums.

Sometime in the night, she did not know the hour, she was wakened by hands shaking her shoulders. She had not been able to sleep early, and when at last her eyes had closed, she had fallen deeply into sleep. Now she came up from a well of darkness and struggling to open her eyes, she heard the voice of her serving woman.

"Wake, wake, Yehonala! You are summoned! The Son of Heaven calls—"

She woke instantly. Her mind leaped to alertness. She pushed back the silken quilts and stepped down from the high bed.

"I have your bath ready," the woman whispered. "Quick—get into the tub! I have poured perfume into the water. I have put out your best robe—the lilac satin—"

"Not lilac," Yehonala said. "I shall wear the peach pink."

Other women were coming into the chamber, waked from their sleep and yawning, the tiring woman, the hairdresser and the keeper of the jewels. Concubines were not given imperial jewels until they were summoned.

Yehonala knelt in her bath and her woman soaped her body well and washed away the foam.

"Now step out upon this towel," the woman said. "I will rub you dry. The seven orifices must be perfumed, the ears especially—the Emperor loves a woman's ears. You have small and beautiful ears. But do not forget the nostrils—and the privacies I must attend to myself."

To all such ministrations Yehonala submitted without a word. Haste —haste was the necessity. The Emperor was awake, he was drinking wine and eating small hot breads filled with flavored meats. The news was brought again and again to the door by Li Lien-ying.

"Do not delay," he hissed in a hoarse voice through the curtains. "If the one he wants is not ready, then he will call for another. His dragon's temper is easily roused, I can tell you."

"She is ready," the serving woman cried. She thrust two jeweled flowers behind Yehonala's ears and pushed her out the door.

"Go, my precious, my pet," she whispered.

"Oh, my little dog," Yehonala cried. The small creature was at her heels.

"No, no," Li Lien-ying shouted. "You may not take your dog!"

But Yehonala, suddenly afraid, stooped and gathered the minute beast into her arms.

"I will take him," she cried, and stamped her foot.

"No!" Li Lien-ying bellowed again.

"Oh, Lord of Hell," the serving woman roared in distraction, "let her take the dog, you piece of cobbler's wax! If you cross her, she will refuse to go, and where are we all then?"

Thus it was that Yehonala went to the Emperor at midnight, bearing in her arms her little lion, her toy dog, and from that day on Li Lien-ying, who was indeed apprenticed to a cobbler before he cut himself into a eunuch, was nicknamed Cobbler's Wax by those who feared and hated him.

In the dark softness of the summer night Yehonala followed Li Lien-ying through the narrow passageways of the city. He held an oiled paper lantern, and the candle within it threw a dim circle of light to guide her. Behind her came her serving woman. The stones upon which they walked were damp with dew and this dew, like light hoar frost, lay upon the small weeds between. Silence surrounded them, except that somewhere a woman wailed.

Though she had never been to the Emperor's palace, yet Yehonala knew, as did every concubine, that it was in the heart of the Forbidden City in the midst of imperial gardens, and in the shadows of the triple shrine, the Tower of Rain and Flowers, whose roofs were upheld by pillars of gold, circled with dragons. In this shrine stood three altars where the Emperor worshipped the gods alone, and so all emperors had worshipped since the time of the great K'ang Hsi and the gods protected them.

She passed the shrine and came to the gate of the entrance courtyard of the Emperor's private palace. It opened silently before her and the eunuch led her through a vast inner courtyard and into a great hall and through this hall again by passageways, silent and empty, except for watchful eunuchs, until at last she reached high double gates, carved with golden dragons. Here the Chief Eunuch, An Teh-hai himself, stood waiting, a tall and splendid figure, his proud face set, his arms folded. His long robe of purple brocaded satin, girdled about the middle with gold, glittered in the light of the candles flaring in high candlesticks of carved and polished wood. He did not speak to Yehonala or make a sign of recognition as she came near, but by a gesture of his right hand he dismissed Li Lien-ying, who fell back in deference.

Now suddenly the Chief Eunuch saw the head of the toy dog peering out from Yehonala's sleeve. "You may not take the dog into the Emperor's bedchamber," he said sternly.

Yehonala lifted her head and fixed her great eyes upon him. "Then I will not enter, either," she said.

The words were brave but she spoke them in a soft indifferent voice, as though she did not care whether she entered or did not.

An Teh-hai looked his surprise. "Can you defy the Son of Heaven?" he demanded.

She made no reply, and stroked the little dog's smooth head with her other hand.

"Elder Brother," Li Lien-ying now said, "this concubine is very troublesome. She speaks like a child but she is more fierce than a female tiger. We all fear her. If she does not wish to enter, it is better to send her home. Truly it is not worth while to compel her, for her mind is more stubborn than a stone."

A curtain behind An Teh-hai was now pulled aside with a jerk and a eunuch's face thrust itself out. "It is asked why there is delay," he cried. "It is asked if he himself must come and settle affairs!"

"Elder Brother, let her go in with the dog," Li Lien-ying urged. "She can hide it in her sleeve. If the beast is a nuisance, it can be taken away and given to the serving woman who will sit here outside the door."

The Chief Eunuch scowled, but Yehonala continued to gaze at him with her great eyes wide and innocent and what could he do but yield? He grunted and quarreled under his breath but he yielded, and again she followed through yet another room, at one end of which hung thick satin curtains of imperial yellow with dragons embroidered in scarlet silk. Behind them were heavy doors of carved wood. The Chief Eunuch put the curtains aside, he opened the doors, and motioned to her to enter. This time she went alone. The curtains fell behind her and she stood before the Emperor.

He sat upright in the huge imperial bed upon a raised platform. This bed was of bronze, the pillars of bronze, and upon them were carved climbing dragons. From the top of these pillars, connected by a framework of bronze, there hung nets of gold thread, woven into patterns of fruits and flowers among curling five-clawed dragons. The Emperor sat upon a mattress covered with yellow satin and his legs were covered by a quilt of yellow satin embroidered in dragons, and behind him were high cushions of the same yellow satin to support him as he sat erect. He wore a bed shirt of red silk, sleeved to his wrists and high about his neck, and his smooth slender hands were folded. She had seen him only the once when he chose her and then he wore his royal headdress. Now his head was bare and his hair was short and black. His face was long and narrow, sunken beneath a forehead too full and overhanging. They gazed at each other, man and woman, and he motioned to her to come near. She walked to him slowly, her eyes fixed on his face. When she was near she stopped again.

"You are the first woman who ever came into this chamber with her head lifted," he said in a high thin voice. "They are always afraid to look at me."

Sakota, she thought, Sakota had surely come in with her head drooping. Where was Sakota? In what room did she sleep not far away? Sakota had stood here, submissive, frightened, speechless.

"I am not afraid," Yehonala said in her soft definite voice. "See, I have brought my little dog."

The forgotten concubines had told her how to address the Son of Heaven. One must never speak before him as though he were only a mortal—Lord of Ten Thousand Years, the Highest, the Most Venerable, these were the words of address. But Yehonala behaved toward the Emperor as though he were a man.

She stroked the little dog's smooth head again and looked down. "Until I came here," she said, "I have never had a dog like this. I used to hear about lion dogs, and now I have one for my own."

The Emperor stared at her as though he did not know what to say to such childish talk.

"Come, sit on the bed beside me," he commanded her. "Tell me why you are not afraid of me."

She stepped up on the platform and sat on the edge of the bed, facing him, and she held her little dog. The small creature sniffed the perfumed air and sneezed, and she laughed. "What is this perfume at which my dog sneezes?" she inquired.

"It is camphorwood," the Emperor said. "But tell me why you are not afraid."

She felt his eyes were upon her, searching her face, her lips, her hands as she stroked the little dog, and she trembled with sudden chill, though it was midsummer and the dawn wind had not yet risen. She bent her head again as if to see the dog, then she forced herself to look up at the man and she forced herself to speak sweetly and shyly and still as though she were a child.

"I know my destiny," she said.

"And how do you know your destiny?" he demanded. He began to be amused, his thin lips curving upward, his shadowed eyes less cold.

"When I was summoned from my home," she said in the same shy sweet voice, "I went into the court of my uncle's house, who is my guardian because my father is dead, and I went to the shrine that stands beneath the pomegranate tree there, and I prayed to my goddess, the Kuan Yin. I lit the incense and then—"

She paused, her lips quivered, she tried to smile.

"And then?" the Emperor inquired, his heart enchanted by the beautiful face, so soft, so young.

"There was no wind that day," she said. "The smoke from the burning incense rose straight heavenward from the altar. It spread into a fragrant cloud and in the clouds I saw a face—"

"A man's face," he repeated.

29

She nodded her head, as a child nods when she is too shy to speak.

"Was it my face?" he asked.

"Yes, Majesty," she said. "Your imperial face!"

Two days, two nights, and she was still in the royal bedchamber. Three times he slept and each time she went to the door and beckoned to her serving woman, and the woman came creeping through the curtains to the boudoir beyond. There the eunuchs had prepared a ready bath, a cauldron of water upon coals, so that the woman needed only to dip the water into the vast porcelain jar and make her mistress fresh again. She had brought clean garments and different robes and she brushed Yehonala's hair and coiled it smoothly. Not once did the young girl speak except to give direction and not once did the serving woman ask a question. Each time when her task was done Yehonala went in again to the imperial bedroom and the heavy doors were closed behind the yellow curtains.

Inside that vast chamber she sat upon a chair near the window to wait until the Emperor woke. What had been done was done. She knew now what this man was, a weak and fitful being, possessed by a passion he could not satisfy, a lust of the mind more frightful than lust of the flesh. When he was defeated he wept upon her breast. This, this was the Son of Heaven!

Yet when he woke she was all duty and gentleness. He was hungry and she sent for the Chief Eunuch and bade him bring the dishes that his sovereign enjoyed. And she ate with the Emperor and she fed the little dog with bits of meat and released him now and then into the courtyard outside the window. When the meal was over the imperial man commanded his Chief Eunuch once more to draw the curtains over the window and hide the sunlight and he bade them leave him alone and not come unless summoned, nor would he meet his ministers that day or the next and not until he felt inclined.

An Teh-hai looked grave. "Majesty, evil news has come from the south, for T'ai P'ing rebels have seized the half of another province. Your ministers and princes are impatient for audience."

"I will not come," the Son of Heaven said peevishly, and fell back upon his pillows.

The Chief Eunuch then could but leave the room.

"Bar the doors," the Emperor commanded Yehonala.

So she barred the doors and when she turned to him again he was staring at her with fearful and unsatisfied desire.

30

"Come here," he muttered. "I am strong now. The meats have made me strong."

Again she must obey. This time it was true that he was strong, and then she remembered something the ladies who lived in the Palace of Forgotten Concubines had told her in their gossip. They said that if the Emperor delayed too long in his bedchamber, a powerful herb was mixed in his favorite dish which gave him sudden and unusual strength. Yet so dangerous was this herb that he must not be roused too far, for then exhaustion followed so extreme that it could end in death.

On the third morning, this exhaustion fell. The Emperor sank into half-fainting silence upon his pillow. His lips were blue, his eyes half closed, he could not move, his narrow face set slowly into a greenish pallor, which, upon his yellow skin, made him seem dead. In great fear Yehonala went to the door to summon help. Before she could call she saw An Teh-hai, the Chief Eunuch, approaching, expecting the summons.

"Let the Court physicians be immediately called," she commanded.

She looked so proud and cold, her great eyes so black, that An Teh-hai obeyed.

Yehonala returned to the bedside. The Emperor had fallen asleep. She looked down on his unconscious face and suddenly she longed to weep. She stood there shivering in the strange chill which had fallen upon her again and again in these two days and three nights and she went to the door and opened it enough to let her slender body through. Outside it her serving woman sat, nodding on a wooden stool, weary with waiting, and Yehonala put her hand on her shoulder and shook her gently.

"Where is your little dog?" the woman asked.

Yehonala stared at her unseeing. "I put it in the courtyard some time in the night—I forget!"

"Do not mind," the woman said, pitying her. "Come, come with me —take your old woman's hand—"

And Yehonala let herself be led down the narrow passageways. It was dawn and the rising sun shone upon the rose-red walls along the way, and thus she came again to her solitary home. And while the serving woman made herself bustling and busy she talked to comfort her mistress.

"They are saying everywhere that never has a concubine stayed so long with the Son of Heaven. Even the Consort spent only a night with him at one time. That eunuch, Li Lien-ying, says that you are the favorite now. You have nothing more to fear."

Yehonala smiled but her lips trembled. "Do they say so?" she said, and she held herself straight and moved with her usual smooth grace.

Yet when she was bathed and clothed in sleeping robes of softest silk in her own bed, though the curtains were drawn, the serving woman gone away, she fell into shivering and deathly chill. Silent she must be so long as she lived, for to no one could she speak. Oh, there was none, for what friend had she? She was alone and never had she dreamed of such loneliness as now was hers. There was not one—

Not one? Was Jung Lu not still her kinsman? He was her cousin, and the ties of blood cannot be broken. She sat up in her bed and dried her eyes and she clapped her hands for her serving woman.

"What now?" the woman asked at the door.

"Send to me the eunuch Li Lien-ying," Yehonala commanded her.

The serving woman hesitated. Upon her round face the doubt was plain enough.

"Good mistress," she said, "do not be too friendly with that eunuch. What can he do for you now?"

But Yehonala was stubborn. "Something that only he can do," she said.

The woman went away, still doubtful, to find the eunuch, who came in great haste and elation.

"What, what, my lady Phoenix?" he inquired when he came to her door.

Yehonala put the curtain aside. She had dressed herself in a dark and somber robe and her face was pale and grave. Beneath her eyes were shadows, but she spoke with high dignity.

"Bring to me here my kinsman," she said, "my cousin-brother, Jung Lu."

"The Captain of the Imperial Bannermen?" Li Lien-ying asked, surprised.

"Yes," she said haughtily.

He went away, wiping the smile from his face with his sleeve.

She let the curtain fall and heard the eunuch's footsteps go away. When she had the power, she told herself, she would raise Jung Lu up, so that no one, not even a eunuch, could dare to say "the guardsman." She would make him at least a duke, a Grand Councilor perhaps. And while she cherished these thoughts in her mind she felt such a yearning arise in her heart that she was frightened for herself. What could she want of her kinsman except the sight of his truthful face, the sound of his firm voice, while he told her what now she should do? Oh, but she was wrong to send for him, for could she tell him what had befallen her in these two days and three nights and how she was changed? Could she say to him that she wished she had never come to the Forbidden City and beg him now to help her to escape? She let herself sink to the floor and she leaned her head against the wall and closed her eyes. A strange pain, deep in her vitals, swelled up into her breast. She hoped he would not come.

Vain hope, for she heard his footsteps. He had come instantly, he was at the door, and Li Lien-ying was calling through the curtain.

"Lady, your kinsman is here!"

She rose then and without thinking to look at her face in the mirror. Jung Lu knew her as she was. There was no reason to be beautiful for him. She went to the curtain and put it aside, and he was there.

"Come in, cousin," she said.

"Come out," he said. "We must not meet inside your chamber."

"Yet I must speak with you alone," she said, for Li Lien-ying waited, his ears outstretched and greedy.

But Jung Lu would not come in and so she was forced to leave her chamber, and when he saw her face, how white it was and how pale were her lips and dark her eyes, he was concerned for her, and he went with her into the courtyard, and she forbade the eunuch to follow there. Only her serving woman stood on the steps nearby, so that it could not be said that she was alone with a man, even her cousin.

Thus she could not touch his hand, nor allow him to touch hers, sorely as she longed for his touch. She moved as far from the door as she could, and she sat down upon a porcelain garden seat, under a clump of date trees at the far end of the courtyard.

"Seat yourself," she said.

But Jung Lu would not sit down. He stood before her as straight and stiff as though he were only a guardsman by the Emperor's gate.

"Will you not sit down?" she asked again and looked up at him with pleading in her eyes.

"No," he said. "I am here only because you sent for me."

She yielded. "Have you heard?" she asked so softly that a bird upon a branch above her could not have known what she said.

"I have heard," he said, not looking at her.

"I am the new favorite."

"That, too, I have heard."

It was all told in these few words, and what more was there to be

33

said, if he would not speak? She kept looking at his face, the face she knew so well, comparing it with that thin narrow sickly face upon the imperial pillow. This face was young and handsome, the dark eyes large and powerful, the mouth set full and firm above the strong chin. Here was a man's face.

"I have been a fool," she said.

He did not answer this. What could be answered to it?

"I want to go home," she said.

He folded his arms and looked carefully above her head into the trees.

"This is your home," he said.

She bit the edge of her lower lip. "I want you to save me."

He did not move. If one watched him he would have said that Jung Lu stood subordinate to the woman who was seated there under the date trees. But he let his eyes slide down to her lovely uplifted face, and in those eyes she saw his answer.

"Oh, my heart, if I could save you, I would. But I cannot."

The heavy pain inside her vitals suddenly eased. "Then you do not forget me!"

"Night and day I do not forget," he said.

"What shall I do?" she asked.

"You know your destiny," he said. "You chose it."

Her lower lip quivered and tears shone silver in her black eyes.

"I did not know how it would be," she faltered.

"There is no undoing what is done," he said. "No going back, no being what you were."

She could not speak. Instead she bent her head to keep the tears from running on her cheeks and she dared not wipe them lest the eunuch lurked near enough to see.

"You have chosen greatness," he said in her silence. "Therefore you must be great."

She swallowed down her tears and still did not dare to lift her head. "Only on your promise," she said, her voice small and trembling.

"What promise?" he asked.

"That you will come when I send for you," she said. "I must have that safety and that comfort. I cannot be always alone."

She saw the sweat start out on his forehead as the sunlight fell through the trees upon his face. "I will come to you when you call," he said, not moving. "If you must, then send for me. But do not send unless you must. I will bribe this eunuch—a thing I have never done before—to bribe a eunuch! It puts me in his power. But I will do it."

She rose. "I have your promise," she said.

She gave him one long look and held her hands hard clasped together so that she could not put them forth to him.

"You understand me?" she asked.

"I do," he said.

"It is enough," she said, and passing him she left him there and went directly to her chamber. Behind her the curtain fell again.

For seven days and seven nights Yehonala would not leave her bed. The palace corridors were busy with whispers that she was ill, that she was angry, that she had tried to swallow her gold earrings, that she would not yield again to the Emperor. For as soon as the Court physicians declared the Emperor recovered from their powerful drugs, he sent for her. She would not obey. Never in the history of the dynasty had an imperial concubine refused herself and no one knew what now to do with Yehonala. She lay in her bed under her rose-red satin coverlets and she would not speak except to her woman. The eunuch Li Lien-ying was beside himself as he saw all his plans astray and his goals lost. Yet she would not allow him to lift the curtain of her door.

"Let them think I want to die," she told her woman. "At least it is true that I do not want to live here."

The woman carried this message to the eunuch and he gnashed his teeth. "If the Emperor were not beside himself with love, it would be easy enough," he snarled. "She could fall into a well or she could be poisoned, but he wants her whole and sound—and now!"

At last the Chief Eunuch, An Teh-hai, himself came and was no more successful. Yehonala would not see him. She kept her earrings beside her bed on the small table where stood her porcelain tea bowl and her earthen teapot bound in silver.

"Let that Chief Eunuch step over the threshold," she declared in a voice raised to reach his ears, "and I swallow my gold earrings!"

So it went through one whole day and then another and another and the Emperor grew peevish and distrustful, believing, he said, that some eunuch was delaying her coming in hope of a bribe.

"She was very obedient to me," he insisted. "She did all that I asked."

None dared to say that His Majesty was hateful to the beautiful girl, and it would not have come to the imperial mind to imagine this alone. Instead he felt that he was potent and able and he did not wish to waste himself on another concubine while he loved Yehonala. Indeed he had never loved any woman as he now loved her, and knowing that with other women his passion died early, he was pleased that after seven days he longed for her presence more than ever and he was therefore the more impatient at delay.

By night of the third day of the seven, An Teh-hai, too, was beside himself and he went to the Dowager Mother and told her what was going on, and how Yehonala, although she knew her power, would not obey the Emperor.

"I have never heard of such a woman in all our dynasty," the Dowager Mother exclaimed with energy. "Let the eunuchs take her by force to my son!"

The Chief Eunuch hesitated. "Venerable," he said, "I question this method. She must be won and persuaded, for I do assure you, Venerable, that she cannot be forced. She is so strong, being both taller and heavier than the Son of Heaven, though slender as a young willow tree, that she will not hesitate to bite him or scratch his face when they are alone."

"What horror!" the Dowager Mother exclaimed. She was old and she had an illness of the liver and spent much of her time in bed, and was indeed now lying in the recesses of a bed so large that she seemed to be looking from a cave.

She pondered. "Is there no one inside the palace who can persuade her?" she inquired.

"Venerable, the Consort is her true cousin," the Chief Eunuch suggested.

The Dowager Mother remonstrated. "It is not usual for the Consort to urge a concubine upon her own lord, the Emperor."

"Neither usual nor proper, Venerable," the Chief Eunuch agreed.

The old lady remained silent for so long that he thought she had fallen asleep. But she had not. She lifted her sunken eyelids after a time and she said, "Well, then, let this Yehonala go to the Consort's palace."

"And if she will not go, Venerable?" the Chief Eunuch inquired.

"How—if she not go?" the Dowager demanded.

"She has refused to go to the Son of Heaven himself," An Teh-hai reminded her.

The Dowager Mother groaned. "I tell you, I have never seen so fierce a female! Well, then, the Consort is gentle. Suggest to her that Yehonala is ill and should be visited."

"Yes, Venerable," the Chief Eunuch said. These were the instructions he wanted and he rose to obey. "Sleep in peace, Venerable," he said.

"Go away," the Dowager Mother replied. "I am too old for the troubles of men and women."

He went softly as she fell asleep, and he went at once to the palace of the Consort and there found Sakota embroidering tiger faces upon a pair of shoes for her child when it should be born.

When he had been announced and presented he exclaimed upon this work.

"Does the Imperial Consort not have many women to embroider for her?" he asked.

"I have," Sakota replied. "But then I myself have nothing to do. I am not clever like my cousin Yehonala. I do not wish to study books or learn painting."

"Ah," he said, standing before her. With a gesture of her little hand she now bade him sit. Upon the middle finger of this hand was her thimble, a ring of gold at the second joint.

"It is about your cousin that I come before you, Lady," he went on, still standing, "and at the command of the Dowager Mother."

She lifted her pretty eyes. "Oh?"

The Chief Eunuch coughed. "Your cousin gives us much trouble."

"Indeed?" Sakota said.

"She will not obey the imperial summons," he went on.

Sakota's little head drooped over her embroidery and she blushed as pink as a peach blossom. "Yet I heard—my women told me—"

"She has won the Emperor's favor," he agreed, "but she will not return to him."

The peach-blossom pink deepened. "What has this to do with me?" Sakota asked.

"It is thought that she might listen to you, the Consort," he suggested.

Sakota pondered this, embroidering slowly and with the utmost delicacy about the yellow eye of the tiny tiger on the shoe. "Is this a proper request to make of me?" she inquired at last.

The Chief Eunuch was blunt. "Indeed, it is not, Lady. Yet must all of us remember that the Son of Heaven is not a common man. He is not to be refused by anyone."

"He likes her so much!" Sakota murmured.

"Can she be blamed?" he asked in reply.

The little creature sighed and folded her embroidery and put it on the inlaid table near her. Then she put her hands together. "We have

37

always been sisters, she and I," she said in her sweetly plaintive voice. "If she needs me I will go to her."

"Thank you, Lady," the Chief Eunuch said. "I will escort you there myself and wait for your return."

So it happened that Yehonala, lying on her bed that same day, tearless and in despair, looked up and saw her cousin standing in the doorway. By now she felt she hated all her life and she was sorry that she had chosen greatness for she did not wish such greatness when she knew the price of it.

"Sakota!" she wailed and held out both her arms.

Sakota flew to her at once, melted by such a cry, and the two young women clasped each other and wept mutual tears. Neither dared to speak of what both remembered, and Sakota knew that the memory was as hateful to her as it was to Yehonala.

"Oh, poor Sister," she wept. "Three nights! I had only one."

"I will not return to him," Yehonala whispered. She all but strangled her cousin, so tightly did she hold her by both arms around the neck and Sakota sank down into the bed.

"Oh Sister, but you must!" she cried. "Else what will they do to you, my dear? We are not our own now."

Then Yehonala, always whispering because of the listening eunuchs, revealed her heart. "Sakota, it is worse for me than you. You love no man, do you? Alas, I know now that I do love. Here is the misery! If I did not love, I could be careless. What is a woman's body? It is only a thing, to be kept or given away. There is no pride in it when one does not love. It is only priceless when one loves—and is loved again."

She had no need to speak the name. Sakota knew it was Jung Lu.

"It is too late, Sister," Sakota said. She stroked Yehonala's smooth wet cheeks. "There is no escape now, Sister."

Yehonala pushed her hands away. "Then I must die," she said, her voice breaking, "for truly I will not live." And she put her head down on her cousin's shoulder again and wept.

Now this little Sakota had the soft heart of a woman in whom is only gentleness, and so while she soothed Yehonala with her hands, stroking her forehead and her cheeks, she plotted in her heart as to what she could do to help her. To leave the palace or even the Forbidden City was not possible. If a concubine escaped there was no place for her in the known world. If Yehonala returned to her uncle's house, who was Sakota's father, then the whole family might be killed for her sin. Yet where else can a runaway woman hide? If she mingles with strangers do they not all inquire to know who she is, for is it not told everywhere with noise and commotion if a concubine runs from the palaces of the Dragon Emperor? Whatever help, whatever comfort, must be found only within the walls themselves. Intrigue there was a plenty, and though no man could sleep within the walls of this city at night, save only the Son of Heaven, nevertheless women had their lovers by day.

Yet how could she, the Imperial Consort, stoop to bargain with eunuchs and so put herself in their power? She could not do this. Not only fear but delicacy, too, forbade.

"Dear Cousin," she said, hiding her thoughts, "you must speak with Jung Lu. Ask him to tell my father that you cannot stay where you are. Perhaps my father can buy you free, or exchange you for some other one, or he can say you have gone mad. Not now, you understand, Cousin, for indeed I hear that our lord is much in love with you. But later, Cousin, when your turn is over, and another takes your place, perhaps it can be done."

Sakota said this innocently, for she loved no man, and was not jealous, but Yehonala felt a prick of pride. What, was she to be displaced? If Sakota said this, then it must be that she had heard it already murmured among the women and the eunuchs. She sat up in bed and pushed her tumbled hair away from her face.

"I cannot ask my kinsman to come to me—you know that, Sakota! Gossip would flare from court to court. But you may send for him, Sakota. He is your kinsman, too. Send for him and tell him I will surely kill myself. Tell him that I care nothing for anyone, only to get myself free again. Here is a prison, Sakota—we are all in prison!"

"I am happy enough," Sakota said, mildly. "It is pleasant here, I think!"

Yehonala turned her eyes sidewise on her cousin. "You are happy anywhere—so long as you can sit in peace and embroider bits of satin!"

Sakota's eyelids fell and her small mouth curved down. "What else is there to do, Cousin?" she asked sadly.

Yehonala flung back her hair and caught it in one hand and twisted it into a great knot behind her head. "There—there—there—" she cried. "It is what I am saying! There is nothing to do—I cannot go on the street, I cannot so much as put my head outside the gate to see if there is a play at the corner, I have not seen one play since I came here and you know I have ever loved to see a play. My books, yes—my painting? Well, I paint. For whom? Myself! It is not enough—not yet! And at night—"

She shivered and drew up her legs and laid her proud head down upon her knees.

Sakota sat silent for a long moment. Then, knowing that she had no comfort for this young and stormy woman, whom indeed she could not understand, since not by storm can a woman change what she is born, she rose.

"Cousin, my dear," she said, in her most coaxing voice, "I will go away now so that you can be bathed and dressed and then you must eat some food, something you like. And I will send for our kinsman and you must not refuse to see him if he comes, for it will be because I have so decided for your sake. And if there is gossip, then I will say that it is I who bade him come."

She put her hand so lightly on Yehonala's head, still bent on her knees, that it felt no heavier there than a leaf, and then she went away.

When she was gone Yehonala flung herself back upon her pillows and lay stone still, her eyes open and staring into the canopy above her. A fantasy wove itself in her mind, a dream, a plan, a plot, possible only if Sakota protected her, Sakota who was the Imperial Consort, whom no one could accuse.

When her serving woman peered in, afraid to speak or call, Yehonala turned her head.

"I will have my bath now," she said. "And I will put on something new—say, my green robe, the apple green. And then I will eat."

"Yes, yes, my queen, my pet," the woman said, well pleased. She let the curtains fall and Yehonala heard her feet trotting down the corridors, hastening to obey.

Sometime in the afternoon of that day, two hours before the curfew fell when all men must leave the Emperor's city, Yehonala heard the footstep for which she waited. She had spent the day alone in her own rooms after Sakota left her, forbidding the entrance of anyone. Only her serving woman sat outside the door. To her Yehonala said honestly:

"I am in sore trouble. My cousin, the Consort, knows my woe. She has commanded our kinsman to come to me, to hear me and to carry my trouble to my guardian uncle. While he is here, you are to stay by the door. You are not to enter, nor let anyone so much as peer into my court. You understand that it is by the Consort's command that he comes."

"Lady, I do understand," the woman said.

Thus the hours had passed, she at the door and Yehonala inside

40

the closed door behind the dropped curtain. She sat idle in body but her mind was exceedingly busy and her heart was in turmoil. Could she prevail upon Jung Lu to foresake his rectitude? It was her will so to prevail.

He came at last, two hours before the curfew. She heard his footsteps, the firm pace measured to his height. She heard his voice inquiring whether Yehonala slept and her woman's reply that she waited for him.

She heard the door open and close, and she saw his hand, that large smooth hand she knew so well, lay hold upon the inner curtain and hesitate. She sat rigid in her chair of carved black wood, waiting and motionless. Then he put the curtain aside and stood there looking at her, and she looked at him. Her heart leaped in her breast, a thing alive and separate from her, and tears welled to her eyes and her mouth began to quiver.

Whatever she could do, this that she did shook all his will. He had seen her weep in pain and he had heard her sob with rage, but he had never seen her sit motionless and weep without a sound, helplessly, as though her very life were broken.

He gave a great groan and his arms went out to her and he strode across the floor. And she, seeing only those outstretched arms, rose blindly from her chair and ran to him and felt them enclose her fast. Thus locked together, in silence and in fearful ecstasy they stood, how long, neither knew. Cheek to cheek they stood, until their lips met by instinct. Then he tore his mouth away.

"You know you cannot leave this place," he groaned. "You must find your freedom here within these walls, for there is no other freedom for you now."

She listened, hearing his voice from afar, knowing only that within his arms she held him.

"The higher you rise," he told her, "the greater will your freedom be. Rise high, my love—the power is yours. Only an Empress can command."

"But will you love me?" she asked, her voice stifling in her throat.

"How can I not love you?" Thus he replied. "To love you is my only life. I draw my breath, my every breath, to love you."

"Then—seal me your love!"

These were the bold words she spoke but in so soft a whisper that he might not have heard them, except she knew he did. She felt him motionless, then he made a sigh. She felt his shoulders shiver and his muscles loosen and his bones yield.

"If once I am made yours," she said bravely, "even here I can live." No answer yet! He could not speak. His soul was still not yielded. She lifted her head and looked into his face. "What does it matter where I live if I am yours? I know you speak the truth. There is no escape for me except by death. Well, I can choose death. It is easy in a palace—opium to swallow, my gold earrings, a little knife to open my veins—can I be watched day and night? I swear I will die unless you make me yours! If I am yours, I will do what you say—forever and my whole life long. I will be Empress."

Her voice was magic, lovely with pleading, deep and soft and gentle, warm and sweet as honey in the summer sun. Was he not a man? He was young and fervent, still virgin because he had loved no one but her whom he now held within his arms. They were prisoners, trapped by old ways of life, jailed within the imperial palace. He was no more free than she was. Yet only she could do what she would. If she said she would be Empress, then none could hold her back. And if she chose death, then she would die. He knew her nature. And would he not devote his life to help her live? And had not Sakota herself imagined some such scene as this when she had bade him come here? At the last moment the Consort had laid her hand on his arm and she bade him do all he could—"whatever Yehonala asks"—those were Sakota's very words.

His soul's voice was stilled, he felt his conscience die and he lifted the beautiful girl in his arms and carried her to the bed.

. . . The drums of curfew beat through the courtyards and the corridors of the city of the Son of Heaven. It was the hour of sunset when every man must be gone from within the walls. The ancient command fell upon the ears of lovers hidden deep within the secret rooms and in Yehonala's bedchamber Jung Lu rose and drew his garments about him while she lay half asleep and smiling.

He leaned over her. "Are we sworn?" he asked.

"Sworn," she put up her arms and drew his face down to hers again. "Forever, forever!"

The drums died down and he made haste, and she rose quickly and smoothed her robes and brushed back her hair. When her woman coughed at the door she was sitting in her chair.

"Enter," she said, and she took her handkerchief and pretended to wipe her eyes.

"Are you weeping again, lady?" the woman asked.

Yehonala shook her head. "I am finished weeping," she said in a small voice. "I know what I must do. My kinsman has made me see my duty."

The woman stood, peering and listening, head to one side like a bird's.

"Your duty, lady?" she repeated.

"When the Son of Heaven summons me," Yehonala said, "I shall go to him. I must do his will."

The heat of summer lingered late in the Forbidden City. One brilliant day followed upon another, the palaces stood in the living light of the naked sun and no rains fell. So hot was the stillness of high noon that princesses and Court ladies, eunuchs and concubines, went to the caves in the imperial gardens and there spent the hours of the full heat. These caves were built of river rock, brought from the south upon barges floating up the Grand Canal. The rocks were shaped by men's hands yet so cunningly contrived that they looked worn by winds and waters. Crouching pine trees hung over the entrances to these caves and inside them hidden fountains dripped down the walls and made pools where goldfish played. In the coolness the ladies did embroidery, heard music, or played at gambling games.

But Yehonala did not enter the caves. She was now always busy at her books, always smiling, silent more often than speaking as she studied her books. Seemingly her rebellion was forgotten. When the Emperor summoned her, she allowed herself to be bathed and dressed afresh and she went to him. His favor did not falter, and this compelled her prudence, for waiting concubines grew restless for their turn, and Li Lien-ying contended among the eunuchs to keep himself her chief servant. Yet if Yehonala knew of strife, she did not let it be known that she knew, unless it could be guessed from her faultless courtesy to all, and from her careful obedience to the Dowager Mother. Each day when she awoke she went first to the Dowager Mother to inquire of her health and happiness. The old lady was often ill and Yehonala brewed herbs in the tea to soothe her, and if she were restless she rubbed the withered feet and hands and soothed the Dowager by brushing her white scanty hair in long and even strokes. No task was too small or too low for Yehonala to perform for the Dowager Mother, and soon all perceived that the handsome girl was not only the favorite of the Son of Heaven, but of his mother, too.

Thus Yehonala knew how eagerly the Dowager Mother waited for the birth of Sakota's child, and it was part of Yehonala's duty daily to accompany the Dowager Mother to the Buddhist temple and wait while she made prayers and burned incense before the gods, beseeching Heaven that the Consort might have a son. Only when this was done did Yehonala return to her own chosen tasks, which were as ever in the library, reading and studying under aged eunuchs who were scholars, or learning music, and she spent herself in learning how to write with the camel's-hair brush after the style of the great calligraphers of the past.

Meanwhile she hid a secret, or thought she did, until one day her woman spoke out. It was a usual day, the air cooler at night and morning than it had been, but still hot at noon. Yehonala slept late, for she had been summoned by the Emperor the night before, as many nights she had been summoned and always she obeyed.

"Mistress," the woman said when she entered the bedroom on this day and closed the door carefully behind her, "have you not marked that the full moon has come and gone and you have no show of crimson?"

"Is it so?" Yehonala asked as if she did not care. Yet how greatly did she care, and how closely she had observed her own person!

"It is so," the woman said proudly. "The seed of the Dragon is in you, lady. Shall I not carry the good news to the Mother of the Son of Heaven?"

"Wait," Yehonala commanded. "Wait until the Consort has borne her child. If he is a son, does it matter what I bear?"

"But if she bears a daughter?" the woman inquired cunningly.

Yehonala threw her a long teasing look. "Then I will tell the Dowager Mother myself," she said. "And if you tell even my eunuch," she said, and made her eyes big and fierce, "then I will have you sliced and the strips of your flesh hung up on poles to dry for dogs' food."

The woman tried to laugh. "I swear by my mother that I will tell no one." But who, her pale face asked, could know when this concubine, too beautiful, too proud, might turn teasing into truth?

While the Court waited, then, upon the Consort, each concubine woke in the morning to ask if there were news and the princes and the Grand Councilor Shun before they entered the Audience Hall at dawn demanded from the eunuchs whether the birth was begun. And still Sakota's child was not born. In his own anxiety the Emperor commanded the Board of Astrologers to study the stars again and to determine from the entrails of freshly killed fowls whether his child would not be a son. Alas, they saw confusion. The signs were not clear. The child might or might not be a son. It was even possible that the Consort would give birth to twins, boy and girl, in which misfortune the girl must be killed, lest she sap the life of her royal brother.

The autumn deepened, and the Court physicians grew anxious for the health of the Consort. She was worn with waiting, her frailty much increased because the child would not be born, and she could not eat or sleep. Once Yehonala went to see her, but Sakota would not receive her. She was too ill, the eunuch in attendance said. She should see no one. And Yehonala went away in doubt. Illness? How could Sakota be too ill to see her own cousin-sister? For the first time she wished Sakota did not know that Jung Lu had come to her in private. True, she knew no more, but even to know so little put a weapon in Sakota's hand—a weak hand that might be used by a stronger one as yet unknown. Alas, she knew by now that intrigue was everywhere throughout the palaces, and she must be strong enough to break through its meshes. Never once again, not for an hour, would she put a weapon of secret knowledge into another's hand.

The days went on, each long, and all omens were dire. Evil news came from everywhere throughout the Empire. The long-haired Chinese rebels in the south had seized the southern capital, Nanking, and many people had been killed. So ferocious were those rebels that the imperial soldiers could not win a single battle. And as a further sign of evil, strange swift winds blew down upon the city, comets crossed the skies at night and in many places rumors rose that women gave birth to twins and monsters.

On the last day of the eighth moon month there appeared at noon a thunderstorm, which changed itself into a typhoon more fit for southern seas than for the dry northern plains upon which the city stood. Even the elders had never seen such lightning nor heard such crashing roaring thunder, and hot winds blew from the south as though devils rode upon the clouds. When rain fell at last it came not in a gentle downpour upon the dried fields and dusty streets but in such floods and lashings and fury that torrents ate the earth away. Whether from fright or deep despair Sakota upon that day felt the pains of birth begin inside her body and no sooner did she cry out than the news spread everywhere through the palaces and all stopped whatever they were doing to wait and hear.

At this hour Yehonala was in the library and at her usual books. The sky had grown so dark that eunuchs lit lamps, and by her lamp she was writing under the eyes of her tutor as he read aloud an ancient sacred text for her to copy. Thus he read:

"Chung Kung, the minister of the House of Chi, asked for advice

45

upon the art of government. The Master said, 'Learn above all how to use your subordinates. Overlook their lesser weaknesses, and raise up only those who are honest and able.'"

At this moment Li Lien-ying appeared at the curtain and behind the tutor's back he made signs to Yehonala whose meaning she understood at once. She laid down her brush and rose.

"Sir," she said to her tutor, "I must hasten to the Dowager Mother, who has sudden need of me."

Long ago she had planned what she would do when Sakota was in labor. She would go to the Dowager Mother and stay with her, soothe her and amuse her, until it was known whether the birth was of a female or a male. Before the tutor could reply she had left the library and was walking ahead of the eunuch toward the Dowager Mother's palace. The lightning darted above the treetops and the courtyards sprang into livid light as she went, and through the roofed passageways the wind blew the rain like spray from the sea. But Yehonala hurried on, and behind her Li Lien-ying followed.

When she reached the palace she went in without speaking to any of the waiting women. The Dowager Mother had gone to bed as she did always in a thunderstorm, and now she lay raised on her pillows, her hands clasped about a jeweled Buddhist rosary, her thin face as white as mutton-fat jade. When she saw Yehonala she did not smile. In a solemn voice she said, "How can a sound child be born at such a time? Heaven itself rages above our heads."

Yehonala ran to her and knelt beside the bed. "Be soothed, Imperial Mother," she coaxed. "It is not because of us that Heaven rages. Evil men have rebelled against the Throne, and the child to be born will save us all. Heaven is angry on his behalf and not against him, or us."

"Do you believe it so?" the old lady replied.

"I do," Yehonala said and she knelt on, speaking soothing words and rising only to fetch hot broth for the Dowager Mother to drink down and uphold her strength. Then she found a pleasant book of tales to read and she played upon a lute and sang a song now and then, and helped the old lady at her prayers and so the hours passed.

At sunset the wind died down and a strange yellow light suffused the palaces and courtyards. Then Yehonala drew the curtains and lit the candles and waited, for she had continuing news, which she did not tell the Dowager Mother, that the birth was very near. After the yellow light the darkness came down suddenly and when night fell the Chief Eunuch, An Teh-hai, came to the palace of the Dowager Mother.

Yehonala went to meet him, and from his face she saw the news was evil.

"Is the child dead?" she inquired.

"Not dead," he said heavily, "but it is a girl—a sickly female—"

Yehonala put her handkerchief to her eyes. "Oh, cruel Heaven!"

"Will you tell the Venerable Mother?" he asked. "I must hasten again to the Emperor. He is ill with anger."

"I will tell her," Yehonala promised.

"And you," the Chief Eunuch continued. "Make yourself ready to be summoned in the night. The Emperor will surely need you."

"I am ready," she said.

Then slowly she went back to the Dowager's bedchamber and gave no heed to the waiting women who had guessed the news and stood with bowed heads and eyes streaming tears as she passed. She entered the great bedchamber again and when the Dowager Mother saw her face she too knew all.

"It is not a male child," she said and her voice was weary with all the weariness of her years of waiting.

"It is a female," Yehonala said gently.

She knelt beside the bed again and took the Dowager Mother's hands and stroked them with her own strong young hands.

"Why do I live?" the Dowager Mother inquired piteously.

"You must live, Venerable Mother," Yehonala said. She made her deep voice tender. "You must live—until my son is born."

Her hope was revealed. She had saved her secret and like a gift she gave it now to the Dowager Mother.

That old face quivered and broke into a wrinkled smile. "Is it true?" she asked. "Can this be Heaven's will? Yes, it is so! The child will become from your strong body, a son! Buddha hears! It must be so. And I called you fierce, I said that you were too strong. Oh, daughter, how warm your hands are on me!"

She looked down into the young and tenderly beautiful face so near her and Yehonala looking up saw adoration in the Dowager Mother's eyes.

"My hands are always warm," she said. "It is true that I am strong. And I can be fierce. And I shall bear a son."

When the Venerable lady heard what Yehonala said she rose out of her bed with such energy that all around her were frightened.

"Save yourself, Imperial Mother," Yehonala exclaimed.

She ran forward to support the Dowager Mother, but the lady

47

pushed her away. "Send eunuchs to my son," she exclaimed in her quavering voice. "Tell him I have good news."

The ladies in attendance heard these words as they waited outside. They looked at one another with doubt and joy, while in great commotion the eunuchs were summoned and sent off.

"My bath!" the Dowager Mother commanded her women, and while they hastened to make the bath she turned again to Yehonala.

"And you, my heart," she exclaimed, "you are more precious to me now than any except my son himself. You are the destined one. I see it in your eyes. Such eyes! Nothing evil must befall you. Return to your own chamber, my daughter, and rest yourself. I shall have you moved to the inner courts of the Western Palace, where the sun falls upon the terraces. And let the physicians be summoned without delay!"

"But I am not ill, Venerable," Yehonala said, laughing. "Look at me!"

She stretched out her arms, she lifted her head, her cheeks were red, her dark eyes bright.

The Dowager Mother stared at her. "Beautiful, beautiful," she murmured. "The eyes so clear, the eyebrows like moth's wings, the flesh as tender as a child's! I knew the Consort would bear only a girl. I told you so, you women—do you remember I said a creature of such soft bone, such slack flesh, would bear only a girl?"

"Venerable, you told us—you told us indeed," the serving women said, one after the other.

And Yehonala said, "I will obey you, Venerable, in all things."

She made her obeisance and retired from the chamber. Outside the doors her own woman waited and Li Lien-ying also. The tall eunuch was rubbing his hands and grinning and cracking his finger joints.

"Let the Phoenix Empress command me," he declared. "I wait for her commands."

"Be quiet," Yehonala said. "You speak too soon."

"Have I not seen destiny over your head?" he cried. "I see it there now with my naked eyes. I say what I have always known."

"Leave me," Yehonala told him. She walked away with swift grace, her woman following. After a few steps she paused and she looked back at the eunuch. "One thing only you may do," she said. "You may go to my kinsman and tell him what you have heard."

The eunuch stretched out his neck, corded like a turtle's neck. "Shall I bid him come to you?" he asked in a hissing whisper.

"No," Yehonala replied in a clear voice for anyone to hear. "It is not fitting that I should speak now to any man, save to my imperial lord."

And she went on her way, her hand resting on her woman's shoulder.

In her own bedchamber she waited, expecting summons from the Emperor when he heard, and her woman bathed her and put fresh inner garments on her and brushed her hair in coils to fit under her jeweled headdress.

"What outer robes will you wear now, Venerable?" the woman inquired fondly.

"Bring me the pale-blue robe embroidered in pink plum blossoms, and the yellow embroidered in green bamboo," Yehonala said.

The two robes were brought but before she could decide which one suited the color of her face today, there was a commotion in the outer courts. A sudden noise of wailing voices rose above the walls.

"What evil has befallen?" the serving woman cried.

She ran out, leaving her mistress with the robes spread out before her on the bed, and at the gate into the court she fell against the eunuch Li Lien-ying. He wore a face as green as a sour peach, and his coarse mouth hung ajar.

"The Dowager Mother is dead," he gasped, and his voice came dry out of his throat.

"Dead!" the woman screamed. "But my mistress was with her two hours ago!"

"Dead," Li Lien-ying repeated. "She came tottering to the Audience Hall supported by her ladies and when the Emperor hastened to her there, she opened her mouth to breathe as though her throat were cut. Then she cried out that he would have a son, and these were her last words, for she fell dead into her ladies' arms. Her soul has gone to the eternal Yellow Springs."

"Oh, Lord of Hell," the woman wailed, "how can you bear such evil news?"

She ran back to her mistress, but Yehonala, hastening to the outer door, had already heard.

"I brought the Imperial Mother too much joy," she said sadly.

"No, but joy came too quickly after sorrow, and her soul was divided," the woman said.

Yehonala did not make reply. She went back to her bedroom and stood looking at the two robes spread out before her.

"Put them away," she said at last. "I shall not be summoned now until the Emperor's days of mourning are ended."

And the old woman, sobbing and moaning at such ill fortune, folded the bright robes and put them away again in the red-lacquered chests from whence she had taken them.

The months slipped quietly into the Season of the First Cold. The Forbidden City was stilled in mourning for the Dowager Mother, and the Son of Heaven, wearing white robes of death, lived without women. Yehonala missed the fondness of the dead Dowager, yet she knew that she was not forgotten. She was free and by the Emperor's command she was also guarded. Whatever she asked for she had, but she must obey the commands sent down to her. Thus she was encouraged to eat the most delicate and delicious foods, fish from the distant rivers, preserved in ice and snow, the yellow carp, the smooth-skinned eels. Fish she craved for every meal, and she drank the soup made from crushed fish bones. Beyond this she asked only to eat the coarse sweets of her childhood that she used to buy at the street vendor's stall, red sugar cakes, sesame toffee, and rice-flour dumplings stuffed with sweetened bean paste, such as peasants eat. Fat pork and roasted mutton and browned duck and other palace meats she could not eat. And most difficult of all to swallow were the herbs and medicines which the royal physicians brewed daily for her to drink down, for they were continually frightened lest the child be born too soon or born deformed, for which evil they would be blamed, as they well knew.

Each morning after Yehonala was bathed and dressed and before she had eaten, the physicians waited upon her in number, to feel her pulse and peer under her eyelids and examine her tongue and smell her breath. Then they conferred for two hours concerning her condition that day, and after they were agreed, they prescribed and themselves prepared what they had chosen. How vile were these bowls of green mixtures and black draughts! But Yehonala swallowed the liquors, for well she knew that what she carried in her was no ordinary child, but one who belonged to all the people as their ruler, and not once did she doubt that she carried a male child. She ate heartily and slept well and she kept down the medicines somehow, and her young body throve with health. Throughout the palaces a grateful joy pervaded like serene music, and this flowed out over the whole country. People said to one another that the times had turned, that evil was past and good was come again to the Empire.

Meanwhile Yehonala herself was changed. Until the day when she knew she had conceived, she had been a girl, willful and mischievous,

50

changeable and impetuous in spite of her love of books and her ambition to learn. Now, while she continued to read the ancient books and to brush the ancient characters, whatever she learned she wove around herself and the child within her. Thus when she came upon the words of Lao Tzu, which are these, "Of all the dangers, the greatest is to think lightly of the foe," she was struck by their present meaning. That wise man had lived how many hundreds of years before her and yet his words remained as fresh as though they were spoken to her this same day. The foe? The realm her son might one day rule was presently beset by foes. She had thought them no concern of hers, but now she knew they were the enemies of her son and so her own. She looked up from the page.

"Tell me," she said to her tutor, "who are our present foes?"

The old eunuch shook his head, "Lady," he replied, "I have no learning in affairs of state. I know only the ancient sages."

Yehonala closed her book. "Send me one to teach me who are my present foes," she said.

The aged eunuch was confounded but he knew better than to question her, and he reported her command to An Teh-hai, the Chief Eunuch, who went to Prince Kung, the sixth son of the last Emperor. His mother was a concubine, and he was therefore half-brother by blood to the present Emperor, Hsien Feng. The two half-brothers had grown up together, studying their books and learning swordmanship under the same tutors. Prince Kung's mind was good, his face manly and good to see. Indeed, his wisdom and intelligence were so high and calm that ministers, princes and eunuchs went to him secretly instead of to the Emperor, nor did he betray anyone and all trusted him. The Chief Eunuch, An Teh-hai, went therefore to the palace of this Prince, which was outside the Forbidden City, and he told him of Yehonala's visit, and he begged Prince Kung himself to teach the young Favorite.

"For she is so strong," he said, "so filled with health, her mind as clever as a man's, that we do not doubt she will bear a son, who will be our next Emperor."

Prince Kung pondered for a while. He was a young man, and it was not seemly for him to come near a concubine. Yet he was related to her now through his imperial brother and custom might be set aside. They were not Chinese, moreover, but Manchu, and Manchu ways were more free than Chinese ways. And he remembered how dire were these times. His elder brother, the Emperor, was dissolute and weak, the Court corrupt and idle, the ministers and princes lifeless, hopeless, powerless, it seemed, to stay the crumbling of the Empire. The treasury was empty, harvests failed and famines starved the people often. And in their angry hunger, the people made rebellion. Secret rebel bands were everywhere plotting against the Dragon Throne, the Chinese declaring that now was the time to drive out the Manchu emperors, who had ruled them for two hundred years. Drive out the Manchu! Restore the ancient Chinese dynasty of Ming! Already such rebels had gathered in a horde under the long-haired madman, Hung, who called himself a Chinese Christ, as if it were not enough that foreigners were Christians and in the name of that same Christ seduced the young in schools and churches to desert their family gods! What hope, then, except to hold hard the remnants of the Empire until an heir was born, strong son of strong mother?

"I will myself teach the Favorite," he said, "but bid her aged tutor stay in her presence while I am there."

The next day, then, when Yehonala went to her books as usual in the Imperial Library, she saw there a man, tall, young, and of powerful handsome looks, beside her tutor. With him was An Teh-hai, who presented Prince Kung, saying why he had come.

Yehonala drew her sleeve across her face and bowed, and Prince Kung stood sidewise, his head turned away.

"Be seated, Elder Brother," Yehonala said in her pretty voice, and herself sat down in her usual chair, while the old tutor took his place at the end of the table. The Chief Eunuch stood behind the Prince, and her four ladies behind Yehonala.

In this fashion Prince Kung began to teach the Imperial Concubine. Without looking at her and his face turned away, he began the lessons which he continued, one day in seven, for many months. He told her the entire state of the nation, described how the weakness of the Throne invited rebellion of its subjects and invasion from enemies beyond the northern plains and eastern seas. He told her how these invaders, three hundred years before, were first men from Portugal, seeking trade in spices. By the riches of their lawless plunder they tempted other men of Europe to do as they had done, and Spanish conquerors came and Dutchmen in Dutch ships, and then the English, making war for their opium trade and after these the French, the Germans.

Yehonala's eyes grew larger and more black. Her face was pale and red by turns and her hands clenched in fists upon her knees. "And we did nothing?" she cried out.

"What could we do?" Prince Kung retorted. "We are not sea-faring people as the English are. Their little lands lie circled by the sea, barren and scanty, and upon the sea they must forage or they starve."

"Nevertheless, I do think—"

Thus Yehonala began but Prince Kung raised his hand.

"Wait—there is yet more."

And he told how continuously the English had made their wars, each time victorious.

"Why?" she demanded.

"They spend their wealth on war weapons," Prince Kung replied.

And he told her how still another enemy came down, this time from the north. "We have long known these Russians," he told her. "Five hundred years ago, Most Favored, the great Kublai Khan, who ruled here, employed Russians to be his bodyguard and so did all the emperors of his dynasty. Two hundred years after him one Yermak, Russian and land pirate, a man of adventure and with a price upon his head, led his wild band across the Ural Mountains to seek furs for those who hired him. He fought the northern tribes who lived in the valley of the great river, Ob, and he took their royal city, called Siber, and he claimed it in the name of the ruler of Russia, who is the Tsar, and thereafter the whole region was called Siberia. And for this deed of conquest his sins were forgiven him and his people call him great even to this day."

"I have heard enough," she said abruptly.

"Yet not enough, Most Favored," Prince Kung said courteously. "The English did not let us be. In the time of Chia-Ch'ing, the son of the mighty Ch'ien Lung, the British sent an envoy, Amherst by name. This man, when summoned to the Audience Hall at the usual hour of dawn, refused to come, saying that his garments of state had not arrived, and that he was ill. The Son of Heaven, then ruling, sent his own physicians to examine the foreigner, and they returned, saying that Amherst feigned illness. The Son of Heaven, then ruling, was angry and ordered the Englishman to go home. The white men are stubborn, Most Favored. They will not bend or kneel before our Sons of Heaven. They tell us that they kneel before none but gods—and women."

"Women?" Yehonala repeated. She was diverted by this image of white men kneeling before women and she put up her hand to hide her laughter behind her sleeve. The sound of laughter escaped her nevertheless and Prince Kung turned his eyes sidewise and caught the mischief in her eyes and himself broke into soundless laughter. Thus encouraged the Chief Eunuch laughed and then the Court ladies laughed, holding up their silken sleeves, too, to hide their faces.

53

"Will white men still not kneel to the Son of Heaven?" Yehonala asked, when her laughter ended.

"They will not kneel," Prince Kung replied.

Yehonala did not speak for a moment. But when my son rules, she was thinking, they will kneel to my son. If they will not kneel and bow their heads to the floor, then I will have them beheaded.

"What now?" she asked. "Are we still helpless?"

"We must resist," Prince Kung said, "though not by arms or battles, for we have not such means. But we can resist by obstructions and delays. We must deny the foreigners their wishes. Now that these Americans, newcomers and followers of the English, insist, too, upon the benefits of the treaties we have been forced to make with other Western peoples, we have demanded that their government may not protect Americans who trade in opium and to this they have agreed."

"What is the end?" Yehonala asked.

"Who knows?" Prince Kung replied. He sighed heavily and shadows fell across his face. It was a bitter face for all its handsome looks, a sad face, the lines deep about the thin mouth and between the black brows.

He rose and bowed. "It is enough, I think, for this one day," he said. "I have brushed a few lines from history for you, Most Favored. Now, if you will, I shall proceed to fill them out until all the truth is plain."

"I pray you do so," Yehonala said, and she rose, too, and bowed.

Thus the day came to an end, and that night she could not sleep. What destiny was hers? Her son must take the Empire back again and drive his foreign foes into the sea.

Yehonala now felt herself no more a prisoner within the palace. She was the center of the people's hope. What she ate, whether she slept well, did she suffer languor or pain, her color, her laughter, her willfulness and whims—all were matters of concern. In the glow of such importance, the winter months came in and passed, day following day, and the clear sunshine of bright and cloudless skies enlivened the whole city. The people were cheerful with their hope, and business was good. In the south the long-haired rebels settled into the city of Nanking, and rumors creeping northward said that the leader was taking many wives and corrupting himself with wines and fine foods. But Yehonala received this good news with no more than mild pleasure, for the Chinese rebel was not her true foe. The foreigners, the white men, were the enemy. And yet why the enemy? Let them return to their own lands, and there need be no enmity even with them. We want but our own, Yehonala told herself.

54

Indeed a mild mood pervaded her spirit in these days, and never had she felt her body grow so sound and whole. Whether it was the brewed herbs she drank or whether it was her own full and vital energy flowering at the demand of motherhood, she did not know. Strangest of all, she no longer hated the Son of Heaven. True, she did not love him, but she pitied him, the shell of a man, wrapped in his golden robes of office. She cradled him in her arms at night, and by day she showed him extravagant respect and honor, for was he not the father of her son? Was he the father of her son? The two-headed question hid in her heart. For all the world to see and to believe, he was the father of her son. Her son must have the Emperor for his father. Yet secret in her own heart was the living thought of Jung Lu and the hour when he had come at her desire.

Into her life there fed two streams, the first her constant deepening pride that she bore within her the Heir to the Throne and the other her secret love. For the one she studied zealously the history of the people whom her son would rule, poring over many ancient books and putting her questions to Prince Kung. Because of the other, she perceived anew the beauty of the world to which one day she would bring her son. Sometimes in the afternoon, instead of closing herself into the libraries, she spent the hours walking with her ladies, her guardian eunuch, Li Lien-ying, following behind. Never did they go beyond the walls of the Emperor's city, but within these walls was enough to see so that it would take her many years to know it all. When the sun was high and no cold winds blew, she walked among the courtyards, down the corridors and between the high rose-red walls of narrow streets that linked the palace courts together. Circling the sacred city were triple walls and in the walls were set four gates, facing the four points of the compass. Within the great first gate were three inner gates leading to bridges and gardens in the palaces and throne halls, these halls facing always south, their colors the symbols of the elements. Even now in winter the gardens were beautiful, the northern bamboo green under snow, and the Indian bamboo bearing scarlet berries under snow. At the Gate of Heavenly Peace stood two winged pillars of white marble, encircled by carved dragons, and to these she returned often, and why she did not know, except that her spirit lifted at the noble sight of these white-winged pillars.

Palace by palace, the throne rooms many, she learned to know the sacred polar city, the center of the earth even as the north star is center of the sky, and in splendid loneliness she walked among her ladies.

55

Ah, she had chosen well to make this city her son's birthplace and his home!

In the third moon of the spring of the new year, on a day chosen by what heavenly decision she did not know, Yehonala gave birth to her son. In the presence of the elder ladies of the Court who took the place of the dead Dowager Mother, her son was born, indisputably the heir, and the midwives so declared him. While Yehonala crouched upon a stool, a midwife caught the child and held him up before the ladies.

"See, Venerables," she announced. "A male child, in full health and strength!"

And Yehonala, half fainting, looked up and saw her son. He lay in the midwife's hands, he moved his arms and legs, and opening his mouth he cried aloud.

When night fell, the soft spring night, the courtyard outside her little private palace was lit by the light of lanterns set upon an altar of sacrifice. From her bed Yehonala looked through the low latticed windows upon the assembly of princes and ladies and eunuchs who stood beyond the table, the candlelight flickering upon their faces and upon their many-coloured robes of satin, embroidered in gold and silver. It was the hour of birth sacrifice to Heaven, and the Emperor stood before the altar to give thanks and to announce his heir. Upon the altar were three offerings, the steamed head of a pig, white and hairless, a steamed cock, naked of feathers except for its head and tail, and between pig and cock a live fish, struggling in a net of scarlet silk.

The rite was difficult. Yet none could make it except the Son of Heaven himself, for this fish had been taken alive from a lotus pond, and it must be returned alive again to that same water, or the Heir would not live to reach his manhood. Nor could the imperial father make haste or violate the solemn dignity of what he did, lest Heaven be offended. In deep silence he raised his arms, in silence he knelt before Heaven, to whom he alone could make obeisance, and he chanted his prayers. Exactly at the right moment he ended, and seizing the still-living fish with both hands he gave it to the Chief Eunuch who hastened to the pool and threw it in, waiting to see if it swam away. If it did not, then the Heir would die a child. He peered into the water, his lantern held high, and in silence the Court waited and the Emperor stood motionless before the altar.

The light fell upon a flash of silver in the water.

"The fish lives, Majesty," the eunuch shouted.

And upon these joyful words the assembly began to laugh and talk. Firecrackers were lit, caged birds in all the palaces were freed, and rockets sprayed the sky with light. While Yehonala leaned upon her elbow, the whole sky seemed to split before her eyes, and from the center she saw floating against the sparkling darkness a huge golden orchid, its petals touched with purple.

"Lady, this is in your honor!" her serving woman cried.

A roar rose up from the city when the people saw the sight, and Yehonala laughed and threw herself upon her pillows. How many times in her life had she wished she were a man but now how glad was she to be a woman! What man could know such triumph as hers, that she had made a son for the Emperor?

"Is my cousin, the Consort, in the courtyard, too?" she asked.

The old woman peered into the lights and shadows of the courtyard. "I see her standing among her ladies," she replied.

"Go out to her," Yehonala commanded. "Invite her to come in. Tell her I long to see her."

The woman went out and approaching proudly she asked the Consort to come to the bedside of her mistress.

"She looks upon the Dragon Consort as her elder sister," the woman said, coaxing.

But Sakota shook her head. "I rose from my bed to attend the sacrifice," she said, "and to my bed I must return. Indeed, I am not well."

She turned away as she said this and leaning upon two ladies, and led by a eunuch with a lantern, she walked into the darkness of a round moon gate.

All were surprised at this refusal and the woman went back to Yehonala to report. "Lady, the Consort will not come. She says she is ill, but I think she is not."

"Then why did she not come?" Yehonala demanded.

"Who can tell how the heart of a Consort changes?" the woman replied. "She has a daughter. The son is yours."

"Sakota is not so small in heart," Yehonala insisted, and yet while she spoke, she remembered that her cousin held over her head the dagger of that secret knowledge.

"Who knows the heart?" the woman replied, and this time Yehonala made no reply.

The courtyard was empty now, the Emperor and his followers gone to their feasts. Everywhere tonight the people feasted and took time for joy. From north to south, from east to west the doors of prisons were opened and all within were freed, whatever had been their crime. In cities and villages no shops were opened for seven days, no beasts killed for food, no fish caught in river or pond, and if they were caught al-

57

ready and still alive in tubs and vats in marketplaces, then they must be thrown back into their waters. Caged birds were loosed, in homes as they had been in the palaces, and men of rank who had been banished could now return and take again their titles and their lands. And all this was done in honor of the newborn child.

Yet in her bed Yehonala felt strangely lonely. Sakota had not come to see her or her son, Sakota who was always gentle, always kind. What then? Eunuchs had been busybodies, surely, they had carried tales, doubtless, and they had made Sakota think evil of her, now that her son was born. The upstart Grand Councilor Su Shun, or his friend Prince Yi, the nephew of the Emperor, these two might be the evil ones, for they were jealous of her. Until she came, Li Lien-ying had told her, it was they whom the Emperor trusted and they were close to him until he drew her closer still by his insatiate love.

I never did them harm, she thought, and I have been more courteous than I needed to be.

The Grand Councilor was haughty and ambitious, though of low birth, and yet she had taken his daughter Mei, a young girl of sixteen, to be her own Court lady. But Prince Kung must be her friend. She remembered his lean handsome face, and she determined to make and hold him as her ally. Lying in the shelter of the great curtained bed, her son curled into the hollow of her right arm, Yehonala pondered her destiny and his. They were alone against the world, she and her son. The man she loved could never be her husband. Alone she might have escaped by death if not by life, but now death too was no longer in her reach. She had borne a son, and he had only her to keep him safe amid the tangle of intrigues within the palaces. The times were evil, the signs of Heaven portentous, the Emperor was weak, and only she could hold the throne secure for her son.

In that night and in many nights thereafter, as many nights indeed as she was to live, there came the small dark hours when she faced her destiny with naked eyes and frightened heart, knowing that only in herself was strength enough to meet the dawn again. She must defy them, enemies and friends, and even Sakota, who knew her secret. This child, her son, here in her arms, must forever be the son of the Emperor Hsien Feng. No other name could she allow. Son of the Emperor and heir to the Dragon Throne! Thus she began the long battle of her destiny.

II

Tzu Hsi

For his first month, by ancient tradition, her son was her own. Not even in the arms of a nurse could he be carried from his mother's palace. Here in this cluster of rooms, around the courtyard bright with peonies, Yehonala spent the hours of day and night. It was a month of joy and pleasure, a month when, pampered and praised as the Emperor's Favorite, she was named Fortunate Mother. All came to look at the child and exclaim upon his size, his ruddy color, his handsome face, his strong hands and feet. All came except Sakota, and here was the one lack in the young mother's joy. The Consort should have been the first to see the child and acknowledge him the Heir, and she did not come. She sent her excuses that her own birth month, by the stars, was the enemy of the child's birth month. How dare she then enter the palace where he was sheltered?

Yehonala heard without reply. She hid her anger in her heart and there it grew for all the remaining days of the birth month. But three days before the month was over she sent the eunuch Li Lien-ying to Sakota with this message:

"Since you, Cousin, have not come to visit me I must come to you to ask your favor and protection for my son, for he belongs to us both, according to law and tradition."

Now it was true that the Consort ought to protect the Heir as her own child, for this was her duty, but Yehonala still feared that some secret jealousy or evil rumor, fostered by eunuchs and princes contending among themselves, had been fed into Sakota's simple heart. Such quarrels infested the Forbidden City and when lesser courtiers made war, they sought also to divide the ones above them, hoping that these too, would take part in the endless struggle for power. But Yehonala, in concern for her son, determined that she would not allow Sakota to be divided from her. She would compel her alliance, were it not given freely.

Therefore on this day she prepared to leave her own palace and go to Sakota. Meanwhile she made every safeguard for the child. She commanded Li Lien-ying to buy from the best goldsmith in the city a chain of small but strong gold links and this chain hung about her son's neck and she fastened the two ends together with a padlock of gold. Its key she put on a fine gold chain around her own neck, next to her flesh, and she did not take it off, day or night. Though her son was thus chained to Earth, by symbol, yet it was not enough. She must offer the child as an adopted son, by symbol, to other powerful families in her clan. Yet what friends had she? She thought and she pondered and she devised this plan. From the head of each of the highest one hundred families in the Empire, she required a bolt of the finest silk. From the silks she commanded the palace tailors to cut one hundred small pieces and from these make a robe for her child. Thus he belonged, by symbol, to one hundred strong and noble families, and under their shelter the gods would fear to harm him. For it is well known that gods are jealous of beautiful male children born of human women and they send down disease and accident to destroy such infants before they grow into god-like men.

On the third day before the end of her son's first moon month Yehonala went to Sakota's palace. She wore a new robe of imperial-yellow satin embroidered in small flowers of pomegranate red, and on her head a headdress of black satin beaded with pearls. Her face was first washed with melted mutton fat and then with perfumed water, and afterward powdered and painted. Her fine eyebrows were drawn with a brush dipped in oiled ink. Her mouth, always lovely, was painted a smooth red, and this mouth betrayed her warm heart for it was full and tender. Upon her hands she wore jeweled rings and one thumb ring of solid jade, and to guard her long polished nails she wore shields of thin beaten gold set with small gems. From her ears hung earrings of jade and pearls. Her high-soled shoes and headdress made her seem taller than she was. When she was attired even her ladies clapped their hands to see her beauty.

She took her son in her arms then, he in scarlet satin from head to foot, embroidered with small dragons of gold, and with him she sat in her palanquin and they were borne, mother and son, to the Consort's palace, the eunuchs walking ahead to announce the arrival and the ladies following. When they came to their destination, Yehonala came down from the palanquin and stepped over the threshold. There in the reception hall she saw Sakota. Pale and yellow Sakota always was, and now more than ever for she had not recovered from the birth of her daughter. Her skin was withered and her little hands were shrunken into such that an invalid child might own.

Before this small timid creature, Yehonala stood strong and handsome as a young cedar tree.

"I come to you, Cousin," she said, after greeting. "I come on behalf of our son. True, I gave him birth, but your duty, Cousin, is even greater to him than my own, for is not his father the Son of Heaven, who is your lord before he is mine? I ask your protection for our son."

Sakota rose from her chair and she stood half bowed, clinging to its arms. "Sit down, Cousin," she said in her plaintive voice. "It is the first time you have walked outside your own courts for a month. Sit down and rest."

"I will not rest until I have your promise for our son," Yehonala said.

She continued to stand as she spoke and she looked steadfastly at Sakota, while she made her black eyes blacker still, their pupils swelling and glowing.

Sakota sank back into the chair. "But—but why?" she stammered. "Why do you speak to me so? Are we not kin? Is not the Emperor our mutual lord?"

"It is for our son that I ask your favor," Yehonala said, "and never for myself. I have no need of anyone. Yet I must be sure that you are for our son and not against him."

Each lady knew what the other meant. In the division of continuing intrigue among the princes and the eunuchs, Yehonala was saying, she must be certain that Sakota would not accept the leadership of those who might plot to destroy the Heir and set another upon the Dragon Throne. By her silence Sakota announced that there was such intrigue and that she did not wish to give her promise.

Yehonala stepped forward while she gave her son to a lady to hold for her. "Give me your hands, Cousin." Her voice was smooth and resolute. "Promise me that none can divide us. We must live out our lives together here within these walls. Let us be friends and not enemies."

She waited while Sakota hesitated and did not put out her hands. Then suddenly, her great eyes furious, Yehonala leaned down and grasped those two small soft hands and crushed them so fiercely that the tears rushed to Sakota's eyes. So Yehonala had used to do when they were children. Whenever Sakota had pouted and rebelled, Yehonala had crushed her hands until they ached.

"I—I promise," Sakota said in a broken voice.

"And I promise," Yehonala said firmly.

She put the two small hands on Sakota's satin lap again, and she saw what all the ladies saw, that the thin gold shields of her nails had cut red stripes into the tender flesh and Sakota put her hands together and let the tears of pain run down her cheeks.

But Yehonala said no word of sorrow for what she had done. She bowed, she waved aside the bowl of tea that a lady offered her.

"I will not stay, Cousin," she said in her usual lovely voice. "I came for this promise and now I have it. It is mine, so long as my life lasts and so long as my son's life lasts. Nor will I forget that I, too, have given my own promise."

With surpassing pride, this proud woman let her eyes circle from one face to another. Then she turned and sweeping her golden robes about her she took back her son and went away.

That night when she had seen her child fed and sleeping in the arms of his nurse she sent for Li Lien-ying. He was never far off from where she was and now when he had come, she commanded him to bring to her the Chief Eunuch, An Teh-hai.

"Tell him I have a trouble that I brood upon," she said.

So Li Lien-ying went and in an hour or two he brought the Chief Eunuch, who said, after greeting, "Forgive me, Venerable, for delay. I was busy in the Emperor's bedchamber and under his command."

"You are forgiven," Yehonala said. She pointed her forefinger at a chair upon which he was to sit, and she sat down in her own thronelike chair by the long carved table set against the inner wall of the room. Her ladies she had dismissed and only Li Lien-ying and her woman remained with her.

Li Lien-ying now made pretense also to withdraw, but Yehonala bade him stay.

"What I have to say is for both of you, for I must count you two as my left hand and my right."

She went on then to inquire of the intrigues which her ladies had whispered into her ears. "Is this true?" she asked of the Chief Eunuch. "Are there those who plot to seize the Throne from my son, if—" She paused, for none who spoke of the Emperor could say the word "death."

"Lady, all is true." The Chief Eunuch nodded his handsome heavy head.

"Say on," she commanded.

"Venerable, you must know," he said, obeying, "that no one among the mighty clans believed that the Emperor could beget a sound son. When the Consort gave birth to a sickly girl, certain of the princes took heart and they plotted how, the moment that the Emperor departed for the Yellow Springs, they would steal the imperial seal. Alas—alas—" again he shook his head, "we may not expect a long reign. The Emperor is young in years, but the Dowager Mother loved him too well. He fed on sweets when he was a child, and when he had pains in his belly she ordered opium for him. Before he was twelve years of age he was debauched by eunuchs and by sixteen he was exhausted by women. Let me speak the truth."

Here the Chief Eunuch put his large smooth hands on his knees and he made his voice so low that Li Lien-ying had to lean to hear it.

"In wisdom," the Chief Eunuch said, his wide face solemn, "we must now count our friends and enemies."

Yehonala sat without moving while he spoke. It was her grace that she could sit for hours motionless and at ease, an upright imperial figure. She looked at him now without a sign of fear.

"Who are our enemies?" she asked.

"First, the Grand Councilor, Su Shun," the Chief Eunuch whispered.

"He!" she exclaimed. "And I have taken his daughter as my court lady and my favorite!"

"Even he," the Chief Eunuch said gravely, "and with him the Emperor's own nephew, Prince Yi, and after him Prince Cheng. These three, Venerable, are your first enemies, because you have given us an heir."

She bowed her head. The danger was as great as she had imagined. These were mighty princes, related by blood and clan to the Emperor himself. And she was but a woman.

She lifted her head proudly. "And who are my friends?"

The Chief Eunuch cleared his throat. "Above all others, Venerable, Prince Kung, the younger brother of the Son of Heaven."

"Is he indeed my friend?" she exclaimed. "Then he is worth all the rest." She was still so young that any hope was hope enough and the red blood ran to her cheeks.

"When Prince Kung saw you," the Chief Eunuch declared, "he said to a clansman standing near, who told me, that you were a woman so clever and so beautiful that either you would bring good fortune to the realm or you would destroy the Dragon Throne."

These words Yehonala received into her thoughtful mind. She pondered them and for a space of time she sat entirely silent. Then she drew her breath in a long sigh.

"If I am to bring good fortune, I must have my weapons," she said.

"True, Venerable," the Chief Eunuch replied and waited.

"My first weapon," she continued, "must be the power of rank."

"True, Venerable," the Chief Eunuch said again and waited.

"Return to the Emperor," Yehonala commanded. "Put into his mind that the Heir is in danger. Put into his mind that only I can protect our child. Put into his mind that he must raise my rank to equal that of the Consort, so that she cannot have power over the Heir, or be used by those who crave such power."

The Chief Eunuch smiled at such cleverness, and Li Lien-ying laughed, cracking his finger joints one after the other to show his pleasure.

"Lady," the Chief Eunuch said, "I will put it in the Emperor's mind that he so reward you on the Heir's first moon birthday. What day could be more auspicious?"

"None," she agreed.

She looked into his small black eyes set deep beneath his high smooth forehead and suddenly her own face dimpled and smiled and her great eyes shone with mischief, mirth and triumph.

The first month of her son's life was completed. The moon had been full when he was born and it was full again. Certain dangers were passed, the danger of the ten-day madness, whereby infants die before ten days are spent; the danger of flux, whereby the bowels of an infant run out like water; the danger of continual vomiting; the danger of cough and cold and fever. At the end of this first month the Heir was fat and healthy, his will already imperious, and his hunger constant, so that his wetnurse must be ready day and night for his demand. This wetnurse Yehonala had chosen herself, a strong young country housewife, a Chinese, whose child was also a first son, and whose milk therefore was suited to the royal nursling. But Yehonala had not been content to have the Court physicians judge the woman sound and healthy. No, she must herself examine the woman's body and taste the sweetness of her milk and smell her breath to discover any taint of sourness in it. And she herself prescribed the woman's diet and saw to it that she was served only the best and richest foods. Upon such milk the princeling throve like any peasant's child.

On this first moon birthday of his heir, then, the Emperor had decreed that feasts must be held throughout the nation. Here in the Forbidden City the day was to be given over entire to feasting and to music, and when he sent the Chief Eunuch to inquire of Yehonala what she would like for her own pleasure on this auspicious day she put her private craving into words.

"I do long to see a good play," she told An Teh-hai. "Not since I came to live beneath these golden roofs have I seen a play. The Dowager Mother did not like actors, and I dared not ask while she lived, and in the months of mourning for her I could not ask. But now—will the Son of Heaven indulge me?"

An Teh-hai could not but smile at the sight of her face, flushed and ardent as a child's, the great eyes hopeful.

"The Son of Heaven will refuse you nothing now, lady," he told her, and he blinked and nodded his head many times to signify that she would indeed receive reward far larger than a play. Then forthwith he hastened off to do her bidding.

Thus it came about that on the day of feasting Yehonala had her lesser desire, too, while she waited for the greater, the pleasure of a play as well as her increase in rank. But first the gifts must be presented and received. For these rites the Emperor chose the throne room named the Palace of Surpassing Brightness. Here at dawn there waited men from all parts of the realm and among them eunuchs passed to and fro to tend the huge lanterns swinging from the beams, whereon were painted the imperial five-clawed dragons. These lanterns were made of horn and they gave forth such a light that, falling on the robes of eunuchs and of guests, it picked out the gold embroideries and the encrusted jewels of the throne. Every hue and color glowed at once, the crimson and the purple deep and strong, the scarlet and the bright blue accenting, and gold and silver glittering for sharpness.

In silence all waited for the coming of the Son of Heaven, and when dawn broke across the sky the imperial procession appeared, its banners streaming in the morning breeze and carried by the guardsmen in their scarlet tunics. Next came the princes, then the eunuchs, marching slowly two by two, in robes of purple belted with gold. In their mist twelve bearers bore the sacred yellow dragon palanquin in which sat the Son of Heaven himself. Within the Throne Hall all fell upon their knees and knocked their heads nine times upon the floor and shouted out their greeting, "Ten thousand years—ten thousand years—ten thousand years!"

The Emperor came down from his palanquin and with his right hand upon his brother's arm and his left upon the arm of the Grand Councilor Su Shun, he mounted the golden throne. There, seated in precise dignity, his hands palms down upon his knees, he received in order the princes and the ministers who presented imperial gifts for the Heir. Their hands did not touch the gifts, for these were placed on trays and silver plates and brought by bearers, but Prince Kung read the lists of gifts and whence they came, from what provinces, what ports and cities, what country regions, and the Chief Eunuch, An Teh-hai, with brush and book, marked down the name of the giver and what the gift was and how much was its worth, and that he might set the value high, the givers had earlier bribed him with secret gifts of goods and money.

Now a screen stood behind the throne as usual, a mighty stretch of scented wood, most cunningly carved with five-clawed dragons, and behind it Yehonala and the Consort sat with their ladies. When all the gifts had been accepted, the Emperor summoned Yehonala to receive his own reward. The Chief Eunuch brought the summons and he led her from her place and she approached the Dragon Throne. She stood there for one instant, tall and straight, her head high, looking neither to the right nor left. Then slowly in obeisance she sank to her knees and laid her hands, one on the other, upon the tiled floor and put her forehead on her crossed hands.

Above her the Emperor waited and now he began to speak. "I do this day decree that the mother of the Imperial Heir, here kneeling, is to be raised to rank of Consort, equal in all ways to the present Consort. That there be no confusion, the present Consort shall be known as Tzu An, the Empress of the Eastern Palace, and the Fortunate Mother shall be known as Tzu Hsi, the Empress of the Western Palace. This is my will. It shall be declared across the realm, that it may be known to all people."

These words Yehonala heard and her blood ran strong and joyful to her heart. Who could harm her now? She had been lifted up and by the Emperor's hand. Three times and three times and yet three times more she touched her forehead to her hands. Then, rising to her feet, she stood until the Chief Eunuch put out his right arm and, leaning on it, she returned again to her place behind the Dragon Screen. But when she was seated, she did not turn her head to look at Sakota, nor did Sakota speak.

While Yehonala had stood before the Dragon Throne the vast multitude in the Banquet Hall was silent. Not one voice spoke except the Emperor's and not one hand stirred. And from that day she was no longer called Yehonala. Tzu Hsi, the Sacred Mother, was her imperial name.

That same night Tzu Hsi was summoned to the Emperor. For three months she had received no summons, the two months before her son's birth and the one month since. But now the time was come. She welcomed the call, for it was proof that the imperial favor still was hers, not only for her son's sake but for her own. Well enough she knew that in these months the Emperor had made use of one concubine and another, and each had hoped that she could displace her who was most favored. Tonight would tell her whether any had succeeded, and eagerly she made herself ready to follow the Chief Eunuch who waited in the entrance of her palace.

Ah, but now how hard it was to leave! The child's bed stood by her bed. His own rooms had been prepared for him before his birth, but she had not let him go from her, even for a night, nor yet tonight. Ready and robed in soft pink satin, jeweled and perfumed, she could not force herself away from the boy who slept, replete with human milk, upon the silken mattress. Two women sat beside him, one the wetnurse, and the other her own woman.

"You are not to leave him for one breath of time," she warned them. "If when I return, though it be at dawn, mind you, if he is hurt or weeping or if a spot of red is anywhere upon his flesh, I will have you both beaten and if he is harmed at all, your heads will be the price."

Both women stared to see her look so fiercely at them, the wetnurse awed, and the woman amazed at the courteous mistress she thought she knew.

"Since the Empress of the Western Palace has borne the child," she said in a mild voice, "she has become a tigress. Be sure, Venerable, that we will guard him better even than you tell us how to do."

But Tzu Hsi had more commands. "And Li Lien-ying must sit outside, and my ladies must not sleep soundly."

"It shall all be so," the woman promised.

Still Tzu Hsi could not go away. She leaned above her sleeping child and saw his rosy face, the pouting lips soft and red, the eyes full and large, the ears close to the head and set low, the lobes long, and these were all signs of high intelligence. Whence did her child receive his beauty? Hers alone, surely, was not enough for this perfection. His father—

She broke off thinking and reached for his hand, first his right hand and then his left, and gently pressing open the curling fingers she smelled the soft baby palms, as mothers do. Oh, what a treasure now was hers!

"Venerable!"

She heard An Teh-hai's voice bumbling from the outer room. The Chief Eunuch grew impatient, not for his own sake, but for her own. She knew by now that he was her ally in the secret palace war, and she must heed him well. She stayed then only to perform one more task. From her dressing table she chose two gifts, a ring of gold and a thin bracelet set with seed pearls. These gifts she gave the two women, the ring to her own woman and the bracelet to the wetnurse, and thus she bribed them to their duty. Then she hastened out and there was Li Lien-ying, her eunuch, waiting with An Teh-hai. To her eunuch she gave a piece of gold without a word; he knew what it meant, and while she went with An Teh-hai, he stayed behind to guard her son.

Inside the bosom of her robe she held gold in a packet for the Chief Eunuch, too, but she would not give it to him until she saw how the Emperor received her. Did the night go well, then he would have his prize. And the Chief Eunuch understood this, and he led her by the well known narrow ways to the imperial center of the Forbidden City.

"Come here to me," the Emperor said.

She stood at the threshold of his vast chamber, that he might see her in all her strong beauty. Upon his command she walked slowly toward him, swaying as she went with that grace she knew so well how to use. She was not humble but she feigned shyness and assumed a sweet coyness which was half real and half pretended. For it was this woman's power that she could be almost what she feigned and planned to be, and so she became nearly what she would be, at any moment and in any place. She was not deceiving, for she deceived herself as much as the person before whom she appeared.

Thus now when she approached the imperial bed, as wide and long as a room inside the yellow curtains and the net of gold, she felt sudden pity. The man who waited for her here was surely doomed for death. Young as he was, he had spent his force too soon.

She hastened the last few steps to him. "Ah," she cried, "you are ill and no one told me, my Lord of Heaven!"

Indeed by the light of the great candles in their golden stand he looked so wan, his yellow skin stretched tightly across the fine small bones of his face and frame, that he seemed a living skeleton propped there against the yellow satin pillows. His two hands, palms upward, lay lifeless on the quilts. She sat down on the bed and put out her warm strong hands and felt his dry and cold.

"Have you pain?" she asked anxiously.

"No pain," he said. "A weakness—"

"But this hand," she insisted. She took up his left hand. "It feels different from the other—colder, more stiff."

"I cannot use it as once I did," he said unwillingly.

She put back his sleeve and saw his bare arm, thin and yellow as old ivory beneath the satin robes.

"Ah," she moaned, "ah, why was I not told?"

"What is there to tell?" he said. "Except I have a slow creeping coldness on this side."

He pulled his hand away. "Come," he said, "come into my bed. None of them has been enough. Only you—only you—"

She saw the old hot light come creeping back into his sunken eyes, and she made ready to obey. And yet as the dark hours passed to midnight and then beyond, she felt a sadness she had never known before. Deep, deep was the woe in this poor man who was the Emperor of a mighty realm. The chill of death had struck his inward life and he was man no more. As helpless as any eunuch, he strove to do his part and could not.

"Help me," he besought her again and yet again. "Help me—help me, lest I die of this dreadful heat unslaked."

But she could not help him. When she saw that even she was helpless she rose from the bed and sat by his pillow and took him in her arms as though he were a child and like a child he sobbed upon her breast, knowing that what had been his chief joy could never be again. Though he was young in years, indeed his third decade not yet come, he was an old man in body, weakened by his own lusts. Too early had he yielded to his desires, too often had the eunuchs fed them, too humbly had the Court physicians whipped his blood alive again with herbs and medicines. He was exhausted and only death remained.

This certainty overwhelmed the woman as she held the man to her breast. She soothed him with pleasant words, she seemed so calm, so strong, that he was at last persuaded.

"You are weary," she said, "you are beset by worries. I know our many foes, and how the Western men with all their ships and armies do threaten us. While I have been living my woman's life, such troubles hide inside your mind and sap your strength. While I have borne my son, you have bent beneath the burdens of the state. Let me help you, my lord. Throw half your burden upon me. Let me always sit behind the screen in the Throne Hall at dawn and listen to your ministers. I can hear the inner meaning of their plaints and when they are gone I will tell you what I think but leaving all decision to my lord, as is my duty."

From unsatisfied desire, she wooed him thus away from love and to the affairs of the nation, the threats of enemies, and the strengthening of the Throne itself, now that he had his Heir. And she saw how weary was this man with all his burdens, for he gave great sighs and then he lifted himself from her bosom and leaned against the pillows again, and holding her hand with his own hand, he tried to tell her his perplexities.

"There is no end to my troubles," he complained. "In the days of my forefathers the enemy came always from the north and the Great Wall stopped them, men and horses. But now the wall is useless to us. These white men swarm up from the seas—Englishmen and Frenchmen, Dutch and Germans and Belgians. I tell you, I do not know how many nations there are beyond the border mountains of K'un Lun! They make war with us to sell their opium and they are never satisfied. Now the Americans are here, too. Where did they come from? Where is America? I hear its people are somewhat better than the others, yet when I yield to those others, the Americans demand the same benefits. This is the year when they wish to renew their treaty with us. But I do not wish to renew any treaty with white men."

"Then do not renew it," Tzu Hsi said impetuously. "Why should you do that which you would not? Bid your ministers refuse."

"The white men's weapons are very fearful," he moaned.

"Delay—delay," she said. "Do not answer their pleadings, ignore their messages, refuse to receive their envoys. This gives us time. They will not attack us so long as there is hope that we will renew the treaty. Therefore do not say yes or no."

The Emperor was struck with such wisdom. "You are worth more to me than any man," he declared, "even than my brother. It is he who plagues me to receive the white men and make new treaties with them. He tries to frighten me by telling me about their big ships and the long cannon. Negotiate, he says—"

Tzu Hsi laughed. "Do not allow yourself to be frightened, my lord, even by Prince Kung. The sea is very far from here, and can there be a cannon long enough to reach as high as our city walls?"

She believed what she said, and he wished to believe what she said, and his heart clung to her more than ever. He fell asleep at last upon his pillows and she sat beside him until dawn. At that hour the Chief Eunuch came to waken the Emperor because his ministers waited for the usual early audience. When he came in, Tzu Hsi rose to command him while the Emperor still slept.

"From this day on," she said, "I am to sit behind the Dragon Screen in the Throne Hall. The Son of Heaven has commanded it."

An Teh-hai bowed down to the floor before her and knocked his head on the tiles. "Venerable," he exclaimed. "Now I am happy."

From that day on Tzu Hsi rose in the darkness of the small hours before day. In the candlelight her women bathed her and put on her robes of state and she entered her curtained sedan and Li Lien-ying went before her with a lantern in his hand to the Throne Hall and she sat behind the great carved screen before which was the Dragon Throne and Li Lien-ying was her guard. He stood near her always, a dagger ready in his hand.

From this day, too, the Heir slept no more in his mother's bed-chamber. He was moved into his own palace and the Chief Eunuch was made his servant, and Prince Kung, the brother of the Emperor, was appointed his guardian.

The cold came soon that year. No rain had fallen in many weeks and already by midautumn the dry and bitter winds blew from the north-west, scattering their burden of pale sand from the distant desert. The city was clothed in the faint gold of the sand and the sun glittered upon the roofs of the houses where the sand drifted into the crevices of the eaves. Only the porcelain tiles of the roofs of the Forbidden City, royal blue and imperial yellow, shed the sand and shone clear in the white glare from the sky.

At noon while the sun still gave forth a mild heat, old people, wrapped in padded garments, stirred out of their houses and sat in sheltered corners between walls, and children ran into the streets and played until the sweat streamed down their brown cheeks. Yet when the sun went away again at nightfall the dry cold congealed the blood of young and old alike. Throughout the night the cold deepened until in the hours after midnight and before dawn it reached its depths. Those beggars in the streets who had no shelter ran hither and thither to keep alive until the sun came up again, and even wild dogs could not sleep.

In such a cold and silent hour and upon a day set by the Board of Imperial Astronomers, Tzu Hsi rose one day to take her usual place in the Throne Hall. Her faithful woman slept near her. When the watchman's brass gong sounded three times three through the streets, the woman got up from her pallet bed and laid fresh charcoal on the brazier and she set on the coals a kettle of water. When it boiled she made tea in a silver and earthen pot, and approaching the vast bed where Tzu Hsi slept she put aside the curtains and touched her shoulder. It needed but a touch, for though Tzu Hsi slept well, she slept always lightly. Now her great eyes opened wide and aware, and she sat up in bed.

"I am wakened," she said.

The woman poured the infused tea into a bowl and presented it with both hands and Tzu Hsi drank it slowly, but not too slowly, gauging exactly the measure of the passing time. When she had drunk the bowl empty the woman took it again. In the bathing room the water was already poured steaming hot into the porcelain tub. Tzu Hsi rose, her every movement graceful and precise, for grace and precision were her habit, and in a few minutes she was in her bath. Her woman washed her gently and then dried her and put on her garments for the imperial audience. Her undergarments were of perfumed silk and over these was a long robe of rose-red satin lined with northern sable and buttoned at the throat and over this again a robe of pale-yellow gauze embroidered in small blue medallions in phoenix design. Upon her feet Tzu Hsi wore lined stockings of soft white silk and over them her Manchu shoes set on high double heels in the middle of the soles. Upon her head, when her hair was dressed, the woman set a headdress made of figures and flowers of satin and gems and veiled with beads of fine small pearls.

They moved in silence, the woman silent because she was weary, and Tzu Hsi silent because her mind was filled with somber thoughts. The times grew more grave. Only yesterday in private audience Prince Kung had said to her, "The people of any nation do not care who their rulers are, if there be peace and order in the realm and if they can laugh and attend plays. But if there be no peace and order is disturbed, then the people blame their rulers. It is our misfortune to rule in these times. Alas that my imperial brother is so feeble! Today neither white man nor Chinese rebel fears the Throne."

"If these white-skinned foreigners had not come from across the seas," Tzu Hsi said, "we could quell the Chinese rebels."

To this he agreed sadly and thoughtfully. "Yet what shall we do?" he inquired. "They are here. It is the fault of our dynasty that our ancestors did not understand a hundred years ago that Western foreigners are different men from all others. Our ancestors at first were charmed with their cunning and their clever toys and clocks, and, thinking no evil, they allowed them to visit us, expecting that in courtesy they would then leave our shores. We know now that we should have pushed them all into the sea, from the very first man, for where one comes a hundred follow, and none goes away."

"It is strange indeed," Tzu Hsi observed, "that the Venerable An-

72

cestor Ch'ien Lung, so great and so wise and ruling so many decades, did not perceive the nature of the men from the West."

Prince Kung, shaking his head, went mournfully on. "Ch'ien Lung was deceived by his power and by his own good heart. It did not come to his mind that any could be his enemy. Indeed, he even likened himself to the American George Washington, then living, and he was fond of saying that he here, and Washington in America, were brothers, though they had never met face to face. It is true their reigns were contemporary."

Such was the stuff of her talk with Prince Kung, and he took pains to teach her often, nowadays. Listening to him and lifting her eyes to that thin handsome face, though sad and weary it was for a man so young, she thought how far better it would have been if this Prince could have been the elder brother and so the Emperor, instead of her own weak lord, Hsien Feng.

"You are ready, Venerable," her woman now said, "and I do wish you would eat a little hot food before you go to sit behind the Dragon Screen. A bowl of hot millet soup—"

"I will eat when I return," Tzu Hsi replied. "I must be empty and my mind clear."

She rose and walked toward the door, her pace measured, her body erect. Her ladies should be with her but she who could be stern and harsh enough when she willed was always mild to her obedient ladies, and she did not require that they rise early. It was enough that her woman rise and that Li Lien-ying, her eunuch, be waiting at the door. Yet one lady often rose, and it was the Lady Mei, the young daughter of Su Shun, prince and Grand Councilor. This morning when her woman opened the door for Tzu Hsi to pass, Lady Mei stood there already, somewhat pale from rising so early, but fresh as a white gardenia flower. She was at this time only eighteen years of age, small of stature and exquisitely shaped, a tender creature so loving in her ways and so yielding that Tzu Hsi loved her much in return, even though she knew that Su Shun was her secret enemy. It was a grace that Tzu Hsi was large of mind and exceedingly just and therefore she did not lay the blame of the cruel father upon the tender daughter.

She smiled now at the young girl. "Are you not early?"

"Venerable, I was so cold I could not sleep," Lady Mei confessed.

"One of these days I must get you a husband to warm your bed," Tzu Hsi said, still smiling.

She spoke these words with careless kindness, not knowing why she said them, but when they had fallen from her lips she knew instantly

73

that they had come from an instinct which she would not recognize. Ah yes, ah yes, the gossip of the women in the courts, where there was little to do except to gossip, had fluttered from mouth to ear, ever since the first moon feast of the Imperial Heir, and she had caught the rumor that Lady Mei had been seen to look more than once at Jung Lu, the handsome Chief of the Imperial Guard and kinsman of the Fortunate Mother. Tzu Hsi heard this as she heard everything, her mind always aware, her eyes seeing, her ears hearing whether she woke or slept. Who could guess all that she knew, who made no confidante?

"Venerable, please, I want no husband," Lady Mei now murmured, her cheeks suddenly pink.

Tzu Hsi pinched the pretty cheek. "No husband?"

"Let me stay with you always, Venerable," the lady pleaded.

"Why not?" Tzu Hsi replied. "This is not to say you shall not have a husband."

Lady Mei went pale and red and then pale again. Unlucky, unlucky to talk of marriage! The Empress of the Western Palace had only to command her marriage to a man and she must obey, whereas her whole heart was—

The gaunt shape of Li Lien-ying appeared before them, large and hideous, the light from the lantern in his hand flickering upward against his coarse features.

"The hour grows late, Venerable," he said in his high eunuch's voice.

Tzu Hsi recalled herself, "Ah, yes, and I must see my son."

For it was her habit every morning to see her son before she went to audience, and she entered her sedan, the curtains fell, and the six bearers lifted the poles to their shoulders and marched forward in swift rhythm until they came to the palace of the Heir, her lady following in a small sedan.

At the entrance to the Heir's private palace, the bearers set down their burden poles by habit and Tzu Hsi descended, her lady waiting while she hastened to her son. Eunuchs stood on guard, and they bowed as she passed to the royal bedchamber. There thick red candles of cow's fat in gold candlesticks stood on a table, and by the guttering light she saw her child. He was sleeping with his wetnurse and she lingered by his bed of quilts laid upon the platform of heated brick. He was pillowed on his nurse's arm, his cheek against her naked breast. Some time in the night he must have wakened and cried and the woman had suckled him and they had both fallen asleep.

Tzu Hsi gazed down upon them with strange and painful longing. She it should have been who heard him weeping in the night and she it should have been who suckled him and then lay sleeping in deep peace. Ah, when she chose her destiny she did not think of such a price!

She forced her heart down again. The moment of choice was gone. By his very birth her son now confirmed her destiny. She was mother not to a child but to the Heir of the Empire, and to that day when he would be Emperor of four hundred million subjects she must give her whole mind. Upon her alone rested the burden of the Manchu dynasty. Hsien Feng was weak but her son must be strong. She would make him strong. To this end her whole life was directed. Even the long and pleasant hours of study in the palace libraries were fewer now, and few, too, the painting lessons with Lady Miao. Some day it might be that she would have time to brush the pictures which her teacher Lady Miao had never let her make, but not yet.

She was soon in her sedan again, the curtains drawn against the winds rising before dawn, the sight of her sleeping baby warm in her heart. She had been ambitious, once, to make herself an empress. How mighty was her ambition now, who must hold an empire for her son!

Through the shifting curtains of the sedan she could see the light of the eunuch's lantern flickering upon the cobbles of the road, and by alleyway and courtyards she was carried until the Throne Hall was reached, and there by a side gate her sedan set down and the curtain lifted. Prince Kung stood waiting to receive her.

"Venerable, you are late," he exclaimed.

"I lingered too long with my son," she confessed.

He looked his reproach. "I hope, Venerable, that you do not wake the Heir. It is necessary indeed that he grow strong and full of health. His reign will be most arduous."

"I did not wake him," she said with dignity. No words passed more than these. Prince Kung bowed and led the way by an inner passage to the space behind the Dragon Throne. Here, shielded by the immense screen carved deep with that bold design of dragons, their scales and five-toed claws gilded and gleaming in the light of the great lanterns that hung from far up in the lofty painted beams, Tzu Hsi took her seat. On her right stood Lady Mei, and on her left the eunuch Li Lien-ying.

Through the interstices of the screen she saw now that the wide terrace in front of the Audience Hall, vast in shadows, was already filled with princes and ministers who had come before midnight in their springless fur-lined carts to bring petitions and memorials to the Emperor himself. While they waited in the courtyard for his arrival they separated themselves according to their rank and stood in groups together, each group beneath its own banner of bright silk and dark velvet. The darkness was still intense around and above, but the terrace was lit by the flaming lanterns in the lower courtyard. There at the four corners stood bronze elephants filled with oil, and this oil fed the torches which the elephants held in their uplifted trunks, and the fire, leaping toward the sky, cast a fierce and restless light upon the scene.

In the Audience Hall itself a hundred eunuchs moved to and fro, mending the huge horn lanterns, arranging their vivid and jeweled robes, whispering now and then as they waited. No voice spoke aloud. A strange silence brooded over all, and as the hour, fixed by the Board of Astrologers according to the stars, drew near, this silence deepened into something like a trance. None moved, all faces stiff and grave, all eyes gazing straight ahead. In the last moment before dawn broke, a courier blew his brass trumpet loudly and this was a sign. The Emperor had left his palace and his imperial procession was on its way, moving slowly through the broad lower throne halls, passing through one great entrance and another into the higher halls to arrive at the exact hour of dawn.

Now the couriers cried out together, "Behold the Lord of Ten Thousand Years!"

At this cry the imperial procession appeared at the entrance to the lower courtyard. Banners of gold waved in the morning wind as the couriers marched onward. Behind them came the Imperial Guard in tunics of red and gold, and at their head Jung Lu walked alone. Behind them bearers in yellow uniform, one hundred in number, carried the Emperor's palanquin of heavy gold, and it in turn was followed by the Bannermen.

Every man and every eunuch fell down upon his knees and shouted the sacred greeting, "Ten Thousand Years—Ten Thousand Years!" Each bowed his face upon his folded hands as he knelt, and thus remained while the bearers carried the imperial sedan up the marble steps to the Dragon Terrace before the Audience Hall. There the Emperor descended, wrapped in his robes of gold embroidered with dragons, and passing between the red and gold pillars he walked slowly to the dais. He mounted its few steps and seated himself upon the Dragon Throne, his thin hands outspread upon his knees, his eyes fixed ahead.

Silence fell again. The kneeling multitude, their heads bowed upon their hands, did not move while Prince Kung took his place on the right of the Throne and standing he read aloud the names of princes and ministers in the order of their rank and the time at which each should appear. The audience had begun.

Tzu Hsi, behind the screen, leaned forward that she might not lose one word of what was said. Thus leaning she saw only the head and shoulders of the Emperor above the low back of the throne upon which he sat. This man, whose front appearance was so pale and haughty, was now betrayed. Beneath the imperial tasseled hat his nape showed thin and yellow, the neck of a sickly youth and not of a man, and this neck sat between two lean and narrow shoulders, stooping beneath the rich robes. Tzu Hsi saw him with mixed pity and repulsion, her mind's eye following those thin shoulders to the thin and sickly body. And how could she keep her swift eyes from reaching beyond the Throne? There Jung Lu stood in the full strength of his youth and manhood. Yet they were as separate, she from him, as north is from the south. Ah, but the hour had not yet come when she could raise him up! Nor could he so much as put out his hand to her. Hers must be the hand to move, but when would be the instant and the chance? Not, and this she knew, until she was strong enough in power to make all men fear her. She must first be so high that none would dare accuse her or soil her name. And suddenly, guided by some instinct she would not acknowledge, her eyes slid sidewise toward Lady Mei. There the girl stood, her face pressed upon the screen, staring at—

"Stand back!" She seized Lady Mei by the wrist and pulled her, twisting her wrist suddenly and cruelly before she loosed it.

The lady turned her head in fright, and her eyes met those eyes, great and black and fierce with anger.

Tzu Hsi did not speak again but she let her eyes burn on until the girl could not bear it. Her head drooped, and the tears ran down her cheeks and only then did Tzu Hsi turn her eyes away. But her will rose hard within her against herself. She would not let her heart beguile her mind. This was the hour of learning how to rule. She would not yearn for love.

At this same moment Yeh, the Viceroy of the Kwang provinces, was before the Throne. He had come by boat and by horseback from the south, where he was the appointed governor of those provinces. Now kneeling, he read aloud from a scroll which he held in both hands. He had a high level voice, not strong but piercing, and since he was a famous scholar, he had written his words in rhythms of four, in the ancient classic style. Only the learned could understand what he said and Tzu Hsi herself, listening with close care, could not have comprehended except that she had so diligently spent her time in studying

77

ancient books. Her intelligence enlightened the words and she guessed what she did not know.

Here was the purport. The traders from the West were pressing again in the south, led by the white Englishmen, who were angry and over so small an affair that he, the Viceroy, was ashamed to mention it now before the Dragon Throne. Yet from such small matters in the past wars had been fought and lost, and he, appointed by the Son of Heaven, could not risk the danger of yet another war. Whenever the white men did not get their way, he said, immediately they threatened battle. There was no reasoning with them, for they were barbarians and uncivilized. Yet the trouble was over nothing more than a flag.

The Emperor murmured something and Prince Kung spoke for him.

"The Son of Heaven inquires the meaning of the word *flag*," he said in a loud clear voice.

"A flag, Most High," the Viceroy replied, not lifting his eyes, "is only a banner."

The Emperor murmured again, and again Prince Kung repeated what he said in the same loud clear voice.

"Why should the Englishmen be angry over what is nothing more, after all, than a piece of cloth and therefore easily replaced?"

"Most High," the Viceroy explained, still not lifting his eyes, "the English are a superstitious people. They are not men of learning and so they attach magic qualities to an oblong cloth, designed in colors of red, white and blue. It is a symbol for them, sacred to some god they worship. They will not tolerate lack of reverence for this piece of cloth. Wherever they place it, it designates possession. In this case, it was attached to a pole on the rear of a small trading vessel, carrying Chinese pirates. Now these Chinese pirates have been the curse of generations past in our southern provinces. They sleep by day and by night they attack vessels at anchor and even coastal villages. The captain of this small boat had paid a sum of money to the Englishmen to allow them the flag, thinking that I, the Viceroy, would then not dare to command them to cease their evil trade. But I, the Viceroy, unworthy servant of the Most High, did not fear. I arrested the vessel and put the captain in chains. Then I commanded the flag to be taken down. When the Englishman, John Bowring, the Commissioner of Trade for the British in Canton, heard of this, he declared that I had insulted the sacred symbol, and he demanded that I apologize on behalf of the Throne."

Horror rushed over the entire assembly. Even the Emperor was aroused.

The Emperor sat up in his Throne and spoke for himself. "Apologize? For what?"

"Most High," the Viceroy said, "those were my words."

"Stand," the Emperor commanded.

"Stand, the Dragon Emperor commands you," Prince Kung repeated. It was unusual, but the Viceroy obeyed. He was a tall aging man, a native of the northern provinces and a Chinese, but loyal, as all scholars were, to the Manchu Throne, since the Throne favored Chinese scholars and when they had passed the imperial examinations with honor, employed them as administrators of government. Thus were the interests of such Chinese cemented to the dynasty in rule, and so it had been for many centuries.

"Did you apologize?" the Emperor asked, again speaking not through his brother but directly, to signify his deep concern.

The Viceroy replied. "Most High, how could I apologize when I, however lowly, am the appointed of the Dragon Throne? I sent the pirate captain and his crew to apologize to the Englishmen. Yet this did not satisfy that haughty and ignorant Bowring. He sent the Chinese back to me, declaring that it was I and not they whom he wanted. Whereupon, in extreme vexation, I had them all beheaded for causing confusion."

"Did this not satisfy the Englishman Bowring?" the Emperor inquired.

"It did not, Most High," the Viceroy replied. "Nothing will satisfy him. He wishes trouble, so that he may have an excuse to make another war and seize still more of our land and our treasure. This Bowring enlarges every cause for quarrel. Thus, although it is against the law to bring opium from India across our borders, he encourages smuggling, saying that as long as any Chinese trader smuggles, Englishmen and Indians and even Americans may be allowed to smuggle the vile weed to demoralize and weaken our people. More than that, guns also are now being smuggled in to sell to the southern Chinese rebels and when the white men from Portugal kidnapped Chinese for the coolie trade, Bowring declared that he would uphold the Portuguese. Moreover, he continues to insist that the English are not satisfied with the land we have allowed them to build their houses upon. No, Most High, now they insist, these Englishmen, that the gates of Canton itself must be opened to them and to their families, so that they may walk upon our streets and mingle with our people, the white males gazing at our women, and the white females, who have no modesty, coming and going as freely as the males. And what is granted to one white tribe will be demanded by all the others as they have done in the past. Is this not to destroy our traditions and corrupt the people?"

The Emperor agreed. "We cannot indeed allow strangers from other countries the freedom of our streets."

"Most High, I did forbid it, but I fear the English will make whatever I forbid an excuse for yet another war, and, small man that I am, I cannot take responsibility."

This is what Tzu Hsi heard behind the screen and she longed to cry out against the interlopers. But she was a woman and must keep silence.

The Emperor spoke. "Have you yourself represented our opinion to this Bowring Englishman?"

He was now so roused that he raised his voice to a feeble shout and this alarmed the Viceroy, for he had never heard the imperial voice raised before, and he turned his head toward Prince Kung, not lifting his face to the Throne.

"Most High," he said. "I cannot receive Bowring because he insists that he be allowed to call upon me as an equal. Yet how can he be my equal when I am the appointed of the Dragon Throne? This would be to insult the Throne itself. I have replied that I will only receive him as I do others from tributary states. He must approach me on his knees as they do. This he will not."

"You are correct," the Emperor said with puny anger.

Thus encouraged, the Viceroy proceeded to further revelation. "Moreover, O Most High, this Bowring insists that I forbid the people of Canton to print wall papers denouncing the white strangers. These papers, Most High, the Chinese paste upon the walls of the city and upon the city gates and Bowring is angry because they call his tribe barbarian and because they demand that all invaders leave our shores."

"They are right," the Emperor exclaimed.

"Entirely right, Most High," the Viceroy agreed. "And how can I forbid the people? It has been their ancient privilege and custom to say what they think and to make known their wishes to their rulers by public protest. Am I now to say that the people may not speak? Is this not to invite fresh rebellion? They were cowed last year when I ordered the provincial armies to kill all rebels. At that time eighty thousand rebels were killed, as I reported to the Dragon Throne, but if one rebel is left alive, ten thousand spring up like weeds. Is it not to put power into the hands of Chinese rebels who continually think that they should be ruled by Chinese and not by Manchus?"

His point struck home. The Emperor raised his right hand to his mouth that he might hide the trembling of his lips. He feared the

Chinese he ruled even more than the white men who pressed upon him. His voice faded.

"Certainly the people must not be restrained," he muttered.

Instantly Prince Kung took up the words and repeated them as was his duty. "Certainly the people must not be restrained," he said in his loud clear voice. Over the kneeling multitude of ministers and princes approval rose in a subdued roar.

"I will send down my command tomorrow," the Emperor said to the Viceroy when silence had fallen again.

The Viceroy bowed his head nine times to the floor and gave way to the next minister. But all knew why the Emperor delayed.

That night when she was summoned, Tzu Hsi knew what she must say. All day she had remained alone and in thought, and she did not even send for her son. Her struggle was with her own anger. Could she have yielded to her anger she would have the Emperor send his armies to attack the foreigners and force them from the shores of China, to the last and youngest child, never to return. But her hour was not yet. She understood well that she must first rule herself if she would rule others, for had she not read in the *Analects* those very words? "When a ruler's conduct is correct, his government is effective without issuing orders. If his personal conduct be not correct, he may issue orders, but they will not be followed." And if such words were true for a male ruler, how much were they true for one who was a woman! How doubly rigorous must she be! Ah, that she had been born a man! She would herself have led the Imperial Armies against the invaders. What sins had she committed in some former life that she was born female in these times when strong men were wanted? She brooded upon the eternal question, sending mind and memory far back into her deepest being. She could not pierce beyond the womb. She was what she was born, and she must do with what she had, a man's mind in a woman's body. Man's mind and woman's body she would combine to do what must be done.

That night when the Emperor received her she found him too frightened for his habitual lust, a desire made fierce because his body could no more obey his mind. He received her eagerly and in his eagerness she read his fear. While he held her right hand in both his hands he caressed her palm, and asked her the question that he had waited to put to her.

"What shall we do with this Bowring Englishman? Does he not deserve to die?"

81

"He does," she said gently, "as any man deserves to die who insults the Son of Heaven. But you know, my lord, that when one strikes a viper, the head must be severed at the first blow, else the creature will turn and attack. Therefore your weapon must be sharp and certain. We do not know what the weapon should be, but we know this serpent is both wily and strong. Therefore I beg you delay and make excuse, never yielding but never refusing, until the way is clear."

He listened, his sallow face wrinkling with anxiety, and every word she spoke he received as though he heard it from Heaven. Indeed, when she had finished he said very fervently:

"You are Kuan Yin herself, Goddess of Mercy, sent to me by Heaven at this dreadful moment to guide and support me."

He had spoken many words of love to her, he had called her his heart and his liver, but what he now said pleased her beyond anything she had ever heard.

"Kuan Yin is my own favorite among the heavenly beings," she replied, and her voice, sweet and powerful as it was by nature, at this moment was also tender.

The Emperor sat up in his bed with sudden energy. "Bid the Chief Eunuch call my brother," he exclaimed. Like all weak men, he was impatient when a decision was made and overquick to act.

Tzu Hsi obeyed, nevertheless. In a few minutes Prince Kung came in, and she felt again as she looked at his grave and handsome face, that this man she could trust. Theirs was a common destiny.

"Sit down—sit down," the Emperor said impatiently to this younger brother.

"Allow me to stand," Prince Kung replied in courtesy, and he remained standing while the Emperor spoke in his high voice, nervous, stammering, seeking for words.

"We have—I have—decided not to attack the white strangers with one blow. They deserve immediate death. But when one steps on a viper —that is to say, a viper should be killed instantly, you understand, his head crushed, or cut off—the question being—"

"I do understand, Most High," Prince Kung said. "It is better not to attack unless we can be sure of destroying the enemy instantly and forever."

"It is what I am saying," the Emperor said peevishly. "Some day, of course, it is what we must do. Meanwhile delay, you comprehend, not yielding, but not refusing."

"Ignoring the white men?" Prince Kung inquired.

"Exactly," the Emperor said wearily. He lay back on his yellow satin cushions.

Prince Kung reflected. Had his brother made such decisions alone, he might have believed that it was from his habitual dread of trouble, the constant lethargy which stayed action. But he knew that this was Tzu Hsi's advice. He heard it, knowing very well the powerful and reasoning brain that was hidden inside the beautiful and shapely head. Yet she was very young—and a woman! Could this be wisdom?

"Most High," he began patiently.

But the Emperor refused to hear him. "I have spoken!" Thus he cried in a high and angry voice.

Prince Kung bowed his head. "Let it be so, Most High. I will myself take your commands to the Viceroy Yeh."

The brittle peace continued. Upon a winter's morning in the last month of the old moon year and the first month of the new solar year, when her son was nine months old, Tzu Hsi woke and, waking, breathed a mighty sigh. Again and again in the night her unsleeping mind had struggled through to consciousness. She felt a loneliness so heavy that it seemed some monstrous and unseen danger from which she could not escape. No more did she waken in the morning as she had once waked at her home in Pewter Lane, her eyes opening on the calm morning sun shining through the latticed windows. Her bed there, shared with her sister, was a refuge to which there was no return, her mother a shelter that was hers no more. Who in this vast tangle of walled passages and courtyards and palaces cared whether she lived or died? Even the Emperor had his many concubines.

"Ah, my mother," she moaned softly into her satin pillows.

No voice answered. She lifted her head and saw the gray light of late dawn steal over the high walls of the courtyard outside her window. Snow had fallen in the night and it lay thickly upon the walls and over the tiled garden. The round pool was hidden beneath snow and the pine trees were bent under its load.

I am too sad, she thought. I feel the very marrow in my bones cold with sadness.

Yet she was not ill. Her arms, lying under the quilts, were warm and strong. Her blood flowed, her mind was clear. She was only heartsick.

If I could see my mother, she thought. If I could see the one who bore me—

She remembered her mother's face, sensible and good, cheerful and shrewd, and she longed to return to her mother and tell her that she was afraid and alone in the palaces. In her uncle's house in Pewter Lane there was no fear or foreboding, no ominous future. The morning dawned only to the simple necessities of food and the day's work. There was no splendor nor demand for greatness.

"Ah, my mother," she sighed again, and she felt the yearning of a child for its own. Oh, that she could return to her source!

The need pervaded her, she rose with it in her heart, and all day she was sad. A sad day indeed, the gray light struggling through the white fall of the snow so that even at noon the lanterns were still lit in the rooms. She went nowhere except into her own library, a place she had taken for herself in a small adjoining palace long unused. Here she had commanded eunuchs to gather the books she liked best and the scrolls she liked to open and to ponder upon. But books did not speak to her today and she sat the hours through with her scrolls, unrolling one after another slowly, until she found the one she sought, a hand scroll, seventeen feet long, painted by the artist Chao Meng-fu in the Mongol dynasty of Yüan. This scroll, five hundred years old and more, had been inspired by her favorite, the great Wang Wei, master of landscape art, who had painted the scenes from his own home, where he lived for thirty years before he died. Now behind the palace walls on this winter's day, where she could see only sky and falling snow, Tzu Hsi gazed upon the green landscapes of continuing spring. One landscape melted into another as slowly she unrolled the scroll, so that she might dwell upon every detail of tree and brook and distant hillside. So did she, in imagination, pass beyond the high walls which enclosed her, and she traveled through a delectable country, beside flowing brooks and spreading lakes, and following the ever-flowing river she crossed over wooden bridges and climbed the stony pathways upon a high mountainside and thence looked down a gorge to see a torrent fed by still higher springs, and breaking into waterfalls as it traveled toward the plains. Down from the mountain again she came, past small villages nestling in pine forests and into the warmer valleys among bamboo grooves, and she paused in a poet's pavilion, and so reached at last the shore where the river lost itself in a bay. There among the reeds a fisherman's boat rose and fell upon the rising tide. Here the river ended, its horizon the open sea and the misted mountains of infinity. This scroll, Lady Miao had once told her, was the artist's picture of the human soul, passing through the pleasant scenes of earth to the last view of the unknown future, far beyond.

"And why," the Emperor asked her that night, when the long lonely day was spent, "why is your mind so far from me? I am not deceived by you. Your body is here but it is lifeless."

He took up her hand, a soft and beautiful hand now, its last roughness smoothed away, the fingers delicate, the palm strong.

"See this hand," he said. "I hold it, it grasps mine, but it could be any woman's hand."

She confessed her humors. "I have been sad today," she said. "I have spoken to no one. I have not even sent for the child."

He continued to stroke the hand he held. "Now why," he asked, "when you have everything, should you be sad?"

She longed to tell her strange fears to him but she dared not. He above all must never feel fear in her upon whom he leaned for strength. Oh, how heavy a burden was this necessity to be strong! And from whom could she draw her own strength? Above her there was none. She was indeed alone.

Tears filled her eyes against her will. The Emperor saw them glitter in the light of the candles that burned beside his bed and he was frightened.

"What is this?" he cried. "I have never seen you weep."

She drew her hand away and wiped her eyes gracefully on the edge of her satin sleeve. "I have yearned all day for my mother," she said. "And I do not know why. Can it be that I have somehow been unfilial? I have not looked upon her face since I entered these walls at your command. I do not know how she is. Perhaps she is dying and that is why I weep."

The Emperor was all eagerness to please her. "You must visit her," he urged. "Why did you not tell me? Go, go, my heart and liver, go tomorrow! I give you leave. But you must come back again by twilight. I cannot have you gone for a night."

So it came about that Tzu Hsi once more returned to her mother for a day and the price she now paid to the Emperor was her grateful ardor. Yet it could not be the next day that she go, for the visit must be announced in order that her uncle's house could be prepared. But the next day after it could be done, and two eunuchs were sent early to say that she would arrive at midday. What excitement now prevailed in Pewter Lane! Tzu Hsi, too, was warmed by her own eagerness, and she rose on the chosen morning with such a heart as she had not known since she came. She spent an hour deciding and then undoing her decisions as to what she should wear.

"I do not wish to be splendid," she explained to her woman, "for then they will think I have grown proud."

"Venerable, you must be somewhat splendid," the woman remonstrated, "lest they think you do not give them honor."

"A middling splendor," Tzu Hsi agreed.

She looked over all her robes, choosing this one and then that, until she selected at last a satin of a delicate orchid purple, lined with gray fur. It was a fine robe, its beauty in the perfection of its embroidered sleeves and hem, and not in the boldness of its design. She was pleased with herself when she was robed in it and she chose for ornaments her favorite jade.

When she was ready and when she had eaten a few mouthfuls of food, which her ladies pleaded with her to swallow, she entered into her sedan that stood waiting in the courtyard, the bearers drew the yellow satin curtains close, and so the journey was begun. For a mile it lay within the walls of the Forbidden City, and she gauged the courts through which she was carried, and the halls by which she passed, traveling always toward the south, for the Emperor in the excess of his love had granted her the privilege of using the chief gate, called Meridian, by which usually only he himself could enter and leave his city. Outside that gate she heard the Commander of the Imperial Guard shout for his guardsmen to stand attendance while she passed. How well she knew that voice! She leaned forward in her chair and put aside the curtains a half-inch and looking through the crack she saw Jung Lu standing not ten feet from her, his face averted, his sword held up before him, his body taut and straight and at its full height. Neither to right nor left did he look when she passed but she knew by the dark flush on his cheeks that he had heard, that he knew it was she. She let the curtain fall.

It was high noon when Tzu Hsi reached the entrance to Pewter Lane, and hidden behind the sedan curtains she knew that she was near her childhood home. She smelled the familiar odors of salty crullers fried in bean oil, the musky fragrance of camphorwood, the reek of children's urine and the choking scent of dust. The day was dry and cold and under the feet of the bearers the earth was frozen hard as stone. Upon this pale dry earth the shadows of the houses on either side of the lane were shrunken small and black against the walls and Tzu Hsi, peering downward between her sedan and the curtains, guessed the hour. So often had she run to and fro along this lane that she could tell within an inch what time it was, the shadows heavy toward the west in the morning and bending eastward in the afternoon. Now in the light of the full sun her sedan approached the well-known gate and she put her eye to the crack of the curtains again and saw that gate opened and her family gathered before it and waiting. There to the right stood her uncle and her mother, and with them the cousins of the elder generation and their wives, and to the left she saw a tall thin young girl who was surely her sister, and with her were the two brothers, grown beyond her memories and behind them Lu Ma. Against the walls on either side were the neighbors and the friends of Pewter Lane.

When she saw their faces grave and welcoming, tears watered into her eyes. Oh, she was the same to them, and somehow she must make them know it! Inside her breast beat the same heart they knew so well. Yet she could not open the curtains or cry out their names, for whatever her heart was, she was now Tzu Hsi, Empress of the Western Palace, and mother of the Imperial Heir, and so she must carry herself wherever she was. She made no sign and the eunuchs led the way to the gate, the Chief Eunuch first of all, for the Emperor had commanded him to go with his treasure and never leave her presence. Up the steps then and through the open gate the six bearers carried her, and they crossed the entrance courtyard and set the sedan down at last before the house. There the Chief Eunuch himself put aside the satin curtains and Tzu Hsi stepped out into the sunlight and saw before her the wide and open doors of her old home. The familiar room was there, the main hall, its tables and chairs polished and clean and the tiled floor swept. Often it had been her task to sweep and clean and set the chairs straight and dust the furniture, and now all was done as though she were still here. A vase of red paper flowers stood on the long table against the wall and fresh candles in the pewter candlesticks, and in front of the square table, between the ceremonial chairs, were small covered dishes of sweetmeats, a teapot and bowls.

She placed her hand upon the lifted arm of the Chief Eunuch and he led her to the highest seat to the right of the square table and she sat down and put her feet together on the footstool. He arranged her skirts and she folded her hands upon her lap. Then the Chief Eunuch returned to the gate and announced that now the family could approach the Empress of the Western Palace. One by one they came, her uncle first and then her mother, and then the elder cousins of the same generation and their wives, and after them her brothers and her sister and the younger cousins of their generation and each bowed down before her while behind her stood the eunuchs, and at her right hand the Chief Eunuch.

At first Tsu Hsi behaved indeed as an Empress must. She received the obeisances of her family with dignity and grave looks, except that when her uncle and her mother bowed before her she motioned to the Chief Eunuch to lift them up and invite them to be seated. When the ceremonies were complete no one knew what to say next. All must wait for the Empress to speak and Tzu Hsi looked from face to face. She longed to come down from her high place and speak as she used to do, and she longed to run about the house and be free as once she had been free. But the Chief Eunuch stood there watching all she did. For a while she considered how she could accomplish what she wished. All were arranged according to the generations, the elders seated and the young ones standing, and still they waited for her to speak first, and how could she speak as her heart longed? Suddenly she tapped her shielded fingernails upon the polished table at her right and she nodded at the Chief Eunuch to signify that she had something to say to him. He came near and leaned down his ear and into this ear she spoke.

"You are to stand aside, you and these eunuchs! How can I enjoy myself when you hear every word I speak and see every motion that I make?"

The Chief Eunuch was concerned when he heard such a command. "Venerable, the Son of Heaven bade me never leave your side," he said in a loud whisper.

Tzu Hsi was instantly incensed. She tapped her foot on the floor and drummed her golden finger shields upon the table and she shook her head at the Chief Eunuch so that the pearls of her headdress trembled on their wires. Her own eunuch, Li Lien-ying, who stood near to hold her jeweled pipe and fan and toilet case, saw her fury rising and, knowing very well what it foretold, he plucked the sleeve of the Chief Eunuch.

"Elder Brother, it is better to let her have her way," he whispered. "Why do you not rest yourself? I will stay near enough to watch over her."

Now whether the Chief Eunuch would have obeyed Tzu Hsi or the Emperor cannot be known, but he was easily weary and already tired of standing on his feet and he grasped the chance to withdraw to another room. Seeing him gone, Tzu Hsi considered her mentor had left her, for Li Lien-ying was to her no more than a piece of furniture whose duty it was to hold whatever possessions she might need. She came down from her high seat now and she went to her uncle and bowed and she put her arms about her mother and laid her head down on that strong shoulder and wept.

"Oh, me," she murmured, "how lonely I am in the palace!"

All were in consternation at this complaint and even her mother did not know what to say and she could only hold her daughter close. And in this long moment Tzu Hsi understood by their silence that even these she loved were helpless. In pride she lifted up her head again and laughed, her eyes still wet, and she cried out to her sister:

"Come, take this heavy thing from my head!"

Her sister came and lifted off the headdress and Li Lien-ying took it and set it carefully on a table. Without this ornament of dignity, all saw now that Tzu Hsi, in spite of her imperial robes and the jewels on her hands and wrists, was the same gay girl that she had ever been. So talk began and the women came near and smoothed her hands and examined her rings and bracelets and exclaimed at her beauty.

"Your skin is white and soft," they said. "What do you rub in your skin?"

"An ointment from India," she told them, "and it is made of fresh cream and pounded orange peel. It is even better than our mutton fat."

"And where do you get the cream?" they asked.

"It is skimmed from asses' milk," she said.

Such small questions they asked, but none dared to ask about her life in the Forbidden City, or of how her lord dealt with her, or of the Heir, lest they use a word which might bring ill luck by chance and inadvertence, as, for example, if one should speak the word "yellow," which being imperial might seem harmless except that it is also a part of the Yellow Springs, which means death, and death may not be mentioned next to the Son of Heaven or the Heir. But Tzu Hsi could not hide her joy in her child, and when none spoke she spoke, and she said in all happiness:

"I did wish indeed that I might bring my little son to show you, but when I asked the Most High, my lord, he said no, it could not be, lest an evil wind or a shadow or some cruel spirit do the child damage. But I assure you, my mother, that he is such a child as would delight your soul, and you must come to visit him since I may not bring him here. His eyes are big like this—" here she measured two circles with her thumbs and forefingers—"and he is so fat, his flesh so fragrant—and he never cries, I do assure you—and he is always greedy for his food and his teeth are whiter than these pearls, and though he is still so small, he wants to stand on his legs, which are like two posts under his strong body."

"Hush!" her mother cried. "Hush—hush—what if the gods hear you, reckless one? Will they not seek to destroy such a child?"

Her mother looked up and down and everywhere around and she cried out, in a loud voice, "Nothing is as you say! I have heard that he is puny and weak and—and—"

Tzu Hsi laughed and put her hand over her mother's mouth. "I am not afraid!"

"Do not say so," her mother insisted beneath the hand.

But Tzu Hsi could only laugh, and soon she was walking everywhere, looking at the rooms she knew so well and teasing her sister, who now had the whole bed to herself, and alone with her mother in one room, she asked concerning the marriage plans for her sister, and proposed that she would find a good husband for her among the young noblemen.

"Indeed," she said, "I will find one young and handsome and bid him wed my sister."

Her mother was grateful. "If you can so do," she said, "it will be a filial deed, and very pious."

So the hours passed, and all the family was merry because Tzu Hsi was merry. In midafternoon a good feast was set, Lu Ma busy everywhere and bawling at the hired cooks, and when this had been shared the day was nearing night and the Chief Eunuch returned to his duty. He approached Tzu Hsi and requested her to prepare for leave-taking.

"The time has come, Venerable," he said. "I have the command of the Most High. It is my duty to obey."

She knew there was no further escape and so she yielded with grace. Once more she became the Empress. Li Lien-ying put back her headdress and she took her seat again in the main room and arranged herself. Immediately the family became her subjects. One by one they came forward and made their obeisances and said their farewells and to each she spoke with suitable words leaving gifts for each, and for Lu Ma money. At last all farewells were said. She lingered a few minutes more in silence, her eyes moving here and there. It had been a day of deep happiness and a renewal of the simple affections of her childhood. And yet somehow she knew it was the last time that ever she could return to this house. All seemed the same, but in spite of her faithful heart, she knew nothing was the same. They loved her still, but their love was entangled with hopes and desires of what she could do for them. Her uncle hinted at debts unpaid, her brother yearned for amusements, and her mother bade her not forget her promise for her sister. In lesser ways the kinfolk, too, had mentioned hardships and lacks. She was pitying and merciful, she made promises for all and she would fulfill them because she could, but her loneliness returned and lay ten times more heavy on her heart, for now she knew she was loved beyond herself. She was loved for what she could do and for what she could give, and her heart shriveled. Though her body had come back and for these few hours her spirit had rejoined the others in this house, the separation was forever. Destiny compelled her onward, and her own she must leave behind. There could be no return.

When this knowledge settled into her being, her gaiety was gone. With firm steps she walked across the room and entered again into her sedan chair, and the Chief Eunuch himself let down the curtains.

So Tzu Hsi returned again to the Forbidden City, and when she approached the great gate of the Meridian, the Imperial Guard announced the end of the day. The drummer stood behind his great drum, beating upon it a rhythm so swift that the sticks fell with heavy blows as steady, one upon another, as the beat of some mighty heart. In the twilight the trumpeters stood in their robes, and each held to his lips a long brass trumpet. These trumpets they raised in unison, then lowered to the same level, and at this moment they blew a long quivering blast of music, beginning in softness and rising to strength, and always following the beating of the mighty drums until, falling away again, the trumpet voices died. Again and again this music was repeated until the last time when the trumpeters allowed the sounds to die so slowly that they were lost in distance. So, too, did the drummer soften the beat of the drum until he made it end by three slow measured beats. A pause of silence followed, and then a bronze bell was struck three times and by Jung Lu.

And the night fell as always it did fall. The watchmen marched to their task, and Tzu Hsi in her sedan entered the vast gates and heard them close behind her.

Winter ended late, and the halting spring was delayed still further by the evil winds that blew down from the north. Sandstorms tortured the city and though the people closed their doors and sealed their windows, yet the wind drove the fine pale sand through every crack and corner. Nor was the news good from the south. The Viceroy Yeh had obeyed the commands from the Dragon Throne. He had dallied and delayed, he had not replied to the many messages from the Englishman Sir John Bowring, and when it was reported to him that a French priest had been killed somewhere, he made no reply to this announcement, either, nor to the demand of the French minister for retribution. Yet, the Viceroy now reported to the Dragon Throne, instead of being subdued by such neglect the white men were more restless than before, and he, the Viceroy, sought further direction from the Son of Heaven. What if war broke out again? And meanwhile there was the small trouble of the families of the beheaded men, who had been the ship's crew of *The Arrow*. They were angry and their sons and nephews had joined the Chinese rebels for revenge against the Viceroy, who stood for the distant Emperor. And worst of all, it was rumored that the Englishman Elgin, a noble lord, very powerful, was threatening to sail English ships northward along the seacoast and enter the harbor at Tientsin in order to attack the Taku forts, which protected the capital itself.

When the Emperor read this memorial he fell ill and took to his bed and would not eat. In silence he handed the document to his brother Prince Kung, whom he summoned, and he commanded that Tzu Hsi read it also and that they two present their advice. Now for the first time Tzu Hsi fell into open disagreement with Prince Kung. They argued in the Imperial Library, their usual meeting place, and in the presence of the Chief Eunuch and Li Lien-ying, who stood as attendants and heard all that was said.

"Venerable," Prince Kung said reasonably, "again I tell you that it is not wise to annoy these white men to the point of anger. They have guns and warships, and they are barbarian at heart."

"Let them return to their own lands. We have tried patience and now patience fails," Tzu Hsi exclaimed. She was very beautiful when she was haughty, and Prince Kung sighed to see such beauty and such pride. Yet he admitted in his secret heart that this woman had an energy which even he had not and surely that his elder brother had not, and indeed the times needed strength.

"We have not the means to force their return," he reminded her.

"We have the means if we have the will," she retorted. "We can kill them every one while they are still few and throw their bodies into the sea. Do dead men return?"

He exclaimed at such recklessness. "Will death put an end to them? When their peoples hear of it, they will send a thousand white men for each one that dies, and they will come with their many ships of war, bearing their magic weapons against us."

"I do not fear them," Tzu Hsi declared.

"Then I do," Prince Kung assured her. "I fear them greatly. It is not only their weapons I fear—it is the white men themselves. When they are attacked they return ten blows for one. No, no, Venerable—mediation is the safe way, and bargaining and delays, as you wisely did advise before. These must still be our weapons. We must still confound them with delays and promises unfulfilled, and we must still put off the evil day of their attack. We must weary them and discourage them, always courteous when we speak, seeming to yield and never yielding. This is our steadfast wisdom."

So in the end it was decided, and that Tzu Hsi might be diverted, for she continued rebellious, Prince Kung advised his elder brother, the Emperor, that she be permitted to spend the hot season at the Summer Palace outside the city of Peking. There among the lakes and gardens she could disport herself with the Heir and her ladies and forget the troubles of the nation.

"The Empress of the Western Palace loves plays and theatricals," he suggested. "Let a stage be built at the Summer Palace and actors be hired to amuse her. Meanwhile, I will consider with the councilors what reply shall be sent south. And it is to be remembered that when the green spring comes again we must celebrate the first birthday of the Heir, and we should announce the occasion soon, that the people may prepare their gifts. Thus all will be diverted while we ponder the dangers ahead."

In this way Prince Kung hoped to allay Tzu Hsi's anger and turn her thoughts to pleasure and away from proud revenge upon the white men. In his secret heart he was very fearful, and he wished to take counsel with the princes and the ministers and any whose wisdom he could trust. For he saw in the future, and not too far, the increasing threat of the men from the West. They had discovered the treasures of ancient Asia, and being men of nations young and poor, could they be asked to leave what they had found? They must be placated, but how he did not know, until defense could be planned. Troubled indeed he was, sleepless at night and never hungry for food any more, for what he pondered was deeper than he could fathom. The old civilized ways of peace and wisdom were menaced by a new brute force. Which would prevail and where lay the final strength, in violence or in peace?

So grave were these times that the Emperor in the fifth month renewed an ancient rite which his ancestors had seldom observed after the end of the preceding dynasty of Ming. At the Spring Feast of the Dead, in this moon year, the Emperor, sorely troubled and afraid, announced that he would worship at the Supreme Temple of Imperial Ancestors. Now this was a very ancient temple and it stood in a vast park where great pines shielded its roofs from the sun. These pines, being older than the memory of man, were gnarled and twisted by the wind and the sand, and beneath them the moss was deeper than piled velvet. Inside the Temple were the sacred shrines of dead emperors,

93

their names carved upon tablets of precious wood and each tablet resting upon a cushion of yellow satin. Only priests in yellow robes wandered about the park and cared for the Temple, and silence hung everywhere as heavy as the centuries that had passed. No birds sang in this still place, but white cranes came in the spring and made their nests in the crooked pines and reared their young and in the autumn flew away again.

To this place then, at the Feast of the Dead, the Emperor came with his princes and dukes, his councilors and high ministers. It was the hour before dawn and mists, unusual in this dry northern climate, rose from earth to sky, so that brother looking at brother could not recognize his face. Two days before the feast day the ancestral tablets of the dead Manchu rulers had been brought from their own private hall near the Imperial Library, and by the light of horn lanterns, so dark were the shadows under the pines, the Chief Eunuch and his eunuchs had arranged them upon the eleven shrines inside the temple.

All was now in readiness for the arrival of the Son of Heaven. He had spent the night in the Hall of Abstinence, neither eating nor drinking nor sleeping. For three days, too, the people of the whole nation had eaten no meat, they had not tasted garlic or oils nor drunk wine nor heard music nor looked at plays, nor invited guests. Law courts were closed for these three days and there was no litigation made by anyone.

At this gray hour before dawn the Court Butcher made his report that he had slaughtered the beasts for the sacrifice, and had poured their fresh blood into bowls, and had buried their bones and fur. The princes and the dukes reported that the sacred prayer was written, which the Son of Heaven was to pray before the guardian Ancestors, whose tablets stood upright and ready upon the imperial-yellow cushions upon the altars.

The Emperor received these reports and he rose to allow the Chief Eunuch to put on him the solemn robes of sacrifice, dark purple trimmed in plain gold and leaning upon two near kinsmen, his first cousins, he entered the Supreme Temple. There his younger brother, Prince Kung, waited to receive him. No strangers were near. Even the eunuchs from the Temple withdrew before the Son of Heaven entered and his kinsmen alone stood at the door. Now the imperial princes came forward to meet the Emperor and after obeisances they led him from one to another of the eleven sacred altars. At each one he made nine obeisances and he offered bowls of food and wine, and before each altar he made the same prayer. The prayer was for peace and for safety against the new enemies that had come from the West. It was a long prayer, and the Emperor read it eleven times, slowly and in as loud a voice as he could muster.

To the Spirits of the Great Dead he reported what the Western men had done, how they had made war and how they had seized territories and how they came as barbarian tribesmen, in ships that spat out fire to frighten the people, and he reported how these men insisted upon unwanted trade.

"We have our own goods, O Venerable Ancestors," the Emperor declared in his prayer. "We have no need of Western toys. What do we lack under the protection of Heaven and Our Guardian Ancestors? We beseech Our Ancestors to protect us now. Let the strangers be driven into the sea! Provide pestilences to destroy them! Send down poisonous insects to sting them and vipers to strike them dead! O Guardians of our people, restore to us our land and give us peace."

When the prayer was ended the hour was already near sunrise and in the dawning light flocks of white pigeons, sleeping under the broad eaves of the Temple, awoke and spread their wings and circled above the ancient pines. The candles faded in the lanterns, and dust motes danced in the pale sunbeams stealing through the wide gates of the Temple. The sacrifice was ended and the Emperor let himself be led away again and entering into his imperial palanquin he returned to his own palaces. Then everywhere over the nation the people took up their accustomed life, comforted and encouraged because the Son of Heaven himself had bowed before the Guardian Ancestors, had made his report and sent up his prayer on their behalf.

These rites at the Spring Feast of the Dead so heartened the Emperor that when the sixth month of the moon year drew near and the heat of summer increased, he himself decided to go to the Summer Palace with his two Consorts, and with him to take the Heir and the Court. Until now, although he had longed to go, the disturbances in the nation had made him uneasy. What if the Chinese rebels were to rise while he was away from the capital, or what if the Western men were suddenly to become incensed and sail their ships northward up the coasts as they had long threatened to do? Yet neither of these ill events had come about and, although the Viceroy Yeh was still gloomy, the delays and the evasions which he made held back both rebels and Western men.

And Tzu Hsi herself coaxed the Emperor upon a certain night when the summer moon was full and her smile enchanting.

"My lord," she said, "come with me to the Summer Palace. The coolness of the hills will restore you to health."

The Emperor was sorely in need of such restoration. The slow paralysis which had weakened him in the last five years lay heavy upon his limbs. Upon some days he could not walk and must lean upon two eunuchs for crutches, and upon other days he could not raise his hands to his head. His dead left side was his constant affliction, and he felt his whole body pervaded with its heaviness. He yielded therefore to this beautiful woman who enlivened him and strengthened him as no other living creature was able to do, and he decided upon a day, then a month hence, for the journey to the Summer Palace, some nine miles outside the city walls.

Now Tzu Hsi, though she could look the Empress and in full majesty, was still so young a creature that the thought of a holiday permeated her heart like warm wine. She did not yet love the severe and noble palaces in which she was doomed to live, although among them she had made small separate places for herself, secret gardens in old forgotten courtyards and terraces where no one walked, and where sometimes she might escape the burdens of state which she must carry. In her own palace she had her pets, a little dog, a female, who bred pups to amuse her, and she kept crickets in cages and birds of many colors. The pets she loved best were not these, however, but the wild creatures who settled sometimes in the trees and upon the pools. She could so imitate the sharp whisper of a cricket that she coaxed the insect to sit upon her forefinger while she stroked its papery wings. With much patience she learned the call of a nightingale at twilight so that the dim brown creature fluttered intoxicated about her head. When this happened she felt a childlike happiness that she was loved for herself alone and not for any favor that she could bestow. Sometimes, when she sat with her son upon her knees, she forgot that he was the Heir and together they watched a flock of ducklings newly hatched or the pups pulling and mauling in play, and then she laughed so loudly that her ladies marveled and smiled behind their fans. But Tzu Hsi had no fear of smiles or reproaches. She was herself and as she was, so she continued to be, a creature as free as those she played with. Yet, though four square miles lay within the Forbidden City, its walls confined her and she longed to be outside all walls and in that place of which she had often heard but where never yet had she gone to live or even to visit.

This Summer Palace had first been built for pleasure several centuries earlier by the emperors then ruling, and they had chosen for its site a place near an eternal fountain which ran so clear and pure, its waters

96

sweet and ever fresh, that it was named the Fountain of Jade. The first Summer Palace was destroyed in a war and rebuilt again two centuries earlier than this time, and by the Imperial Ancestor K'ang Hsi, then ruling, but the Imperial Ancestor, his son Ch'ien Lung, then ruling, brought all the separate buildings together, uniting them into a vast park threaded with lakes and rivers and crossed by marble bridges or bridges of ironwood, painted and carved by master workmen. Dearly indeed did Ch'ien Lung enjoy what he had done, so that when he heard that the King of France, then ruling, had also such pleasure grounds in that distant land, Ch'ien Lung inquired of French ministers and Jesuit priests what the French king had that he had not, for Emperors in those days were diverted by Western men and even welcomed them, not dreaming that they could have a later evil intent. When Ch'ien Lung heard of the beauties that the French king had made he wished for them, too, and he added Western beauty to the Summer Palace as well as that which belonged there. The Jesuit priests, for their part, thinking to find favor with the great Ch'ien Lung, brought with them from France and Italy pictures of the palaces of Europe, which Ch'ien Lung studied closely, and he took from them anything which caught his fancy. After Ch'ien Lung's time, however, the Summer Palace was long closed, for his Heir, Chia Ch'ing, loved better the Northern Palace in Jehol and there was struck by lightning one summer's day when he was in the company of his favorite concubine and so died. And T'ao Kuang, his son, the father of the Emperor Hsien Feng, now ruling, was a miser and would not allow the Court to move even in the hot season to the Summer Palace, because he feared expense.

In high mood, therefore, the Court set forth one summer's dawn. The day was fine, a dewy day, the morning moist and warm with unusual mists. Tzu Hsi had risen early and had commanded her women to dress her in simple garments, befitting the country. Thus the women put on her a thin silk, made of pineapple fiber imported from the southern islands, a pale water-green in color, and she wore no jewels except her pearls. In her haste she was ready hours before the Emperor bestirred himself to waken and be dressed and eat his morning meal. Yet it was still midway between dawn and noon when the imperial procession set forth, the Bannermen going first, then the princes and their families and at last the Imperial Guards upon horses, and Jung Lu was at their head upon a great white stallion. Behind them and before the yellow-curtained palanquin of the Emperor, Tzu Hsi followed in her own palanquin with her son and his nurse and beside her was Sakota, the Empress of the Eastern Palace, in her palanquin. Not for many

97

months had these two ladies met, and seeing her cousin's pale face this morning Tzu Hsi blamed herself again and said in her heart that when she had time to spare she would renew her kinship with her sister Consort.

The streets through which the imperial procession passed were emptied and silent. Flags shaped in yellow triangles had been placed at early morning along the route chosen for the Son of Heaven and these warned the people that no man or woman or child should be upon the streets at this hour. The doors of all houses were closed, the windows curtained, and wherever a cross street gave into the main highway curtains of yellow silk forbade the entrance of any citizen. When the Son of Heaven left the Gate of the Meridian, drums beat and gongs roared to give the signal and at this noise the people went into their houses and hid their faces. Again the drums beat and gongs roared and those who smoothed the highway with yellow sand also retired. Upon the third warning of drums and gongs the nobles of the Manchu clans, all in their best robes, knelt on the sides of the highway before the Son of Heaven as he passed, surrounded by his thousand guardsmen. In the old days the emperors rode always upon great Arabian horses, bridled with gold, the saddles covered with jeweled velvet. But Hsien Feng, now ruling, was not able to sit upon a horse and so he must ride in his palanquin. He was shy, too, because he knew himself so thin and sallow, and he would not allow the eunuchs to lift the curtains. Hidden and in silence he was carried along the yellow-sanded highway, and the kneeling noblemen neither saw him nor heard his voice.

At the village of Hai T'ien, outside the city walls, the road turned eastward, and through this village the palanquins of the Emperor and his two Consorts passed with all the Court. The little town was bustling with good business, for here the Imperial Guardsmen were to live, and in the countryside nearby the princes and the dukes and other noblemen had summer palaces on their own estates, that they might more easily wait upon the Emperor at the Summer Palace. Everywhere the villagers were in high mood, for when the Court took residence at the Summer Palace of Yüan Ming Yüan, they grew rich.

At sunset the imperial procession approached the gate of the Summer Palace itself and, peering through the cracks between her curtains, Tzu Hsi saw the lofty gate of carved white marble, guarded by two golden lions. It was open and waiting, and she was carried over the high threshold and into the quiet of the vast park. Now she could not forbear opening her curtains with her hands to look out and she saw a dreamlike scene. Pagodas hung as though suspended on the green hillsides, clear brooks ran smoothly rippling beside the winding roads paved with marble, and bridges carved of white marble led the way to a hundred pavilions, each different from the others and beautiful in gold and colored tile. A lifetime would not be enough to know it all. And with much that she could see, there was more unseen, the great palaces themselves, designed so long ago and enriched by every emperor in his time, the famous water clock whose twelve animals spouted water from the Fountain of Jade, each for two hours at a time. And every palace, so she had heard, was filled with treasures not only of the East but of Europe and the West. Her pleasure-loving soul rejoiced and she was impatient to be free to wander as she would.

At sunset she felt her palanquin set down, the curtains put aside by Li Lien-ying, and she rose as one who greets a fairy country, bewitching and unknown. She looked about her and by a strange chance at this very moment her look fell, unwary and unprepared, on Jung Lu. He stood alone, his men behind the Emperor, whose palanquin was already at the great Hall of Entrance. Not expecting, he lifted up his head and looked into the eyes he knew so well. She caught his look, and he caught hers, and for one instant their hearts entangled. They turned their heads in haste, the moment passed. Tzu Hsi entered her assigned palace and her ladies followed. But a sudden happiness sprang up in her. She overflowed with lively joy at all she saw as she went from one room to another. This palace, now hers, was named the Palace of Contentment. It was old, and its very age enchanted her. Here emperors and their courts had come for pleasure and to escape from their burdens, and here they had found peace in gaiety. When she had seen all that could be seen today she returned to its entrance and standing upon the threshold of the wide doors, thrown open to the sunset, she stretched out her arms to the landscape, exquisite and calm in the clear brightness of the evening sun.

"The very air is mellifluous," she said to her ladies. "Breathe it, and feel how light it is in the lungs! Compare it with the weight of the air inside the city walls!"

The ladies breathed in as she commanded and they cried out their agreement with her. Indeed, the air was pure and cool but not chill.

"I wish I could spend all my life here," Tzu Hsi exclaimed. "Would that I need never return to the Forbidden City!"

Her ladies cried out against this. How, they inquired, could she be spared in that center of the nation's life?

"At least let us not speak of anything not joyful," Tzu Hsi insisted.

99

"Whatever is sorrowful or rouses anger or gives pain must here be forgotten."

Her ladies agreed to this in a chorus of mild murmurs and sighs, and Tzu Hsi, eager to continue her discovery of the manifold variety of palaces and gardens, lingered in the doorway. Alas, the day was at its end, the sun slipped down behind the spires of the pagodas, and the afterglow faded from the lakes and streams. Soon even the shadows of the marble bridges no longer lingered upon the waters, and the day was ended.

"I shall retire early," Tzu Hsi said, "and I shall rise at dawn. However many tomorrows are allotted to this joyful place, they will not be enough to see all that is to be seen here or to take our fill of pleasure."

Her ladies agreed and the moon had scarcely risen before Tzu Hsi went to her own apartments. A light meal of sweetmeats and tidbits was served to her, she drank her favorite green tea, and then, bathed and in fresh silk garments, she lay down to sleep. At first she said she could not sleep, so sweet was the night air, and twice, after her weary women slept, she rose from her bed to look from the open windows. The palace stood high above the low encircling walls, and she could see beyond them to the distant mountains, pale in the moonlight. Peace stole over her spirit, so deep a peace that it seemed the prelude to sleep itself, and yet she was awake in every sense. Before her lay the golden moonlit landscape, she smelled the fragrance of night-blooming lilies, she heard the clear call of the harvest bird, early in its season. Her loneliness subsided, the fear of wars and troubles died away, her impetuous heart grew gentle and her thoughts kindly. Beyond the terrace, to the right, stood the Palace of the Floating Cloud, assigned to Sakota. Tomorrow—no, not tomorrow, but some day when her happiness was full enough she would stay by her resolve and renew her sisterly friendship with Sakota. How strange to think that they who had grown up beneath the same roof in Pewter Lane should now live side by side in their two palaces, their one lord the Emperor!

And then, because her mind was never long at rest, she thought of Jung Lu, her kinsman, and how she had seen him for a moment today, how their unwary eyes had met, had clung and then had parted again, unwillingly, and she longed fiercely, of a sudden, to hear his voice and know him near. And why should she not summon him as her kinsman —say, for some advice she needed? What advice did she need? Her mind roamed in search of its excuse. Her promise to her mother, still unredeemed, her promise to wed her sister to a prince—for that, surely, she could ask advice from a kinsman? And her own eunuch, her faithful one, Li Lien-ying, to him she could say honestly:

"I have a family matter, a promise I made to my mother, and I wish to ask my kinsman, the Commander of the Imperial Guard—"

The moonlight grew more golden, the air more fragrant than it had been and she sighed with happiness. Here in this magic place, could not magic be accomplished? She smiled at herself with secret mockery. There was an edge to her joy, a thin sharp edge of old desire, a teasing memory waking to renew itself. Well, let it be no more, she thought. She need not put a guard upon herself—he would do that. His rectitude would be her guard, the lock to which he held the key. Him she could trust, for he could not be corrupted.

Suddenly she longed for sleep and stealing to her bed and walking softly among her women sleeping on their pallets on the tiled floors, she parted the curtains and lay down.

The morning dawned clear again and calm, a day without wind, yet cooled by some distant northern storm, and she let this day pass, forgetful of everything except her childlike pleasure in what she saw about her. Many days must pass before she could see all there was to see, for when palaces and lakes and courtyards, terraces and gardens and pavilions were visited, there remained the treasure houses, the annexes to Yüan Ming Yüan, and in these were stored the gifts that had been given for two hundred years to the emperors of the ruling dynasty. Silks by lots of a thousand bolts apiece, furs by bales from beyond the Siber River, curios from every nation in Europe and from the British Isles, tributes from Thibet and Turkestan, gifts from Korea and Japan and all those lesser nations who, though free, acknowledged that their guide and leader was the Son of Heaven, fine furniture and precious wares from southern provinces, jades and silver toys and boxes, vases of gold and gems from India and the southern seas, all these waited for her searching eyes and quick hands to judge their weights, shapes and textures.

And in the evening of every day, by the Emperor's command, a play was presented to the Court by the Imperial Players, and for the first time Tzu Hsi could indulge to fullness of her desire her love of theater. She had read books about the past, and she had studied well the old paintings and writings, but in the plays she saw men and women of history come to life again before her eyes. She lived with other consorts and empresses, and saw her own self, born earlier to rule and die. And thoughtful thereafter she went to bed at night if the play were thoughtful, and merry if the play were merry, and whatever she did was all pleasure.

Among the treasures which she mused upon more than the rest was the library which the Ancestor Ch'ien Lung himself had caused to be collected and created from the great books of the past of four thousand years. By his command these books had been copied by the scholars of his reign into one vast treasure. Two sets of the manuscripts these scholars made, the one to remain in the Forbidden City and the other here, lest fire or invading enemies destroy either. Tzu Hsi had not herself laid hands upon these libraries which the scholars had made, for inside the city the one was stored in the Hall of Literary Glory and kept under lock and key, except for a single season each year, this at the Feast of Classics, when it was the duty of the highest scholars to take out the ancient writings and expound their meaning to the Emperor, then ruling. For ever since the First Emperor eighteen hundred years ago had burned the books and buried scholars to put an end to ancient learning, and make himself supreme, it had been the first care of scholars to preserve books by teaching reverence for them, first from the Emperor and then from all his subjects, and that the words of the sage Confucius could not be destroyed by willful rulers, the Four Books and the Five Classics were even carved on stone and these stone monuments stood in the Hall of Classics, whose gates were barred. But here at Yüan Ming Yüan Tzu Hsi, though a woman, could read the ancient writings and so she promised herself she would do, if on a day it rained, or if she were sated with the sights to be seen.

Yet whatever she did for some twenty days, not only while she enjoyed outdoor feasts upon the imperial houseboats with the Court, not only while she walked among the flower gardens, or played with her imperial son, who throve in this pure air, not even when she was summoned to the Emperor's bedchamber, she did not forget her wily wish to speak again with Jung Lu, her kinsman. It lay twisted in her brain, that enchanting plan, the germ within a seed, ready to come to life when she so chose.

One day, made reckless with much freedom and incessant pleasure, she did so choose, and suddenly deciding, she beckoned Li Lien-ying to her side, waving her jeweled fingers to him. He was always near and always watching and when he saw her raised hand, he came at once and knelt before her, his head low, to hear what she would command.

"I find my mind troubled," she said in her clear imperious voice. "I cannot forget a promise I made to my birthmother concerning the marriage of my younger sister. Yet the months pass and I do nothing. Meanwhile at my childhood home they wait anxiously. Yet to whom can I turn for good advice? Yesterday I remembered that the Commander of the Imperial Guard is our kinsman. It is he alone who can help me in this maternal family matter. Summon him to come to me."

She said this purposely before her ladies, for she who was so high could have no secrets. Let all know what she did. When she had spoken she sat calmly on her pretty throne, a seat delicately carved and inlaid with ivory from the tusks of elephants of Burma. Around her stood her ladies, and they heard and made no sign of any thought not innocent.

As for Li Lien-ying, he knew his sovereign well by now and when she spoke he obeyed at once, for nothing could rouse her temper higher than delay in what she wished. The thoughts in that dark heart of his none knew and none asked, but surely he remembered another day when he had obeyed such a command and had brought Jung Lu to Yehonala's door. In the courtyard outside the closed door that day the long hours of afternoon had crept by, while he had let none enter. Only he and the serving woman had known that Jung Lu was there. At sunset when the tall guardsman had come out, his face proud and troubled, they had not spoken, nor had Jung Lu so much as looked at the eunuch. The next day Yehonala had obeyed the summons of the Emperor. In ten moon months the Heir was born. Who could say—who could say? He went grinning and cracking his knuckles to find the Commander of the Imperial Guard.

Where before she had received her kinsman in secret now Tzu Hsi recieved him openly and among her ladies. Seated on her throne in the great hall of her palace, she waited for Jung Lu. Magnificence became her, as always. The walls were hung with painted scrolls, behind the throne was an alabaster screen and porcelain pots of blooming trees stood to right and left. Her little dogs gamboled with four white kittens upon the floor, and here was the woman in the Empress. Tzu Hsi, in the midst of her splendor, laughed at her pets so much that at last she came down from her throne, possessed by mirth and playfulness. And while she went here and there she praised one lady for her fresh looks and another for her headdress and she trailed her silken kerchief to make the kittens follow her, and only when she heard the eunuch's footsteps followed by a certain steadfast tread did she make haste to sit upon her throne again and fold her jeweled hands and look proud and grand, while her ladies smiled behind their fans.

Her face was grave, her lips demure, but her great eyes sparkled when Jung Lu stepped across the high threshold of the entrance, wearing his guardsman's tunic of scarlet satin and black velvet trousers. He took nine steps forward and did not raise his face to hers until he knelt. Then before he bowed his head, he took one full look at her he loved.

"Welcome, cousin," Tzu Hsi said in her pretty voice. "It has been a long time since we met."

"A long time, Venerable," he said and waited, kneeling.

She gazed down on him from her throne, the corners of her mouth deepening in a smile. "I have something to plead advice upon, and so I have summoned you."

"Command me, Venerable," he said.

"My younger sister is old enough to wed," she went on. "Do you remember that child? A naughty wailing little thing, do you remember? Always clinging to me and wanting what I had?"

"Venerable, I forget nothing," he said, his head still bowed.

Tzu Hsi received the secret meaning in these words and hid the treasure in her heart.

"Well, now my sister needs a husband," she went on. "She has outgrown her naughty ways and is a woman, very nearly, a slender pretty thing—fine eyebrows she always had—like mine!"

Here she paused to lift her two forefingers and smooth her eyebrows, shaped like the leaves of a willow tree. "And I promised her a prince, but what prince, cousin? Name me the princes!"

"Venerable," Jung Lu replied carefully, "how can I know princes as well as you do?"

"You do know them," she insisted, "for you know everything. All is gossiped at the palace gates, I daresay."

She paused for him to answer and hearing not a word she changed her mood upon the instant, and turned upon her ladies.

"Go—all of you," she commanded. "You see my cousin will not speak before you! He knows that you will seize his words and scatter them as you go. Retire—retire, you listening ears—leave me with my cousin!"

They fluttered off like frightened butterflies, and when they were gone, she laughed and came down from her throne. He did not move and she stooped and touched his shoulder.

"Rise, cousin! There is no one near to see us, except my eunuch—and what is he? No more than a table or a chair!"

He rose unwillingly and kept his distance. "I fear any eunuch," he muttered.

"Not mine," she said heartlessly. "If he betrayed me by a word I'd pinch his head off as I would a fly's." She pinched her thumb and forefinger together as she spoke.

"Sit down yonder on that marble chair," she commanded, "and I will sit here—the distance is enough, I think? You need not fear me, cousin.

I remember that I must be good. Why not? I have what I want—my son, the Heir!"

"Be silent!" he cried in a low and angry voice.

She lifted her dark lashes at him, innocently.

"And what prince shall I choose for my sister?" she asked again.

Sitting stiffly upon the edge of the chair she had assigned, he considered this question of a prince.

"Of my lord's seven brothers," she mused, "to which one shall I give my little sister?"

"It is not fitting that she be a concubine," Jung Lu said firmly.

She opened her eyes wide at him. "Why not, pray? Was I not a concubine until my son was born?"

"To the Emperor," he reminded her, "and now you are the Empress. The sister of an empress cannot be a concubine even to a prince."

"Then I must choose the Seventh Prince," she said. "It is only he who has no wife. Alas, he is the least handsome of all princes—that heavy mouth drawn down, the eyes dull and small, a proud solemn face! I hope my sister does not love beauty in a face as well as do I!"

She looked sidewise at him from beneath her long straight lashes and he looked away.

"Prince Ch'un's face is not evil," he rejoined. "It is lucky if a prince be at least not evil."

"Oh," she said most mockingly. "You think that important? In a prince? Is it not enough that he be a prince?"

He ignored her mockery. "I think it not enough."

She shrugged her shoulders. "Well, kinsman, if Prince Ch'un be your advice, I'll choose him, and send a letter to my mother."

She was angry of a sudden at his hardness toward her and she rose to signify the audience was ended, then paused. "And you—" she said carelessly, "I suppose you're wed by now?"

He had risen with her and he stood before her, tall and calm. "You know I am not wed."

"Ah, but you must," she insisted. A sudden happiness made her face soft and young, as he remembered it.

"I wish you would wed," she said wistfully and locked her hands together.

"It is not possible." He bowed and without farewell he left her presence and did not once look back.

She stood there alone, surprised at his being so swiftly gone and before she had dismissed him. Then her quick eyes caught the movement of a curtain in a doorway. A spy? She stepped forward and twitched the curtain and saw a shrinking figure. It was Lady Mei, her pretty favorite, the youngest daughter of Su Shun.

"You? Now why?" Thus Tzu Hsi demanded.

The lady hung her head and put her forefinger in her mouth.

"Come, come," Tzu Hsi insisted. "Why do you spy on me?"

"Venerable, not on you." This came forth in the smallest whisper.

"Then on whom?" Tzu Hsi demanded.

The lady would not speak.

"No answer?"

Tzu Hsi stared at the childish drooping figure and then without a further word she took the lady by her ears and shook her vehemently.

"On him, then!" she whispered fiercely. "Ah, he—you think him handsome? You love him, I daresay—"

Between her jeweled fists the small face looked helplessly at her. The lady could not speak.

Again Tzu Hsi shook with all her strength. "You dare to love him!"

The lady broke into loud sobs and Tzu Hsi loosed her ears. So harshly had she seized them that blood dripped where the earrings had cut into the flesh.

"Do you think he loves you?" Tzu Hsi asked scornfully.

"I know he does not, Venerable," the lady sobbed. "He loves only you —we all know—only you—"

At this Tzu Hsi was in two minds what next to do. She ought to punish the lady for such a charge and yet she was so pleased to hear it said, that whether she must smile or slap the girl's cheeks she did not know. She did both. She smiled and seeing the heads of her other ladies peeping here and there in doorways to know why there was such commotion, she slapped the girl's cheeks with a sound but not with hurt.

"There—and there," she said heartily. "Go from me before I kill you out of shame! Do not let me see you for seven full days."

She turned and sauntering with exquisite grace she sat down on her throne again, half smiling, and listening she heard the patter of the lady's little feet, running down the corridors.

From that day on the face and figure of Jung Lu were fixed anew in Tzu Hsi's mind and memory. Though she could not summon him again, she planned and plotted how they could meet, not by contrivance and seldom but freely and often. He was present in her thoughts wherever she went in the day and when she woke in the night he was there. While she sat at a play he was the hero at whom she looked and if she listened to music, she heard his voice. As the summer days passed and she grew accustomed to her pleasure palace she indulged herself much in thoughts

106

of love. Indeed, she was a woman compelled to love, and yet there was no man for her to love. Meanwhile the Emperor received the overflow of this need, and he thought himself beloved, but he was no more than the image upon which she hung her dreams.

Yet this woman was not one to be content with dreams. She longed for flesh and blood to match her own. Out of dreaming then she let herself proceed to purpose. She would raise Jung Lu high enough so that she could keep him near her, always maintaining their cousinship beyond doubt but using it for what she willed. How could she raise him without drawing all eyes toward her? Within the close walls of palaces scandals breed like foul fevers. And she recalled her enemies, Su Shun, the Grand Councilor, who hated her, because she was above him, and with him were still the Princes Cheng and Yi, for they were Su Shun's friends. She had an ally in An Teh-hai, the Chief Eunuch, and him she must keep loyal. She frowned, remembering the gossip that he was no true eunuch and that he pursued the ladies of the court in secret.

This led her on to thinking of Lady Mei again, who, it could not be forgotten, was Su Shun's child. Well, she must not let that lady hate her, too. No, no, she would keep the daughter her friend and within her power, so that the father could not use the daughter as a spy. Well, then, was it not useful to know that the lady loved Jung Lu? Why had she shown such jealous anger? She must undo what she had done. She would send for Lady Mei and bid her take heart, for she, the Empress of the Western Palace, would herself speak for her to the Commander of the Imperial Guard at some opportune time. Such a marriage would serve a double purpose, for it would give excuse to raise Jung Lu to high place. Yes, here, she saw all at once, was her means to raise up her beloved.

She paused, prudent after the instant of decision, and when the forbidden seven days had passed, she sent Li Lien-ying to find the Lady Mei and bring her here. Within an hour he brought his charge, who fell at once upon her knees before her sovereign. Tzu Hsi today was seated on her phoenix throne in the Pavilion of the Favorite, a small secondary palace she claimed also for her own.

When she had let the lady kneel awhile in silence, Tzu Hsi rose and came down from her throne and lifted her up.

"You have grown thin these seven days," she said kindly.

"Venerable," Lady Mei said, her eyes piteous, "when you are angry with me I cannot eat or sleep."

"I am not angry now," Tzu Hsi replied. "Sit down, poor child. Let me see how you are."

She pointed to a chair, and herself sat down on another next it, and she took the lady's soft narrow hand and smoothed it between her own and went on talking.

"Child, it is nothing to me whom you love. Why should you not wed the Commander of the Imperial Guard? A handsome man, and young—"

The lady could not believe what she heard. Her face flushed delicately, tears came to her dark eyes, and she clung to the kind hands.

"Venerable, I do adore you—"

"Hush—I am not a goddess—"

"Venerable," the lady's voice trembled, "to me you are the Goddess of Mercy herself—"

Tzu Hsi smiled serenely, and put down the little hand she held. "Now—now—no flattery, child! But I have a plan."

"A plan?"

"We must have a plan, must we not?"

"Whatever you say, Venerable."

"Well, then—" and here Tzu Hsi put forth her plan. "When the Heir completes his first full year since birth, you know that there is to be a great feast. At that time, child, I will myself invite my kinsman so that all may see my intent to raise him. When this is clear, then step can follow step, and who will dare to stop my kinsman? It is for your sake I raise him, so that his rank may equal your own."

"But Venerable—"

Tzu Hsi raised her hand. "No doubts, child! He will do what I say."

"No doubts, Venerable, but—"

Tzu Hsi examined the pretty face, still pink. "You think it is too long to wait so many months?"

The lady hid her face behind her sleeve.

Tzu Hsi laughed. "Before one journeys to a new place the road must be built!"

She pinched the lady's cheeks and made them still more red and then dismissed her.

"For two hundred years," Prince Kung said, "the trade of these foreign merchants was confined to that one southern city of Canton. Moreover, such trade could only be through the licensed Chinese merchants."

Summer was ended, the autumn half gone, and Tzu Hsi, listening to her lesson, gazed pensively beyond the wide doors open to the sun of midafternoon. Porcelain pots of late chrysanthemums bloomed in red and gold and bronze. She heard and did not hear, the words falling on her ears and floating on her mind like fallen leaves upon the surface of a pool.

Prince Kung spoke sharply to recall her from her dreaming.

"Do you hear, Empress?"

"I hear," she said.

He looked doubtful, and went on. "Recall then, Empress, that the end of the two Opium Wars left our nation defeated. This defeat taught us one bitter lesson—that we could not consider the Western nations as tributaries. Their greedy, ruthless men, though never our equals, can become our masters through the brute force of the evil engines of war they have invented."

These words, spoken in his powerful deep voice startled her, and she woke from her dreaming memories of summer now gone. How hateful was it to return again to these high walls and locked gates!

"Our masters?" she repeated.

"Our masters, unless we keep our wits awake," the Prince said firmly. "We have yielded, alas, to every demand—the vast indemnities, the many new ports opened by force to this hateful foreign trade. And what one foreign nation gains, the others all gain, too. Force—force is their talisman."

His handsome face was stern, his tall figure wrapped in gray satin robes drooped in the carved chair below the phoenix throne which Tzu Hsi made her favorite seat here in the Imperial Library. Near her Li Lien-ying leaned against a massive wooden pillar, enameled red as all the pillars were.

"What is our weakness?" Tzu Hsi demanded. Her indignation roused her. She sat upright, hands gripping the sides of her throne. Jung Lu's face, so clear to her mind a moment before, faded into dimness.

Prince Kung looked sidewise at her, his melancholy eyes seeing as always her powerful beauty informed by the strength of her lively mind. How could he shape her so that these could save the dynasty? She was still too young, and, alas, forever only a woman. Yet she had no equal.

"The Chinese were too civilized for our times," he said. "Their sages taught that force is evil, the soldier to be despised because he destroys. But these sages lived in ancient times, they knew nothing of the rise of these new wild tribes in the West. Our subjects have lived without knowing what other peoples are. They have lived as though this were the only nation on the earth. Even now, when they rebel against the Manchu dynasty, they do not see that it is not we who are their enemies, but the men out of the West."

Tzu Hsi heard these fearful words and instantly her mind caught their meaning.

"Has the Viceroy Yeh let these white men enter the very city of Canton?"

"Not yet, Empress, and we must prevent it. You will remember that I told you how, nine years ago, they fired their cannons at our forts at the mouth of the Pearl River, upon whose banks the city stands, and by this force compelled us to grant them a great tract of land on the south bank for their warehouses and their homes. At that time they demanded also that in two years the gates of Canton were to be opened to them, but when the time came the Viceroy denied the agreement, and the British did not press. Yet this is not peace. If these foreigners seem to yield, be sure it is only while they plan some larger victory."

"We must put them off," Tzu Hsi insisted. "We must ignore them until we are strong."

"You speak too simply, Empress," Prince Kung replied and again sighed the heavy sigh that had become his habit. "It is not a matter of white men alone. The knowledge of foreign weapons, the sight of cruel force instead of skillful reason, is changing even the Chinese people in subtle ways. Force, they say now, is stronger than reason. We have been wrong, the Chinese say, for only weapons can make us free. This, Empress of the Western Palace, this is what we must understand in all depth and distance, for I do assure you that in this one concept hides a change so mighty in our nation that unless we can change with it, we who rule, Manchu and ourselves not Chinese, our dynasty will end before the Heir can sit upon the Dragon Throne."

"Give them weapons, then," Tzu Hsi said.

"Alas," Prince Kung sighed, "if we give the Chinese weapons wherewith to repel the enemy from the West, they will turn first on us, whom they still call foreign although our ancestors came down from the north two hundred years ago. Empress, the throne is trembling on its foundations."

Could she comprehend the peril of the times? His eyes rested most anxiously upon the beautiful woman's face. He could not read the answer that he sought, for he knew that woman's mind is not an instrument apart from her other being. She does not separate herself as man does, now flesh, now mind, now heart. She is three in one, a trinity complete and unified. Thus while Prince Kung could only guess how Tzu Hsi's mind received what he taught, in fact her mind was working through her every sense. It was not the dynasty alone the white men threatened, it was her and hers, the son, the Imperial Heir, imperial not only because he was the next to sit upon the Dragon Throne, but imperial because she had made him, her energy conceived him and created him, and now her instinct rose to save him.

That day, when Prince Kung left her and she had returned to her own palace, she sent for the child. While she played with him, holding him in her arms, laughing with him, singing to him the songs that she had heard her mother sing, counting his small toes and fingers, coaxing him to stand and catching him when he fell, as all mothers do, her mind was busy planning how she could destroy his enemies. The nation —yes, but first her son! And when the play was over she gave him to his nurse again and from that hour she applied herself with fresh will to read the memorials presented to the Throne from each province but especially from that place where the white men quarreled to gain entrance for their trade, the southern city of Canton. There, although both Chinese and white merchants grew rich on trade, neither could be satisfied. She wished she dared to risk a war, but it was too soon. The turmoil of foreign war heaped upon Chinese rebellion might indeed destroy the Dragon Throne and force the Emperor to abdicate before a people's wrath. No, she must play for time until her son was grown and then he in his manhood could lead the war. Year by year—

But when the first snow fell upon the palaces news came by courier from the Viceroy of the Kwang provinces that new ships of war had anchored in the harbor near Canton, and these ships brought not only weapons of greater strength than before, but also envoys of high rank from England. In fright and fury the Viceroy thus memorialized the Throne. He did not dare, he said, to leave his city, else would he come himself before the Son of Heaven and cry his shame that he had not been able to prevent these enemies from crossing the black seas. What therefore were the commands of the Most High? Let them be sent by special courier and he would obey.

The Emperor, distracted, could only call his government to consultation. Day after day at bitter dawn they met in the Audience Hall, the Grand Secretariat, whose four First Chancellors, two Manchu and two Chinese, two assistant chancellors, one Manchu and one Chinese, and four sub-chancellors, two Manchu and two Chinese, met with the Council of State, who were the princes of the blood, and the grand secretaries, presidents and vice-presidents of the six Boards, the Board of Revenue, the Board of Civil Office, the Board of Rites, the Board of War, the Board of Punishments and the Board of Works. These chief ruling bodies heard Prince Kung read the memorial before the Dragon Throne. After much discussion each body separated to decide apart what advice to give to the Son of Heaven and their advice was written down and presented to him, and he received it, the next day to return it with his own comment, written with the imperial-vermilion brush.

Now all knew that it was not the Emperor who used the vermilion brush but the Empress of the Western Palace. All knew, for Li Lien-ying boasted everywhere that each night Tzu Hsi was summoned to the royal bedchamber, and not for love. No, while the Emperor lay in his bed, half sleeping in an opium dream, she pondered long and alone upon the written pages, studying every word and weighing every meaning. And when she had decided what her will was, she lifted the vermilion brush and crossed out the words of those who advised action or war or retaliation against the intruders. "Delay," she still commanded. "Do not yield, but do not resist—not yet. Promise, and break the promises. Is not our land vast and mighty? Shall we destroy the body because a mosquito stings a toe?"

None dared to disobey, for to her handwriting she set the imperial seal, and she alone, except the Emperor, could lift it from its coffer in the imperial bedchamber. All that she commanded was printed in the Court Gazette, as imperial decrees, essays and memorials had been printed daily for eight hundred years. This gazette was sent by messenger to every province and its viceroy, to every city and its magistrate, so that everywhere the people could know the royal will. And this will now was the will of one woman, young and beautiful, who sat alone within the royal chamber while the Son of Heaven slept.

Prince Kung, reading the vermilion words, was sick with fear.

"Empress," he said when next they met in the wintry shadows of the Imperial Library, "I must warn you again and yet again that the temper of these white men is short and savage. They have not lived the centuries that our people have. They are children. When they see what they want they put out their hands to snatch it. Delays and promises not kept will only anger them. We must bargain with them, persuade them, even bribe them, to leave our shores."

Tzu Hsi flashed her splendid eyes at him. "Pray, what can they do? Can their ships sail a thousand miles up our long coast? Let them harass a southern city. Does this mean that they can threaten the Son of Heaven himself?"

"I think it possible," he said gravely.

"Let time tell," she retorted.

"I hope it will not be too late," he sighed.

She pitied his careworn looks, too grave for a man still young and handsome, and she coaxed him with pleasant words. "You make your own load heavy. You revel in your melancholy. You should take pleasure as other men do. I never see you at the theater."

To this Prince Kung made no reply except to take his leave. Ever since her return from the Summer Palace Tzu Hsi had kept the Court actors near her, and supported by the imperial funds, they enjoyed good food and a pavilion of their own to live in outside the walls of the Forbidden City and another for their theater inside the walls. On every feast day Tzu Hsi commanded that they give a play, and to it came the Court, sometimes the Emperor, but certainly the ladies and the royal concubines, the eunuchs, and the lesser princes and their families. By sunset all must be gone, men and their families, but the play lasted two hours or three of every day and in such diversions winter passed to spring, and peace held.

With the first flowering of the tree peonies the Court prepared to enjoy the birthday feast of the Heir. The spring was favorable. The rains fell early and dispelled the dust, the air was mild and so warm that already mirages hung over the landscape like painted scenes from some distant country. The nation, informed by the gazettes, welcomed opportunity for feasting, and the people prepared gifts. A slumberous peace pervaded every province and Prince Kung wondered if the Empress of the Western Palace had a private wisdom of her own. The ships of the white men delayed at the port near Canton, and daily quarreling went on, but no worse than it had been. The Viceroy still ruled the city, nor did he yet receive the envoy from England, Elgin, a lord of high rank. For this lord still would not bow himself to the floor, in acknowledgment of his inferiority, and the Viceroy Yeh, proud and mindful of his place, would not receive an emissary not willing to bow before him, who stood for the Emperor. Neither yielded and each maintained his place for the sake of each his ruler.

In this vague and shallow peace the people seized upon the chance to make a feast and have some pleasure, while the Court made ready for the birthday of the Heir. Everywhere men looked at neighbors and agreed that they would not think beyond the day and therefore let the future wait upon the feasting. For Tzu Hsi this birthday gala had another meaning, too. All through the winter and its troubles she had been patient with time and stern with her own heart. Yet while she had resolutely studied and read her books, she had remembered Jung Lu and her purpose to advance his rank. One day before the birthday, she chanced in passing, or it seemed chance, to see that Lady Mei looked pensive. She put up her hand and stroked the lady's smooth cheek.

"Do not think I have forgotten, child!"

She gazed into the pretty eyes that looked up at her startled and knew that this woman whom she called "child" understood her meaning. It was Tzu Hsi's secret strength that while she put her mind to the large matters of state, pondering long into the night and far beyond what Prince Kung thought she did, yet she could at the same time remember her own hidden wishes. Thus a few nights before the birthday, as she lay in the Emperor's arms, seeming half asleep, she murmured words.

"Almost I forgot—"

"Forgot what, my heart and liver?" he inquired. He was in good humor because this night he had found satisfaction, enough to make him feel himself still a man.

"You know, my lord, that the Commander of the Imperial Guard is my kinsman?" This she said, still seeming half asleep.

"I know—that is, I have so heard."

"Long ago I made my uncle Muyanga a promise concerning him and I have never kept that promise—oh, me!"

"So?"

"If you invite him to our son's birthday feast, my lord, my conscience will not tease me."

The Emperor was languidly surprised. "What—a guardsman? Will it not stir jealousy among the lesser princes and their families?"

"There is always jealousy among the small, my lord. But do as you will, my lord." So she murmured.

Nevertheless in a little while she made slight movements of withdrawal from him. Then she yawned and said that she was tired.

"My tooth aches," she said next, and lied, for all her teeth were white and solid as pure ivory.

After this, she slipped from the bed and put on her satin shoes, and said, "Do not summon me tomorrow night, my lord, for I shall not like to tell the Chief Eunuch that I will not come, if so be you send him for me."

The Emperor was alarmed, knowing her relentless will and that she did not love him, and not loving, how he must plead for her favor and bargain for it. He let her go, troubled though he was, and so passed two nights, and she did not come and he dared not send for her, lest there be laughter in the palace if the eunuchs heard she had refused him again. They knew her tricks, and how often the Emperor had been compelled to send her gifts before she would return to him. The last time had been vexatious indeed, for she would not show obedience until he had sent a eunuch to the south, five provinces away, to find some hornbill ivory, that strange rare substance of the helmeted hornbill's beak, which lives only in the jungles of Malaya and Borneo and Sumatra. Tzu Hsi had heard of this bird and she craved an ornament made of the yellow ivory on its high beak, covered with a skin of scarlet. This ivory came first to the imperial court as tribute from Borneo, centuries ago, and it was so rare that only emperors could wear the ivory in buttons and buckles and thumb rings and its scarlet sheath was used to cover their ceremonial belts. In the dynasty now ruling the princes of the imperial house still loved this ivory so well that no woman was allowed to wear it, wherefore Tzu Hsi longed for it and would have it. When the Emperor explained to her with patience that she could not have it, and how the princes would be angry if he yielded to her, she said she would have it nevertheless, and she withdrew herself for weeks until in despair he yielded, knowing how relentless and unchangeable she was where her will was concerned.

"I wish I did not love so troublesome a woman," he groaned to his Chief Eunuch next day.

An Teh-hai groaned, too, to show respect. "We all wish it, Most High, and yet we all love her—except some few who hate her!"

Now again the Emperor yielded and sent her his promise, and on the third night, the last before the birthday feast, he summoned Tzu Hsi and she went, very proud and beautiful and gay, and being generous and just when she could have her way, she gave him full reward. That same night Jung Lu received the imperial invitation to the birthday feast.

The day of the feast dawned fine and fair, the air blown clean by earlier sandstorms, and Tzu Hsi woke to noise and music. In every courtyard in the city families set off fire crackers when the sun rose, and they beat gongs and drums and blew trumpets. This was true in each city in the realm and in all villages, and for three days no one was to work.

She rose from her bed early, imperious beyond anything she had ever been, yet careful as her habit was to be courteous to each woman in her place, as tenderly careful of her serving woman as of the highest of her court ladies. She was bathed, she allowed herself to be dressed, she ate her morning sweetmeats. The Heir was then presented to her in his royal robes of scarlet satin, wearing on his head the imperial hat of his unique rank. She took him in her arms, her heart near breaking with love and pride. She smelled his perfumed cheeks and the perfumed palms of his little hands, plump and firm with healthy flesh, and to him she whispered, "I am most fortunate of all women born upon this earth today."

He smiled his baby smile at her and tears came to her eyes. No, she would not be afraid, even of jealous gods. She was strong in herself and none could assail her on earth or in heaven. Her destiny was her shield and buckler.

Now, the hour having come, she summoned her ladies and preceding the Heir in her palace sedan she went to the Supreme Throne Hall, the very center of the Forbidden City, and the place the Emperor had chosen for receiving the birthday gifts. This central and most sacred hall in length was two hundred feet, in width one hundred feet, in height one hundred and ten feet, and it was the largest of all the palaces. Flanked by two lesser halls, it rose from a broad marble terrace, known as the Dragon Pavement, and below this terrace were five tiers of marble steps, carved between with dragons. Upon the terrace stood gilded cisterns and incense burners and sun dials and grain measures, symbols of Heaven and Earth, and it was surrounded by marble balustrades whose pillars repeated the sacred numbers of the gods. Today the roof of the hall shone golden in the sun. No weed or wild grass marred its smoothness, for when the tiles were laid in ancient times a certain poison had been mixed with the mortar and this poison killed all windblown seeds of weeds and trees.

Alas, so sacred was this Supreme Throne Hall that no woman had ever entered it, and not even the pride and beauty of Tzu Hsi could admit her on this day. She gazed at the golden roof, the carved doorways and the painted eaves and then withdrew into a lesser hall and one she chose, the Hall of Central Harmony, preferring it to the other, the Hall of Exalted Harmony.

Yet the Emperor was mindful of her. When he had seated himself upon the Dragon Throne, and had there received gifts from the nation, the Heir beside him in the arms of Prince Kung, he commanded that all gifts be taken by eunuchs to the Hall of Central Harmony. Thus Tzu Hsi was shown them and she examined them and made appraisal and although she would not express her pleasure at magnificence, for no gift could be too splendid for her son, yet all who watched her face saw pleasure in her bright eyes and vivid looks, for indeed the tribute was very rich and valuable.

The day was not long enough for the receiving of the gifts, and when the sun set, those gifts still remaining to be seen, all from the lower princes and lesser persons, were put aside. The moon rose and this was the hour for the feasting in the Imperial Banquet Hall, where only mighty feasts were held. Here the Emperor and his two Empresses preceded all and they sat at a table set apart, and at a table near them the Heir sat upon the knees of his uncle, Prince Kung. The Emperor could not keep his eyes from the child, and indeed the little boy was in the gayest mood. His large eyes, so like his mother's, traveled from one huge candle to another as they swayed in tasseled lanterns above the tables, and he pointed at them and clapped his hands and laughed. He wore a robe of yellow satin which reached from his neck to his velvet shoes and upon it were embroidered small dragons in scarlet silk. Upon his head he wore a hat of scarlet satin, plumed with a little peacock feather, and around his neck was padlocked as always the chain of gold which Tzu Hsi had placed there when he was born, to keep him safe from evil spirits who might wish him dead. All admired the Heir but none spoke aloud their praise, nor mentioned his health and good growth, lest cruel demons hovered near.

Only Sakota, the Empress of the Eastern Palace, looked at him sadly, and mild as she was, she could not forebear a peevish word or two. When the Emperor in courtesy urged her to taste some dish she shook her head and said she could not eat, she was not hungry, and of all the dishes this one she liked the least, and when Tzu Hsi deferred to her she pretended not to hear. She sat there at the feast table, thin as a bird, her little clawlike hands heavy with jewels too large, and under her high headdress her face was pale and pinched. Who could blame the Emperor when he turned from this Consort to the other? Never had Tzu Hsi been so beautiful and so endowed with grace. To Sakota's peevishness she replied with most perfect patience, and all who saw her felt the largeness of her spirit.

Among the low tables set for the thousand guests who sat on scarlet cushions eunuchs garbed in bright robes moved in silent swiftness to serve them all. At the far end of the hall were the Court ladies, the wives of princes and ministers and noblemen, and at the other were the noblemen themselves. Nearest to Tzu Hsi, indeed at her right hand, the Lady Mei had her seat, and Tzu Hsi looked down upon her and smiled. Both knew where Jung Lu sat, though at a distant table. Guests wondered doubtless why the Commander of the Guard had been so honored, but when the question was put behind a hand to some eunuch passing by he had the answer ready.

"He is the kinsman of the Empress of the Western Palace and here by her command."

To this no further question could be made.

Meanwhile the hours of feasting passed, the Court musicians played upon their ancient harps, their flutes and drums, and the theater went on for those who cared to see. The stage was raised high enough for the

Emperor and his Consorts but not above them. The Heir fell fast asleep at last, the Chief Eunuch carried him away, the candles burned and guttered, and the feast drew near its end.

"Tea for the nobles," Prince Kung commanded the Chief Eunuch when he had returned.

Then eunuchs served tea to all the nobles but none was served to the Commander of the Guard, who was not noble. Tzu Hsi, seeming not to see, saw all, and she beckoned with her jeweled hand, and Li Lien-ying, always watching, moved quickly to her side.

"Take this bowl of tea from me to my kinsman," Tzu Hsi commanded in her clearest voice. She put the porcelain cover upon her own bowl she had not tasted, and gave it with both hands into the two hands of the eunuch. And Li Lien-ying, proud to be the bearer, carried it in both hands to Jung Lu, who rose to receive it in his two hands. He set it down and turning toward the Empress of the Western Palace he bowed nine times to signify his thanks.

All talk ceased, and eyes turned to eyes. But Tzu Hsi seemed not to notice. Instead, she looked down at Lady Mei and smiled again. This moment also passed. The Chief Eunuch motioned to the musicians and fresh music soared into the air while the last dishes were presented.

The moon was high, the hour was late. All waited for the Emperor to rise and make his way again to the terrace where his sedan waited. But he did not rise. He clapped his hands and the Chief Eunuch cried out for the music to be stilled.

"What now?" Tzu Hsi inquired of Prince Kung.

"Empress, I do not know," he said.

Silence fell once more upon those feasting and eyes turned to the doors through which the eunuchs came and went.

The Son of Heaven leaned toward his beloved. "My heart," he whispered, "look toward the great doors!"

Tzu Hsi looked and she saw six eunuchs bearing a tray of gold so heavy that they had lifted it upon their heads and crouched beneath it. Upon this tray stood the image of a hugh peach, gold on one side, red on the other. A peach? It was the symbol of long life.

"Announce my gift to the Fortunate Mother of the Heir!" the Emperor now commanded his brother.

Prince Kung rose. "The gift of the Son of Heaven to the Fortunate Mother of the Heir!"

All rose and bowed, while the eunuchs brought the tray to Tzu Hsi and stood holding it before her.

"Take the peach with your hands," the Son of Heaven now commanded.

She put her hands upon the giant sweet. It split and fell apart. Inside she saw a pair of shoes made of pink satin and embroidered with fine stitches into flowers of gold and silver thread, and in the threads were caught gems of every hue. The heels, high and set in the Manchu fashion beneath the middle of the soles, were studded with pink pearls from India, so closely that the satin was encrusted.

Tzu Hsi lifted brilliant eyes to the face of the Son of Heaven.

"For me, my lord?"

"For you alone," he said.

It was a daring gift, the symbol of man's lustful love for woman.

Evil news came up from the south, and soon. Evil enough it had been before, but Yeh, the Viceroy, of the Kwang provinces, held back the worst until the holiday was over. Now he could no longer conceal fresh disaster. He sent couriers by relay on horseback to the capital, saying that the Englishman, Lord Elgin, again made threats to attack the city of Canton, this time with six thousand warriors who waited upon his battleships in the harbor at the mouth of the Pearl River. Even were there no Chinese rebels hidden in the city, the Imperial Armies could not have held the gates. Alas, the city was rotten with these rebels who called themselves Christians under the leadership of the madman, Hung, that ignorant and powerful man who declared continually that he was sent by a foreign god named Jesus to overthrow the Manchu throne.

When this desperate news came to the imperial city, Prince Kung received it first and he dared not present it to the Emperor. Since the Heir's birthday feast the Emperor had not risen from his bed. He had eaten too well and drunk too much and then to quiet his pains he had smoked opium until now he could not tell day from night. Prince Kung sent word therefore to Tzu Hsi, asking audience at once. That same day, an hour after noon, Tzu Hsi went to the Imperial Library and took her seat behind a screen, for Prince Kung did not come alone. With him were the Grand Councilor Su Shun and his ally, Prince Ts'ai, and with them Prince Yi, who was a younger brother of the Son of Heaven, a prince yielding and without wit and less wisdom, but given to envy and peevishness. These four, surrounded at a distance by the eunuchs who followed to serve, now heard the news which Prince Kung read from the scroll upon which the Viceroy had written with his own brush.

"Very grave—very grave," Su Shun muttered.

He was a tall broad man, his face powerful and coarse, and Tzu Hsi wondered how he could be the father of so delicate a beauty as her favorite, Lady Mei.

"Very grave," Prince Yi agreed in a high little voice.

"So grave," Prince Kung said, "that we must ponder the question of whether this Elgin, having seized the city of Canton and there entrenched himself, may demand that he be received here at the Imperial Court."

Tzu Hsi struck one hand upon the other. "Never!"

"Venerable," Prince Kung said sadly, "I venture to suggest that we cannot refuse so strong an enemy."

"We must use cunning," she retorted. "We must still promise and delay."

"We cannot prevail," Prince Kung declared.

But the Grand Councilor Su Shun now came forward. "We did prevail two years ago when the Englishman Seymour broke into the city of Canton. You will remember, Prince, that he was driven out again. At that time a bounty of thirty silver pieces was offered for every English head, and when such heads were presented to the Viceroy he ordered that they be carried through the streets of the city. He commanded also that the foreign warehouses be burned down. Upon this the English withdrew."

"They did, indeed," Prince Yi agreed.

Still Prince Kung refused to agree. He stood tall and handsome and strong, too young to speak so boldly as he did before these men. Nevertheless he spoke. "The English withdrew only to send for more armies. Now those armies have come. Moreover, this time the French, desiring to seize our possession, Indo-China, have promised to aid the English against us and once more they have used the excuse of a French priest tortured and killed in Kwangsi. Moreover, again, it is said that this Lord Elgin has received instructions from his ruler, the Queen of England, to demand residence here in our captial for a minister from her court whenever she shall so wish."

Tzu Hsi was unchanged in her will but such was her respect for Prince Kung and her desire to keep his loyalty that she spoke courteously.

"I do not doubt that you are right, and yet I wonder if you are. Surely my sister-queen of the west does not know what this lord demands in her name. Else why is it that all this did not happen to us before when we drove them away?"

Prince Kung explained, still patiently. "The delay, Empress, has been caused only by the Indian mutiny of which I told you some months ago.

You remember that the whole of India is now conquered by England and when rebellion rose there recently and many Englishmen and women were killed, the English armies put it down with frightful force. Now they come here for further conquest. I fear—I fear—it is their intent one day to possess our country as they do India. Who knows how far their greed will reach? An island people is always greedy, for when they multiply they have nowhere to spread. If we fall, the whole of our world will fall with us. This we must prevent at any cost."

"We must, indeed," Tzu Hsi agreed.

She was still unbelieving. Her voice was not grave nor her manner concerned as she went on. "Yet the distances are great, our .walls are strong, and I think disaster cannot happen soon or easily. Moreover, the Son of Heaven is too ill to be disturbed. Soon we must leave the city for the summer. Let action be postponed until the hot season is past and we have returned from the Summer Palace. Send word to the Viceroy to promise the English to memorialize the Throne and present their demands. When we receive the memorial we will send word that the Son of Heaven is ill and we must wait until the cold weather comes before he is well enough to make decisions."

"Wisdom," the Grand Councilor cried.

"Wisdom, indeed," Prince Tsai now said, and Prince Yi nodded his head up and down. Prince Kung kept silent, except for the heavy sighs he drew up from his bosom.

But Tzu Hsi would not heed these sighs and she put an end to the audience. From the Imperial Library she went to the palace where her son lived with his nurses and his eunuchs and she stayed with him for hours, watching him while he slept and holding him upon her knees when he woke, and then when he wished to walk, she let him cling to her hand. In him was the source of her strength and resolution, and when she felt afraid she came here and renewed her courage. He was her tiny god, her jewel in the lotus, and she adored him with all her heart and being. Her heart was soft with love and she caught the child to her and held him close to her and longed that she could keep him as safe as once he had been in her own body.

From these hours with the child Tzu Hsi returned to her own palaces refreshed and she set herself to her continuous task, to study all letters and memorials which came before the Throne and to decide what the Emperor must command in reply.

In these months before the summer she arranged for the marriage of her sister to the Seventh Prince, whose name was Ch'un, his personal name I-huan. She had private audience with this Prince, that she might observe him herself on her sister's behalf, and though he had an ugly face and a head too large for his body, she found him to be honest and simple, a man without ambition for himself and grateful to her for the alliance with her sister. The marriage was made before the departure of the Court for Yüan Ming Yüan, but there was no feasting, in respect for the illness of the Emperor, and Tzu Hsi herself only knew that on the appointed day her sister went with proper ceremony to Prince Ch'un's palace, which was outside the walls of the Forbidden City.

The summer passed sadly even at Yüan Ming Yüan, for while the Emperor was ill no music could be made, no theatricals allowed, no merrymaking enjoyed. The glorious days followed one upon another, but Tzu Hsi, mindful of her dignity, did not so much as command a boating party on the Lotus Lake and she lived much alone. Nor did she dare to recognize still further her kinsman, Jung Lu, for gossip had sprung up after the birthday feast like smoke in a dry forest and it was everywhere known that to him she had once been betrothed. Until her power was beyond assail, she could not do more for Jung Lu, lest what she did be used against her to the Emperor, or if he died, against her son. Young though she was and passionate, she was mistress of herself, and when she wished she could be strong in patience.

The Court returned early in the autumn of that year to the Forbidden City, the harvest feasts were observed quietly, and as the peaceful months passed by Tzu Hsi believed that she had decided wisely not to allow a war to be made against the foreigners. For the Viceroy Yeh sent up better news. He reported that the Englishmen, though angry at delays, were helpless, and that their leader, Lord Elgin, "passed the days at Hong Kong stamping his feet and sighing."

"Proof," Tzu Hsi declared in triumph, "that the Queen of the West is my ally."

Only the Emperor's ill health made Tzu Hsi sad. She did not pretend even in her own heart to love the motionless pallid figure that lay all but speechless upon his yellow satin cushions, but she feared his death because of the turmoil of the succession. The Heir was still so young that were the Dragon Throne to fall to him now, there would be mighty quarrels over who should be Regent. She, and she alone, must be the Regent, but was she able yet to seize the Throne and hold it for her son? Strong men in Manchu clans would come forward to assert their claims. The Heir might even be set aside and a new ruler take his place. Ah, there were plots everywhere. She knew it, for Li Lien-ying brought her news that Su Shun was plotting and persuading Prince Yi to plot with him and Prince Cheng made an evil third. There were lesser plots and weaker plotters. Who could know them all? Her fortune was that her advisor, Prince Kung, was honorable and made no plots, and that the Chief Eunuch, An Teh-hai, with all his command in the palaces and over the other eunuchs, was loyal to her, because she was the beloved of his master, the Emperor. From habit first and then because he had fared well under his master, the Chief Eunuch loved this frail ruler and he stayed always near the vast carved bed upon which he lay, unmoving and seldom speaking. It was the Chief Eunuch who heard when the Emperor whispered and he who leaned over him to hear what was wanted. Sometimes in the night when others slept, the Chief Eunuch went alone to fetch Tzu Hsi, to tell her that the Emperor was afraid and that he craved the touch of her hand and the sight of her face. Then, wrapped in dark robes, she followed the Chief Eunuch along the silent passageways and she entered the dim chamber where the candles always burned. She took her seat beside the great bed, and she held the Emperor's hands, so chill and lifeless, between hers, and she let him gaze at her and made her eyes tender toward him, to comfort him. Thus she sat until he slept and she could steal away again. The Chief Eunuch, watching from a distance, perceived her perfect patience and her steadfast courtesy and careful kindness, and he began from that day to fix upon her the same devotion and loyalty that he had given the Emperor since first he came into the gates, a child of twelve, castrated by his own father that he might serve inside the imperial city. He was a thief sometimes, this eunuch, he took what he liked for himself from the vast stores belonging to his master, and all knew that he had heaped great treasures for himself. He could be cruel, too, and men died by rope and knife when he held his thumb downward to make the sign of death. But in that lonely heart of his, hidden beneath the layers of his increasing flesh and fat, he loved his sovereign, and him only, and when he saw the Emperor daily nearer death, he transferred that strange and steadfast devotion, hour by hour, to the woman, young and beautiful and strong, whom the Emperor loved above all others and would so love until he ceased to breathe.

None were prepared, therefore, for the hideous news which reached the palace gates one day at twilight, in the early winter of that year. It was a day like others, a gray day, chill and threatening snow. The city had been quiet, some business done, but without liveliness. Within the palace there had been little coming to and fro, no audience, for matters of importance had come before Prince Kung on the Emperor's behalf, and decisions were postponed.

Tzu Hsi had spent the day in painting. Lady Miao, her teacher, stayed by her side, no longer instructing or forbidding, but watching while her imperial pupil brushed a picture of the branches of a peach tree in bloom. It was no easy task to please her teacher and Tzu Hsi took pains and worked in silence. First she must ink her brush in such a way that at one stroke she could give the branch its outline and also its shading, and this she did, with care and perfectly.

Lady Miao commended her. "Well done, Venerable."

"I am not finished," Tzu Hsi replied.

With equal care she drew another branch, intertwining with the first. To this Lady Miao remained silent. Tzu Hsi gathered her eyebrows into a frown.

"You do not like what I have done?"

"It is not what I like or do not like, Venerable," the lady said. "The question you must ask yourself is whether the master painters of peach blossoms would so have intertwined two branches in this fashion."

"Why would they not?" Tzu Hsi demanded.

"Instinct, not reason, rules where art is concerned," the lady said. "Simply, they would not."

Tzu Hsi made her eyes big and pressed her red lips together, and prepared contention, but Lady Miao refused to contend.

"If you, Venerable, wish to intertwine the branches thus, then do so," she said mildly. "The time has come when you paint as you wish."

She paused and then said thoughtfully, her delicate head lifted to gaze at her pupil, "You are an amateur, Venerable, and it is not needful that you should be professional, as I must be, for I am an artist, and all my family have been artists. Yet were you free to be an artist, bearing no burdens of nation and state, you, Venerable, would have been among the greatest of all artists. I see power and precision in your brush, and this is genius, which needs only use to be complete. Alas, your life has not time enough for this greatness to be added to all the others you possess."

She could not finish. While Tzu Hsi listened, her great eyes fixed upon her teacher's face, the Chief Eunuch burst into the pavilion where the ladies sat. Both turned to him, amazed and startled, and indeed he was a fearful sight. He had run all the way from somewhere, his eyes were rolling and ready to burst, his breath coming out of him in gasps that tore his breast, his bulk of flesh pale and wet with sweat. Two streams were running down his jellied cheeks, in spite of cold.

"Venerable," he bawled, "Venerable—prepare yourself—"

Tzu Hsi rose instantly to hear the news of death—whose death?

"Venerable," the Chief Eunuch roared, "a messenger from Canton—the city's lost—the foreigners have seized it—the Viceroy is taken! He was climbing down the city wall to escape—"

She sat down again. It was disaster but not death.

"Collect your wits," she said sternly to the trembling eunuch. "I thought from your looks that the enemy was inside the palace gates."

Nevertheless she put down her brushes, and Lady Miao withdrew silently. The Chief Eunuch waited, wiping his sweat away with his sleeves.

"Invite Prince Kung to join me here," Tzu Hsi commanded. "Then do you return and take your place with the Emperor."

"Yes, Venerable," the Chief Eunuch said humbly, and made haste away.

In a few minutes Prince Kung came alone, bringing no councilor or other prince. He knew the worst, for he himself had received from the exhausted courier the memorial written in an unknown hand, but bearing the Viceroy's own seal, and he brought it with him.

"Read it to me," Tzu Hsi said, when she had acknowledged his obeisance.

He read it slowly and she listened, sitting upon her little throne in her own library, her eyes thoughtful upon the pot of yellow orchids on the table. She heard all that the courier had told the Chief Eunuch, and much more. Six thousand Western warriors had landed and they had marched to the gates of Canton and there had attacked. The imperial forces had made a show of noise and bravery and then had fled and the Chinese rebels hiding inside the city had opened the gates and let the foreign enemy come in. The Viceroy, hearing the evil news, had run from his palace to a parquet on the city wall and then his officers had let him down by a rope. But halfway down the Chinese had seen him dangling and they shouted to the enemy, who swarmed up the wall and cut him down and took him prisoner. All high officials were taken prisoners, and the Viceroy was deported to Calcutta in distant India. Then the Western men, arrogant and honoring no one, set up a new government, all Chinese, and thus defied the Manchu dynasty. Still worse, the memorial continued, the Englishmen declared that they had new demands from their own Queen Empress but they would not say what these were. Instead, they insisted that they would appear before the Emperor in Peking and tell him what they would have.

In this quiet place, where an hour ago Tzu Hsi had painted peach blossoms, the dreadful news now fell upon her. She heard it and said not one word. She sat musing, and Prince Kung, looking sidewise at her, pitied the beautiful and lonely woman and waited for her to speak.

"We cannot receive these hateful strangers at our court," she said at last. "And still I do believe they use Victoria's name without her knowledge. Yet I cannot reach her distant throne, nor reveal to our people the mortal illness of the Emperor. The Heir is still too young, the succession is not clear. We must deny the foreigners entrance. At any cost, we must still delay and promise and delay again, making winter our excuse."

He was greatly sorry for her in the midst of his own deep alarm and he spoke gently.

"Empress, I say what I have already said. You do not understand the nature of these men. It is too late. Their patience is at an end."

"Let us see," she said, and that was all she would say. To his pleadings and to his advice she shook her head, her face pale, and the black shadows creeping beneath her tragic eyes. "Let us see," she said, "let us see."

Heaven helps me, Tzu Hsi told herself, and indeed that winter was cold beyond any that man had known. Day after day when she rose and looked from her window the snow lay deeper than the day before. Imperial couriers to the south took three times as long as usual to reach the capital and it was months before her reply could reach Canton again. The aged Viceroy Yeh was now wasting away in a prison in Calcutta, whither the English had transported him, but her heart was hard against him. He had failed the Throne and no excuse was strong enough to forgive him such defeat. Let him die! Pity and mercy she would keep for those who could serve her.

Winter crept slowly by and spring came again, a bitter and uneasy spring. She longed for the first leaves to bud on the date trees and for the bamboo sprouts to crack the earth. Inside the palaces the sacred lilies bloomed, warmed by the burning charcoal smothered in ashes in which their bowls were placed. Dwarf plum trees, coaxed by hot stoves, stood blossoming in porcelain jars. She made a mock spring from such flowers in her halls and in the branches of the potted trees she commanded birds in cages to be hung so that she could hear their songs. When she thought of the peril in which the nation stood it comforted her to open the cages and let the birds fly out and settle on her shoulders and her hands and take food from her lips, and she played tenderly with her dogs. To such creatures her love flowed out because they were so innocent.

Innocent, too, was her little son, and she knew, and this was her deepest joy, that he loved her and her alone, as yet. When she came into the room where he was, though he had not seen her for a day or two if she were busy, he forgot all others and ran into her arms. She could be cruel, and anyone who crossed her will felt instantly her relentless cruelty; and yet this tenderness flowed from her toward all weak and innocent creatures and certainly toward others who loved her. Thus she bore with the evil of the eunuch, Li Lien-ying, because he worshipped her. She winked at his thieving and his mischief and his demand for bribes from those who sought her for the Emperor's favor. In the same mood, she forgave the Emperor his helplessness and decadence and his folly with women. For he would have women with him nightly because with her he was impotent, but not always with little young women. Yet her he loved and those he did not. She could forgive him because she did not love him, and she was tender to him because he loved her.

All this Prince Kung knew, and she knew that he knew, and that never would he put his knowledge into words, for she saw understanding in his eyes and she heard it in the gentleness of his voice. But she was lonely as only the high can be lonely, and since she could never speak her loneliness, he was the more steadfast in his loyalty, not as a man, for he had his own beautiful and beloved wife, a quiet woman, sweet of heart, who fulfilled his every need. She was the daughter of an old and honorable mandarin, Kwei Liang by name, a man of good common sense who was at all times faithful to the Throne and who gave wise counsel always to the Emperor Hsien Feng, now ruling, as he had also to T'ao Kuang, the Emperor's father, now dead.

The spring crept slowly on. It deepened into summer and still Tzu Hsi could not decide if it were safe to go to the Summer Palace. She longed for its peace. All winter she had not looked beyond the walls of the Forbidden City and she was sick for the sight of the lakes and mountains of Yüan Ming Yüan. Never had she longed for beauty as she did now, when all was uncertainty about her, and she yearned for the natural beauty of sky and water and earth. When she slept at night she did not dream of lovers but of gardens not enclosed and of the peacefulness of moonlight on the bare and distant hills. She spent hours poring over landscape scrolls and painted scenes, imagining she walked beside rivers or the sea and that at night she slept in pine forests or in a temple hidden in a bamboo grove. When she woke she wept, for these dreams were as real as memories, clear and never to be forgotten, but which she could never see.

But one day, suddenly as a storm comes down, the rumors of the evil for which she felt herself always waiting came rushing northward and instantly she put aside all hope of Yüan Ming Yüan. The Western men were moving up the coast in ships of war. Imperial couriers in relay ran day and night to tell the news before the ships could reach the Taku forts at Tientsin, which city was a scant eighty miles from the capital itself. Now consternation fell on everyone, on commoners as well as on courtiers. The Emperor bestirred himself and he commanded his Grand Councilors and ministers and princes to gather in the Audience Hall and he sent a summons to the two Consorts to seat themselves behind the Dragon Screen. There Tzu Hsi went, leaning on her eunuch's arm, and she sat herself upon the higher of the two small thrones there. In a while Tzu An, the Empress of the Eastern Palace, came, too, and Tzu Hsi, always courteous, rose and waited while she sat on the other throne. That Empress was aging beyond her years, for she was not yet thirty-two. Her face had grown long and thin and melancholy, and she made a faint sad smile when Tzu Hsi pressed her hand.

Yet who could think of one when all were threatened? In silence the noble assembly listened to Prince Kung as he stood to announce the evil news. The Emperor, in his golden robes and seated on the Dragon Throne, bowed his head low, his face half hidden by a silken fan he held in his right hand.

When proper greetings had been made Prince Kung proceeded to the hard truth he must tell. "In spite of all the Throne has done to prevent them, the aliens have not remained in the south. They are even now on their way up our coast, their ships armed and carrying warriors. We must hope they will halt at the forts of Taku, and not enter into the city proper at Tientsin, from whence it would be but a short march to this sacred place."

A groan burst from the kneeling assembly and they bowed their heads to the floor.

Prince Kung faltered and went on. "It is too soon for me to speak. Yet I fear, I fear, that these barbarians will obey neither our laws nor our etiquette! The least delay, and they will come even to the gates of the imperial palaces, unless they are bribed and persuaded to return south again. Let us face the worst, let us cease dreaming. The last hour is come. Ahead is only sorrow."

When the full text of the memorial which Prince Kung had written was read and presented, the Emperor ended the audience, commanding the assembly to withdraw and consider its judgment and advice. So saying he rose, and supported by two princes, his brothers, he was about to come down from the Throne when suddenly Tzu Hsi's clear voice rose from behind the Dragon Screen.

"I who should not speak must nevertheless break my proper silence!"

The Emperor stood uncertain, turning his head left and right. Before him the assembly knelt with heads bowed to the floor and they remained motionless. None spoke.

In the silence Tzu Hsi's voice rose again. "It is I who have counseled patience with these Western barbarians. It is I who have cried delay and wait, and now it is I who say I have been wrong. I change, I declare against patience and waiting and delay. I cry war against the Western enemy—war and death to them all, men, women and children!"

Had her voice been that of a man, they would have shouted yea or nay. But it was the voice of a woman, though she was an empress. None spoke, none moved. The Emperor waited, his head drooping, and then, still supported by his brothers, he came down from the Throne, while all heads were bowed to the floor, and he entered his yellow palanquin and, surrounded by Bannermen and guards, he returned to his palace.

After him in proper time the two Consorts also withdrew, saying not a word to each other, except what was necessary for courtesy, but Tzu Hsi could see that Tzu An shunned her and looked away. And Tzu Hsi returned to her own apartments while the day passed to wait for the imperial summons, but none came. In silence she pored over her books, her mind distracted. When evening came near and she was not called, she inquired of Li Lien-ying, her eunuch, and he told her that the Emperor had dallied all day with one and another of his lesser concubines and had not mentioned her name. This he had heard from the Chief Eunuch, who had been compelled to stay by his master's side, and bear with his whims.

"Venerable," Li Lien-ying said, "be sure the Son of Heaven has not forgotten you, but he is afraid now of what may happen. He waits for the judgment of his ministers."

"Then I am defeated!" Tzu Hsi exclaimed.

This was speech too plain against the Emperor and Li Lien-ying pretended he had not heard. He felt the teapot and muttered that it was cold and he bustled away with the pot in his hands, his ugly face blank and unsmiling.

The next day Tzu Hsi heard the news she had foreseen. There was to be no resistance, even now, against the invaders from the West. Instead, by advice of his councilors and ministers, the Emperor appointed three honorable men to go to Tientsin to negotiate with the Englishman, Lord Elgin. Among these three the chief was Kwei Liang, the father of Prince Kung's wife, a man known for his good sense and his caution.

"Aie, alas!" Tzu Hsi cried when she heard his name. "This excellent man will never oppose the enemy. He is too old, too careful and too yielding."

She was right indeed. On the fourth day of that seventh month, Kwei Liang signed a treaty with the Western warriors, which was to be sealed in a year from that day by the Emperor himself. The three noblemen then returned with their treaty. At point of sword, the Englishmen and the Frenchmen, supported by their friends, the Americans and the Russians, had gained their demands. Their governments were to be allowed ministers resident in Peking, their priests and traders could travel throughout the realm without submitting to its laws, opium was to be called the stuff of legal trade, and the great river port of Hankow in the heart of the Empire, a thousand miles from the sea, was named a treaty port where white men could live and bring their families.

When Tzu Hsi heard such terms she retired to her bedchamber, and for three days she did not wash herself nor take off her garments nor eat food. Nor would she admit any of her ladies. Her woman grew frightened and her eunuch went to Prince Kung secretly to report that the Empress of the Western Palace lay on her bed like one dead, exhausted with weeping and weariness.

Prince Kung received the report in his own palace outside the Forbidden City and he begged audience with her. Tzu Hsi roused herself then and was bathed and dressed and she drank a broth that her woman brought to her, and leaning on her eunuch's arm she received the Prince in the Imperial Library. There, sitting upon her throne, she listened to his reasonable words.

"Empress, do you think that so honorable a man as my father-in-law would have yielded to the enemy if he could have resisted? No choice was given us. Had we opposed their demands they would have marched forthwith upon this imperial city."

Tzu Hsi thrust out her red underlip. "A threat!"

"No threat," Prince Kung repeated firmly. "One thing I have learned about the Englishmen. What they say, they do."

Whether this good Prince were right or wrong, Tzu Hsi knew him loyal and true and wise beyond his years and she could not argue, now that the treaty was made. Indeed, she was too sad. Were her hopes already lost because her son was too young to fight for himself? She made a gesture of impatient dismissal and when the Prince was gone she returned to her own chamber. There alone in days and nights to come, she planned her secret ways. She would conceal her heart and her mind, she would make friends of all, she would subdue herself wholly to the

Emperor, sparing him the smallest reproach, and she would wait. And with this she made her will as hard as iron, as cold as stone.

Meanwhile, content with their victorious treaty, the Western men did not move northward. The year passed as other years had passed, and the new summer of the next year brought the day for the treaty to be sealed. Now Tzu Hsi had determined to win her way against the sealing, and she won, not by talk and threat, but by seduction of that weak man, the Emperor. When he found during this year that she was always gentle, always willing, he became her captive again, his mind with his body. Upon her advice, which she made subtle nowadays, he sent ministers to the white men ruling the city of Canton through the Chinese governors they had appointed, and these ministers were to coax and bribe the white men not to come north again because the treaty was not sealed.

"Let them be content with their southern trade," the Emperor commanded. "Tell them we are friendly if they remain where they are. Did they not come here for trade?"

"What if they refuse?" Prince Kung asked.

Remembering what Tzu Hsi had said in the long night when they were alone together, the Emperor replied, "Tell them, if you must, that we will meet them later at Shanghai to seal the treaty. This is to go halfway toward them. Can they complain that we are not generous?"

For Tzu Hsi had said, feigning indifference to matters of state, "Why sign the treaty? Let them hope, and if they are impatient, say it will be signed at Shanghai, halfway up the coast. If they come there, then it will be time to decide what to do."

This she said, while secretly she held war as the final weapon. If the invaders came to Shanghai, would it not be proof that only death could end their advance?

The noblemen departed early in the year with these commands and that same spring, as soon as the earth was free of frost, the Emperor commanded that the Taku forts near Tientsin were to be strengthened and to be manned with guns and cannon bought from Americans. This was to be done secretly, so that the English knew nothing of it. Such plans were seeded into his mind in idle hours while Tzu Hsi amused him and made dutiful love to him, and roused him by reading tales and verses from the forbidden books she had found in the eunuchs' libraries.

What dismay, then, when in early summer couriers brought news from the Emperor's ministers that the Western men would make no compromise, that once again their ships were sailing northward up the coast far past Shanghai, this time under the Englishman Admiral Hope! But the Court and the commoners of the city declared themselves not afraid. The Taku forts were strong and the imperial soldiers had been promised good reward for bravery. In calm and courage they waited for the attack.

This time, by the help of Heaven, they did indeed repulse the enemy and with such force that three ships of war and more than three hundred of the enemy were destroyed. The Emperor was overjoyed and he praised Tzu Hsi and hearing his praise she encouraged him to refuse everything to the invaders. The treaty was not sealed.

The white men retreated, and peace was proclaimed. The whole nation exclaimed their surprise at the wisdom of the Son of Heaven, who, they declared, had known when to delay and when to make war. Observe, they cried, how easily the invaders were overcome! Yet could they have been so overcome had not the stratagem of delay and compromise persuaded them to false estimates of weakness in the capitol and their own strength? A master of cleverness and wisdom, they declared their Emperor.

Yet all knew who was the Emperor's advisor. The Empress of the Western Palace was called powerful and magic, her beauty was extolled in private, for it would not have been seemly to speak of it in public, and in the palaces every eunuch and courtier deferred to her smallest wish.

Only Prince Kung was still fearful and he said, "The Western men are tigers who retire when they are wounded and return again to attack."

He was wrong, it seemed, for a year passed, another strange quiet year. Tzu Hsi deepened her knowledge of books, and the Heir grew strong and willful. He learned to ride his horse, a black Arabian, he loved to sing and laugh and was always in high humor, for everywhere he looked he saw only friendly faces. Serene in her present power, Tzu Hsi felt no fear while she watched her son increase in beauty. The spring grew late, the summer came again, and she made her plans to go to the Summer Palace with her ladies and her son. This year had passed in peace and she could take delight in holiday.

Alas, who could know what was to come? The Court had only just made its summer journey to Yüan Ming Yüan when those warriors of England, without warning and aided and supported by other warriors from France, came roaring in full force up the coast, furious for revenge. In the seventh month of that year, two hundred vessels of war, as if they dropped from the sky, and carrying twenty thousand armed men, landed at the port of Chefoo, in the province of Chihli, and pausing neither for treaty-making nor for bargaining, they prepared instantly to invade the capital.

Couriers ran day and night to bring the black tidings. In the Forbidden City there was no time for reproach or for delay. Kwei Liang, that wise old man, accompanied by other noblemen, was sent to persuade the invaders to stand.

"Make promises," the frightened Emperor commanded when they came to make farewell obeisance. "Concede and yield! We are outdone!"

Tzu Hsi stood at the Emperor's side, the place his private audience chamber.

"No, no, my lord," she cried. "That's shameful! Do you forget your victory? More soldiers, my lord, more strength—now is the time for battle, my lord!"

He would not hear her. He put out his right arm, suddenly grown strong, and pushed her back. "You hear what I save said," he told Kwei Liang.

"I hear and obey, Most High," the old man replied.

With this command he and his escorts entered their mule carts and made haste to Tientsin, for, alas, the invaders had again seized the forts of Taku. But when Kwei Liang was gone, Tzu Hsi, stern with anxiety for her son, in secret used her clinging arms, her coaxing lips and tender eyes, and by such means she made the Emperor uncertain again.

"What if the white men will not be persuaded?" she argued in the night, in the Emperor's bedchamber. "It is wisdom to be ready to save the lives of our own." And then she persuaded the Emperor to order Seng-ko-lin-chin, his Mongol general, to lead the Imperial Armies in ambush against the white men. This general belonged to the house of Korchiu princes of Inner Mongolia, favored by the Manchu emperors for their loyalty, and he was called Prince Seng. A brave man, he had by his courage and skill prevented the southern rebels from invading the northern provinces and twice he had slaughtered them in battle, the first time when they were only twenty-four miles from Tientsin, and again he captured them in their retreat in Lien-chin, and he had pursued those remnants who fled into the province of Shantung.

To this invincible man Tzu Hsi now turned. The Emperor yielded, not daring to tell even his brother that he did so, and Prince Seng, receiving the private orders, led his men forthwith into ambush near the Taku forts, determined that he would drive the white men into the sea as he had driven away the rebels. Meanwhile, the English and French emissaries, knowing nothing of the ambush, came forward, they thought, to meet the Imperial Commission under Kwei Liang, their leader bearing a white flag of truce. But this flag Prince Seng took to be the sign of surrender. He summoned his men, who ran forward shouting and raging, and they fell upon the Western contingent and took the two leaders captive, and then seized all who were with them. The flag was torn and stamped into the dust, the captives were imprisoned and put to torture for their boldness in daring to invade the country.

In great joy this good news was carried back to the capital. Once again the Western men were routed. The Emperor praised Tzu Hsi heartily and gave her a gold coffer filled with jewels. Then he announced seven days of feasting in the nation and in the palaces special theatricals were arranged for the enjoyment and relief of the Court, while high honor and rich reward were announced for Prince Seng when he should return to the capital.

The joy was planned too soon, and the feasting and the plays were never finished. When the Western men heard of the treachery done their comrades, they gathered in a solid square for battle and then attacked the Mongol general and his men so strongly that these men were bewildered by such fury and fled, dying as they fell, for they had no foreign guns. The invaders then marched in triumph toward the capital and none stopped them until they came to a certain marble bridge, called Palikao, which crossed the river Peiho, near the small city of Tungchow, but ten miles away from Peking itself. At this bridge they were met by imperial soldiers, sent in haste and distraction by the Emperor, who by now had heard by courier from Prince Seng of the disaster. A battle took place, a sad battle in which the imperial soldiers were altogether routed. They ran back to the capital, crying their own destruction, and were joined by villagers and weeping people who crowded their way into the walls of the capital, hoping that the gates would be quickly barred and they be saved from the fierceness of the foreign enemy. The whole city was soon in turmoil, the people running everywhere and yet not knowing where to run to save themselves. Women and children wailed aloud, men shouted and cursed one another and called upon Heaven to rescue them. Merchants put up the boards of their shop fronts lest invaders loot their goods, and all citizens who had young and beautiful wives and concubines and daughters hastened to leave the city and escape with them into villages and countryside.

In the Summer Palace all was in like confusion. The princes gathered in haste to decide how to save the Throne and the Heir and how to protect the Empresses and the imperial concubines, and they could not decide what to do for none agreed with another, while the Emperor trembled and wept and declared that he would swallow opium.

Prince Kung alone remained himself. He went to the Emperor's private chambers and found Tzu Hsi there with the Heir, surrounded by eunuchs and courtiers, all protesting the decision of the Emperor to kill himself.

"Ah, you have come," Tzu Hsi cried when she saw the Prince. What comfort indeed to see this man, his face composed, his garments ordered, his manner calm!

Prince Kung made obeisance and spoke to the Emperor, not as to an elder brother but as to the ruler of the people.

"I dare to give advice to the Son of Heaven," he said.

"Speak—speak," the Emperor groaned.

Prince Kung continued. "With such permission I beg to be allowed to write a letter to the leader of the approaching enemy and ask a truce. To this letter I will set the imperial seal."

Tzu Hsi heard and could not speak. What this Prince had foretold had come to pass. The tiger had returned for revenge. She continued in silence, holding her child in her arms, cheek pressed against his head.

"And you, Sire," Prince Kung went on, "must escape to Jehol and with you must go the Heir and the two Empresses and the Court."

"Yes—yes," the Emperor agreed too eagerly and the ladies and the eunuchs murmured their applause.

At this Tzu Hsi rose from the chair where she sat, and still holding her son in her arms, she cried out against Prince Kung.

"Never should the Emperor leave his capital! What will the people think if he deserts them now? They will yield themselves to the enemy, and be utterly destroyed. Let the Heir be taken away and hidden, but the Son of Heaven must remain, and I will stay at his side to serve him."

All eyes turned to gaze at her when she spoke. Not one could deny the fire and majesty of her beauty. Prince Kung himself could only pity her.

"Empress," he said in his gentlest voice, "I must protect you from your own courage. Let the people be told only that the Emperor is going north on a hunting trip to his palaces in Jehol. Let the departure be a few days hence, without haste and in the usual manner. Meanwhile, I will hold the invaders with my plea for a truce and promises to punish the Mongol general."

She was defeated and she knew it. All were against her, from the Emperor himself to the lowliest eunuch. What could she say? In silence she gave her child to his nurse, and making deep obeisance she withdrew from the imperial hall, her ladies following.

Within five days the Court departed, taking the northwest road toward Mongolia. The city gates were locked against the enemy and bearing their heavy burdens, the long procession of sedans and mule carts set forth on their journey of a hundred miles, a thousand souls in all. Ahead of the imperial array marched Bannermen, carrying their banners of many hues, and behind them came the Imperial Guard on horseback, led by their commander, Jung Lu. The Emperor rode in his curtained palanquin, the color of which was yellow and its frame of gold. Behind him followed the Empress of the Eastern Palace in her own mule cart, and behind her was the Heir with his nurses in his cart. Behind the Heir Tzu Hsi rode alone, for she would allow no one to be with her now. She longed for freedom to weep for hours if she wished, so that she could empty her heart. Ah, what loss was hers! Her spirit was brave but even courage was not enough for this hour. What now would happen? When could she return? Was all lost indeed?

Who could answer? Not even Prince Kung, upon whom the nation depended. He had remained but not in the city inside the locked gates, for he must meet the enemy outside the gates if the worst befell, so that the city itself would be spared. He waited therefore at his own summer palace near Yüan Ming Yüan.

"Gain what you can," the Emperor had whispered when he crept into his cushioned palanquin. He was ill and weary, and the Chief Eunuch had lifted him this morning in his arms as though he were a child to put him in the cart.

"Trust me, Sire," Prince Kung had replied.

But Tzu Hsi could not weep forever, even now. Her tears dried at last, she felt listless, and forced to accept her present fate. The hours crept by too slowly, for the road was paved with rough stones and the springless cart tossed her from side to side and the satin cushions could not save her from bruises. Soon the procession halted for the midday meal which couriers had been sent ahead to prepare.

Now Tzu Hsi was still so young that after weeping, when she came down from her mule cart and looked about her, when she saw the fresh green fields, the tall corn, the fruiting trees, she could not keep down her heart. She was alive, her son was clamoring for her, and she reached out her arms for him. All was not lost so long as she lived and he was in her arms. And never had she seen the Northern Palaces of Jehol. Her mind, always lively and ready for fresh adventure, revived at the prompting of her heart.

At this moment her glance chanced to fall upon Lady Mei, standing near. They smiled, and the lady ventured to make some cheerful talk.

"Venerable, I hear the Northern Palaces are the most beautiful of all the imperial places."

"I, too, have heard it," Tzu Hsi replied. "Let us enjoy them since we must go there."

Yet later, when she was about to enter her mule cart to take up the journey again, she looked backward to the city, her eyes involuntary and following the direction of her heart. There upon the edge of sky and land she saw a mass of darkening smoke. She cried out, alarmed, to those around her:

"Can it be our city is afire?"

All looked and all saw the black, curling clouds mounting against the deep blue sky of midsummer. The city was on fire.

"Haste—haste!" the Emperor cried from his palanquin and all made haste to climb into carts and the procession went on with fresh speed.

That night the Court rested at a bivouac prepared for them but in her tent Tzu Hsi could not rest. Time and time again she sent Li Lien-ying to see if there was word concerning the beloved city. At last, near midnight, a courier came running and Li Lien-ying, watching, caught him by the collar and hauled him before his imperial mistress. Tzu Hsi was still waiting, for she had forbidden her women to prepare her for the night, although they lay sleeping about her on the carpet spread over the bare ground beneath the tent. When she saw the eunuch and the pallid courier, she put her finger to her lips.

"Venerable," the eunuch hissed, "I brought the fellow here because I knew the Son of Heaven was sleeping. The Chief Eunuch told me that he had prepared twice the usual opium."

She fixed her great eyes on the frightened courier. "What news do you bring?"

"Venerable," the man gasped, while the eunuch pushed him to his knees, "the enemy came in full force soon after dawn. The truce holds as of tonight. But this whole day the barbarians have spent in doing evil which they say they do to punish Prince Seng because he tortured those prisoners he took, and because he tore down that white cloth banner."

Tzu Hsi's blood chilled and her heart slowed with dread.

"Loose this man," she said to the eunuch.

When Li Lien-ying loosed him the man slid to the carpet like an empty bag and lay there with his face hidden. She gazed down at him.

"Did the city gates not hold?" Her mouth was dry, so dry her tongue could scarcely make the words.

The man knocked his head on the earth at her feet.

"Venerable, they did not try the gates."

She asked, "What was that smoke I saw against the sky today as high as thunder clouds?"

"Venerable," he said, "Yüan Ming Yüan is no more."

"The Summer Palace?" she shrieked. She put her hands before her staring eyes. "I thought the city burned!"

"No, Majesty," the man whimpered, "the Summer Palace. The barbarians looted all its treasures. Then they burned the palaces. Prince Kung hastened to prevent them and failed and barely kept his own life, escaping by the small gate in the eunuchs' court."

She heard a fearful din inside her skull. Her mind whirled, she saw flames and smoke and porcelain towers and golden roof tops crashing down. She stared at the crouching man.

"Is nothing left?" she whispered.

The man did not lift his head. "Ashes," he muttered, "only ashes."

"Close the windows," Tzu Hsi commanded.

The hot dry wind blew steadily from the northwest over Jehol, a wind she could not bear. The flowers in the courtyard were dead and the leaves of the date trees were torn to shreds. Even the needles of the gnarled pines were yellowing at their base. And the Emperor had not once sent for her since they reached this fortress palace.

Her woman closed the windows.

"Fan me," Tzu Hsi commanded.

From behind a pillar Li Lien-ying stepped forward and standing by her he waved a large silken fan to and fro. She leaned back in the great carved chair and closed her eyes. She was an exile, a stranger, her roots pulled up. Why had the Emperor not sent for her? Who had taken her place? On the Emperor's last birthday, the fifth day of the six moon, now a month ago, he had received good wishes and gifts from the whole Court. Only she had not been summoned. She had waited in these rooms, robed in satin and wearing her finest jewels, but he had not summoned her. Through the hours she had waited until the day was done, and then in fear and anger she had torn off her robes and had lain sleepless on her bed all night.

Since then he had been ill, always weaker, so she heard, but still she was not summoned. And his illness deepened, in spite of good omens proclaimed before the imperial birthday by the Board of Astrologers, a fair conjunction of the stars, a comet crossing the northwestern skies. Now he lay dying, so she heard, and still she was not summoned.

"Stop fanning me," she commanded.

Li Lien-ying's arm dropped. He stood motionless.

She sat erect, and opening her great eyes she fixed them upon nothing. Indeed, she must know what went on in the Emperor's bedchamber. Yet she could not go there without summons. Were Prince Kung here, she could ask his advice, but he was far away and still in the capital. That city was now in the hands of the barbarians while he begged and bargained for a truce. But this was eunuchs' rumor, for she did not know what messages he sent to the Emperor, since she was not summoned. She lived here in her own wing of this palace. Two days ago, when in restless loneliness she had sent word even to Sakota that she wished to visit her, the Consort had made excuse that she had a headache.

"Come here before me," Tzu Hsi commanded now.

Li Lien-ying stepped before her and bowed his head.

"Fetch me the Chief Eunuch," she commanded.

"Venerable, he is not allowed to leave the bedchamber," he replied.

"Who forbids him?" she demanded.

"Venerable, the Three—"

The Three, Prince Yi, Prince Cheng, and the Grand Councilor, Su Shun, her enemies now in power because she was alone and barbarians ruled in the capital!

"Fan me," she said.

She leaned back her head and closed her eyes and the eunuch began again to fan her slowly. Her thoughts ran hither and thither, and she could not control them. She was more than alone, she was homeless. Yüan Ming Yüan was gone, the home of her heart was heaped ruins. The foreigners, barbarians that they were, had looted its treasure, they had set fire to the carved and paneled walls and screens. Monstrous stories had spread throughout the palace from the lips of the courier sent to tell it and in secret she had sent for the courier again to hear all for herself.

The imperial family had scarcely left the Summer Palace, he said, before the foreign warriors arrived. The Englishman Lord Elgin, moved by the beauty of the Summer Palace, had indeed forbidden its destruction but he could not control his barbarous hordes. When Prince Kung protested from a nearby temple where he had taken shelter, Lord Elgin replied that his men were maddened by the torture and murder of their comrades at the hands of Prince Seng. She heard this and was silent. It was she who had sent the Mongol warrior to attack the white men. Alas, alas!

"My head is bowed in the dust," the courier had said. "Nevertheless

I must report that all which could be carried away was looted. The golden plates were stripped from the ceilings and the golden images from the altars. The gems inset in the imperial thrones were torn out and jeweled screens were carted away. Fine porcelains were broken and ground into the earth, except where some more clever robber perceived their value. Jade pieces were stolen or smashed. Yet with all this robbery, less than one tenth of our treasures were saved even to be enjoyed by our enemies. The rest of our precious and delicate possessions, the bequeathed inheritance of our Imperial Ancestors, was crushed into pieces by the butts of the barbarian guns or tossed into the air by howling white men in wild games. Last of all, the whole palace was set afire. For two days and nights the sky was lit by flames, the clouds dark with smoke. Yet, not satisfied, the barbarians pushed into the uttermost folds of the hills and destroyed every pagoda and every shrine and pavilion, and be sure that close behind the barbarians came the local thieves and robbers."

Tears crept from under Tzu Hsi's closed eyelids as she now remembered what the courier had said, and her woman, watching, wiped them away with a kerchief.

"Do not weep, Venerable," she said tenderly.

"I weep for what that which is no more," Tzu Hsi said.

"Venerable, this palace, too, is beautiful," Li Lien-ying said to comfort her.

She did not answer. To her Jehol was not beautiful. Centuries ago the Ancestor Emperor Ch'ien Lung had built this fortress palace a hundred miles north of Peking, and he loved well the wild and sand-hued landscape in which it stood, the miles of sand and rock and in the distance the mountains of bare sand and rock stretched against a sky as endless blue. In contrast to this barren land Ch'ien Lung had made the palace the more gorgeous. The walls were hung with brocaded silks and embroideries of many colors, the ceilings paneled with scarlet and gold and across them gold dragons spread their jeweled length. The table and chairs and vast beds, brought from the south, were carved and inlaid with gems.

Ah, but she longed for gardens and lakes, for fountains and brooks! Here water was more precious than jade. It was carried upon the backs of bearers from little wells, dug into the desert, and when these failed, from a distant oasis. Within her heart a fever of anger burned night and day because Yüan Ming Yüan now lay in ashes, because in the capital Prince Kung stood a suppliant before the barbarians, because here in this remote and dreadful palace, prevented by her enemies, she could not approach the Emperor. She was frantic with anger and anxiety and the discipline she enforced upon herself to hide what she felt, drained the strength from her very bones.

And how could she prevail against her enemies when here she had no friends? The Three had declared themselves against her on that fearful day when the Court had fled the Summer Palace. For she had not ceased to resist flight even while the Court had fled. But they, her enemies, had persuaded the weak and foolish man who was Emperor that he was in danger of his life. She remembered how easily he had yielded and so swiftly that he had left his pipe, his hat, his papers, on the table of his bedchamber. It smote her now to think that when the barbarians had pushed into that imperial place they must have seen these things and laughed loudly to know how frightened was the Son of Heaven. Why should this be an arrow into her heart when all else was gone?

She rose abruptly from her chair, pushing aside with her hand the fan that Li Lien-ying again wielded with slow patience, and she began most restlessly to pace the floor, up and down, up and down, while outside the closed windows the hot winds howled.

Well she knew what the plot was. Su Shun and his allies and their subordinates had taken flight with the Emperor but they had seen to it that the ministers and councilors who might have helped her against them were left behind. She had perceived the conspiracy too late and she was helpless.

No, she had one ally, only one, for even Su Shun could not prevent the Imperial Guard from its duty to protect the Emperor.

She turned imperiously to Li Lien-ying.

"Summon my kinsman, the Commander of the Imperial Guard! I would ask his counsel."

Now Li Lien-ying had never before failed to obey immediately whatever command she put upon him. What was her surprise to see him hesitate, the fan hanging in his hand!

"Come, come," she insisted.

He fell upon his knees before her. "Venerable," he begged, "do not compel me to obey this one command."

"Why not?" she asked, severely. Surely it could not be that Jung Lu himself was against her.

"Venerable, I dare not say," Li Lien-ying stammered. "You will have my tongue cut out if I speak."

"I will not," she promised.

He continued afraid, nevertheless, and she could not pull the words out of him until at last she flew into a great rage and threatened to have him beheaded if he did not speak without delay. Thus beset, he whispered that the Emperor would not summon her because her enemies had told him that—that—she and Jung Lu—

"Do they say we are lovers?" she demanded.

He nodded his head and hid his face in his hands.

"Liars," she muttered, "Liars—liars—"

She had to vent her anger somehow and she struck the kneeling eunuch with her foot and he fell over and lay there motionless while she went raging up and down the great hall, coming and going as though she climbed mountains.

Suddenly she stopped before the silent eunuch.

"Get up," she commanded. "I daresay you have not told me all. What else do you know that I am not told?"

He crawled to his feet, and wiped his sweating face with his sleeve. "Venerable—I have not slept a night since I heard what those three plot."

She made her eyes wide and terrible. "What do they plot?"

"Venerable," he faltered. "I cannot speak the traitorous words. They plot—they plot—to seize the Regency themselves—and then—and then—"

"Kill my son!" she shrieked.

"Venerable, I promise you—I did not hear so far as that. I beg you, calm yourself—"

"When did you hear it?"

She sat down in her great chair again and smoothed her hot cheeks with her palms.

"I heard a first rumor many months ago, Venerable—a small rumor, a whisper—"

She cried out. "And you were silent!"

"Venerable," he said, pleading, "if I told you every rumor I hear you would cast me in prison to silence me. Those who sit in high places must always be surrounded by the swarming insults of gossip. And you, Venerable, were higher than all the rest. Who could have thought that the Son of Heaven would have heeded these lower ones?"

"You should have used that stupid brain of yours," she cried. "You should have remembered that in the years before I came it was Su Shun who was the well beloved of the Emperor. They were young men together, and because the Emperor was weak and gentle he loved that wild strong youth, who hunted and drank and gambled and lived like a savage. Recall how this same Su Shun rose from a small position in the Board of Revenue to be Assistant Grand Secretary and how he brought about the death of Po Ch'un, that good and honorable man, so that he himself could have the power!"

It had been so, indeed. In the days before her child was born, when she had won the Emperor's love, one day there had come to her an aged prince, the Grand Secretary Po Ch'un. She had been too young then, too new to palace ways, to comprehend the tangles of intrigue. Therefore she had listened without thought while the good old man besought her to speak for him to the Emperor.

"I do not have his ear now, lady," he said mournfully, while he stroked his scanty beard, already white.

"Of what are you accused by Su Shun?" she inquired.

"Lady, I am accused of enriching myself at the Throne's expense. This fellow, this Su Shun, has whispered to the Emperor that I hold back monies from the Imperial Treasury."

"Why should he say so?" she asked.

"It is he who is the robber and he knows I know it," the old Prince said.

She could not doubt his plain and honest looks, and too innocent, she promised to speak for him to the Emperor, and had done so. But in those days the Emperor still favored Su Shun, and he believed him, and so the old man had been beheaded and Su Shun then took his place. Her anger mounted afresh as she remembered how Su Shun began to hate her. Only the Emperor's quickly growing love for her had saved her against Su Shun's anger. Ah, she had been too sure of her power—look at her now!

Suddenly, unable now to bear the heat within her heart, she stood up and lifted her right hand and slapped Li Lien-ying first on one cheek and then on the other until his eyes watered and he could not get his breath. But he said nothing, for to bear such anger was his duty.

"There," she cried, "and there and there—not to tell me at once! Oh, evil silence!"

With this she sat down again and put her palms to her cheeks and sighed for full five minutes or so, while Li Lien-ying knelt like a stone before her, for never had he seen her in such a rage as this.

Another five minutes and her mind cleared. She rose from her seat and walked with impetuous grace to her writing table. There she sat down, prepared her ink slab and wet her brush and when this was done she took a small piece of silk parchment and on it wrote a letter to Prince Kung, telling him of her plight and asking his immediate help. She folded it and pressed her own seal upon it and beckoned Li Lien-ying to her side.

"You are to go to the capital this very hour," she commanded. "You are to deliver this parchment into the hands of Prince Kung and from him bring reply, and all this is to take no longer than four days."

"Venerable," he protested, "how can I—"

She cut him off. "You can because you must."

He looked sorrowful and struck his breast and groaned, but she did not melt and so he could only make haste to obey.

When he was gone she went pacing up and down the hall once more, until her woman was weary of watching her and her Court ladies came and peered through the curtains at her and went away, not daring to speak or even to let their presence be known.

At the end of four days Prince Kung himself arrived and he came dusty and travel-worn to that wing of the mighty palace where Tzu Hsi lived. She had not left these rooms, she had eaten little and slept less, while all her hope was pinned on word from this prince. What was her joy then when he was announced by Li Lien-ying, who, haggard and unwashed, had not stopped to sip even a bowl of millet gruel.

But she paid no heed to that faithful eunuch, hungry though he was. She rose and ran to the hall outside her bedchamber where Prince Kung waited, and there she gave greetings and thanked the gods and wept. Never had gaunt face looked so kind nor man so powerful and trustworthy, and she felt her heart ease in his presence.

"I have come," he said, "but secretly, for I should have gone first to my elder brother, the Emperor. Yet I had already news by courier from the Chief Eunuch, who sent to me a lesser eunuch, his own servingman, disguised as a beggar, to tell me that these infamous Three have dared to denounce me to the Dragon Throne. They have told my elder brother that I am plotting against him, that I am in secret alliance with the enemy in Peking, that I am bribed by their promises to let me take his place. When your letter came, Venerable, I could only hasten to untie this mighty tangle."

Before he could speak another word, Tzu Hsi's woman came running from the outer courtyard.

"Venerable," she sobbed, "Oh, lady, my mistress, your son, lady, the Heir—"

"What of him?" Tzu Hsi shrieked. "What have they done to him?" She laid hold on the woman's shoulder to shake the words from her.

"Speak, woman!" Prince Kung shouted to the half demented creature. "Do not stand gaping at us!"

"He has been stolen away," the woman sobbed. "He has been given to the wife of Prince Yi! She was summoned this morning to the Hunting Lodge Palace, and all other ladies have been dismissed. She and her women, they have him—"

At this Tzu Hsi fell back in her chair. But the Prince would not let her yield to fright.

"Venerable," he said firmly, "you cannot allow yourself the luxury of fear."

He did not need to speak again. She bit her lips, she wrung her hands together.

"We must move first!" she cried. "The seal—we must find the great imperial seal first of all—then we have the power with us."

He cried out his admiration. "Was there ever such a mind? I bow myself before you."

She rose, not hearing, from her chair.

But the Prince put up his hand. "Do not leave these rooms, I beg you. I must find out first the full danger to the Heir. The plot has swelled beyond our knowledge. Wait, Venerable, for my return."

He bowed and walked swiftly away.

How could she wait? Yet so she must, in agony, for were she way-laid and murdered in some lonely corridor, then who would save her son, the Heir? Poor child of hers—oh, little pitiful Heir to the Dragon Throne!

She stood motionless when Prince Kung had gone. She heard the wind howling among the many towers of the palace and she turned her head to look from the window. The gusts caught up the sand and drove it against the stone battlements until it fell sliding down the walls into the moat. The waters of the moat were dried, the very clouds in the sky were dried by the most merciless wind. It was the wind, she did not doubt, that burned away the life still lingering in the Emperor's body while he was borne in his palanquin across the desert plains. How could she save her son?

She was idle only for a moment. Then swiftly, while her woman and her eunuch watched her, she went to her writing table and prepared to write. In delicate haste she poured the water on the ink stone, she rubbed the stick of dried ink into it and made a thin paste and wet her camel's-hair brush in the paste until it was pointed sharper than a needle. Then she began to write in bold black strokes a decree of imperial succession.

"I, Hsien-feng," she wrote, "I, Emperor of the Middle Kingdom and of the dependencies of Korea and Thibet, of Indo-China and the islands of the south, am this day summoned to join My Imperial Ancestors. I, Hsien-feng, in full possession of My mind and My will, do hereby declare that the Heir is the male child borne to Me by Tzu Hsi, Empress of the Western Palace, and that he shall be known to all as the new Emperor, who shall sit upon the Dragon Throne after Me. And as Regents, until he shall have reached the age of sixteen years, I do appoint My two Consorts, the Empress of the Western Palace and the Empress of the Eastern Palace, on this day of My death————"

Here Tzu Hsi left a space, and after it she added these words:

"And I set My name and the imperial dynastic seal to this My will and My decree."

Here again she left a space.

She rolled the parchment and put it in her sleeve. Yes, she would take Sakota as Regent with her, compel her to be her ally, and thus prevent her as an enemy. Tzu Hsi could still let a smile flicker on her lips at her own cleverness.

Meanwhile her woman and Li Lien-ying stood watching her and waiting for her commands. Weary though he was, the eunuch did not dare to ask for rest.

Suddenly the woman turned her head toward the closed door. She had the sharpest ears, this woman, made keen by years of listening to hear her sovereign's call.

"I hear footsteps," she muttered.

"Whose footsteps?" the eunuch muttered.

He caught his robes in his right hand and strode to the door. He drew the bar and slipped through the crack and the woman hastened after him and stood with her back to the door, closed again, and she heard the flat of a hand pounding softly. She opened the door a crack and looked through. She turned to her mistress.

"Venerable," she said under her breath, "it is your kinsman."

Tzu Hsi, still at the writing table, turned her head sharply. "Let him come in."

She rose as she spoke. The woman opened the door further and Jung Lu came in. The woman closed the door and drew the bar while outside the door the eunuch stood on guard.

"Kinsman, greeting." Tzu Hsi's voice was smooth and sweet.

Jung Lu did not speak. He walked forward and made swift obeisance.

"Kinsman," she said, "do not kneel. Sit down on yonder chair and let us be as we have always been."

But Jung Lu would not sit. He rose and stepping nearer to her he fixed his eyes on the floor between them and began to speak. "Venerable, we have no time for courtesy. The Emperor is dying and the Chief Eunuch sent me to tell you. Su Shun was there less than an hour ago and with him the Princes Yi and Cheng. They had their plot—a decree for the Emperor to sign, appointing them as Regents for the Heir! He would not sign it and he fell unconscious when they tried to force him, but they will come again."

She did not pause a moment. She flew past him. He followed her swiftly and Li Lien-ying came after. She tossed commands across her shoulder to the eunuch as she went.

"Announce me—tell the Son of Heaven that I bring the Heir with me!"

As though the winds bore her she went to the Hunting Lodge. She burst into the door and none dared to stop her. She heard a child crying, she paused to listen, and recognized her son's voice. Oh, fortunate weeping, that led her to him! She pushed aside the frightened women, she ran through the rooms until she found the room where he was crying. She burst through those doors and saw a woman nursing her son but he would not be comforted. She swept him in her arms and carried him away, he clinging to her neck with both his arms, silenced by astonishment but not afraid. She hastened through passages and corridors, up steps of stone, through halls and chambers until she reached the innermost of all, and there without pause, she went straight through the door that the Chief Eunuch held open for her.

"Does the Son of Heaven still live?" she cried.

"He breathes," the Chief Eunuch said. His voice was hoarse with weeping. The great bed was raised like a bier and around it the eunuchs knelt, weeping in their hands. She passed through them as though they were trees bowed in a forest. Straight she went to the Emperor's side and there she stood, her child in her arms.

"My lord!" She called the two words in a loud clear voice. She waited and he did not answer.

"My lord!" she called again. Ah, would the old magic work?

The Emperor heard, his heavy eyelids lifted. He turned his head, the dying eyes looked up, he saw her face.

"My lord," she said, "here is your heir."

The child's eyes stared down, his eyes big and dark.

"My lord," she said, "you must declare he is your heir. If you hear me, raise your right hand."

All watched the dying hand. It lay motionless, a yellow piece of skin and bone. Then while they watched it moved with such effort that those watching groaned.

"My lord," she said imperiously, "I must be the child's Regent. None

147

but I can guard his life against those who would destroy him. Move your right hand once more to signify your wish."

Again they saw the slight slow movement.

She stepped forward to the bed and lifted up the yellow hand.

"My lord," she called, "my lord, come back for one more moment!"

With great effort did his soul return when her voice called. He moved his dim eyes to rest upon her face. She took the parchment from her breast and quick as her own wish, Jung Lu brought the vermilion brush from the writing table nearby and put it in her hand. Then he took the child from her arms.

"You must sign your will, my lord," she said distinctly to the dying Emperor. "I take your hand—so. Your fingers about the brush, so—"

He yielded her his hand, she held it, and the fingers moved, or seemed to move, to make his name.

"Thank you, my lord," she said, and put the parchment in her bosom. "Rest now, dear lord."

She motioned with her hand for all to withdraw. Jung Lu carried the child from the room, and the eunuchs stood at the far end and waited, their sleeves at their eyes. She sat down then upon the bed, and lifted the Emperor's head to rest upon her arm. Did he still live? She listened and heard a flutter in his breast. He opened his eyes wide, and drew in his breath.

"Your perfume—sweet!"

He held his breath an instant, it quivered in his throat and then he blew it out in a great sigh and with it died.

She put his head down gently upon the pillow and leaned over him and moaned twice. "Ah—" and "Ah—" and she wept a little, her tears pure pity that a man should die so young and never loved. Oh, that she could have loved him and for a moment she grieved because she could not.

Then she rose and walked from the imperial chamber, but slowly, as a widowed Empress walks.

Swifter than the winds the news of death swept through the palace. The Emperor lay in state in the Audience Hall, whose gates were barred and padlocked against all the living. At each gate of the great building stood one hundred men from the Imperial Guard, appointed by Jung Lu. Only the birds were free to come and go and nest among the gold dragons that reared themselves upon the two-tiered roofs. Silence lay deep beneath the heavy eaves along the pillared outer corridors but there was no peace in such a silence. Throughout the palace these walls hid the struggle of power but who knew where the final battle would take place?

Tzu Hsi was now the Empress Mother, the mother of the Heir. She was still young, a woman not yet thirty years of age. Princes of the blood surrounded her and heads of strong and jealous Manchu clans. Could she prevail, even as Empress Mother? All knew that Su Shun was her enemy, and with him the two princes, both brothers of the dead Emperor. Was Prince Kung still her ally? The Court waited irresolute, not knowing where to give its loyalty, and each courtier kept to himself, and each was careful to be cool and make no sign of either friendship or hostility to any other.

Meanwhile this same Su Shun, Grand Councilor that he was, had summoned the Chief Eunuch, as soon as his spies had reported the death of the Emperor, and he bade the eunuch take a message to the Empress Mother.

"Tell her," Su Shun said arrogantly, "that I and Prince Yi were appointed Regents by the Son of Heaven himself before his spirit left us. Say that we come to announce ourselves to her."

The Chief Eunuch made obeisance, saying nothing, but he hastened to do what he was told. Yet on the way he paused to whisper his business to Jung Lu, who waited on guard.

Jung Lu took command at once. "Proceed as quickly as you can to bring the Three to the Empress Mother. I'll hide myself outside the door and the moment that they leave I'll enter."

Meanwhile Tzu Hsi sat in her own palace hall, white-robed from head to foot, her headdress white, her shoes white, to signify the deepest mourning. Thus she had sat since the announcement of the Emperor's death. She had not eaten food nor drunk tea. Her hands were folded in her lap, her great eyes fixed on distance. Her ladies, standing near, wept and wiped their eyes upon their silken kerchiefs. But she did not weep.

When the Chief Eunuch came she heard him, and still gazing far off she spoke wearily, as though a duty pressed her that she would be rid of.

"Bring the Grand Councilor Su Shun here, and with him the Princes Cheng and Yi. Tell these three great ones that surely my lord, now dwelling in the Yellow Springs, must be obeyed."

He went, and in less time than can be told, she saw the Grand Councilor come in, and with him the two Princes. She turned her head and spoke softly to her favorite, Lady Mei, who was Su Shun's daughter.

"Leave us, child. It is not seemly that you stand here by me in the presence of your father."

She waited until the slender girl had slipped away. Then she accepted the obeisances of the Princes, and to show that she was not proud, now that her lord was dead, she rose and bowed to them in turn and sat down again.

But Su Shun was proud enough for two. He stroked his short beard and lifted his head to look at her with eyes bold and arrogant. She noted very well this breach of propriety, but she did not speak to correct it.

"Lady," he said, "I come to announce the Decree of Regency. In his last hour the Son of Heaven—"

Here she stopped him. "Wait, good Prince. If you have a parchment, and it bears his imperial signature, I will obey his will, in duty."

"I have no parchment," Su Shun said, "but I have witnesses. Prince Yi—"

Again she stopped him. "I have such a parchment, signed in my own presence and in the presence of many eunuchs."

She looked about to find the Chief Eunuch, but that prudent fellow had stayed outside the doors, not wishing to be present when the tigers met. She was not daunted. She drew from her bosom the parchment which the dying Emperor's hand had signed. In a smooth calm voice, every word distinct as the stroke of a silver bell, she read the decree from the beginning to the end, while Su Shun and the two Princes listened.

Su Shun pulled at his beard. "Let me see the signature," he snarled.

She held the parchment where he could see the name.

"There is no seal," he cried. "A decree without the imperial seal is worthless."

He did not wait to hear her answer or even to see the look of consternation on her face. He turned and fled, the princes his following shadows. She knew at once what made their haste. The imperial seal was locked within its coffer in the death chamber. Whoever seized it first was victor. She gnashed her teeth against herself that she had not waited for the seal. She tore the headdress from her head and threw it on the floor, she pulled her ears with both her fists and was beside herself with rage.

"Stupid!" she shrieked against herself. "Oh, stupid, stupid woman, I, and more stupid Prince, who did not warn me early, and stupid kinsman and treacherous eunuchs who did not help me sooner! Where is the seal?"

She ran to the door and jerked it open, but no one stood outside, no Chief Eunuch, not even Li Lien-ying. There was none here to give chase.

She threw herself upon the floor and wept. The years were lost, she was betrayed.

At this moment Lady Mei, peeping through brocaded curtains, saw her mistress lying there as dead and she ran in and knelt beside her.

"Oh, Worshipful," she moaned, "are you wounded? Did some one strike you?"

She tried to lift her weeping mistress but she could not and so she ran to the door still open and met there Jung Lu, and behind him the eunuch Li Lien-ying, just now arrived.

"Oh," she cried and shrank back, her blood flooding upward from her heart into her cheeks. But Jung Lu did not see her. He carried something in his hands, a lump wrapped in yellow silk.

He set it down when he saw the graceful figure lying on the stones, and he stooped and lifted the Empress in his arms and looked into her face.

"I have brought the seal," he said.

She got to her feet then, and he stood tall and straight beside her, his countenance grave as was its habit nowadays. And he, avoiding her direct gaze, took up the seal again in both his hands, a solid rock of jade whereon was deeply carved the imperial symbol of the Son of Heaven. This was the seal of the Dragon Throne and had been for eighteen hundred years and more, designed by the command of Ch'in Shih-huang, then ruling.

"I heard Su Shun," he said, "while I stood at the door to guard you. I heard him cry out that the parchment bore no seal. It was a race between us. I went one way and sent your eunuch by another to hold him if he reached the death chamber first."

Here Li Lien-ying, always eager to claim a prize for himself, put in his own tale.

"And I took a small eunuch with me, Venerable, and I crept into the death chamber through a vent, for you know the great gate is padlocked for fear of robbers in this wild country, and while the little eunuch watched, I went through head first and I smashed the wooden coffer with a vase of jade, and took out the seal. The little eunuch pulled me through again, even as I heard the Princes at the lock and forcing the key into the hole, and I wish that I could have stayed to see their faces when they saw the empty coffer!"

"Now is no time for laughter," Jung Lu said. "Empress, they will try to take your life, since they have not destroyed your power."

"Do not leave me," she implored him.

Tzu Hsi's woman had all this time been standing at the door, her ear

151

pressed against the panel. Suddenly she opened it. Prince Kung came in, his face pale, his robes wrapped about him for swiftness.

"Venerable," he cried, "the seal is gone! I went myself to the death chamber and ordered the guards to open the doors that I might go in. But the doors were open already at the order of Su Shun, and when I went in the coffer was empty."

He stopped. At this moment his eyes fell on the imperial seal covered with yellow silk. His jaw dropped, his dark eyes opened, the tip of his tongue touched his upper lip in a rare smile.

"Now I see," he said, "now I know why Su Shun says that such a woman as you must be killed or she will rule the world."

They looked at one another, Empress, Prince and eunuch, and they broke into triumphant mirth.

The imperial seal was hidden underneath Tzu Hsi's bed and the rose-red satin curtains overhung it, so that in the whole palace only she and her woman and her eunuch knew it was there.

"Do not tell me where it is hidden," Prince Kung had commanded. "I must be able to say I do not know."

With the imperial seal secure, she could do as she wished. Her fever left her and peace took the place of restlessness. She could and did ignore the ferment in the palace when it was known that the seal was gone, and none knew where. All guessed that she had taken it, and courtesy and obedience took the place of creeping impudence and growing arrogance. Her three enemies kept far from her, and well she knew that they were beside themselves, since they could not carry out their plot. Amid this confusion and consternation she went sweetly and at ease and her first deed was to send her eunuch to thank the Lady Yi for caring for her son, and to assure her that she would not put this trouble elsewhere, for she could care for him herself, since now, to her grief, her time was no more needed for the Emperor. So was restored to her the Heir.

Her next deed was to go weeping to her cousin, there to sit beside her, and tell her how the Emperor had decreed that they two should be the Regents while the Heir was yet a child. "You and I, dear Cousin," she said, "will now be sisters. Our lord willed us to be united for his sake, and I swear my loyalty and love to you so long as we both live."

She took Sakota's little hand and smiled tenderly into the wistful face, and how could Sakota dare to make reply? She smiled back again, half gratefully, and with something like her old childish honesty she said:

"To tell the truth, Cousin, I am glad to be friends."

"Sisters," Tzu Hsi said.

"Sisters then," Sakota amended, "for I always feared that Su Shun. His eyes are fierce and shifty, and though he promised me very much, I never knew—"

"Did he promise?" Tzu Hsi inquired too gently.

Sakota flushed. "He said that while he was regent, I was always to be called the Empress Dowager."

"And I was to be put to death, was I not?" Tzu Hsi asked in the same quiet voice.

"To that I never did agree," Sakota said too quickly.

Tzu Hsi maintained her usual courtesy. "I am sure you did not and now all can be forgot."

"Except—" here Sakota hesitated.

"Except?" Tzu Hsi demanded.

"Since you know much," Sakota said, unwillingly, "you must know that it was their plot to kill all foreigners everywhere in our nation, and put to death, too, the brothers of the Emperor who would not take their side in the plot. The edicts for these deeds are written and ready for the seal."

"Indeed, and is it so?" Tzu Hsi murmured, smiling, but in her heart aghast. How many lives had she saved besides her own!

She pressed Sakota's hand between her hands. "Let us have no secrets from each other, Sister. And fear nothing, for these plotters do not have the imperial seal, and so these edicts which they planned are nothing. Only that one who has the ancient seal, which has come down to us from the Ancestor Ch'in Shih-huang himself, and upon which are carved the words 'Lawfully Transmitted Authority,' can claim succession to the Dragon Throne."

She looked so high and pure and calm that Sakota dared not put a question as to that seal and where it was now. She bowed her head and murmured in a faint voice, "Yes, Sister." She put her kerchief to her lips and touched her eyelids, and said, "Alas—alas," to signify her grief that her lord was dead, and upon this Tzu Hsi took her leave and all was amity.

While the days passed until she must return to the capital she had only to await the further revelations of her enemies, and this she did with calm spirit, tinged with private mirth. But of such hidden mischief she showed nothing. Outwardly she was grave as a good widow should be and she wore white robes and put aside her jewels.

Meanwhile Prince Kung returned to the capital, there to prepare a special truce with the enemy which would allow the return of the dead Emperor for his imperial funeral.

"I have but one warning," Prince Kung told her in parting. "Do not, Majesty, allow any meeting between yourself and your kinsman, the Commander of the Guard. Who can value his loyalty and his courage more than I do? Yet enemies will have their eyes upon you now to see if there be truth in old gossip. Instead, put your trust in the Chief Eunuch, An Teh-hai, who gives his service whole to you and to the Heir."

Tzu Hsi cast reproachful looks upon the Prince. "Do you think me stupid?"

"Forgive me," he said, and these were his parting words.

Although she did not need it, yet his advice was good for her against temptation. For she was woman, and her heart was hot, and now that the Emperor was dead she did often in the night let her wild and secret thoughts go creeping through dark corridors and lonely halls and past empty rooms to that gate lodge where the Imperial Guard was stationed. There she found him whom she loved and her thoughts circled about him like mourning doves, remembering him as he had been when they were children, he always tall and straight, inclined to stubbornness, it was true, never yielding unless it was his will to yield, stronger than she, however strong she was, handsome then as now, but male, and never delicate or womanish, as the poor Emperor had been. Against such thoughts and memories, it was well that she had Prince Kung's warning, a shield to keep her from her own desire. She made her outer calm invincible, while within the fire burned.

And indeed she could not indulge her heart. Her task was still not finished. She must not give comfort to her enemies, nor freedom to herself until the Throne was hers, to hold for her son. She must exert her every charm, her dignity and courtesy toward everyone, and so well she did this that all except her enemies were drawn to her, and especially the soldiers of the Imperial Guard to whom she granted gifts and kindness, without once seeming to show a difference between these men and their commander. To them, too, she sent her daily thanks for their protection of the imperial corpse.

Meanwhile she took for her own ally the Chief Eunuch, An Teh-hai, and he was near her always as he had once been to the Emperor. From him she heard the troubles of her enemies, and how distracted the Three were, and their followers with them. For on the day after the imperial death they had sent out edict declaring themselves appointed Regents by the Emperor on his deathbed and she was forbidden any part in government. The next day, however, when they could not find the seal, they made haste to placate her, and sent out another edict proclaiming the Consorts both Empress Dowagers.

"This, Venerable," the Chief Eunuch told her, chortling and snickering, "is not so much that you are the mother of the new Emperor, but because you have won to your side the Manchu soldiers who guard this palace."

Tzu Hsi's smooth cheeks dimpled. "Am I still to be killed?" she inquired too innocently.

"Not until they are sure of their place in the capital."

They laughed and parted, he to make his report to Prince Kung by daily courier, and she to play her part of lovely woman. When she met by chance any of the Three, her courtesy was so perfect, her manner so indifferent to her danger, that Prince Yi at least could not believe she knew them still plotters.

On the second day of the ninth moon month, truce having been made with the invaders, the Board of Regents declared that the cortège of the dead Emperor must set forth on the journey homeward to the capital. Now it was the custom of the centuries that, when an emperor died away from his burial place, the Consorts must travel ahead, so that they could be ready to welcome the Imperial Dead to his final home. With due gravity and mourning, Tzu Hsi prepared herself and her son. The ancient custom gave Tzu Hsi her advantage and she hid her joy that this was so. For those Three, who were still her enemies, were by duty forced to follow with the imperial catafalque, and its great weight, borne by one hundred and twenty men, compelled their pace to such slowness that the journey to the capital must take ten days with resting places every fifteen miles. But in her simple mule cart the Empress Mother could reach the city in half the time, and there establish her place and power before Su Shun could prevent her.

"Venerable, your enemies despair," the Chief Eunuch told her the night before departure. "Therefore we must watch them at every step."

"I depend on your ears," she said.

"This is their plot," the Chief Eunuch went on. "Instead of our loyal Manchu guards, Su Shun has ordered his own soldiers to accompany you, Venerable, on the plea that the Imperial Guards are needed for the dead Emperor. And even I have been commanded to attend the bier and with me your own eunuch, Li Lien-ying."

She cried out, "Alas—"

The Chief Eunuch put up his huge hand.

"I have worse to tell. Jung Lu is ordered to remain behind to guard this Jehol palace."

155

She wrung her hands together. "Forever?"

The Chief Eunuch nodded his immense head. "He tells me so."

"What shall I do?" she asked in sharp distress. "This means I am to die. In some lonely mountain pass, who will hear me when I cry out to be saved?"

"Venerable, be sure your kinsman has his own plan. He says you are to trust him. He will be near you."

With this faith only to uphold her, she set forth the next morning at dawn, her son's cart in front, then hers and Sakota's, and surrounded by the alien guard. Yet all saw her calm and unafraid, she spoke courteously to everyone, directing here and there and asking last, as though she all but forgot, that her large toilet case be put beneath her, lest she wish for kerchief or perfume. There in her toilet case was hidden the imperial seal, but none knew it save her faithful woman.

When all was ready, she seated herself inside her curtains and so began the sad journey. She had longed to leave that somber palace and yet it seemed a shelter now that she did not know what lay ahead nor even where that night she must sleep. The summer drought had broken, and rain fell steadily as the day went on, a clean hard rain that soaked into the sandy soil and swelled the mountain streams and choked the narrow roads between the mountains. By nightfall, thus delayed, they were far from any resting place, and the rivers were so high that they were forced to stop in a certain gorge of Long Mountain, and make shelter as they could in the tents with which they traveled.

Here in darkness while the bearers raised the tents, there was further mischief. The captain of the hostile guard declared that the Empress Dowager and the Heir must have their tent set well apart from all the rest, because their station was so high.

"I will myself be your guard, Venerable," he said. He stood before her in his soldier's garb, a coarse and loud-mouthed churl, his right hand on a sword that hung down to his heels while he made a show of courtesy.

She kept her eyes down and so her eyes chanced to fall upon that right hand of his. Upon the thumb, and shining in the lantern light, she saw a ring of pure red jade. Such jade was not common, and its color caught in her mind.

"I thank you," she said calmly, "and when our journey is ended, I will reward you well."

"I do my duty, Venerable—I only do my duty." Thus he boasted and bustled off.

Night deepened. The winds and rain roared through the narrow gorge and at its bottom the river swelled high as it rushed on its way down the mountain. Rocks cracked from the mountainside and thundered past the tent where Tzu Hsi sat beside the child. His nurse slept and at last her own serving woman slept and the child went to sleep holding his mother's hand. But Tzu Hsi could not sleep. She sat silent in her tent watching the candle gutter in the horn lantern, while she kept guard of the imperial seal, inside her toilet case. The seal was the treasure, and for it she might lose her life. She knew her danger. This was the hour for her enemy. Alone, with helpless women and the child, she was too far away to be heard if she cried out. And who would hear her? All day she had no sign to tell her where her kinsman was. She searched rocks and hillsides as she passed, but he was not hidden there. Nor had he mingled with the guards, disguised as common soldier. If she cried out to be saved, would he be near to hear? She could only wait while time passed, each moment separate torture.

At midnight the guard beat the hour upon a brass drum to signify that all was well, and she pretended reproach for her own anxiety. Why should her enemies choose this place, this night, rather than another, to kill her? Would it not be easy to bribe a palace cook to put poison in her food, or an assassin eunuch to hide behind some door where she must pass? She toyed with each thought, coaxing herself free from fear, saying that it would indeed be annoyance to have the body of a dead empress to hide, and would not her subjects inquire what had befallen her, and could even her enemies take the risk of their anger?

The next hour passed more quickly and now she only dreaded the dying of the candle. If she moved the child would wake, and he was sleeping sweetly, his hand folded into hers. Then she must call but softly, to rouse her woman to put a fresh candle in the lantern. She lifted her head so to call, and her gaze, which had been fixed upon the child's sleeping face, at this moment caught the movement of the leather curtain of the tent. It was the wind, doubtless, or the rain pouring down, but still she could not move her eyes away nor did she call. And while she watched, a short sharp dagger cut the leather silently and now she saw a hand, a man's hand, and upon the thumb it wore a red jade ring.

Without a sound she snatched up the child and ran across the tent but in that same instant another hand reached out and seized the hand that held the dagger, and forced it back and the slit fell shut again. Ah, she knew well that saving hand! She stood and listened and heard men struggle and she saw the side of the tent tremble when they fell against it. She heard a moan, then silence.

"Let that be an end to you," these words she heard Jung Lu mutter.

157

Such comfort now came flowing into her being that she was shaken to the heart. She put down the sleeping child and stole across the carpet to the door of the tent, and looked out into the stormy night. Jung Lu was there. He took three steps toward her and they gazed at each other full.

"I knew that you would come," she said.

"I will not leave you," he said.

"Is the man dead?"

"Dead. I have thrown the body down the gorge."

"Will they not know?"

"Who can dare to speak his name when they see me in his place?"

They stood, eyes meeting eyes, yet neither took the next step toward the other.

"When I know what reward is great enough," she said, "then I will give it to you."

"Because you live I am rewarded," he replied.

Again they stood until he said, uneasy, "Venerable, we must not linger. Everywhere we are surrounded by our enemies. You must retire."

"Are you alone?" she asked.

"No, twenty of my own men are with me. I pressed ahead, my horse the swiftest! You have the seal?"

"Here—"

He stepped backward, turned and went into the darkness. She let the curtain fall and stole back to her bed. Now she could sleep. No more was she afraid. Outside her tent he stood on guard. She knew it, though the night hid him, and for the first time in many weeks she slept deeply and in peace.

At dawn the rains ceased and the clouds rolled away. She looked from the door of the tent upon a blue sky and valleys green between the bare and rocky hills. As though the night had never been, she spoke courteously to the nurse and to her woman and taking her child's hand, she led him outside the tent and in the sand she searched for small bright stones to please him.

"I will tie them in my kerchief," she said, "then you may play with them while we travel."

Never had she been more calm. Those who saw her remarked her quiet resignation. She did not laugh or smile, for that would be unseemly in a funeral procession, but she seemed comforted and resolute. Nor could anything be said when it was seen by all that the captain's place had been taken by Jung Lu, and that he was surrounded by twenty of his own men. In such uncertain times no questions could be asked, but all knew that she had won a victory, and each stepped more quickly to do his duty.

When she had eaten, the tents folded and the carts made ready, the journey began again. Beside the Heir and his imperial mother Jung Lu rode on a high white horse, and his men rode with him, ten on each side. Still no question could be asked, nor did Tzu Hsi take notice of the change of guard. She sat silent in her cushioned seat, the curtains parted wide enough to see the landscape, and if any glanced toward her, not once did he see her face turned toward the Commander of the Guard. What her thoughts were who could know?

She was scarcely thinking, her restless mind for once was in repose. These few days of travel were her own, for she was safe. The climax of her struggle, the final battle for the Dragon Throne, must come when she received the imperial catafalque. Traveling now at such steady speed, she would enter the Forbidden City five days before the cortège. As soon as she reached her palace, she must summon her clansmen and the dead Emperor's loyal brothers, and they must plan together how to seize the traitors, not by force for then the people would protest, but with order and decorum, proving their wickedness and her own right as Regent on the Heir's behalf. Beyond the edge of her mind these deeds of state loomed dark and threatening, but she had the trick of taking pleasure when she could, and therefore was refreshed and strong when the hard moment came.

And surely this was pleasure, to ride through the autumn countryside, the dangerous mountains hourly more distant while Jung Lu rode beside her, silent, it was true, and proud, so that they could not speak or look toward each other. But he was there and her life was in his keeping. Thus passed the days. She slept sweetly in the nights and woke hungry in the morning, for the fresh northern air made her blood lively.

On the twenty-ninth day of that ninth month of the moon year, she saw the walls of the capital rise up from the surrounding plains and the gates were open. Inside the city the streets were cleared of folk but Tzu Hsi put down her curtains lest she see a foreign enemy. There were none. The city lay silent in suspense, for news traveled faster than human feet, and the poorest citizen knew that tigers were at war, and victory was not clear. At such times the people wait.

Tzu Hsi had planned her course. She entered the palace in deep mourning, her robes of white sackcloth, and she wore no jewels. Looking not to right or left, she descended from her cart while eunuchs knelt on either side. Then in perfect courtesy she went to Sakota's cart and helped her to descend, and holding her left hand within her own right, she led her into the palaces they knew so well. Still courteous, she escorted her co-Regent to her Eastern Palace before she went into her own.

Scarcely had an hour passed before she had messages from Prince Kung, by eunuch, who said:

"The Younger Brother Prince Kung asks pardon, for he knows the Empress Mother is weary with grief and travel. Yet so urgent are the affairs of state that he dares not delay, and he bids me say that he is waiting for audience in the Imperial Library, and with him are his brother princes and the noble headmen of the Manchu clans."

"Tell the Prince I come without delay," she answered. Without waiting to change her garments or to take food, she went again to Sakota's palace and entered without ceremony. Her cousin was lying on her bed, her women at her side, one to brush her hair, one with tea, another with her favorite perfume.

Tzu Hsi put them aside, "Sister," she said, "get up, if you please. We must not rest. We must give audience."

Sakota pouted, but what she saw in that proud and beautiful face forbade complaint. She sighed and rose, her women put on her outer robes, and leaning on two eunuchs she followed Tzu Hsi to the courtyard where sedans waited. The two ladies were carried swiftly to the Imperial Library and there descending Tzu Hsi took Sakota's hand and so they entered side by side into the hall. All rose and made obeisance. Then Prince Kung came forward gravely, as befitted his mourning clothes of white sackcloth, and he led the ladies to their thrones and took his place at Tzu Hsi's right hand.

In secret conference the hours went on. The doors were guarded, and the eunuchs sent to the ends of the vast hall where they could not hear what plans were made.

"Our problem is severe," Prince Kung said at last. "Nevertheless, we have one great strength. The Empress Mother has the imperial seal in her secret keeping, and this seal alone is worth a mighty army. The legitimate succession is therefore hers as Regent for her son, together with the Empress Dowager of the Eastern Palace as her sister-Regent. Yet we must move with every care and righteousness, with all decorum and propriety. How then shall we seize the traitors? Shall violence be used while the Emperor, no longer ruling, comes to his own funeral scene? There is no precedent for such a course. To battle enemies in the presence of a sacred Ancestor is indeed too impious. The people would not accept such rulers, and the Heir's reign would begin under an evil cloud."

All agreed that Prince Kung spoke well, and at last, with much pondering and talking to and fro, it was decided that each step be taken slowly, with caution and dignity, conforming to the high tradition of the dynasty. To this Tzu Hsi agreed, as mother of the Heir and the new reigning Empress, and Sakota bowed her head and did not lift her voice for or against what was said.

Three days passed, and now came the hour for which all waited. Tzu Hsi had spent these days in meditation, planning every moment and every motion of how she would appear and what she would do when the imperial cortège came to the gates of the capital. She must not show one sign of weakness, and yet she must be faultless in all courtesy. Boldness must combine with dignity and ruthlessness with righteousness.

Hourly through those days couriers came to announce when the catafalque would arrive until on this morning of the second day of the twelfth month of the moon year the last courier declared that the cortège would come to the East-Flowered Gate of the Forbidden City. Tzu Hsi was prepared. The day before, by her command, Prince Kung had stationed an army of loyal soldiers near this gate, lest the traitorous Three might use the arrival of the dead Emperor to proclaim themselves Regents for the new Emperor. In the palace all was mournful peace. When it was known that the imperial cortège was near, the Empress Dowagers set forth to meet their dead lord, and with them went the Heir. Through the silent empty streets they went, their sedans covered with white sackcloth and followed by guardsmen in white. Behind them upon horseback came the princes and the heads of the royal clans, all in robes of mourning. The procession went slowly with grieving looks and in silence except that Buddhist priests, who were funeral musicians, played sadly upon their flutes while they led the way for the imperial mourners.

At the mighty gate into the city they halted and all came down from their sedans and their horses to kneel as the huge coffin appeared, carried by its hundred bearers. First and in front of others knelt the Heir, wrapped in white sackcloth. Tears of frightened sorrow streamed down his rosy face. Behind him Tzu Hsi knelt and with her Sakota, Imperial Dowagers. Behind them knelt the princes and the heads of clans and officials, each in his rank. Loud lamentations and sobs and sighs rose into the air, and people listening behind closed doors and windows heard the voices of those who ruled them.

The three traitors, Prince Yi, Prince Cheng and the Grand Councilor,

Su Shun, having performed their duty in bringing the dead Emperor safely home, must finish it by making full report to the Heir, and for this rite a great pavilion had been built inside the gate. There Tzu Hsi now went with her son, and Sakota, silent and shrinking but obedient nevertheless, went with them. The princes and the officials of the court led by two Grand Secretaries gathered around. Tzu Hsi sat at the right hand of the Heir, and on his left Sakota. Without delay, in her calm graceful fashion, as though it was her right, Tzu Hsi began to speak to the traitors.

"We thank you, Prince Yi, Prince Cheng, and Grand Councilor Su Shun, for your faithful care of him we hold most dear. In the name of our new Emperor, the Son of Heaven now ruling, we give you thanks, since we, the two Consorts of the late Emperor, are the duly appointed Regents, by the decree signed by the late Emperor himself. Your duties are now fulfilled and it is our will that you be relieved of further cares."

This was the meaning of what Tzu Hsi said, and she spoke with every small grace and delicate courtesy, but all understood the immovable will behind the gemlike words.

Prince Yi, hearing, was immediately in severe distress. Above him he saw the handsome child sitting upon the throne, and to one side the helpless Empress Tzu An. On the right hand of the young Emperor sat the true ruler, the beautiful powerful woman who feared no one and by whose charm and strength all were subdued. Behind these stood the princes and the headmen of the royal Manchu clans, and behind these again the Imperial Guard. Prince Yi looked at Jung Lu, standing formidable and fierce, and his heart shook within him. Where was his hope?

Here Su Shun leaned to whisper in his ear, "Had that female fiend been killed early, as I advised, then would we be safe at this hour! But no, you shilly-shallied, you did not dare, you chose a halfway plan, and now our heads are loose upon our shoulders! You are the leader now, and if you fail we die."

Prince Yi mustered his poor courage therefore and he stepped nearer to the young Emperor and trying boldness, though his lips trembled, he thus addressed the Throne:

"It is we, Most High, who are your appointed Regents. Our Imperial Ancestor, your father, did appoint me and Prince Cheng and the Grand Councilor Su Shun, we three, to act on your behalf. We are your faithful servants, and we pledge our loyalty. As Regents, duly appointed, we hereby decree that the two Consorts have no authority beyond their station, and they are not to be present at audience, except by our permission, as ruling Regents."

While he spoke these brave words in a trembling voice, the little Emperor looked here and there and yawned and played with the cord that tied his sackcloth garments about his waist. Once he reached for his mother's hand, but firmly she put his hand back upon his knee, and he obeyed her and sat with his hands upon his knees and waited for the old man to stop talking.

When Prince Yi stepped back, Tzu Hsi did not hesitate. She lifted her right hand and thrusting her thumb downward, she commanded in her clearest voice, "Seize the Three Traitors!"

Immediately Jung Lu strode forward, and with him his guardsmen. They seized the Three and wrapped ropes about them. Those traitors did not move or struggle. Who dared to aid them now? No voice spoke. In dignity and order the funeral procession formed again, the young Emperor following the great catafalque, the Empress Dowagers to right and left, and behind them nobles and princes. Last of all came the traitors, walking in the dust, their faces downcast. For them remained no hope. The streets were lined with loyal soldiers and every eye was on them.

Thus did the Emperor Hsien Feng come home again and thus was he united to his Ancestors. His bier rested in the sacred hall, guarded night and day by his Imperial Guardsmen, and candles burned without ceasing while Buddhist priests prayed his three souls to Heaven and placated his seven earthly spirits by burning incense and chanting many psalms.

And Tzu Hsi, mindful that every act must be confirmed in due order and according to ancient precedent, sent forth an edict and this was its purport: the realm, she declared, had been disturbed too much by enemies, and this was the fault of Prince Yi and his allies, who had brought shame upon their country by tricking the white men. These then became enraged and burned the Summer Palace in revenge. Yet the traitors persisted in their evil, she declared, and they pretended that the late Emperor, before he died, had appointed them as Regents, and taking advantage of the present Emperor's extreme youth, they had set up themselves in power, disregarding the express wish of the Emperor, no longer ruling, that the two Consorts, the Empress Dowagers, should be the Regents.

"Let Prince Kung," the edict ended, "in consultation with the Grand Secretaries, the Six Boards and the Nine Ministries, consider and report to the Throne the proper punishment to be inflicted upon these traitors, in proportion to their offences. Let them consider and advise, moreover, how the Empress Dowagers shall act as Regents, and let a memorial be submitted as to procedure."

To this edict, the Empress Mother affixed the imperial seal. When the edict had gone out to the people, she prepared a second edict to which she set her own name and the co-Regent's, as Empress Dowagers, and she decreed that the traitors were to be stripped of all their honors and their ranks. Then she sent forth yet another edict, signed this time by her name only, which said:

"Su Shun is guilty of high treason. He has usurped authority. He has accepted bribes and has committed every wickedness. He has used blasphemous language to Ourselves, forgetting the sacred relation between Sovereign and subject. Moreover, he kept his wife and concubines with him while he escorted the Imperial Catafalque from Jehol, and this on his own responsibility, although all know that to allow women the privilege to accompany the Imperial Catafalque is a crime to be punished by death. Therefore We decree that Su Shun shall die by slicing, his flesh to be cut into a thousand thousand strips. His property shall be confiscated, both in the capital and in Jehol, and let no mercy be shown him or his family."

This decree was bold indeed, for Su Shun was the richest man in the history of the dynasty, except for one Ho Sh'en, who lived in the reign of the Ancestor Ch'ien Lung, and him the Emperor, then ruling, had commanded to be put to death because he had grown rich by theft and usury.

By this edict, Su Shun's vast wealth was given to the Throne, as Ho Sh'en's had been in the earlier age. How vast it was none knew, but under Tzu Hsi's command Su Shun's libraries were seized, and with them his records of all the treasure in his storehouses. Among these records was found one which made known a thing strange and comforting to her, and it was that Lady Mei was no true daughter of Su Shun. When this was reported to Tzu Hsi she commanded that the record be brought to her, and there she read with her own eyes a private note, appended by some unknown secretary who held a grudge against Su Shun, his employer. Here were the words, written very small, beneath an accounting of certain lands and houses:

"Let it be told here that these properties belonged to a nobleman of the clan of the Plain White Banner. Su Shun, when he had seized this treasure, found in the household of the nobleman, whom he had caused to be put to death on false accusation, one infant, a girl. This girl he took into his own household. She grew up to be the Lady Mei, now in waiting upon the Empress of the Western Palace."

When Tzu Hsi read these words she sent at once for Lady Mei, and showed her the record. The lady wept awhile, then dried her eyes on her white silk kerchief and she said, "I often wondered why I could not love Su Shun as father. How sinful did I feel! Now I can let down my heart."

She knelt before Tzu Hsi and thanked her and from that day on she loved her mistress even more faithfully than before.

"For I am orphaned," she said, "and you, Venerable, are my mother and my father."

With all her vengeance against Su Shun, Tzu Hsi could not be content. She pursued her vengeance and placed her decrees before the princes, ministers and members of the Boards and they bowed their heads. Prince Kung alone dared to raise his voice.

"Majesty," he said, "it would become the Empress Dowagers to show some mercy in the manner in which Su Shun is to die. Let him be beheaded rather than sliced."

None dared to lift his eyes to see Tzu Hsi's face, stern and beautiful, when she heard these words. She heard against her wish, all knew, for minutes passed before she answered.

"Let it be by our mercy, then," she said at last, "but the beheading shall be public."

So it came about that Su Shun's head was cut off in the marketplace of the city. It was a fair and sunny morning, and the people made a holiday to come and see him die. He walked bravely before the throng, villain though he was, his head held high and his bold face unmoved. Proud to the end he laid his head upon the block and the headsman lifted up the broadsword and brought it down. With this single blow, Su Shun's head was severed from his body, and when it rolled into the dust, the people howled with joy, for he had injured many.

The Empress Mother had commanded the Princes Jui and Liang to stand by to see the head roll off and they reported to the Throne that Su Shun was dead indeed.

Since the Princes Yi and Cheng belonged to the Imperial House, these two were not beheaded but were ordered to the Empty Chamber, which was the prison of the Imperial Court, and there were told to hang themselves. And Jung Lu gave to each a silken rope, and he stood by, and each did hang himself upon a beam, one at the south end of the Chamber and the other at the north. Prince Cheng died resolutely and at once, but Prince Yi took long to get his courage up until, weeping and sobbing, he forced himself at last.

165

So died the Three, and those who had hoped to rise with them were sent in exile. From this day on Tzu Hsi assumed publicly the title of Empress Mother, which the dying Emperor in Jehol had bestowed upon her. Thus began the reign of the young Emperor but all knew that whatever her propriety and her courtesy to all, the Empress Mother reigned supreme.

III

The Empress Mother

WINTER crept down from the north and the city of Peking shriveled in the cold. The trees in the courtyards, so green and blooming in the summer that they made a vast tropical garden, now dropped their leaves and their skeletons, gray with frost, loomed above the roofs. Ice edged the lakes and froze upon the gutters. The people in the streets shivered and bent their heads against the wind. The vendors of roasted sweet potatoes did good business, for the earthy food warmed the hands and put heat into the bellies of the poor. When a man opened his mouth to speak, his breath curled into the air like smoke, and mothers bade their children not to cry lest they lose their inner heat.

It was a winter cold beyond any that could be remembered, and the cold was more than that of the flesh. Chill crept into the bones and into the hearts of all. Now that the body of the dead Emperor rested in the palace temple until burial, now that the succession was decided, the years stretched somberly before the nation and sensible minds did not deceive themselves. The treaty which Prince Kung had made with the white invaders was a treaty which acknowledged the victory of the enemy.

The Empress Mother sat alone in her private throne room one winter's day, the parchment of that treaty spread upon the table before her. She was alone and yet never alone, for near enough to hear her voice the eunuch Li Lien-ying always waited. It was his life to wait until she moved or spoke. Meanwhile she forgot him as though he were not there.

On this cold morning she read the treaty again and yet again, carefully and without haste, pondering each word, while her imagination livened every meaning. From now on, forevermore, there would be in Peking men from England and France and other countries, the constant representatives of alien governments. This meant that there would be also their wives and their children, their servingmen and their families, their guards and couriers. Wild white men would find ways to lie with lovely Chinese women, doubtless, and this would be confusion under Heaven.

Moreover, the treaty said, the Empress Mother and Regent must find thousands of pounds of gold for the foreigners, as recompense for the war which the invaders had forced. Was this justice, that a war which her people had not wanted should be paid for by them rather than by those who had brought it to pass?

And, furthermore, the treaty said, new ports were to be opened to these white men from the West, even the port of Tientsin, which was less than a hundred miles from the capital itself. Did this not mean that goods as well as men would be continually brought hither, and when the people saw foreign goods, would not false desires rise in their unenlightened hearts? This would bring further confusion.

And foreign priests, the treaty said, bringing their own religions, were to be allowed to wander through the country at will, settling where they liked and persuading the people to new gods. This had already brought disaster to the nation.

Of these and many like evils the Empress Mother read during that dark day in her lonely palace, and she spoke to no one. When food was brought she did not eat. Night fell but she paid no heed. None dared to speak to her or beg her to sleep. Her eunuch set a pot of her favorite green tea on the table and poured a bowl where her hand could reach it, but she did not look up or put out her hand.

Sometime in the small hours she set the parchment aside. Yet still she did not rise from her chair to go to her bedchamber. The great red candles burned low into the sockets of the golden candlesticks, and their flames, leaping up, made strange shadows on the painted beams of the high ceiling. The eunuch, ever watchful, came forward and put in fresh candles and went away again. She sat on, her chin in her right hand, in meditation deeper than she had ever known. The young Emperor, her son, was but five years old, his sixth birthday still half a year away. She, his mother, was twenty-six years of age. He could not sit upon the Dragon Throne before his sixteenth birthday. For ten years of her young womanhood she must rule in her son's place. And what was her realm? A country vaster than she could guess, a nation older than history, a people whose number had never been counted, to whom she was herself an alien. In peace this realm would have been a monstrous burden, and there was no peace. Rebellion raged, the country was divided, for the rebel Hung ruled as Emperor in Nanking, the southern capital of the last Chinese Ming dynasty. The Imperial Armies fought incessantly against him but his power held, and between the armies the beggared people starved. Her armies, as she well knew, were little better than the rebels, for they were seldom paid, and to keep themselves from starving they fed from the people, robbing as they fought, until the country folk, their villages burned and their crops laid waste, hated rebels and imperial soldiers with an equal hatred.

This was her burden.

At the same time, a new rebellion had risen among the Muslim in the southern province of Yünnan. These Muslim were the offspring of mideastern tribes, Arabs who had come as traders in earlier centuries and had stayed to marry Chinese women and rear mongrel children. They clung to their own gods, and as the number of their children grew, the worshippers of these alien gods grew bold. When Chinese Viceroys, appointed by the Dragon Throne but living far away, ruled over them with greed and hardship, the Muslim, rebelling, vowed that they would cut off their lands from the realm and set up their own government.

This was her burden.

And of her burdens there was yet another. She was a woman. The Chinese did not trust a woman for their ruler. Women, they said, were evil rulers. The Empress Mother acknowledged some truth here. She had read history well in long lonely hours and she knew that in the eighth century, in the dynasty of T'ang, the Empress Wu, wife of the great Emperor Kao Tsung, had seized the Throne for herself against her own son, and her wickedness had sullied the name of all women. Men rose against her, and freed the young Emperor from the jail in which his own mother had cast him. Yet he was still not safe, for then his wife, the Empress Wei, in her turn coveted the Throne, and she hid behind curtains and listened to gossip and stirred up such mischief that death alone could quiet her. No sooner was she in her grave, a heavy stone upon it to hold her down, than the Princess T'ai-p'ing, her enemy, plotted to poison the Emperor's son, the Heir, and she, too, must be killed. But this same Heir, when he was the Emperor Hsüan Tsung, fell under the power of his beautiful concubine, Kuei-fei, who did so bewitch the Emperor by her beauty and the brilliance of her mind, and did so ruin him by her love of gems and silks and perfumes, that the people again rebelled, and their leader forced Kuei-fei to hang herself before her royal lover's eyes. Yet the glory of T'ang died with her, for the Emperor would not rule again but hid himself in perpetual mourning. The history of these women was evil and they were still her enemies, though long dead. Would the people now believe that a woman could rule justly and well?

This was her burden.

Greatest of all her burdens was the burden of herself. Though she was learned beyond the reach of many scholars, she knew her faults and dangers and that, still young and of passionate heart, she could be betrayed by her own desires. Well she knew that she was not all of a piece, one woman molded whole. A score of various women hid within her frame, and not all were strong and calm. She had her softness, her fears, her longing for one stronger than she was, a man whom she could trust. Where was he now?

Upon this question she put an end to her meditation. She rose, chilled to the heart, and Li Lien-ying came forward.

"Venerable, surely now you will take your rest."

So saying he put out his arm, and she placed her hand upon it, and let him lead her to the closed door of her bedchamber. He opened it before her, and her woman, waiting there, received her from the eunuch and closed the door.

Sharp winter sunshine woke her from sleep, and she lay in her bed considering her mood of the night before. She had her burdens, but did she not have also the means of bearing them? She was young, but to be young was strength. She was a woman, but she had borne a son who was the Emperor. She would not follow in the evil path of those dead women who had put themselves above all others, even their sons, that they might rule alone. She would think only of her son. In these ten years while she was Regent, she would speak softly, be courteous to all, think never of her own good, be angry only when she saw her son forgotten, be careful always for his future power. She would build the Empire strong and sound for him, and when he ascended to his place, she would retire, for none should be his rival, not even she. She would prove a woman could be good. Youth came to her aid, and health and will, and she rose from her bed renewed by her own energy.

From this day on, all saw a new Empress, a strong, gentle and mild-mannered lady, who looked no man in the face, who turned her head away from eunuchs and spoke courteously to low and high alike. She was distant, far above them all. None was her intimate and none knew her thoughts and dreams. She lived alone, this Empress, the walls of her courtesy impregnable and inviolate, and through that wall there was no gate.

As though to cut herself off from the past, she moved from the palaces which had so long been her home, and she chose instead a distant palace in the imperial city, the Winter Palace, in that part called the Eastern Road, its six halls and many gardens built and furnished by the Ancestor Ch'ien Lung. Near to it was a vast library, built also by that Ancestor and filled with thirty-six thousand most ancient books, in which were enshrined the minds and memories of all great scholars. At the entrance to the palaces there stood a spirit screen, upon which were nine imperial dragons made of porcelain in many colors. Behind this screen the largest hall was the Audience Hall, and it opened upon a wide marble terrace. Behind this hall were the other halls, each with its courtyard. One she chose for her private throne room, where princes and ministers who wished for conference alone could kneel before her. The next was her living place. Behind it was her bedchamber, small and quiet, the bed built into one wall, its mattress yellow satin, its curtains yellow gauze embroidered with the red pomegranate flowers she loved. The next hall she kept as her secret shrine and here above the marble altar a gold Buddha stood, and beside him on the right a small gold Kuan Yin and on his left a gilded Lohan, who was the guiding spirit of wisdom. Behind the shrine was a long room where her eunuchs stayed on guard, out of sight and sound and yet near her always.

These rooms in which the Empress now lived were furnished with the luxury that she loved, with inlaid tables, chairs and couches cushioned in scarlet satin. Here were her many clocks, her flowers and birds, her embroidered pallets for her dogs, her books and desk for writing, her cabinets of scrolls. Between each two rooms were vermilion-painted doors, overhung with gilded rooflets. A side door led from her most private court into a garden, much loved by the Ancestor Ch'ien Lung. Here he had sat when he was old, and in the sunshine filtering through the bamboo leaves he dreamed. The doors to this garden were moon-shaped and framed in marble delicately carved, and the walls were set with many colored marbles in mosaic. Beneath the ancient pines, bent to the earth with age, the moss grew deep, and when the sun shone down the scent of pine needles perfumed the air. In a far corner, where the sun fell warm, stood a locked pavilion, to which the Empress held the only key, and here Ch'ien Lung, the Great Ancestor, had slept in his coffin while he waited for the auspicious day of burial.

In this silent ancient place, the young Empress Mother walked often and always alone, her burdens upon her shoulders, and she felt their growing weight. None but the strong could endure the life which she now set for herself. She rose daily in the cold and bitter dawn and when she was dressed she went in her imperial yellow-sedan to the Audience Hall. She would not go alone however, for, mindful of her firm will to be always modest and invincible in courtesy, she commanded her sister-Regent to sit with her on a second throne behind a curtain. And the Empress Mother would not sit without this curtain. The Dragon Throne was empty and would be empty, she declared, until the young Emperor could himself rule the nation. Behind the silken curtain, then, the two Empress Dowagers sat side by side, surrounded by their ladies and eunuchs, and to the right of the empty throne Prince Kung stood and heard the memorials of princes and ministers and all who brought their petitions.

Foremost among the suppliants were some who came one winter's day to beseech the Regents to end the rule of the rebel Hung in the southern city of Nanking. The Viceroys of those provinces had been driven away and now they appeared to ask for redress.

The elder Viceroy, who had long ruled the province of Kiangsu, was old and fat. A little beard hung from his chin and two long ends of gray hair on his upper lip were mingled with his scanty beard. He knelt uneasily, the cold marble of the floor creeping through the horsehair cushions to his knees. Yet kneel he must before the empty Throne and the hanging silken curtain.

"This rebel Hung," he declared, "began his evil career as a Christian. That is, he ate a foreign religion. Nor is he a true Chinese. His father was a farmer, an ignorant man of no learning, one of the dark-skinned Hakka tribe of southern hillmen. But this Hung, whose name is Hsiu Tsuan, wished to rise and he studied and went up for imperial examination, hoping to become a governor. He failed, and tried again and failed again. Three times he failed, but somewhere as he came and went he met a Christian who told him of the descent to earth of the foreign god Jesus and his incarnation as a human being, so that when he was killed by enemies he rose again and ascended once more on High. Therefore Hung, downcast by failure, envied the god and he began to have dreams and visions and he declared himself the reincarnation of Jesus, and he summoned all discontents and rebellious sons to follow him, so that he could with their help overthrow the dynasty and set up a new kingdom under his own rule which was to be called the Kingdom of the Great Peace, and he swore that the rich would all be made poor and the poor would become rich, those that are high be brought low, and the low raised up. With such promises his followers were many and their number has swelled into the millions. By robbery and murder he has taken lands and gold, and he has bought guns from the white men. Bandits and disorderly persons join themselves to him daily and they call him Heavenly King. Under his magic powers his followers fall into trances and see visions. It is said that this Heavenly King can cut soldiers out of paper and breathe upon them and they become men. Good people everywhere are distracted with terror. Indeed, our whole country will be lost unless this devil is destroyed. Yet who dares to approach him? Without conscience, without fear, caring nothing for right or wrong, he confounds the righteous."

Behind the yellow silk curtain, the Empress Mother heard this memorial with increasing anger. Was one man to destroy the nation while her son was but a child? The Imperial Armies must be reorganized. New generals must be raised up. She could be lenient where it was well to be lenient, but she would not longer tolerate this rebel, lest he eat up the realm, and then who could drive him out?

After audience that day, when Prince Kung came as usual to her private throne room to confer with her, he found a woman cold, haughty, determined. This was her other self. For she had two selves among her many, and these two as different as man from woman. She could be lenient so that the people called her Our Benevolent and Sacred Mother, and Kuan Yin of the Benign Countenance, and she could be hard and cruel as a headsman at the block. On this day Prince Kung found no Benevolent Mother nor Benign Countenance but a strong, angry queen, who would have no weakness in her ministers.

"Where is that general who commands our Imperial Armies?" she demanded from her throne. "Where is that Tseng Kuo-fan?"

Now Tseng Kuo-fan, Commander of the Imperial Armies against Chinese rebels, was the son of a great country family in the mid-southern province of Hunan. His grandfather had taught him wisdom and learning, and, inspired by this ancestor, the young man studied well and went up for the imperial examinations, at which he early won high honors, and he was soon received at the capital and given a post in government. When the rebellion rose, Tseng Kuo-fan, already experienced in the affairs of government, was appointed by the Throne to go south, there to organize the imperial armies which were being routed by the rebel Hung. Tseng Kuo-fan then trained the noble army called the Hunan Braves, and before he sent them against the rebels he seasoned them in war against local bandits. Indeed, so long did he train those peasant warriors that other generals were angry, for the rebel Hung was winning half the south away, and they complained against Tseng Kuo-fan for his long delay. The Empress Mother now enforced the complaints of warriors by her own command.

"This Tseng Kuo-fan," she told the Prince Kung, "how dare he keep back the full force of the Braves while every day the rebels rob us of more southern provinces? When the realm is gone, what value are his Braves?"

"Most High," the Prince replied, "the Braves cannot be everywhere at once, even when they attack."

"They must be everywhere at once," the Empress Mother declared. "It is their leader's duty to send them everywhere, striking here where the rebels gather, there where they plan to attack and anywhere that they threaten to break through our ranks. A stubborn man, this Tseng Kuo-fan, pursuing his own plans alone!"

"Most High," the Prince said, "I venture to propose a strategy. The English, with whom we presently are in a state of truce, have urged us to accept an English warrior to organize our resistance to the rebels. At first these white men approved the rebel Hung because he calls himself a Christian, but now they see him as a madman, and we have the advantage."

The Empress considered what Prince Kung had said. Her slender hands had rested on the carved arms of her throne, as peaceful as jeweled birds. Soon her fingers began a restless drumming, her golden nail shields striking against the hard wood.

"Does Tseng Kuo-fan know the English make this offer?" she inquired.

"He knows," Prince Kung replied, "and will have none of it. I do believe this general is so stubborn that he would rather lose the realm to a rebel of our own than win by a foreigner."

She began suddenly to like this Tseng Kuo-fan. "His reason?" she inquired.

"If we accept help from the English, he says they will surely ask a price."

The jeweled hands gripped the chair. "True, true," she cried. "They will claim the land they saved for us. Ha, I begin to trust this Tseng Kuo-fan! But I will have no more delay. He must cease his preparations and begin attack. Let him surround the city of Nanking and gather all his forces in a closing circle about that place. If the leader Hung is killed, the followers will disperse."

"Most High," the Prince said coldly, "I venture at my own risk to say that I doubt it wise for you to advise Tseng Kuo-fan in matters of war."

She flashed her great eyes at him sidewise. "I do not ask for your advice, Prince."

Her voice was gentle but he saw her face grow white with rage and her frame trembled. He bowed his head, controlling his own anger, and immediately he withdrew from her presence. When he was gone she came down from her throne and went to her writing table and there wrote her own edict to the distant general.

"Hard pressed though you may be," she wrote, after greeting, "it is time now to put forth all strength. Bring to your side your younger brother, Tseng Kuo-ch'uan. Call him from Kiangsi to advance on Anhuei province with you. Seize Anking, the provincial capital, and make it the first step in the large plan to seize Nanking. We know that Anking has been held for nine years by the rebels, and doubtless they call it their home. Dislodge them, that they may know what it is to be driven from entrenchment. Next, recall from his guerrilla warfare the general, Pao Ch'ao. This man is fearless, brave in attack, and loyal to the Throne. We recall how he struck down the rebels at Yochow and Wuchang, though often wounded. Keep this general flexible, ready to move swiftly with his armies, so that when you encircle the central city of Nanking, tightening the circle day by day, Pao Ch'ao may be detached to fly to the rear if the rebels rise again behind you in Kiangsi. For you have a double task—to kill the leader Hung, and while you press toward this end, to scotch every uprising that may spring up behind your circle. Meanwhile, do not memorialize the Throne with difficulties. You may not complain. What must be done, shall be done, if not by you, then by another. Reward will be generous when the rebel Hung is dead."

In such words, interspersed with frequent courtesies and compliments, the Empress Mother shaped her edict and with her own hands she stamped the imperial seal upon the parchment and summoning the Chief Eunuch she sent the edict to Prince Kung to be copied for the records and then taken south by courier to Tseng Kuo-fan.

The Chief Eunuch returned with the jade emblem that was Prince Kung's reply to prove he had received the edict and would obey. This the Empress Mother received and she smiled, her eyes like dark jewels beneath her black lashes.

"Did he say a word?" she asked.

"Benevolent," the Chief Eunuch replied, "the Prince read the edict line by line, and then he said, 'An emperor sits inside this woman's brain.' "

The Empress Mother laughed softly behind her embroidered sleeve. "Did he—did he, indeed!"

The Chief Eunuch, knowing how she loved to hear such praise, added to it.

"Most High, I say the Prince speaks truly. So say we all."

He touched the tip of his tongue to his handsome lips, and grinned and went away before she could reproach him.

Still smiling when he was gone, she fell into reflection. What should be the name for her son in his new reign? The Three Traitors had chosen the name Chi Hsiang, which is "Auspicious Happiness." She would not have the empty windy words, signifying nothing. No, she craved a sound strong peace, founded on unity within the nation, the people willing subjects and the Throne benevolent. Peace and benevolence—she loved good words fitly placed, suited to their time, exact in meaning. Her taste in words had been shaped by masters in prose and poetry, and now after long thought, she chose two words to be her son's name as Emperor. These words T'ung, meaning to pervade, and Chih, meaning peace, a tranquil peace, rooted deep in heart and spirit, she chose. It was a bold choice, for the times were troubled and the nation was beset by enemies. Yet by this name she announced her will for peace, and for her to will was also to do.

She had won the people's faith. Affairs large and small of the whole realm were brought daily to her Audience Hall. Such small matters as the curbing of a distant magistrate who oppressed his region cruelly, or in a city the price of rice which rose too high because a handful of men had bought the surplus of the last year's harvest, or a decree that since snow had not fallen in late winter when the wheatfields needed snow as fertilizer, the gods must be persuaded by three days of public reproach, the priests carrying the gods out from their pleasant temples to survey the dry and frozen fields, from such small matters to the great ones of protecting coastlines from the ships of foreign enemies and regulating the hateful opium trade with white men, the Empress Mother found patience for all.

Yet she remembered also her vast household in the palaces. She took most jealous notice of her son, keeping him beside her each day for as long as she could, he running about her Audience Hall or in her private library where she read memorials and wrote her commands, and while she worked she lifted her eyes often to watch him and paused to feel if his flesh were solid and cool, the skin moist but not damp, and she looked at the color of his eyes, the dark luminous and black and the white very pure, and she looked inside his mouth to see the soundness of his teeth and if his tongue were red and his breath sweet, and she heard his voice and listened for his laughter. And while she did this, she thought beyond him of the needs of all. She scanned the household bills, the records of food received as tribute, of foods bought, of silks and satins received and stored, and not one bolt of silk was taken from the storehouses without her private seal set to the order. She knew well how thievery within a palace spreads at last to all the nation, and she let every serving man and woman and every prince and minister feel the coldness of her watching eyes upon him.

Yet she rewarded richly and often. A eunuch who obeyed her well was given silver and a faithful serving woman gained a satin jacket. Not all rewards were costly. When she had eaten her fill of dishes on the imperial table, while her ladies waited, she would summon one who pleased her to eat of her own favorite dish and by this mark of favor insure the lady's place within the palace, for all made haste to serve one favored by the Empress Mother.

None knew except herself the great rewards she planned for those two, Jung Lu and Prince Kung. She had delayed the presentations until she could decide which should come first. Jung Lu had saved her life and the Emperor's and for this he deserved whatever she willed to give him. But Prince Kung had saved the capital, not by arms but by the skill of his bargaining with the enemy. True, much was lost. The treaty lay heavy on the Throne, and she did not let herself forget that within the walls of the capital white men now lived and with them their aides and families. Yet the city was not destroyed as the enemy had threatened to destroy it. The Summer Palace she had resolutely forgotten, until she remembered against her will the gardens and the lakes, the rockeries and grottoes, the fairy pagodas hung against the hills, the treasure houses of tribute from around the four seas, the libraries, the books and the paintings, the jade, the splendid furniture. At such times her heart hardened against Prince Kung. Could he not have prevented somehow the fearful loss? More loss was it than to herself who loved the Summer Palace, more loss even than to one nation, for such stores of beauty belonged to beauty everywhere, a sacred treasure. Then Jung Lu she would put first. He at least had not allowed destruction. Yet her hardening heart could still be prudent and prudence told her that she must summon Prince Kung and pretend to ask his advice.

She waited, therefore, for a fortunate day, and this came after heavy snowfall, for the gods, besought and urged and blamed, had seen at last the dry fields and hungry peasants and thus sent a heavy snow to cover city and countryside, so deep that it was full three weeks before the last white drift was gone. The fields which had been bitter dry were now a soft green beneath the snow, and when the sun had shone a few mild days, the winter wheat sprang up as far as eye could reach. For this the Empress Mother was given full thanks, and the people said it was her grace and power that had compelled the gods.

This, then, was the fortunate day, a day in late winter and so near to spring that a warm mist hung over the city, as hot sun shone down upon cold earth. The Empress Mother sent the Chief Eunuch to summon Prince Kung to her private Audience Hall. He came soon, splendid in his robe of state, a blue brocade from neck to ankle, a dark hue, for the Court was still in mourning and must be for three years after the death of an emperor. He looked so proud, so stately, as he approached her throne, that she was displeased. He bowed, she fancied, somewhat slightly, as though he grew familiar. A thrust of secret anger stabbed her breast, but she put it aside. She had the task of winning him to something that she wished. It was not the time to reproach him for his pride.

"I pray you let us not stand on ceremony," she said, her voice pure music. "Let us confer together. You are my lord's brother, upon whom he bade me always lean when he was gone."

Thus invited he sat down at the right side of the hall and now she did not like the readiness with which he did what she had bade him do. True, he made a show of protest, though only with a word or two, before he sat in her presence.

"I have in my mind," she said, "to bestow a reward upon the Commander of the Imperial Guard. I do not forget that he saved my life when the traitors would have taken it. His loyalty to the Dragon Throne is like the Mount of Omei, never to be shaken, steadfast in every storm. I do not value my life overmuch, yet had I died, those traitors would have kept the throne for themselves, and never would the Heir have been the Emperor. The reward is not for my sake but for my son, the Emperor, and through him the people, for had those traitors won their way, the Throne would have fallen."

Now Prince Kung did not look at her face while she spoke, but his acute hearing and his clever mind perceived inner meaning in what she said.

"Most High," he said, "what reward have you in mind?"

She seized the moment boldly. It was not her habit to evade a crisis. "The post of a Grand Councilor has been empty since Su Shun's death. It is my will to put Jung Lu there."

She lifted her head that she might look into the Prince's face, but when he felt her powerful gaze upon him he returned the look.

"It is impossible."

These were his words, while eyes met eyes.

"Nothing is impossible if I will it."

These were her words, and her eyes flamed against his eyes. But he was ruthless.

"You know that gossip creeps unending through the Court. You know how rumor whispers its way from eunuch to eunuch. Deny rumor as I do always for the honor of the Throne and for my clan, yet I cannot kill it."

She made her eyes innocent. "What gossip?"

He could not be persuaded of her innocence and yet since she was so young a woman, it might be she was still innocent. And speak he must, having said so much, and he spoke plainly.

"Some doubt the young Emperor's paternity."

She looked away, her eyelids fluttered, her lips trembled and she put her silk kerchief to her mouth.

"Oh," she moaned, "and I thought my enemies were dead!"

He said, "I speak for your sake. I am no enemy."

Tears, hanging on her lashes, dried in rage. "Yet you should have put to death the ones who spoke such filth against me! You should not have let them live an hour. If you did not dare, then should you have told me and I would myself have seen them die!"

Was she innocent? He did not know, and would never know. He stayed silent.

She drew herself erect upon her throne. "I ask advice no more. Today, as soon as you are gone, I shall proclaim Jung Lu my Grand Councilor. And if any dares to speak against him—"

"What will you do?" he asked. "What if the whole Court is swept by gossip?"

She leaned forward and forgot courtesy. "I'll silence them! And I bid you, Prince, be silent!"

Never in all their years had these two come to open anger. Then they recalled the mutual need of loyalty, each to the other.

The Prince was first. "Most High, forgive me." He rose to his feet and made obeisance.

She replied in her gentlest voice. "I do not know why I spoke so to you, who have taught me all I know. It is I who must ask you to forgive me."

He would have made protest quickly, but she put up her hand to prevent him.

"No, do not speak—not yet. For I have long had it in my mind to give to you the best reward of all. You shall receive the noble title of Prince Advisor to the Throne with full emolument. And by my special decree—that is to say, by our decree, the two Regents, my sister Consort and myself—the title of the Duke of Ch'in, which my late lord bestowed upon you in gratitude for loyalty, shall now be made hereditary."

These were high honors and Prince Kung was bewildered by the sudden bestowal. Again he made obeisance and he said in his usual kind and mellow fashion,

"Most High, I wish no reward for what was my duty. My duty first was to my elder brother, then to my Emperor who chanced by birth to be my elder brother. My duty now is first to his son and then to that son as the young Emperor. Next is my duty to you, the Empress Mother, and to both of you, two Empresses, who are the Regents. You see how full my duty is and for none of it should I be rewarded."

"Indeed, you must accept," the Empress Mother said, and thus began a courteous battle between them, she insisting and he refusing, until at last they came to graceful agreement.

"I beg to be allowed at least to refuse a title which my sons can inherit," Prince Kung said at last. "It is not in our tradition that sons inherit what their fathers win. I would have my sons win their own honors."

To this the Empress Mother could but agree. "Then let the matter be postponed until a time more lucky. Yet I ask a gift from you, too, most honored Prince."

"It is given," Prince Kung promised.

"Let me adopt your daughter, Jung-chun, as princess royal. Give me this happiness to comfort me and let me feel you have some small reward for your true and loyal aid against the traitors at Jehol. Did you not answer my summons? I remember no delay."

It was now the Prince's turn to yield, and he did so with magnanimity. From that time on his daughter was a princess royal and so faithfully did she serve her sovereign mistress that at last the Empress Mother bestowed upon her a palanquin whose satin curtains were imperial yellow, to use as a perpetual right, as long as she lived, as though she were indeed a princess born.

So the Empress Mother made her plans. She did nothing carelessly or in haste. A plan began with the seed of a wish, a longing, a desire. The seed, planted, might lie fallow for a year, two years, ten years, until the hour came for it to grow, but the flowering came at last.

It was summer again, a pleasant season when winds came from the south and the east, bringing mists and gentle rain and even the scent of the salt seas of which the Empress Mother had heard and had never seen, though she loved water in pools, in fountains and in lakes. As the deep and slumberous heat of high summer crept behind the high walls of the Forbidden City, she longed for the palaces of Yüan Ming Yüan which were no more. She had never seen the ruins nor beheld the ashes, for that she could not endure. Yet, she told herself, there remained the famous Sea Palaces. Why should she not make for herself there a place of repose and pleasure?

So thinking, she decreed a day when her ladies and eunuchs should accompany her palanquin in their sedans and mule carts and on horseback, each according to habit, and though the journey to the Sea Palaces was short, not more than half a mile away, the stir and commotion of the Court procession was such that the streets were cleared by the Imperial Guard lest an evildoer be tempted to raise his hand. The pleasure parks of the Three Sea Palaces were not new to the Empress Mother, for she had visited them many times to make sacrifices in spring on the Altar of Silkworms to the God of Mulberries, and then, entering the Hall of Silkworms, there to offer sacrifices again before the Goddess of Silkworms. This was her yearly duty, but she came sometimes, too, for boating on one of the three lakes called seas, or in winter she came to watch the Court make skating parties on the lake called the North Sea, and she liked to see the eunuchs in bright garments as they skated skillfully on the thick ice smoothed by hot irons before the fête. These lakes were ancient, and were first made by the emperors of the Nurchen Tartars, five hundred years earlier. Yet those emperors could not dream of the beauty which Yung Lo, the first emperor of the Chinese dynasty of Ming, had later added. He caused them to be deepened and bridges to be built to small islands where were pavilions, each carved and painted and each different from the others. Mighty rocks, curiously shaped by rivers, were brought from the south and from the northwest to make gardens, and palaces and halls were built in these gardens and ancient twisted trees were planted and tended as carefully as though they were human, and indeed to some of these trees were given human titles, such as duke or king. In the Hall of Luster was a great Buddha, called the Jade Buddha, although the image was not jade but carved very cunningly from a white clear stone from Thibet. The Ancestor Ch'ien Lung loved the Sea Palaces and he made a library among them and named it Pine Hill, and named its three halls the Hall of Crystal Waters, the Veranda of Washing the Orchids, this rite of orchid-washing taking place on the fifth day of the fifth month of the moon year, and the Hall of Joyful Snow, so named from the poem by the poet Wang Shi-chih, who, while writing on one winter's day, was overjoyed by a sudden fall of snow. The verses he made, though carved upon marble, were lost for centuries until a common workman found the stone among ruins and gave it to the Ancestor Ch'ien Lung, then ruling, who placed it in this suitable hall.

Every part of the Sea Palaces was enriched with such legends, and the Empress Mother knew them all from her much reading of many books. No part of that pleasure place did she love better than the pavilion by the South Sea, called the Pavilion of the Thoughts of Home. This pavilion was two-storied, built thus by Ch'ien Lung, so that his favorite, the Fragrant Concubine, whose name was Hsiang Fei, because the sweat from her delicate body was sweet as perfume, could look toward her lost land. This Fragrant Concubine had been taken from her husband and her home in Turkestan, where she was a princess of Kashgaria. Booty of war she was, for Ch'ien Lung had heard of her magic beauty and especially of the softness of her white skin, and he commanded his generals to bring her to him, by force if they must. But she was faithful to her husband and she would not leave her home for any reason, and so a war began for her sake. When her husband was defeated and took his own life, then this princess had no defense and she was compelled to come to the Emperor of China. Yet she would not yield herself to him, and although he loved her at first sight, he would not take her by force, desiring the full and subtle pleasure of her yielding. Therefore he built the pavilion from whose tower she could look toward her lost home and he waited patiently until she would have him, and this he did against the advice of the Empress Dowager, his mother, who in anger bade her son send back the beautiful and invincible woman to Turkestan again. For the Fragrant Concubine would not tolerate so much as the approach of the Emperor to her side, saying that if he touched his palm to her hand she would kill herself and him.

One winter's day, when it was his duty to worship at the Altar of Heaven on behalf of his people, his mother, the Empress Dowager, sent for the Fragrant Concubine and commanded her either to yield to the Emperor or take her own life. The princess chose to take her life, and when the Empress Dowager heard the choice, she commanded her to be led to an empty building and given a silken rope, and there the lonely lady hung herself. A faithful eunuch took the news in secret to the Emperor, who, though he was fasting in the Hall of Abstinence to purify himself for the sacred sacrifice, forgot his duty and hastened to his palace. He was too late. His beloved had escaped him and forever. Such was the legend.

For her own the Empress Mother now chose the many halls and courtyards, the pools and flower gardens of the Palace of Compassion, which stands near the Middle Sea. She loved especially the rock gardens, and though she allowed herself no parties or gay gatherings, such as she had used to make at the Summer Palace of Yüan Ming Yüan, where she and her ladies wore costumes of goddesses and fairies, as her playful mood enjoyed, yet now for the first time since the death of the Emperor, her late lord, she did allow herself to look at plays, not large plays or merry ones, but sad quiet plays, portraying the wisdom of the soul. For this purpose she caused to be opened a gate from her rock gardens into an unused courtyard beside a closed hall, and she ordered those eunuchs who were carpenters and painters and masons to make a great stage near a pleasant space where she and her ladies could sit in secluded comfort and watch the actors. Her royal box was as large as a room, and she had it raised beyond a narrow brook which ran through the courtyard, and this flowing water softened the voices of the actors and made music of their words. A marble bridge, no wider than a footpath, spanned the brook.

To this place one day, when she felt her secret plans were ripe, the Empress Mother commanded Jung Lu to be summoned. It was her way never to tie two deeds too close, so that none could say, "First she did this, and then she did that," and so comprehend by chance her private mind. No, she let a full two months pass by after she had made Prince Kung's daughter her adopted child before she took the next step and sent for Jung Lu as though upon today's whim, she who was too wise for whims.

The play was going on before her eyes, the actors all eunuchs, for since the time of the Ancestor Ch'ien Lung no female could play a part upon the stage because his own mother had been an actress, and to honor her he allowed no woman to be like her. The play that day was one well known, *The Orphan of the Clan of Ch'ao,* and the Empress had seen it many times and her ears grew weary with the singing. Yet she did not wish to wound the actors and so while she sat listening and delicately tasting sweetmeats, her mind went to her secrets. So, she thought, why not summon Jung Lu here, where all were assembled, and while the play went on, make known to him her will? She must hear his own willingness to take Su Shun's place, before she could reward him in public.

She beckoned Li Lien-ying to her side. "Bid my kinsman to come hither. I have a command."

He grinned and made obeisance and went away cracking his knuckles, and the Empress Mother turned her head to the stage and seemed absorbed again in the play. Her ladies sat in their places around her. Did any see her eyes fall upon her, then that one would rise. In a few minutes, therefore, Lady Mei, always watchful of her sovereign, felt a gaze upon her and looking from the play she saw that the Empress Mother was looking at her with long and thoughtful eyes. She rose at once and bowed. The Empress Mother beckoned with her down-turned hand and half timidly the lovely girl went to her.

"Lean your ear to me," the Empress Mother commanded. The singing on the stage silenced her voice to all but the lady herself, who leaned her head and in her ear she heard her sovereign say these words:

"I have not forgot my promise to you, child. This day I will fulfill it."

Lady Mei continued to stand, her head bowed to hide her blushing face.

The Empress Mother smiled. "I see you know what promise."

"Can I forget a promise that Majesty has made?" This was Lady Mei's reply.

The Empress Mother touched her cheek. "Prettily said, child! Well, you shall see—"

By this time Jung Lu was walking to the royal box. The afternoon sun shone down upon his tall figure and upright head. He wore his uniform, dark blue in mourning for the dead Emperor, and from his belt hung his broad sword, the silver scabbard glittering. With firm steps he approached the dais and made obeisance. The Empress Mother inclined her head and motioned to a seat near her low throne. He hesitated and sat down.

For a while she seemed not to heed him. The star of the play came on the stage to sing his most famous song and all eyes were upon him, and so were hers. Suddenly she began to speak, not turning her eyes from the stage.

"Kinsman, I have had in mind all this while a good reward for your service to me and to the young Emperor."

"Majesty," Jung Lu said, "indeed, I did no more than my duty."

"You know you saved our lives," she said.

"That was my duty," he insisted.

"Do you think I forget?" she asked in reply. "I forget nothing then

184

or now. I shall reward you, whether or no, and it is my will that you take the place left empty by the traitor Su Shun."

"Majesty—" he began impetuously, but she put up her hand to silence him.

"You must accept," she said, still gazing at the stage. "I need you near me. Whom can I trust? Prince Kung, yes—I know his name is on your lips. Well, I trust him! But does he love me? Or—do I love him?"

"You must not speak so," he muttered.

The voice upon the stage soared high, the drums beat, the ladies cried out their praises and threw flowers and sweets to the singing eunuch.

"I love you always," she said.

He did not turn his head.

"You know that you love me," she said.

Still he was silent.

She turned her eyes to him then.

"Do you not?" she asked clearly.

He muttered, staring at the stage, "I will not have you fall from where you have risen and because of me."

She smiled and though she turned her head away again her great eyes shone. "When you are Grand Councilor, I may summon you as often as need be, for the burden of the realm will fall upon you, too. The Regents lean upon the Princes, the Grand Councilors and ministers."

"I shall not obey such summons save in company with all councilors."

"Yes, you shall," she said willfully.

"And spoil your name?"

"I'll save my own name and by this means—you shall wed a lady whom I choose. If you have a wife young and beautiful, who can speak evil?"

"I will wed no one!" His voice was bitter between his teeth.

Upon the stage the famous actor made his last bow and sat down. The property man ran forward to bring a bowl of tea. The actor took off his weighty many-colored helmet and wiped his sweat away with a silk kerchief. In the small theater the serving eunuchs wrung soft towels from basins of perfumed water steaming hot and tossed them here and there where hands were raised to catch them. The eunuch Li Lien-ying brought a hot perfumed towel on a gold salver to the Empress Mother. She took it and touched it delicately first to her temples and then to her palms, and when the eunuch was gone again, she spoke low and sharply.

"I do command you to wed Lady Mei. No, you shall not speak. She is the gentlest woman in our Court, the truest soul, and she loves you."

"Can you command my heart?" he cried beneath his breath.

"You need not love her," she said cruelly.

"If she is what you say, then I would do her such injustice as is against my nature," he retorted.

"Not if she knows you do not love her and still longs to be your wife."

He pondered this awhile. Upon the stage a new young actor stood and sang his best, while serving eunuchs brought trays of sweetmeats, hot and cold, to feed the throng. Since the actor was unknown, he was not heeded, and eyes crept toward the Empress Mother. She felt them on her, and she knew she must dismiss Jung Lu.

She spoke between her set teeth. "You may not disobey me. It is decreed that you shall accept this marriage, and on the same day you shall take your seat among the Councilors. And now retire!"

He rose and made his deep obeisance. His silence gave assent. She inclined her head. With careful grace she lifted her head again and seemed intent upon the stage.

In the night, when she was alone, the scene returned to her. She could not remember what story the actors played upon the stage when he was gone, nor what songs they sang. She had sat fanning herself slowly, the stage a blur before her eyes, and then, her whole body tense in agony, she had folded the fan and stayed motionless, gazing at the stage while pain pervaded all her being. She loved one only and she would love him until she died. He was the lover whom she craved, the husband she denied herself.

And as her mind fluttered here and there like a caged bird against the bars, she thought of a queen, an English queen, Victoria, of whom Prince Kung had told her. Ah, fortunate queen, who was allowed to wed a man she loved! But then Victoria was not concubine or widow to an emperor. She was born to her throne and she could lift up the man she loved to sit beside her. But no woman could be born to sit upon the Dragon Throne, and she could only seize it for herself.

And thus am I, the Empress Mother said to herself, so much the stronger than that English Queen. I have seized my throne—

But is strength comfort for a woman?

She lay in her great bed, still wakeful, though the watchman struck his brass gong twice to signify that midnight was two hours past. She lay motionless while pain ran through her very blood and her breath caught deep and hard inside her bosom. And why was she not all woman? Why could she not be content to yield the throne and be his wife whom she so loved? What pride possessed her to rise to yet higher power? How did it serve her, a woman, if a dynasty held or fell?

186

She saw herself at last, a woman in her secret need and longing, yet not a woman in her lust for more than love. Place and power, the pride of being above all—these too were her necessity. But surely she was woman in her love for her son? Her relentless self replied that though he to her was all child, and she to him all mother, yet beyond the closeness of their blood-bond was another bond. He was the Emperor and she the Empress Mother. The common boons of womanhood were not enough. Oh, cursed woman to be born with such a heart and brain!

She turned upon her pillow and wept with pity for herself. I cannot love, she thought. I cannot love enough to make me willing to yield myself to love. And why? Because I know myself too well. Were I to cramp myself into my love, my heart would die, and having given all, I would have nothing left but hatred for him. And yet I love him!

The watchman beat his bronze gong again and called his cry. "Three hours past midnight!"

She pondered then awhile on love, weeping when thought grew too sorrowful. Suppose, when Jung Lu was wed to Lady Mei, that she could persuade him to meet her in some secret room of a forgotten palace. Her eunuch could be watchman, she would pay him well and did she suspect his loyalty, a word would put a dagger in his heart. If, once or twice, a few times, say, in her life years, she could meet her love as only woman, then she could be happy, having so much, if not all. Did she not hold his heart?

Ah, but could she hold his heart? While she sat upon her throne another woman would lie in his bed. He being man, could he remember always that it was the Empress whom he loved and not the woman in his arms?

Her tears burned dry in sudden jealousy. She rose in her bed and threw aside her silken coverlet and drawing up her knees she laid her forehead down and bit her lips and sobbed silently, lest her woman hear.

The watchman beat his gong again and called, "Four hours past midnight!"

When she was spent with bitter weeping she lay down once more, exhausted. She was born what she was, a woman and more than a woman. The very weight of genius was her destruction. Tears trembled on her eyelids again.

And then from somewhere in herself an alien strength welled up. Destruction? If she allowed herself to be destroyed by her own love and jealousy, then call it true destruction, because she was not great enough to use the size of her own nature.

Yet how strong I am, she muttered. Yes, she would make of strength a comfort. The tears dried on her eyelids and through her veins came the old powerful faith in what she was. She reckoned up her thoughts and separated true from false. Madness, folly, vain dreaming, to imagine a secret room in some forgotten palace! He would never take such yielding. If she would not give up all for love, he would be too proud to be her private lover. Once—yes, once, but only once, when he was still a boy on that past day—and she had found him virgin. Well, she had that first fruit, a memory to keep, yet not to think about but put away, forever unforgotten. He would not yield again.

And now there came a thought to her so new that she was struck with wonder. Grant that she could not love any man enough to forsake all and follow after love. Let it be so, for so she was born. Yet was it not a gift for him if she let him love her with all his heart and pour his love into her service?

It may be that I love him best, she thought, when I accept his love for me and let it be my refuge.

With this wisdom a strange peace came flowing gently through her veins and stilled her restless heart. She closed her eyes.

The watchman's gong beat once again. She heard his morning call.

"Dawn," he sang, "and all is well!"

She set the wedding day early. Let it be soon, that it might be the sooner irrevocable! Yet Lady Mei could not be married from the imperial palaces, though she had no other home.

"Summon the Chief Eunuch," the Empress Mother commanded.

Li Lien-ying, standing silent in his usual place by the door of the Imperial Library, where the Empress had now spent four days without speaking to anyone except to give commands, went with all speed to obey. The Chief Eunuch was in his own rooms, taking his midmorning breakfast, a meal of various meats, which he ate slowly and with relish. Since the death of his late sovereign he had comforted himself with pleasures, but now he hastened to obey the summons.

The Empress Mother looked up from her book when he appeared before her and when she saw him she spoke with much distaste.

"You, An Teh-hai, do you dare to let yourself become so smug? I swear you've put on fat even in these days of mourning."

He tried a look of sadness. "Venerable, I am full of water. Prick me and liquid flows. I am ill, your Majesty, not fat."

She heard this with her usual look of sternness when she felt it necessary to reproach one beneath her. Nothing escaped her notice, and though her mind and heart were occupied with her own secret woes, she could, as usual, turn her thought for the moment to so small a matter as the Chief Eunuch's waxing fat.

"I know how you eat and drink," she said. "You grow rich, you know you do. Take care that you do not grow too rich. Remember that my eyes are on you."

The Chief Eunuch made humble reply. "Majesty, we all know your eyes are everywhere at once."

She continued to look at him severely for a moment, her immense eyes burning upon him, and though he could not in proper courtesy lift his eyes to her face, nevertheless he felt her look and began to sweat. Then she smiled.

"You are too handsome to grow fat," she said. "And how can you play the hero on the stage if your belt does not meet around your middle?"

He laughed. It was true he loved to act a hero in court plays. "Majesty," he promised, "I'll starve myself to please you."

In good humor then she said, "I did not call you here to talk about you, but to say it is my will that you arrange for the marriage of Lady Mei to Jung Lu, Commander of the Guard. You know he is to wed her?"

"Yes, Majesty," the Chief Eunuch said.

He knew of the marriage as he knew everything within the palace walls. Li Lien-ying told him all that he heard, and so did every eunuch and serving woman, and the Empress Mother knew this.

"The lady has no parents," she continued. "I must therefore stand in the place of parent to her. Yet as Regent I stand also in the place of the young Emperor and it would not be fitting to give her the appearance of a princess by my presence at her marriage. You are to take her to my nephew's house, the Duke of Hui. Let her be accompanied with all honor and ceremony. From that house my kinsman, the Commander, will receive her."

"Majesty, when is this day to be?" he inquired.

"Tomorrow she shall go to the Duke. You are to go today and bid the household prepare for her. He has two old aunts, and let them be her motherly companions. Then you shall go to the Commander and announce that I have decided that the marriage must take place two days from now. When it is over you are to come and tell me. Until she is his wife, do not trouble me."

"Majesty, I am your servant." He bowed and went away. But she had already turned to her book and she did not lift her head.

Upon her books she seemed intent for two whole days. Late at night while serving eunuchs mended candles and hid their yawns behind their sleeves, she read slowly and carefully through one book and then an-

189

other. These were books of medicine, of which she knew nothing, but she was determined to know everything, and whatever she was most ignorant of, that she longed most to know. This was not only her true craving for knowledge and her curiosity concerning the universe, but also it was that she might always know more than any person to whom she spoke. Thus in these two days, while the marriage she had ordained took place, she rigorously denied her imagination and she forced her whole brain upon an ancient work of medical jurisprudence. This work, in many volumes, was well known to all courts of law, and even local magistrates in petty courts throughout the nation studied its precepts before judging the case of any who died from unknown causes. The Board of Punishments shaped its practice by this work, and some eighteen years ago the Emperor, T'ao Huang, then ruling, annoyed by the disorder of the earlier volumes, had commanded a well-known judge, named Sung Tz'u, to compile all past versions into one edition. This great book, too, the Empress now studied, closing her mind to all else.

Thus she compelled herself to learn that the human body has three hundred and sixty-five bones, the number being the same as the number of days that the sun rises and sets within a solar year, that males have twelve ribs on each side, eight long and four short, though females have fourteen ribs on each side. She read that if parent and child or husband and wife cut themselves and let their blood flow into a bowl of water, the two bloods will mix into one, but the blood of two strangers not related by such bonds will never mingle. She learned, too, the secrets of many poisons, how they can be used for illness or for death, and how their use may be concealed.

At the end of two days she had not once left the Imperial Library except to go to her palace for food and sleep. On the morning of the third day the eunuch Li Lien-ying coughed in the distance to announce himself. She looked up from the page where she was reading of the power of mandrake as a poison.

"What now?" she asked.

"Majesty, the Chief Eunuch is returned."

She closed the book and took the corner of the silken kerchief which hung from her jade shoulder button and touched it to her lips.

"Let him approach," she said.

The Chief Eunuch came and made his obeisance.

"Stand behind me to say what you have to say," she commanded.

He stood behind her and while she listened she gazed beyond the open doors into the great courtyard, where chrysanthemums blazed scarlet and gold in the calm and brilliant sunlight of that autumn day.

"Majesty," he began, "all has been done with due honor and propriety. The Commander sent the red bridal sedan to the palace of the Duke of Hui and the bearers withdrew. The two elder aunts of the Duke, as I instructed them under Your Majesty's order, then escorted the lady as the bride and they led her to the sedan and placed her therein and drew the inner curtain and locked the door. The bearers were called and they lifted the sedan and carried it to the palace of the Commander and the two elders accompanied it in their own sedans. At the palace of the Commander, two other elder ladies, who were the cousins of his father, met the bridal sedan and the four elders together led the bride into the palace. There the Commander waited, and with him stood his own generation, his parents being dead."

"Did the elders not powder the face of the bride with rice powder?" the Empress Mother inquired.

The Chief Eunuch made haste to correct his memory. "Majesty, they did so, and they dropped the maidenhood veil of red silk to cover her. Then she stepped over the saddle as the rite demands—the Commander's own Mongol saddle it was, which he had from his ancestors—and then she stepped over charcoal embers and so she entered into his palace, surrounded by the elder ladies. There an aged marriage singer waited and he bade the bridal couple kneel twice and give thanks to Heaven and to Earth. Then the elder ladies led the bride and groom into the bedchamber and they told the two to sit down on the marriage bed together."

"Whose robe was uppermost?" the Empress Mother asked.

"His," the Chief Eunuch replied and gave a snort of laughter. "He, Majesty, will rule in his own house."

"Well I know it," she said. "He has been stubborn from his birth. Proceed!"

"Then," the Chief Eunuch went on, "the two drank wine from two bowls wrapped in red satin, and they exchanged bowls and drank again and they ate rice cakes together in the same proper fashion. After that was held the wedding feast."

"Was it a great feast?" the Empress Mother asked.

"A proper feast," the Chief Eunuch said carefully, "neither too much nor too little."

"And it ended, doubtless," she said, "with dough strings in chicken broth."

"Signifying long life," the Chief Eunuch said.

He paused, waiting for the last question, the one most weighty, that must be asked the next morning after every wedding night throughout the nation. After long pause the question came.

"Was the marriage—consummated?" Her voice was small and strange.

"It was," the Chief Eunuch said. "I stayed the night and at dawn the bride's serving woman came to tell me. The Commander lifted the lady's bridal veil at midnight, using the fulcrum of a weight scale in ritual fashion. The serving woman then withdrew until the hour before dawn, when she was summoned. The elder cousins gave her the stained cloth. The bride was virgin."

The Empress Mother sat silent now, until the Chief Eunuch, hearing no dismissal, coughed to show he was still there. She started as though she had forgot him.

"Go," she said, "you have done well. I send reward tomorrow."

"Majesty, you are too kind," he said and went away.

She sat on then, watching the sunlight fall upon the brilliant flowers. A late butterfly hung quivering upon a crimson blossom, a creature of imperial yellow. An omen? She must remember to inquire of the Board of Astrologers to know what such an omen meant, a lucky sign surely, appearing at this instant when her heart was breaking. But she would not let it break. Hers was the hand that dealt the wound and hers the heart.

She rose and closed the book, and followed at a distance by her ugly, faithful eunuch, she returned to her own palace.

From this day on the Empress Mother changed the center of her life and fastened it upon her son. He was the cause of all she did, the reason for all she had done, and around his being she wound her concern and her constant thought. He was her healing and her consolation. In the many nights she could not sleep, when imagination presented scenes she could not share, in loneliness she rose and went to find her little boy. While he slept she sat beside him, holding his warm hand, and if he stirred she made it the excuse to lift him into her arms and let him sleep against her breast.

He was strong and beautiful, so fair-skinned her ladies said it was a pity that he was not a girl. Yet he was more than beautiful, for he had a mind which already the Empress knew was brilliant and most able. When he was four years old she had chosen tutors for him, and at five he could read not only his native Manchu, but Chinese books as well. His hand by instinct held the brush as an artist does, and she recognized in the still-childish writing a boldness and a firmness which would one day make him a calligrapher of strength and style. His memory was prodigious, he had but to hear a page read to him a time or two and he knew it. But she would not allow his tutors to spoil him with praise. She scolded them when she heard one exclaim his excellence.

"You must not compare him to any other child," she said. "You shall only compare what he does with what he can do. Say to him that his Ancestor Ch'ien Lung did far better than he, at five years of age."

While she thus commanded his tutors, she herself instilled into the child a pride as strong as her own. Not even his teachers might sit before him save only she, who was his mother. Did he dislike a tutor for some manner or for a trick of look or garb, then that one was dismissed, nor would she allow the least question or complaint.

"It is the Emperor's will," she said.

Had his been a smaller nature, surely he would have been changed and ruined by power given him so young, but the genius of this child was that he could not be spoiled. His place he took for granted as he accepted sun and rain, and he was tenderhearted, too, so that if a eunuch were whipped for some fault the little Emperor flew to rescue him. The Empress Mother could not so much as pull her woman's ears for clumsiness, for if she did, the little Emperor burst into tears.

She doubted at such times whether he were strong enough to be a ruler of a vast subject people, and yet at another time he could flash such heat and fury, he could be so imperious, that she was consoled. Indeed, she had once to intervene because her eunuch Li Lien-ying did not please His Majesty, who had commanded him to bring a music box from the foreign shop in the city. As was his duty, the eunuch had first inquired of the Empress Mother whether he should obey the little Emperor, and hearing what the son wished to have she forbade it in these words:

"Surely he shall have no foreign toy. Yet we must not refuse his will. Go to the marketplace and bring him back toy tigers and other beasts to amuse him. He will forget the music box."

Li Lien-ying obeyed, and he returned to the little Emperor with a basket of such toys, saying that he could not find the foreign shop but on the way he had found these clever creatures made of wood and ivory and with eyes of gems.

The little Emperor saw himself deceived and he turned into a baby tyrant. He pushed aside the toys, he rose from his small throne and strode about his nursery, his arms crossed upon his breast and his eyes, big like his mother's and as black, glittering with rage.

"Throw them away!" he cried. "Am I an infant that I play with toy animals? How dare you, Li Lien-ying, defy your sovereign? I will have you sliced for this! Send me here my guardsmen!"

And he gave command that the eunuch was indeed to be sliced, the flesh stripped from his bones for insubordination to the Throne. None dared to disobey. The guardsmen came and stood hesitating, reluctant, until a eunuch went in haste to find the Empress Mother, who came at once, her robes flying.

"My son," she cried, "my son, you may not put a man to death—not yet, my son!"

"Mother," her child said, very stately, "your eunuch has disobeyed not me but the Emperor of China."

She was so struck with this distinction between himself and his destiny that she was speechless for a moment, nor would she assert her own power.

"My son," she said, coaxingly, "think what you do! This eunuch is Li Lien-ying, who serves you in a hundred ways. Have you forgot?"

The little monarch stood his ground, he would have the eunuch sliced, until the Empress Mother summarily forbade it.

Nevertheless, this small matter forced her to see for herself that the boy needed a true man to take the place of the father that he never had.

Upon this she sent resolutely for Jung Lu, now Grand Councilor by her own decree. She had not seen him face to face since his marriage, and to shield her own heart from his penetration, she put on robes of state and sat in her private throne room surrounded by her ladies. True, the ladies stood apart, but there they were, their brilliant garments bright as hovering butterflies.

Jung Lu came in, no longer wearing his commander's uniform, but gowned as a councilor, his robe of gold brocaded satin reaching to his velvet boots, about his neck a chain of jewels hanging to his waist. Upon his head he wore a hat set with a button of red jade. She had known him always kingly in his looks but at this sight of him her heart quivered like a bird in hand. All the more then must she control her heart, who alone knew its secret. She let him kneel before her and she did not bid him rise. When she spoke it was half carelessly, her eyes imperious and weary.

"My son is old enough to ride a horse and draw a bow," she said, after greetings. "I remember that you sit a horse well and that you have the trick of being its master. As for the bow, it seems I once did hear that you are a hunter better than the best. I command you then to begin a new duty. Teach my son, the Emperor, to shoot an arrow straight to its target."

"Majesty, I will," he said, and did not lift his eyes.

How proud and cold he is, she thought, and now I see his revenge. Love or hate, he will never let me know what is between him and his wife—oh, me, desolate!

But her look did not change. "Begin tomorrow," she commanded.

"Let there be no delay. Take him with you to the archery fields. Each month hereafter I will see for myself what progress he has made and judge how able you are as a teacher."

"Majesty," he said, still kneeling, "I obey."

From that day on, after his morning with his tutors, the little Emperor spent his afternoon with Jung Lu. With tender pains the tall strong man instructed the boy, anxious when the bold boy beat his black Arabian to a gallop and yet he would not cry out his fear because he knew this child must never be afraid. And he was proud to find in this same princely child a true eye upon the arrow and a firm hand upon the bow. When each month the Empress Mother walked along the archery field, surrounded by her ladies, with what confidence did he display the child!

And she, seeing man and boy growing daily nearer to each other, spoke only a few words of cool praise. "My son does well, but so he should," she said.

Of her own yearning heart she showed not a glimpse. She let it burn inside her breast with pain and joy to see these two, whom she loved, as close as son and father.

"Majesty," Prince Kung said on a certain day thereafter, "I have summoned to the capital our two great generals, Tseng Kuo-fan and Li Hung-chang."

The Empress Mother, about to walk to the archery fields as was her habit each day, paused upon the threshold of her private throne room. Her ladies immediately surrounded her in their bright-hued semicircle. Prince Kung was the only man with whom she spoke face to face and by law he was her kinsman, the brother of the late Emperor, and she violated no custom in thus speaking to him, still young and handsome though he was. Nevertheless she was annoyed. He had come today when she had not summoned him, and this was an offense. None should so presume.

She stood, quelling the sudden anger in her breast. Then with her usual dignity and grace she turned and walked to the small throne in the middle of the hall. There she seated herself and she assumed the usual pose of Empress, her hands clasped lightly on her lap, her wide sleeves falling over them. She waited for the Prince to stand before her and was not pleased when, having made his obeisance, he sat down uninvited on a chair to the right of the low dais upon which her throne stood. To show her displeasure she said not a word, but she fastened upon him the piercing gaze of her great black eyes, not meeting his eyes, which would have been unseemly, but fixing her look upon the green jade button which fastened his robe at the throat.

But he did not wait for her to speak first. Instead, he began in his direct fashion to say why he had come.

"Majesty, I have purposely not troubled you with such affairs of state as were small enough for me to attend to for you. Thus I have received day by day the couriers from the south who bring the news of the continual war being waged by the Imperial Armies against the rebels."

"I am aware of that war," she said. Her voice was cold. "Did I not a month ago command this same Tseng Kuo-fan to attack the rebels on all sides?"

"He did," Prince Kung replied, not seeing her anger, "and the rebels drove him back. Fifteen days ago they announced their attack on Shanghai itself. This has stirred up the rich merchants in that city, not only the Chinese but also the white traders, and they are forming their own army, fearing that our soldiers will not be able to defend their city. I therefore sent for our two generals in order that I might know their strategy."

"You take too much upon yourself," she said with displeasure.

Prince Kung was amazed at this reproof. Until now the Empress Mother had been usually gracious and ready to approve what he did, and in his zeal to serve the Throne it was true that he had gradually assumed great responsibility. She was, moreover, a woman in spite of all, and he believed that no woman could master the affairs of state and the conduct of a ferocious war such as was now being waged, which did indeed shake the very foundations of the nation. These rebels had spread still further over the southern provinces, destroying city and town and burning villages and harvests, and the people were running everywhere in confusion. Millions had been killed, and in spite of years of fighting, the imperial soldiers were not able to end the rebellion, which now broke out everywhere like a forest fire. He had heard that the small army of Shanghai volunteers, which had been led by a white man surnamed Ward, was to be strengthened and improved by a new leader, one Gordon, an Englishman, for Ward had been shot in battle. This was clear and good enough, except that yet another white man, an American surnamed Bourgevine, was jealous of Gordon and wished to take the leadership for himself and in this he was supported by his fellow Americans. But the rumor was that Bourgevine was an adventurer and a scoundrel whereas Gordon was a good man and a proved soldier. Nevertheless if Gordon were successful in quelling the rebels, would not the English cry out that they had won the victory and must be rewarded?

It was not a matter of simple war. Harried and beset, Prince Kung had sent for the two imperial generals, Tseng Kuo-fan and Li Hung-chang, and only when they arrived did he bethink himself of what he had done and that it might not please the proud Empress Mother. Nor would be acknowledge that he was jealous in his heart because he had heard that the Empress Mother sought the advice of Jung Lu now above all. He had heard the rumor, and he dared not inquire of the Chief Eunuch, for all knew that An Teh-hai was the ally of the Empress Mother, and whatever she did was right in his eyes.

"Majesty," he said, striving to be humble, "if I have overreached myself I ask your pardon and I excuse myself because what I did I have done for your sake."

She did not like this proud apology. "I do not excuse you," she said in her cold and beautiful voice. "Therefore it scarcely matters if you excuse yourself."

He was confounded, and pride meeting pride, he rose and made obeisance. "Majesty, I leave your presence. Forgive me that I came without your summons."

He went away, his noble head held high, and she watched him thoughtfully. Let him go, for she could always recall him. Meanwhile she would find out for herself what the news was from the south, and prepared with her own knowledge she could accept or refuse his counsel. Until she knew all she could not judge advice. She sent her eunuch therefore to fetch the Chief Eunuch. In a few minutes that sleeper arrived, his eyes still drowsy, and he knelt before her and rested his head on his hands to hide his yawns.

"You are to summon the two generals, Tseng and Li, to the Audience Hall tomorrow," she told him. "Inform Prince Kung and the Grand Councilor Jung Lu that I shall require their presence. Invite the Eastern Empress Dowager to come an hour earlier than usual. We have grave matters to hear."

She turned to Li Lien-ying, "Say to the Grand Councilor that I shall not come to the archery field today, and he is to take care that the black horse my son rides is fed no grain, lest he become restive under the bridle."

"Yes, Majesty," the eunuch said, and went off to do his duty. In a few minutes he was back while she was still sitting on her throne, pondering what Prince Kung had said. He made obeisance.

"What now?" she asked. "Why am I troubled again?"

"Majesty," he said, "the young Emperor is weeping because you are **not** there to see his new saddle. The Grand Councilor prays you come."

She rose immediately, for she could not bear to hear that the child was weeping, and her ladies following her, she went to the archery field, where the young Emperor was sitting on his horse. Jung Lu stood by, his own silver gray Arabian saddled and waiting and held by a eunuch.

How kingly handsome was her son! The Empress Mother paused to look at him before he saw her. He sat upon the new saddle, made of sand-colored leather set upon a blanket of black felt embroidered in many colors. His short legs, stretched astride, could barely reach across the wide back of the horse and only the tips of his velvet boots touched the golden stirrups. His scarlet robe was gathered under his jeweled girdle and his yellow brocaded pantaloons showed to the waist. He had taken off his imperial hat, and his hair, braided in two braids and tied with stiff red silk cord, stood out from his head. Jung Lu, his handsome face uplifted to the child in love and laughter, was listening to the high gleeful voice. Suddenly the little Emperor saw his mother.

"My mother!" he cried. "See the saddle Jung Lu has given to me!"

So she must go and look at the saddle and inspect its wonders and her eyes met Jung Lu's in mutual pride and laughter. And then upon an impulse she said in a low voice while the child brandished his whip:

"Do you know that the two generals have come from the south?"

"I have heard it," he said.

"They propose to let the merchants of Shanghai build a stronger army, under a new foreign leader. Is this wise?"

"The first task," he replied, "is to put an end to the rebellion. As it is, there are two wars at the same time, one with the rebels and one with the white men. Between them we shall be so squeezed that we cannot survive. Crush the rebels, using whatever means is to be found, and then with strength the white men can be driven away."

She, nodding and smiling all this time as though she thought only of the child, now watched him gallop around the field. Jung Lu mounted his own horse to be at his side, and she stood there, her ladies somewhat at a distance, the wind fluttering her long blue satin robe, for she was still in mourning for the late Emperor. She gazed at these two whom she loved, the child so small and gallant, the man straight and tall, as they sat erect and pliant upon the galloping horses. The man's face was turned to watch the child, to speak a word of counsel, ready at any moment to catch him if he fell. But the child looked well ahead, his head high, his hands holding the reins with a mastery wonderful to see.

"An emperor born," she thought, "and he is my son!"

When they had drawn their horses to a standstill at the opposite end of the field she waved her kerchief and, followed by her ladies, she returned to her own palace.

In the chill gray dawn of the next day the two Empress Dowagers sat, each on her own throne upon a raised dais. It was the hour of the Audience of the Grand Council and before the two Empresses hung the thin curtain of yellow silk through which they could see dimly, without being seen, the figures of the Councilors as they came in, one by one, in order of their seniority, Prince Kung entering first in accordance with his rank. Now it was the duty of the Chief Eunuch to announce each Councilor and even Prince Kung must wait for the call of the Chief Eunuch, but today he did not, and Li Lien-ying leaned to whisper to the Empress Mother:

"Majesty, it is not my business, but jealous of your dignity, I see that Prince Kung has come in without waiting for his name to be called."

So attuned was this eunuch to every mood and thought of his sovereign that somehow already he had caught from her the odor of her displeasure with Prince Kung.

The Empress Mother seemed not to hear but he knew she had heard and she put down in the inexorable record of her memory this second discourtesy of the Prince. She was too wise to act swiftly until she knew all. Surely he could not be her enemy. Yet she could trust no one except Jung Lu, and even he was now wed to another woman.

She put aside such thoughts. Intrigue she must always suspect and for her own safety, but not at this moment. Nevertheless, Prince Kung, living outside the Forbidden City, was able to come and go as he pleased, whereas she must always stay locked inside these walls, and could he not intrigue as he liked without her knowledge? What guarantee had she of his honor except his word? She sighed, knowing herself forever alone. This, too, she must accept. It was her destiny.

Beside her Sakota sat musing, hearing and seeing nothing. She hated these audiences at dawn, for she was one who did not wake before noon, and now, half drowsing, she waited to return to her bed. Meanwhile the Grand Council assembled. All knelt before the Dragon Throne, their faces to the floor, and Prince Kung began his recitative of the memorial he held in both hands. He read well, his voice deep and sonorous, and he made every word as clear and shaped as gems set separately from each other upon a chain of gold.

"In the fourth month of this moon year," he read, "and the fifth month of this solar year, the Chinese rebels, called T'ai P'ing, became exceedingly troublesome in the countryside surrounding the city of

Shanghai. Not content with setting up their kingdom in the southern capital of Nanking, they came close to Shanghai and in sorties they ventured even into the settlements and burned several houses. The local army of Shanghai, called the Ever-Victorious, pursued them but did not kill many, for the rebels knew the ditches and gullies of the terrain and leaped over them easily and escaped. Meanwhile the peasants are terrified and more than fifteen thousand of them are crowding into the city, creating disorder. The foreign merchants are angry, for they see that among these peasants are many strong young men who ought to be fighting the rebels instead of taking refuge with the women and children and old persons. In order to persuade all young men to resist, they now propose to summon one Gordon, an Englishman known for his fearless nature and great rectitude, to lead the Ever-Victorious. This memorial of the two generals Tseng and Li is before the Throne."

Behind the silken curtain the Empress Mother bit her lips. She was not pleased that Prince Kung had presented the memorial. She said, her voice clear and firm:

"Let us hear what the two generals themselves wish to declare before the Dragon Throne."

Prince Kung, thus rebuked, could only summon first General Tseng, as the elder, who prostrated himself before the Dragon Throne, and he said, after greetings:

"I pray that my brother general, Li Hung-chang, may speak for both of us, since he is the acting governor of the province of Kiangsu and his headquarters are in the city of Shanghai. Though but thirty-nine years of age, Li Hung-chang is the most able of my younger generals and I present him to the Dragon Throne with full recommendation."

Again without waiting for the Empress Mother to command, Prince Kung said:

"Let Li Hung-chang come forward."

Behind the screen the Empress Mother did not speak but her secret anger increased. Nevertheless she held it controlled until the affairs of state were settled. Li Hung-chang came forward and prostrated himself before the empty Dragon Throne and he said, after greetings:

"In the third month of this moon year, or as the foreigners have it, in the fourth month of the solar year, I led my army into the city of Shanghai, under the command of my superior, General Tseng Kuo-fan. There I found the city protected not by Imperial Armies, which indeed were elsewhere engaged, for nearly the whole of the province is in rebel hands, but by the Ever-Victorious, who are mercenaries in the pay of the city merchants and led by an American mercenary, surnamed Ward.

This Ward was a good soldier but unfortunately he was killed in a rebel attack in the ninth month of this solar year, which is the eighth month of the moon year. A second American, surnamed Bourgevine, then sought his post but this man is an adventurer. Although he is well loved by the mercenaries, for he divides with them whatever spoils he takes, yet he is insubordinate to our command. He thinks of himself as a king and the mercenaries of the Ever-Victorious Army as his private army and, counting upon their loyalty, he makes war only when and where he pleases. Thus when I commanded him to proceed to Nanking, for my superior officer had sent word that the situation there was critical and ordered me to send reinforcements at once, Bourgevine refused to go. For this I deprived him of his post, and I reproved him, whereupon Bourgevine attacked the treasure houses of the Merchants' Guild, which collects the money for the Ever-Victorious Army. He hit this guard and that in the face with his right hand and ordered the soldiers to take forty thousand silver taels from the coffers, a sum, which, it is true, was in arrears, and he distributed the taels among the mercenaries, thereby winning even stronger loyalty from them. I then discharged him and threatened to disband the Ever-Victorious Army, knowing that unless the leader be under my orders, as I am under the orders of my superior officer, the soldiers may themselves become the nucleus for a new rebellion."

"This leaves the Ever-Victorious Army without a leader," Prince Kung observed.

"It does indeed, Highness," Li Hung-chang replied.

Now the Empress Mother had listened to this memorial with the greatest care, and though she could not see Li Hung-chang clearly, she discerned through the silk curtains a tall man, and she could hear his voice, decisive and deep, and all he said was plain and well spoken. Here was a man who could be useful to her, and she marked him in her mind. But she said nothing, for she was again displeased that Prince Kung had spoken without first waiting for her reply. She could not blame Li Hung-chang for answering Prince Kung, who was his superior in rank, but she could and did blame the Prince.

"Do you still wish to disband the mercenaries?" she inquired after silence. Her voice, silvery clear, proceeding thus from behind the yellow curtain, startled the two men. Both looked toward her without being able to see her.

"Majesty," Li replied. "Those soldiers are well trained and though they are arrogant to a degree, we cannot afford to lose their skill against the rebels. I propose to invite the Englishman surnamed Gordon to take the leadership of the Ever-Victorious Army and proceed to battle."

"Does any one of you know this Gordon?" the Empress Mother now asked.

Prince Kung made obeisance toward the Throne. "Majesty, by chance I know something of him."

"What chance?" she asked.

All could perceive displeasure in her cold voice, but Prince Kung, unthinking, replied without pause. "Majesty, when the invaders destroyed the palaces of Yüan Ming Yüan, I could not restrain myself from hastening thither to see if by any means I could save our national treasure. Alas, already the flames reached as high as Heaven, and man could do nothing. While I stood there grieving and sick at heart I saw a tall pale man near by. He wore the uniform of an English officer and he leaned upon a bamboo cane, and when I looked at his face I saw to my amazement that he, too, was sorrowing. When he in turn saw me, he came near and speaking very tolerably in Chinese, he told me that he was ashamed to see his compatriots and fellow-Europeans so greedy for plunder, even destroying what they could not carry. The mirrors, the watches, the clocks, the carved screens, the screens of carved ivory, the coral screens, the heaps of silk, the treasures in the storehouses—"

"Silence!" The voice of the Empress Mother came strange and strangled from behind the curtain.

"Majesty," Prince Kung persisted, "I saw a French soldier pay a looter a handful of small coins for a string of imperial pearls which next day he sold for thousands of silver dollars. Gold ornaments were burned as brass and the ebony which lined the Throne Hall—"

"Silence!" the Empress Mother's voice rang out again.

Prince Kung was still too proud to yield and he spoke sternly indeed. "Majesty, I claim the right to speak. I then inquired of Gordon. I asked, 'Can you not call off your soldiers?'"

"He said, 'Why did your Emperor allow the torture of our officers and our men, sent in good faith under a white flag to proclaim a truce, so that fourteen of them died?' Majesty, how could I answer?"

"Be quiet!" the voice of the Empress ·Mother cried out insistent from behind the curtain. She was bitter with fury, for she knew that Prince Kung reproached her publicly because she had persuaded the Emperor, now dead, to send Prince Seng, the Mongol general, to seize the foreign truce party. She bit her lips and was silent for a full minute. Meanwhile Prince Kung bowed to the Dragon Throne and he stepped back into his place. All waited for the voice of command from behind the yellow curtain.

"We give permission for this Englishman to serve us," the Empress Mother said at last and she made her voice calm and resolute. She paused while all again waited, and then she said, "We must accept, it seems, the service even of the enemy."

And so saying, she dismissed the audience.

But when she had returned that night to her own palace she sat brooding and aloof for many hours, and none dared ask her thoughts. She was alarmed that Prince Kung, whom she had trusted, could put himself above her. Was this a portent of her failing power? Her mind went roving over the year past, searching for signs of omen, good or ill. Then she remembered that on the twenty-sixth day of the fourth month of the solar year a strange dust storm had fallen out of season on the countryside, and so heavy that it brought early darkness. The sky turned black and mighty columns of darkening dust came sweeping down upon the wings of a hurricane wind. The canal between Peking and Tientsin, fifty miles long, eighteen feet wide and seven feet deep, was filled with dust, barges lay on sand piles and the waters were absorbed. The storm lasted for sixteen hours and many travelers were lost. Some were driven into ditches by the force of the wind and lying there were suffocated by the dust and of those who struggled through the blackness to some kind of shelter many were forever blind and others mad. In the palaces the lanterns were lit by three o'clock in the afternoon and here was the strangest part of the storm, that when one column of dust had blown past, the blue sky shone clear and bright for a moment until the next cloud came.

When the storm was over and the sandbanks cleared away, a task of many days, the Board of Astrologers sent report to the Throne that such a storm had great portent and in conjunction with the stars it signified that some vast struggle was about to take place in the nation, and though many would be killed, yet a stranger from the West would come like the mighty wind and he would bring victory to the Imperial Armies.

This she recalled and she was comforted and her spirit rose high again. No, she would not fail. Victory was foretold, and what victory could this mean except over the southern rebels? And was not Gordon the stranger from the West? Whom need she fear? She would act now to prove to Prince Kung that she, not he, was Regent until her son sat upon the Throne. Thousands of years ago the Viscount Kê had advised the Emperor Wu, then ruling, in this fashion:

"In times of disorder, the government should be strong. In times of good order, it should be mild. But whatever the time, do not permit a prince or a minister to usurp the royal prerogatives."

And while her will worked again like tonic in her veins a thought came to her as though clouds parted above her and the Eye of Heaven shone through upon a beam of sunlight. She would do more than bring a proud prince low. She would seat her son now, this very day, upon the Dragon Throne. He would sit there, an Emperor, and she behind the Throne would whisper her commands for him to speak aloud as his own.

She moved the more swiftly to perform her plan, for within a few days the Chief Eunuch came in secret to report to her that Prince Kung had twice presented himself to Sakota, her co-Regent, and eunuchs in waiting there had told him that Prince Kung had much reproached the Empress Dowager for her weakness and had said that she should not allow the Empress Mother to have her way always.

The Chief Eunuch, enjoying intrigue, pretended nevertheless to be much offended at what he had to tell. "And then, Majesty, Prince Kung said since you give ear daily to Jung Lu, whom you, Majesty, he said, now permit to act almost as a father to the young Emperor, that he most sorrowfully gave some credence to a tale he had refused to hear before—"

"Enough!" the Empress Mother cried. She rose, her robes flying, and she drove the Chief Eunuch from her presence by the fury in her long black eyes. He retired, content nevertheless with the seed he had sown, for he knew her quick imagination could see a story whole in a handful of words.

As for the Empress Mother, she went that very afternoon to call upon her cousin Sakota, the Empress Dowager, and speaking sweetly and giving no hint of what she knew, she used greetings and pleasant small talk and gracious flattery. Then changing her voice and manner, she said:

"Sister, my true purpose in coming to you today is to say that you must act with me to bring down the pride of Prince Kung, who has outstripped himself. He goes beyond his place, taking power away from you. I do not speak of myself."

She saw at once that the Empress Dowager caught her meaning. Something of the old childish Sakota still hid inside this wasted frame. A sickly flush spotted the thin face.

"I see you feel as I do," the Empress Mother said. "You marked how this Prince spoke ahead of me at our last audience. And much else I find, now that I put my mind upon it. He even comes into the Throne Hall without waiting to be announced by the Chief Eunuch."

The Empress Dowager put forward her weak defense. "Surely he has proved his faithfulness."

"I do not forgive him that he dares to presume because he thinks he saved my life," the Empress Mother made retort.

The Empress Dowager made a small show of courage. "And did he not save your life?"

"He should not remember it if he did," the Empress Mother said, and her red lips curved in contempt. "Does a large-minded man boast of having done his duty? I think not. And how, pray, did he save my life? By coming to Jehol when I commanded? I think not." She paused and then said boldly, "It was our kinsman, Jung Lu, who dashed aside the assassin's dagger."

The Empress Dowager said nothing, and the Empress Mother, seeming not to notice her silence, went on, her great eyes flashing in bright triumph, her lovely hands eloquent in gesture. "And do you hear how Prince Kung raises his voice when he speaks to us? As though we were stupid women!"

The Empress Dowager smiled faintly. "I am stupid, I know."

"I am not," the Empress Mother declared. "Nor are you—I will not have it so. And did we grant that we are stupid, for men think all women stupid, though they are the fools who think so, still Prince Kung must behave with humble courtesy, for we are the Regents, Empresses in our own right, and much more than women. I tell you, Elder Sister, if we do not put this prince down, he will one day usurp the Regency and we shall be imprisoned somewhere in secret rooms inside these walls and who will rescue us? Men will follow a man, and our end will be unknown forever. No, you must act with me, Sakota."

She spoke the childish name and bent her black brows into a frown upon her cousin. Sakota shrank away, as she had always done, and hastened to agree.

"Do as you think best, Sister," she said.

With this timid permission, the Empress Mother rose and made obeisance and took her leave while all the ladies watched from the distance, seeing but too far to hear.

Yet this bold and most beautiful woman could bide her time once her plan was perfected. She waited, her plan ripening all the while within her mind. She waited for the rebels to be quelled in the South while the year passed. For the Englishman Gordon did not rush his soldiers into battle. No, he would not risk the least defeat. With proud modesty he asked that he be allowed to make a military survey of the countryside around Shanghai before he became leader of the Ever-Victorious Army, in order that he might know what he must face in battle. Impatient as she was, the Empress Mother gave him his time. Alas, while Gordon prepared slowly, a lesser white man was for the time being put in his place, a pompous small man, who sought glory for himself. With that mixed army of mercenaries of men of many nations, the Ever-Victorious, twenty-five hundred in all, and an imperial brigade of twice the number, he laid siege to the walled city of T'aitan, near Shanghai, dreaming that when he won that city, he could attack Nanking itself. Yet such was his stupidity that he did not go to see how T'aitan stood, but he believed what Chinese mandarins had told him, that the moat surrounding the city wall was no more than a dry ditch. But on the morning when he marched his men to cross it, they found it thirty-five feet wide and brimming with water, and no boats near. Nevertheless he ordered his men to cross it somehow on the bamboo ladders which they had brought to breach the walls, but the ladders broke in midstream and many men fell into the water and were drowned, while on the city wall the rebels stood and fired their guns at those who struggled across, jeering at the drowning men.

"Oh, how we laughed!" the rebels boasted after victory. "We watched the Ever-Victorious Army come nearer to the creek with no bridges upon which to cross. How we laughed when we saw their ladders grow weak and fall into the moat! Our Heavenly King laughed loudest of all! 'What general is he?' he cried, 'who sends his men to take a city without finding out first whether there is water in the moat?' Then he grew angry to see the small number of the enemy who had come to conquer us. 'Do they think we are cowards?' he asked. 'Arise!' he shouted to us, 'drive these devils from the land!' We rose together and we shouted with one mighty voice, 'Blood—Blood—Blood!' And we advanced upon the foolish Ever-Victorious ones and we pursued them until all were dead or scattered, the English officers among them. These English did wrong in overstepping the boundary that they themselves had set between us, and we let them suffer. Indeed, we thank the English captain for the guns he left behind for us, and for the thirty-two pounders which we have now mounted on our walls as proof of our victory. It is not possible to believe how foolish he was, for he took the small guns before he removed the large ones and thus had no weapons wherewith to cover his retreat. Meanwhile let not the Imperial Armies think that they alone have the help of the foreigners. In our armies, too, are many white men, and it was a Frenchman who directed the guns at T'aitan. As for us, we will not transgress the boundary line, but the country we possess we will hold and we will utterly destroy those devils who come against us."

When this monstrous boast was presented to the Dragon Throne the Empress Mother rose up in her wrath and she sent her emissaries to Gordon and commanded him at once to take the leadership of the Ever-Victorious and the Imperial Armies, and to avenge the Throne for the loss of T'aitan. Gordon obeyed, but he would not avenge that city alone. Indeed, he obeyed no one, but still taking such time as he thought needful, he sought in battle to find the very heart of the rebellion. Thus he trained his men to strike sudden blows where they were not expected, changing his ground with vigor and speed, always winning until he had forced the rebels into defense. He worked in closest union with Li Hung-chang, all forces converging upon the pivotal cities of Chanzu and Quinsan, near Shanghai, and from there he advanced steadily toward victory.

Meanwhile, lulled by the Empress Mother's mildness during this crisis, Prince Kung had forgotten earlier rebukes, and worn with his cares and grown familiar with her ways, more often than ever he omitted small courtesies in her presence. She saw and still said nothing until one day, his mind upon affairs of state, he rose unbidden from his knees when holding audience with her. Swift as a tigress she pounced upon him.

Her eyes fixed under frowning brows, her voice majestic, she said, "You forget yourself, Prince! Is it not law and custom, declared by our ancestors, that all must kneel before the Dragon Throne? The purpose of this law is to protect the Throne from sudden attack. Dare you stand when every other must kneel? You plot treachery against the Regents!" She turned to the eunuchs. "Summon the guards and let Prince Kung be seized!"

Now Prince Kung was so dazed that he only smiled, thinking the Empress Mother jested. But the waiting eunuchs heard the command and they made haste to call the Imperial Guards who laid hold upon the Prince to force him from her presence.

He protested. "What—after all these years?"

She forbade him even one complaint. "None, however many years, nor if he be a kinsman, no, not one, may violate the safety of the Dragon Throne."

He gave her one long look and let himself be led away. And she that same day sent out an edict sealed with the imperial seal upon her own name and the Empress Dowager's as Regents. "Inasmuch," thus she declared, "as Prince Kung has shown himself unworthy of Our confidence and has shown unrighteous favor to his own nephews in appointing them to high office, he is relieved of his duties as Grand Councilor and all other high offices wherewith he has been rewarded are taken from him. By this act We do sternly check his rebellious spirit and usurping ambition."

Not one dared to plead the Prince's cause though many went secretly to Jung Lu to beg that he would speak for this noble Prince, whom none believed disloyal. But Jung Lu would not speak—not yet.

"Let the people say what they think," he told them. "When she finds that the people do not approve her she will change. She is too wise to oppose her will to them."

For a month all waited, and it was true that everywhere the people complained in rising accord that the Empress Mother as Regent had been unjust to the brother of the late Emperor and her loyal subject. They recalled how Prince Kung had risked his life to stay in the capital when the late Emperor fled, and how he, with Kwei Liang, had made the treaty which provided peace, and how again and again he had negotiated with the foreigners to hold them off from battle.

The Empress Mother heard these complaints and seemingly without concern. She listened, her beautiful face as calm as a lotus flower. Yet secretly she measured the exact reach of her power and when she saw that Prince Kung submitted to his sentence and made no effort to oppose her, thus signifying that he accepted reproof, and when she heard the people muttering much against her, she issued two more edicts, both signed in the names of the Empress Regents. The first edict explained to the people that she must in duty punish with equal severity all who failed in humility before the Throne. In the second edict she wrote:

"Prince Kung has now repented him of evil and he has acknowledged his faults. We have no prejudice against him, being compelled to act only with pure justice. It was not Our wish to deal harshly with a Councilor so able, or to deny Ourselves the aid of such a Prince. We restore him now to the Grand Council but not to his place as advisor to the Throne. We admonish him from this day forward to reward Our leniency by greater faithfulness to duty, and We advise him to purify himself of evil thoughts and jealousies."

So Prince Kung returned and ever after did his work with proud dignity and correct humility.

From now on the Empress Mother did not allow the Dragon Throne to be empty before the yellow curtain in the Audience Hall. She set her son there and taught him to hold his head high and to place his hands upon his knees and listen to the ministers when they memorialized the Throne. There the boy must sit, dressed from head to foot in yellow satin robes of state, embroidered with five-toed dragons, a ruby button at his shoulder, and on his head the imperial hat. Early in the winter mornings and before dawn in summer, she caused the boy Emperor to be waked and they two walked together in fair weather, for she liked to walk, or rode in palanquins were the weather foul, and in the Audience Hall they took their places, he on the Throne, and she behind the yellow curtain but so close that her lips were at his ear.

When a windy prince had made his plea, or an ancient minister had droned his way through a long memorial, the little Emperor turned his head to whisper, "What shall I say, Mother?" and she told him what to say and he repeated it after her, word by word.

Thus the hours passed, and he, often weary and apt to twist his button or trace the curling dragons with his forefinger, sometimes forgot where he was. Then his mother's voice struck sharply across his ears.

"Sit up! Do you forget you are the Emperor? Do not behave as would a common child!

She was so tender to him elsewhere that he was shocked and straightened, frightened by a power in her that he did not know.

"What do I say now, Mother?"

It was his constant question, and as often as he asked it, she answered.

As eagerly as though they were love letters the Empress Mother read the daily memorials which her mighty general, Tseng Kuo-fan, sent her from the south. The greatness in herself, like lodestone, sought and found the greatness in others, and next to Jung Lu she now valued best this general. He was no mere mass of brawn and bombast, as soldiers often are, but a scholar, as his grandfather and father had been, and so to his skill was added wisdom. Yet she felt no warmth toward her general. Her interest was in what he did, in the excitement of battles, in the danger of failure, in the pride of victory.

While these prescribed years of mourning for the dead Emperor came nearer to their end, and that peace might be secure before the great day of his burial, the Empress Mother thus devoted herself wholly to crushing the rebels in the south. Daily her couriers ran between the imperial city and Nanking, in relays so swift that in a single day men's feet covered four hundred miles. Each night at midnight the Chief Eunuch, An Teh-hai, delivered to her the packet containing the day's news from Tseng Kuo-fan, and she read the pages alone in her chamber by the light of the great twin candlesticks beside her pillow. Thus throughout the chill winter months she read of his masterful strategy and how with the help of two other generals under his high command, one P'eng

Yu-lin and the other his own younger brother, Tseng Kuo-ch'uan, he attacked the rebels by land and water, recovering during that one winter more than a hundred cities in the four provinces of Kiangsu, Kiangsi, Anhui and Chekiang. More than a hundred thousand rebels were slain, and slowly all retreated to their stronghold in Nanking.

Each day before dawn and the hour of audience the Empress Mother walked through the palace corridors to the temple of the Great White Buddha, he of the thousand heads and hands, and before this image of the Unknown Source she knelt and gave thanks and besought help for Tseng Kuo-fan. The priests prostrated themselves while she prayed, and remained motionless while she lit incense in the golden urn. And Buddha heard her prayers so that in the summer of that same year, in the sixth moon month and the seventh solar month, on the sixteenth day, Tseng Kuo-fan, having captured the outer ramparts of Nanking, ordered great bombs filled with gunpowder to be laid beneath the city wall and so made breaches through which his men poured by the thousand into the city. The palace of the Heavenly King was their last goal, but it was surrounded by desperate defenders. Nevertheless, an iron bomb filled with gunpowder was thrown into the center of the buildings to set a fire, and at one hour after noon of that day, flames burst as high as heaven, and the dwellers in the palace rushed out like rats from a burning house. They were all seized and put to death, except for the leader, one Li Wan-ts'ai, who was kept alive. This man, when questioned, confessed that the Heavenly King had killed himself by poison some thirty days before and that his death had been hidden from his followers until his son could be proclaimed king in his place. Now this son, too, was killed.

When the Empress Mother read these memorials from Tseng Kuo-fan she sent out the news in one edict after another so that all the people might know that the rebels were dead, and she proclaimed a month of feasting. Then she commanded that the body of the Heavenly King be dug up from its grave and the head cut off and sent everywhere throughout the provinces so that all her subjects might see it and know the fate of rebels, and those leaders of the rebels who still survived were to be brought to the imperial city and questioned and then put to death by slow slicing of their flesh. As for herself, she declared that she would accompany the young Emperor to all the imperial shrines and temples and give thanks to the gods for their fortunate aid, and to the Imperial Ancestors for their ever-present protection.

When Tseng Kuo-fan himself came to report to the Throne, he told further of strange and pitiful doings of the Heavenly King, reported to him by captives before they were put to death. This Heavenly King, in truth only a common fellow whose mind had gone awry, nevertheless had boasted mightily even when he knew his cause was doomed. He sat upon his throne and he said to his dwindling followers, "The Most High has issued to me his sacred decree. God the Father and my divine Elder Brother, Jesus Christ, commanded me to descend into this world of flesh and to become the one true Lord of all nations and kindreds upon earth. What cause have I then to fear? Remain with me or leave me, as you choose; my inheritance of this empire will be protected by others if you will not protect it, for I have a million angels at my side, a heavenly host. How then can a mere hundred thousand of these cursed imperial soldiers take my city?"

Nevertheless by the middle of the fifth moon month, the Heavenly King knew he was lost and he mixed a deadly poison with wine and drank it in three gulps. Then he cried out, "It is not God the Father who has deceived me, but it is I who have disobeyed God the Father!" So he died, and his body was wrapped in a cover of yellow satin embroidered with dragons and he was buried without a coffin, secretly and by night, in a corner of his own palace grounds. His followers plotted to put his sixteen-year-old son on the throne in his place, but the rebels heard of his death, too, and they lost hope and yielded the city.

All this Tseng Kuo-fan reported in the Imperial Audience Hall, before the Dragon Throne, upon which now sat the young Emperor, and behind the yellow silk curtain the Empress Mother listened to hear every word, while Sakota sat beside her motionless.

"Was not the body of this rebel king already decayed?" the Empress Mother inquired.

"It was strangely clean," Tseng Kuo-fan replied. "The silk which wrapped the whole body, even the feet, was of fine heavy quality, and protected the flesh."

"What sort of man was this rebel king in his looks?" the Empress Mother inquired again.

"He was very large and tall," Tseng Kuo-fan replied. "His head was round, his face massive, and he was bald. He wore a beard, streaked with gray. The head was cut off according to imperial command to be taken from province to province. As for the body, I ordered it to be burned and I myself saw it in ashes. The two elder brothers of the Heavenly King were captured alive, but they had lost their wits, too, and they could only mutter unceasingly, 'God the Father—God the Father'—and so I ordered them both beheaded."

Then before this rebel's head was sent to the provinces for the people to see, the Empress Mother announced that she wanted to look upon it with her own eyes.

"These many years," she declared, "I have carried on war against the rebel king, and now I am victor. Let me set my eyes upon my enemy who is vanquished."

The head was brought to her then by a horseman who carried it in a basket slung from his saddle, and Li Lien-ying received it, wrapped in yellow satin, stained and soiled, and he brought it with his own hands into the private throne room of the Empress Mother.

There she sat upon her throne, and she commanded Li Lien-ying to put the head down upon the floor before her and unwrap it. This Li Lien-ying did, the Empress Mother steadfastly gazing while he did so, until the satin fell away, and the ghastly face was revealed. The Empress Mother sat transfixed, her eyes held by the staring eyes of the dead, which none had taken time to close. These dead eyes stared back at her, black and bitter in the bloodless face. The mouth was pale and made more pale by the sparse black beard around it, streaked with gray, and the lips were drawn back from strong white teeth.

The ladies who stood about the throne shielded their eyes with their sleeves from the fearful sight, and one lady, always timid and shy, retched to vomit and cried out that she was faint. Even Li Lien-ying could not forbear a groan.

"A villain," he muttered, "and villainous even in death."

But the Empress Mother put up her hand for silence. "A strange wild face," she observed. "A desperate face, too sad to look upon. But it is not a villain's face. You have no feeling, you eunuch! This is not a criminal face. It is the face of a poet, gone mad because his faith was vain. Ah me, it is the face of a man who knew himself lost when he was born."

She sighed and leaned her head down and covered her eyes with her hand for a moment. Then her hands fell and she lifted her head.

"Take away the head of my enemy," she commanded Li Lien-ying, "and let it be shown everywhere to my people."

Li Lien-ying took the head away again, the horseman put it into the basket and he began the long journey. In every city of every province the head was set high upon a pole for the people to see, until at last its flesh dried and peeled away, and only the skull was left. And wherever the head was shown peace followed.

So ended the T'ai P'ing Rebellion in the solar year 1865. For fifteen years this cruel war had been waged back and forth across nine provinces of the realm and twenty million people died or starved to death. Nowhere had the Heavenly King stayed to build his kingdom, but he went everywhere with his followers, first killing and then looting, and among those followers were also many rootless white men, drifters, lost to their own peoples. But some, a few, believed in the Heavenly King because they were Christians and he used the name of Christ. These, too, were killed.

When this great rebellion was put down, the Imperial Armies, encouraged by what Gordon had taught them concerning warfare, put an end also to two lesser rebellions, one in the southern province of Yünnan, whence came the landscaped marble as tribute to the Dragon Throne, and the other a rebellion of Muslim in the province of Shensi. These were small frays compared to the great rebellion, and were soon ended. The Empress Mother, surveying the realm, saw only peace and in peace and prosperity, and the people praised her for that under her advice all rebels were defeated. Her power rose high, she knew it, and she moved swiftly at last to establish her power inside the Court as well and so make the dynasty secure.

Meanwhile she did not forget the Englishman Gordon. While Tseng Kuo-fan had led the Imperial Army against Nanking, Gordon led the Ever-Victorious Army against the same rebels in the region of the lower Yangtse where Li Hung-chang led the imperial soldiers. Had it not been for Gordon's victories, Nanking could not have fallen so easily, and Tseng Kuo-fan was great enough to say so before the Throne.

Now the Empress Mother desired exceedingly to see this Englishman, but she could not yield to her personal wish, for never had a foreigner been received at the Imperial Court. She read every report of him, however, and listened to all that was said concerning him by those who had seen him.

"The strength of Gordon," Li Hung-chang wrote in a memorial, "lies in his rectitude. He declares that he believes it his duty to put down the rebels for the sake of our people. Truly I have never seen a man like Gordon. He spends his own money to give comfort to his men and to the people who have been robbed and wounded by the rebels. Even our enemies call him 'great soul,' and declare that they are honored in defeat by such a one."

When the Empress Mother received this memorial she commanded that the Order of Merit of the First Rank be awarded Gordon, and that he be given a gift of ten thousand taels for his share in the honors of victory. But when the imperial treasure bearers came into his presence bearing the bullion upon their heads in great bowls, Gordon refused the gift and when the bearers, unbelieving, did not retire, he raised his cane and drove them away.

The news of this refusal went over the whole nation and yet not one citizen could believe that a man would refuse such treasure. Then Gordon made known why he would receive no gifts. Here was his reason. Li Hung-chang, in excess of triumph when the great city of Soochow was captured, had ordered the murder of many of the enemy leaders who had already surrendered. Now Gordon had promised these leaders that their lives would be saved if they surrendered, and when he found that he had been betrayed, his promise voided by Li Hung-chang, he fell into such a frenzy of temper that even Li was frightened and withdrew for a while into his own house in Shanghai.

"I will not forgive you so long as I live," Gordon had howled, and Li, staring at that white set face, indeed saw no forgiveness in the frost-blue eyes.

And Gordon, forever unforgiving, sent this proud letter to the Dragon Throne:

"Major Gordon received the approbation of His Majesty with every gratification, but regrets most sincerely that, owing to the circumstances which occurred after the capture of Soochow, he is unable to accept any mark of His Majesty the Emperor's recognition, and therefore respectfully begs His Majesty to receive his thanks for the intended kindness and to allow him to decline the same."

The Empress Mother read this document a few days later as she sat in the winter garden of the Middle Sea Palace. She read it twice. Then most thoughtfully she considered what man this Gordon was, who could for so high a reason refuse vast treasure and great honor. For the first time it came into her mind that even among the Western barbarians there were men not savage, not cruel, not venal. There in the quiet garden, this thought shook her to the soul. If it were true that there could be good men among the enemy, then indeed she must still be afraid. If righteous, the white men were stronger than she reckoned, and she kept this fear hidden in her so long as she lived thereafter.

The Empress Mother held Tseng Kuo-fan in the city for many days while she pondered what reward he should have for his bravery and successes, for by now this imperious woman asked no advice of prince or minister, and at last she commanded that he be made Viceroy of the great northern province of Chihli, and that he live thereafter in the city of Tientsin. On the sixteenth day of the first moon of the new year, she presided at a Court banquet whose dishes were beyond reckoning, and while all feasted, Tseng Kuo-fan sat in the highest seat of honor and the court actors presented six famous plays. Only after all this merrymaking did the Empress Mother bid Tseng Kuo-fan to depart for Tientsin and there find peace.

Yet he had no peace, for sudden rioting burst out in that city against some French nuns. These nuns, who kept an orphanage, offered a reward of money to any who would bring them a child, and trouble then followed, for evildoers began to kidnap children to sell them to the nuns who received them without asking to whom they belonged, and would not give them up again when their parents came to claim them, since they were paid for.

The Empress Mother sent for Tseng Kuo-fan again.

"And why," she inquired of him, "do these foreigners want Chinese children?"

"Majesty," the learned man replied, "I believe, for myself, that they wish to make converts to their religion, but alas, the ignorant people of the streets are full of superstitions and they declare that the magic medicines of the foreigners are made from the eyes and hearts and livers of human beings, and it is for this that the nuns want the children."

She had cried out in horror. "Can it be so!"

But he assured her, "I think it is not so. The nuns do often take the children of beggars already half dead on the streets, or they search for the newborn female infants of the very poor, whose parents expose them on the roadsides to die, and it is sure that most of such children cannot be saved, and yet the nuns take them and baptize them and count them as converts. Then such as die are buried in their Christian graveyards and it is considered to the merit of the nuns to baptize so many."

Whether Tseng Kuo-fan was right or wrong, she did not know, for he was a man of tolerance, believing no ill even of his enemy. Nevertheless, in the fifth month of that same year, a curse of the gods had fallen upon the nuns in the city of Tientsin, so that many children in the French orphanage had died and a horde of rabble-rousers and ne'er-do-wells, who called themselves the Turgid Stars, went everywhere saying that the foreign nuns were killing the children left in their care. The people were angered, and the nuns, in fear, agreed that certain chosen men should be allowed to come in and see for themselves that the orphanage was a place of mercy and not of death. Alas, the French Consul was angered in his turn at such inspection and he came and drove out those chosen, and although Chung Hou, the Superintendent of Customs in Tientsin, warned him that this was dangerous indeed, yet that foreigner was too proud to deal with him and demanded that an officer of high rank be sent to the Consulate. Then, although the city magistrate did his best to placate his people, they continued in their rage, and they went to the church and the orphanage of the foreign nuns, threatening them with fire and weapons, whereupon that foolish French Consul ran into the street with his pistol in his hand to succor the nuns. But he was seized by the people and put to death in some unknown manner, for none ever saw him again.

Prince Kung then came to the aid of Tseng Kuo-fan and he negotiated with all his skill, and by luck and by chance at this moment France itself went to war with Prussia, and in such trouble was more willing to close the negotiation. Nevertheless, the Empress Mother had been compelled to agree to pay to France four thousand silver taels from the Imperial Treasury as the price for the dead Frenchman's life and the fright caused the nuns, and Chung How, the Superintendent of Customs in Tientsin, was ordered to go to France in person to make apology for the Throne.

Before Tseng Kuo-fan could bring this trouble to an end, the Empress Mother sent for him again, for she had received a memorial from the south that brought grave news. Though the Heavenly King was dead, the city of Nanking and the four provinces were still not peaceful, the people so unruly and restless after the many years of rebellion that they had assassinated her Viceroy. For this reason she sent in haste for Tseng Kuo-fan and commanded him to take the dead man's place in Nanking. The weary, aging general was compelled to leave his post and come to the capital and once more in the Imperial Audience Hall at dawn he knelt upon the cushion before the Throne, whereon sat the young Emperor. Behind the yellow silk curtain the two Empresses sat on their thrones, the Empress Mother to the right and her co-Regent to the left.

When the kneeling general heard the voice of the Empress Mother commanding him to return to the south and take up new duties in Nanking as Viceroy, he begged her patience while he told her that indeed he was not well, that his eyesight was failing, and therefore he prayed to be excused from such a task.

She interrupted him from behind the curtain. "Though your eyes fail you," she declared, "yet you are able to supervise those under your command." And she would not hear his plea.

He reminded her then that he had not yet settled the troubles in his present province of Chihli, where a French officer in Tientsin had been murdered by Chinese rowdies while he tried to protect the nuns who were his countrywomen.

"Have you not executed those miscreants?" she demanded.

"Majesty," Tseng Kuo-fan replied, "the French Minister and his friend the Russian Minister insist upon sending deputies to watch the beheadings, and they have not yet arrived. I have left my supporting general, Li Hung-chang, to finish the task. The beheadings were to have taken place yesterday."

"Oh, these foreign missionaries and priests!" the Empress Mother exclaimed. "I wish we could forbid them our realm! When you take up your duties in Nanking, you must maintain a large and disciplined army to control the people, who hate all foreigners."

"Majesty, I purpose to build forts along the entire Yangtse River," Tseng Kuo-fan replied.

"These treaties Prince Kung has made with the foreigners are too irksome," the Empress Mother went on. "Especially irksome are the Christians, who come and go everywhere as though theirs were the country."

"Majesty, it is true," Tseng Kuo-fan replied. He was still on his knees, and since Court custom compelled him to kneel without his hat on his head, he felt the chill of the wintry dawn creeping into his bones. Nevertheless he continued with courtesy to agree with the Empress. "It is true," he said, "that missionaries cause trouble everywhere. Their converts oppress those who do not wish to eat the foreign religion and the missionaries always protect the converts and the consuls protect the missionaries. Next year when the time comes to revise the treaty with France, we must reconsider carefully the whole matter of allowing religious propaganda to be spread among the people."

The Empress Mother said with still more irritation, "I cannot understand why we must have a foreign religion here when we have three good religions of our own."

"Nor I, Majesty," the old general replied.

After silence the audience ended, and since this was the year of Tseng Kuo-fan's sixtieth birthday, the Empress Mother again made a great feast for him and gave him many rich gifts. She composed a poem in her own vigorous handwriting in which she praised him for his age and accomplishments, and with it she sent a carved tablet upon which were the words "To One Who Is Our Lofty Pillar and Our Rock of Defense." She sent also a gold image of Buddha, a scepter made of sandalwood inlaid with jade, a robe embroidered with gold dragons, ten rolls of imperial silk and ten other rolls of silk crêpe.

So powerful was the influence of Tseng Kuo-fan that the restlessness of the people subsided when he entered the Viceregal palace in Nanking. His first duty was to discover the assassin of the former Viceroy and condemn him to death by slicing. He made this death public, deeming it well that the people watch with their own eyes what befell such a criminal, and they watched in silence while the thin strong blade of the headsman's knife cut the man's living body into strips of meat and fragments of bone.

Thereafter the people returned to their daily work and to their usual amusements. Once more the flower boats plied their way upon Lotus Lake and lovely courtesans sang their songs, playing upon lutes while their clients listened and feasted. Tseng Kuo-fan was pleased to see the old peaceful life return, and he reported to the Throne that the south was now as it had been before the great T'ai P'ing Rebellion.

Yet in spite of his honors and his high place and his rectitude, Tseng Kuo-fan had not long to live. In early spring of the next year he was struck down by the gods while he sat in his sedan chair on the way to meet a minister whom the Empress Mother had sent with messages from Peking. As was his habit when alone, he was reciting to himself certain passages from the Confucian classics when suddenly he felt his tongue grow numb. He motioned to his attendants to take him back to the palace. He felt dazed and confused, spots floated before his eyes, and he lay silent upon his bed three days.

Twice again he was struck, and then he summoned his son to his side and with difficulty he gave him these commands:

"I am about to cross over to the Yellow Springs. Alas, I am useless, for I leave behind me many unfinished tasks and problems. I command you to recommend to the Empress Mother my colleague, Li Hung-chang. As for me, I am like the morning dew which passes swiftly away. When the end comes and I am encoffined, let my funeral services be performed with the old rites and Buddhist chants."

"Father, do not speak of death," his son exclaimed, and the tears overran his eyelids and rolled down his cheeks.

At this Tseng Kuo-fan seemed to rally, and he asked to be taken into the garden to see the blossoming plum trees. There he was stricken once more, but this time he would not be taken to his bed. Instead, he motioned that he was to be carried into the Viceregal Audience Hall, and they carried him in and put him upon the Viceroy's throne, and there he sat as though he conducted an audience and so he died.

At the moment of his death a great cry went up from the city, for a shooting star fell from the sky and all saw it and feared catastrophe. When he heard that the Viceroy was dead, every man felt that he had lost a parent.

The Empress Mother, hearing the evil news two days later, bowed her head and wept for a time in silence. Then she said:

"Let there be no merrymaking, no feasting or plays, for three full days of mourning."

And she sent out a decree over the whole nation ordering that a temple be built in every province to the honor of this great and good man, who had brought peace to the realm.

On the evening of the third day she sent for Jung Lu, who came to her private audience hall and knelt before her, and she put a question to him.

"What do you think of this Li Hung-chang whom Tseng Kuo-fan put before me in his place?"

"Majesty," Jung Lu replied, "you may trust Li Hung-chang above all other Chinese. He is brave and enlightened, and the more you depend upon him, the more loyal he will be to the Throne. Nevertheless, reward him often and generously."

She listened to these words, her great eyes wistfully upon his face, and she said:

"It is only you who seek no reward for all you do for me."

When she saw that he would make no reply to this, but continued to kneel before her in silence, she touched his shoulder with her foiled fan and she said:

"I pray you guard your health well, kinsman. Next to you, I valued Tseng Kuo-fan, and since he is gone, I tremble lest the gods in some wrath that I do not understand are set upon snatching from me my every support and stay."

"Majesty," he said, "you are to me what you ever have been, since the days of our childhood together."

"Stand," she said. "Stand and let me see your face."

He stood then, stalwart and strong, and for one instant their eyes met full.

In the autumn of the next year, the Board of Imperial Astrologers proclaimed the day for the burial of the late Emperor. During these several years between death and burial, his jeweled casket had rested in a temple in a distant part of the palace, but now most solemn preparations were made for the imperial funeral. The building of the new tomb had taken five years, and as a sign of her renewed confidence in Prince Kung, the Empress Mother had commanded him to be responsible for the collection of the vast sums needed. Without complaint Prince Kung had performed this duty, though indeed the task was severe, for the southern provinces, the richest in the Empire, whence should have come most of the tribute monies, were too poor from wars and rebellions to give their share. Ten million silver taels he collected by force and persuasion, levying taxes on every province and guild, and from this sum he must allow commissions to officials high and low, from ministers and lesser princes and viceroys to eunuchs and tax gatherers. Each one must be paid for his effort and in the privacy of his own palace Prince Kung complained to his gentle wife, in whose presence alone he could speak his heart.

"Yet must I obey the She-dragon," he sighed, "for if I offend her again she will destroy us all."

"Alas," his lady replied, "I wish, my lord, that we were poor folk so that we might be at peace."

But he was born a prince and as a prince he must conduct himself, and so he did.

Four years Prince Kung spent in the building of the tomb, for time was needed not only for collecting the funds but also to carve the great marble beasts and warriors who stood in pairs to guard the entrance of the tomb. Blocks of marble weighing from fifty to eighty tons were brought from the marble quarries a hundred miles distant from the imperial city, and each block was carried upon a six-wheeled cart, drawn by six hundred horses and mules. Such blocks were oblong in shape but for the twin elephants they were fifteen feet long, twelve feet wide and twelve feet thick. The horses and mules were harnessed together between two thick hempen ropes interwoven with wire and the length of these ropes was a third of a mile. Upon the cart an imperial Bannerman sat to hold up the dynasty flag, and with him were four eunuchs. The cavalcade halted every half-hour for rest, and when the time came to halt or to start again, one of the eunuchs beat a large brass gong. In front of the horses and mules a guardsman rode with a signaling flag. Thus it was with each of the fifty huge blocks of marble which, when they reached the place of the tomb, were immediately set upon by the finest sculptors who with mallet and chisel shaped beast and man.

The tomb itself was domed and it was made of marble, and in its center stood a vast jeweled pedestal of gold inlaid with jewels upon which the imperial coffin was to rest. There one clear cold day in the autumn of that year the dead Emperor was brought amid many mourners. In the presence of the Empress Mother and the Empress Dowager as Regents, and of the young Emperor and the princes and the ministers of the Court, the great coffin was placed upon the pedestal, while candles flamed and incense smoldered. The coffin was of catalpa wood, finely smoothed and polished, and before it was sealed, gems were laid upon the dead Emperor's wizened body. Rubies and jade and emeralds from India and a necklace of perfect yellow pearls were laid upon him. Then the lid of the coffin was sealed with pitch and a glue made from the tamarisk tree, which hardens into a substance invincible as stone. Upon the coffin were carved sutras of Buddha, and around it eunuchs placed kneeling figures made of silk and paper upon bamboo frames, to symbolize those who in ancient and less civilized days would have been human beings of flesh and blood, doomed to be buried with their lord, so that he would not be alone beyond the Yellow Springs. With the dead Emperor was buried his first Consort, the elder sister of the Empress Dowager, whose name was also Sakota. For fifteen years the body of this Consort had rested in a quiet temple in a village seven miles from the city, waiting for the death of the Emperor. Now she rejoined her lord, and her coffin was placed upon a low and simple pedestal at his feet.

When priests had chanted prayers and the Regents and the young Emperor had prostrated themselves before the dead, all withdrew from the tomb. Only the candles were left to burn, their flickering lights glowing upon the jeweled ornaments and upon the painted tablets which bedecked the walls of the tomb. The great bronze doors were closed and sealed and the imperial mourners returned to their palaces.

The day after the funeral the Empress Mother issued this edict of complete forgiveness for Prince Kung:

"Prince Kung has for the last five years busied himself under Our command with the funeral arrangements of the late Emperor. He has shown decorum and diligence, and Our grief has been somewhat assuaged by the splendor of the Imperial Tomb and the solemnity of the funeral ceremonies. So that the white jade of Prince Kung's fair name may not be marred in the records of Our reign, We decree that the record of his previous dismissal be erased and that he stand again in all his honor. Thus do We reward Our good servant, and may his name be forever clear."

At the end of that day the Empress Mother walked alone in her favorite garden. It was a gentle autumn evening, the sky a mild gray and the sunset a faint rose in the sky. She was melancholy but not sorrowful, for she felt no grief. Her spirit dwelt in loneliness, but to this she was accustomed. It was the price of greatness, and she paid it day after day, and night after night. Yet she was still woman and now for a moment her mind, lit by her too vivid imagination, saw a house, a home, where a man lived with a woman and where he begat children. For on this day of mourning her eunuch had told her that a son was born to Jung Lu. At three o'clock, before dawn, Lady Mei had given birth to a healthy male child. Again and again during the day of sorrow the Empress Mother had thought of this child. Yet Jung Lu stood among the mourners and she had seen no sign of joy upon his face. It was his duty to show no joy but now, tonight, when he returned to his home, could he refrain from joy? She would never know.

She paced slowly up and down the garden path between the late flowering chrysanthemums, her dogs following her faithfully, strong Mongol beasts who guarded her night and day and small sleeve dogs for her amusement. Then, as so often she had done before, she summoned her will and drew her mind and imagination inward again, to face the great tasks of her power.

On a certain day two summers later when the Empress Mother had moved the Court to the Sea Palace for enjoyment of the gardens, she sat upon her throne before the Imperial Theater to watch a play. It was not an ancient play but one written by a witty scholar only two hundred years before, in which the villain was a big-nosed man from Europe, a Portuguese sea captain with a great sword on his belt and beneath his nose a mustache like the outspread wings of a raven. The hero was the Prime Minister of the Chinese Court and this part was played by the Chief Eunuch, An Teh-hai, who was an actor of genius.

Suddenly the eunuch Li Lien-ying, who had been laughing loudly, was stricken silent and he rose from his stool near his imperial mistress and endeavored to steal quietly away. The Empress Mother, however, her eyes always seeing, motioned to him to return to her, which he did somewhat shamefaced.

"Where are you going?" she demanded. "And is it respectful of you to leave the theater when your superior is on the boards?"

"Majesty," Li Lien-ying said in a whisper, "the sight of this foreign rascal has made me remember a promise I gave yesterday to the young Emperor, which I had forgot until now."

"What is it?" she asked.

"He has heard somewhere of a foreign cart which can run without horse or man, and he bade me buy him one to see. But where can I find this cart? I inquired of the Chief Eunuch and he said that it may be I can find it in the shop kept by a foreigner in the Street of the Legations. Thither I now go."

The Empress Mother drew down her beautiful black brows. "I forbid it," she exclaimed.

"Majesty," the eunuch coaxed her, "I pray you remember that the young Emperor has a temper and I shall be beaten."

"I will tell him that I still forbid him a foreign toy," the Empress declared. "A toy, indeed, when he is no longer a child!"

"Majesty," the eunuch begged, "it was I who said a toy, seeing that I had no hope of finding a real spirit cart in our whole land."

"Toy or not, it is a foreign object," the Empress Mother insisted. "And I forbid it. Sit down again."

Li Lien-ying could do no more than obey, and so he sat, not laughing any more, although An Teh-hai upon the stage outdid himself to make the Empress Mother laugh. But she did not laugh either, and after an hour or so, while her handsome face remained grave, she signified to her ladies that she would withdraw and she did so, proceeding to her own palace, where, after further thought, she sent for the Chief Eunuch.

He came, a tall and handsome man in spite of his growing fat. He had bold dark eyes, but he subdued their gaze upon his imperial mistress, and she did not like him less for knowing that elsewhere his eyes could be impudent enough. It was rumored often that An Teh-hai was no true eunuch and that he even begot children inside the imperial walls, but the Empress Mother had learned not to inquire where she did not wish to know. Now she looked severely at her henchman.

"How dare you plot with Li Lien-ying?" she inquired.

"Majesty," he gasped. "I? Plot, Majesty?"

"To bring a foreign spirit cart to show my son!"

He tried to laugh, "Majesty, is this a plot? I thought merely to amuse him."

"You know that I do not want him to have foreign objects," she said in the same severe tone. "What, shall his soul be weaned away from his own people?"

"Majesty," the Chief Eunuch begged, "I swear I had no such intent. We all do what the Emperor wishes, and is this not our duty?"

"Not if he wishes for what is wrong," she said, implacable. "I have told you that I will not have him learn such vices as his father learned. If you can be so foolish as to yield in this, where else have you not yielded?"

"Majesty—" he began.

But the Empress Mother frowned. "Get out of my sight, you faithless servant!"

Upon this the Chief Eunuch was frightened. He had long been her favorite, yet every eunuch knew that the favor of a ruler is less stable than sunlight in early spring. At any moment it can be withdrawn, and as soon can a eunuch's head tumble from his shoulders.

He flung himself at her feet and wept. "Majesty, when my whole life is yours! When your command is above every other to me!"

But she pushed him away with her foot. "Out of my sight—out of my sight!"

He crept away then upon his hands and knees and once beyond the door he fled to the only one he knew who could save him from her anger. He went to Jung Lu, whose palace was a mile distant, running all the way.

At this hour of the day it was Jung Lu's habit to study the memorials which would next day be presented before the Throne. Once it had been Prince Kung's task to do this, but now, as Grand Councilor, Jung Lu took his place. Alone he sat in his library before a vast desk of black-wood, his head bent over the pages before him.

Behind the servant who announced him the Chief Eunuch pressed, and as soon as his name was spoken he made obeisance and gave greeting.

"Why have you come?" Jung Lu inquired.

In a few words An Teh-hai told of his trouble. "I beseech you to save me from the imperial wrath," he begged.

To his alarm Jung Lu did not at once give his promise. Instead, he motioned the Chief Eunuch to a chair nearby and after a moment, he said:

"I have been concerned for the last year or two at what I see in the Emperor's palace."

"What do you see, Venerable?" the Chief Eunuch asked, pale in the candlelight.

Jung Lu made his face stern. "The young Emperor's father, Hsien Feng, was ruined by his eunuchs, of whom you were one, An Teh-hai. True, you were not in those days the Chief Eunuch, but you had it in your power to persuade the Emperor, then regnant, to clean thoughts and righteous acts. Instead, you pandered to him, and he loved you because you were a young man and very handsome, and instead of helping him to righteousness you guided him downward, playing upon his weakness and his lusts, so that he died an old man before he was forty. Now you have his son—"

He broke off, his face was moved, and he put his right hand to his mouth, a strong hand, a strong mouth.

An Teh-hai trembled with fright. He had come hoping for support and instead he was attacked anew.

"Venerable," he said, "it is very hard to be a eunuch and disobey one's lord."

"Yet it can be done," Jung Lu said. "And in the end you would be honored. For there is in every man, even in an emperor, both good and evil. In childhood one is destroyed and the other kept alive. You chose the evil."

"Venerable," the eunuch stammered, "I made no such choice—it was never given me to choose."

"You know what I mean," Jung Lu said yet more sternly. "You know that when the Emperor, now dead, was in pain you fed him opium. When he was fretful you soothed him in evil ways. You taught him to seek refuge in vice whenever he was troubled or ill. Before he was a man his manhood was destroyed."

An Teh-hai was no coward, neither was he stupid. The time had come for him to use a dangerous weapon. "Venerable," he said, "if the Emperor's manhood was destroyed, how is it that he begot a son and one so sturdy as the young Emperor?"

Jung Lu's face did not change. He looked steadfastly at the eunuch. "If this imperial house fall," he said, "you must fall with it, and so must I, and with us the dynasty. Shall we then destroy this young man, who is our only hope?"

Thus did Jung Lu put to one side the dagger that the Chief Eunuch thrust at him. And the Chief Eunuch understood that they were to be allies and not enemies, and he pretended to be abashed and he mumbled, "I came here only to ask that I be saved from the wrath of the Empress Mother. And what this is all about I do not know, seeing that it began with a toy, a toy train, that Cobbler's Wax Li forgot to buy for the young Emperor. I do not know how it is that inside these walls a small thing can blow itself up bigger than a man's life."

Jung Lu passed his hand wearily over his eyes. "I will speak for you," he promised.

"Venerable, it is all I ask," the Chief Eunuch said, and making obeisance he went quickly away. He was well content. His cruel question had served him better than a sword, and Jung Lu had only parried it.

In his library Jung Lu sat long alone and so long that his gentle wife came stealing in between the curtains to look at him and go away again, not daring to speak when his face was so grave. She knew very well, this lady, that she could never have his true love, but she loved him so well that she contented herself with what he gave her, a mild affection, a tenderness always courteous and patient. Never did he come close to her, and even when he slept in her bed and held her in his arms he was not close. She did not fear him, for his kindness was unchanging, but she could not reach across the distance that lay between them.

Tonight grew so late that anxiety had compelled her, and she came to his side, her feet silent in satin slippers, and she put her hand on his shoulder so lightly that he did not feel it.

"It is nearly dawn," she said, "and do you still not come to bed?"

He was startled and turned his face all naked to her eyes, and she saw such wild pain there that she threw her arms about his neck.

"Oh, love," she cried, "what's wrong?"

He stiffened and in the next instant loosed her arms. "Old troubles," he muttered, "old problems, never to be solved! I am a fool to think upon them. Come, let's sleep."

And side by side they walked down the corridors to their rooms, where at the door to her bedroom he took his leave, saying as though it had only come to his mind, "And are you better with this child within you than you were with the first?" For she was big with child a second time.

"I thank you, I am well," she said.

To which he smiled and said, "Then we will have a daughter, if I remember old wives' tales I heard in childhood. It is the sons who struggle against the womb."

"And shall you mind if I give you a daughter?" she asked.

"Not if she looks like you," he said most courteously, and bowed to her and left her there.

Next day when the water clock had marked the third hour after noon, the eunuch Li Lien-ying, overzealous today to please his royal mistress, announced that the Grand Councilor Jung Lu sought audience with her when it was her convenience.

To which she said at once, "When is it not convenient for me to welcome my kinsman? Bid him come now."

So in a brief time Jung Lu was in her private audience hall, where she sat on her throne to receive him, and when she had motioned to the eunuch to stand at a distance, she bade Jung Lu rise from his knees and seat himself below her throne.

"Now pray you," she said, "let us be easy together. Put courtesy aside and say what is in your mind for once. You know that underneath the Empress there is always I, the one you knew as child and maiden."

She spoke freely and he was the more easily alarmed because of the Chief Eunuch's thrust. He turned his head this way and that to see if a curtain moved, or if Li Lien-ying held his ears alert. But no, that eunuch read some book or other, and the curtain did not sway. So vast was the hall that unless one stood near the throne, he could not hear what his beloved said, for she had made her voice small and sweet. Yet he would not yield beyond a long look that passed between them, he with his right hand covering that strong mouth of his.

"Take your hand from your mouth," she said.

His hand dropped and she saw him bite his lower lip.

"Those teeth of yours," she said, "are white and strong as any tiger's teeth. Spare yourself, I pray you—do not bite your lip so cruelly."

He forced his eyes away from hers. "I came to speak about the Emperor."

He used his own guile, knowing that only her son could divert those dark eyes from his face.

"What of him?" she cried. "Is something wrong?"

He was free again, the bond was loosened between them, that bond which never broke.

"I am not pleased," he said. "These eunuchs with their pandering hands pervert a young lad by their own perversion. You know what I mean, Majesty. You saw their evil wreak its doom upon the late Emperor, a foul corruption. Your son must be saved before it is too late."

She flushed and did not answer for an instant. Then she said calmly, "I am glad you speak as a father to my fatherless son. I, too, am much concerned, but being only woman, what can I do? Can I foul my tongue to speak of deeds I should not so much as know about? These are men's affairs."

"So I am here," he said, "and I do advise you that you betroth your son early. Let him choose the one he likes, with your consent, and though he is too young to wed for two years more, for he should not wed before he is sixteen, I daresay, yet the image of her whom he has chosen will keep him clean."

"How can you know that?" she inquired.

"I know it," he said bluntly, and would say no more, and when she sought to get his eyes again to hers, he turned his head away.

She sighed at last, yielding to his stubborn goodness. "Well, I will do as you bid me. Let the maidens be called together soon, to be prepared —as I was. Oh, Heaven, how the years have passed so that it is I who sit, as the Dowager Mother once did sit beside the Emperor, to mark his choice! Do you remember she did not like me?"

"You won her afterwards as you do win all," he muttered, and still did not turn his head toward her.

She laughed softly, her red mouth trembling as though to speak some mischief, but she withheld it and rose, again the Empress.

"Well, let it be so, kinsman! And I thank you for advice."

She spoke so clearly that Li Lien-ying, still distant, heard and thrust the book into his bosom, and came to escort the Grand Councilor from the hall. Jung Lu bowed low to the floor, the Empress Mother inclined her head and so they parted yet again.

Meanwhile the Chief Eunuch was uneasy. He had thought his place as secure as the Throne itself. Emperors came and went, but eunuchs remained, and above all eunuchs was the Chief Eunuch. Yet the Empress Mother could be angered even with him! He was shaken, he felt uncertain, and he longed to escape for a while from the walls of the Forbidden City, where he had spent his life.

"Here I have lived," he muttered in himself, "and I have never seen what is beyond." And he drew out of his memory an old dream he had forgotten and with it he went to the Empress Mother.

"Majesty," he said, "I know that it is against the law of the Court for a eunuch to leave the capital. Yet it has been my secret longing all these years to sail on the Grand Canal southward and view the wonders of our land. I pray you let me go for such a pleasure, and I will surely return."

When the Empress Mother heard this request, she was silent for a time. She knew that she was often blamed privately by princes and ministers and Court ladies, because she gave heed and honor to eunuchs. Only once in the dynasty had such heed and honor been given to eunuchs. It was two hundred and fifty years earlier when the Emperor Fu Lin, then ruling, had let eunuchs control the affairs of the palaces. This Emperor, being prone to books and meditation and desiring much to become a monk, was deceived by those greedy and powerful eunuchs, who became the lords of the palace, corrupting all they touched. One day, Prince Kung, saying nothing, had put before the Empress Mother a book telling the history of the reign of the eunuchs of the Empress Fu Lien, which was called the period of Shun Chih, and she read it, her face flushing with anger as she read. When she had finished she closed the book and returned it in silence to Prince Kung, and though she gazed severely at him, he did not lift his head to meet her eyes.

Nevertheless she had pondered on the present power of eunuchs. She used them as spies everywhere, rewarding them richly when they brought her rumors and gossip. Above all, she had honored An Teh-hai, the Chief Eunuch, for not only was he loyal, but he was also handsome and gifted as an actor in the Imperial Theater and as a musician he knew how to coax sadness from her spirits. So reflecting, she had excused herself for her dependence upon eunuchs, saying to herself that she was, alas, a woman, and when a woman rules there is none she can trust, for though a man who sits upon a throne has his enemies, he has also those loyal to him for their own sakes, but a woman knows no such loyalty. Spies are her necessity, that she may learn enough to act before the enemy suspects her knowledge.

"What a trouble you make for me," she now exclaimed to An Teh-hai. "If I let you go, then all will put blame on me for breaking the law and the tradition."

He sighed sadly. "It is sacrifice indeed that I have made, to give up manhood and wife and children, and beyond that it seems I must be content with the walls of one city as long as I live."

He was a creature still young enough to claim good looks, his height noble and his face brave and proud. Corruption, indeed, had done its work in the sensual lines of his square mouth and in the blurred planes of cheek and brow, and he had grown too fat. But he had a melodious voice, not small as the voices of eunuchs are, and he spoke with classical perfection, carving each word with proper tone and emphasis so that all he said was music. To these graces he added surpassing grace when he moved, even in the gestures of his large and beautiful hands.

The Empress Mother did not deny that his beauty pled his case, and remembering now his constant loyalty to her, not only in obedience but in amusing and comforting her, she yielded. "I might," she said thoughtfully, examining the gold nail shield of the little finger on her left hand, "I might send you to the southern city of Nanking to inspect the imperial tapestries being woven there. I have commanded special fabrics for my son, the Emperor, against the day of his marriage and accession, for such stuffs need time to weave. And though I sent exact instructions, yet I know how easily mistakes are made. I remember in the time of our Ancestors the Nanking weavers sent bolts of satin of a yellow too pale to be imperial. Yes, go there and make sure that the yellow at least is a true gold, and that the blue is not faint, for you know that clear blue is my favorite color."

When she had thus decided, the Empress Mother as usual allowed no sign of possible mistake to escape her, and she held her head high above any who cried against what she did. In a very few days the Chief Eunuch set sail for Nanking, his entourage on six great barges, each flying imperial banners, and upon the barge where he lived he commanded to be raised the Dragon insignia itself. When the barges passed through any town and city upon the Grand Canal the magistrates saw banners and insignia and they hastened to bring gifts to An Teh-hai and to bow before him as though he were the Emperor. Thus encouraged, the proud eunuch demanded bribes not only of money but of lovely maidens, for though he was eunuch, yet he used them in his own hateful ways. Thus the barges became abodes of evil, those eunuchs who were with him taking heart for license from their chief's example.

The stink of this reached northward to the ears of Prince Kung, for magistrates sent secret memorials to him, knowing now the Empress Mother favored eunuchs, and at the same time eunuchs who hated An Teh-hai for some past cruelty and secret injustice carried tales of what he now did to Sakota, the Empress Dowager of the Eastern Palace, so that she sent privately for Prince Kung, and when he had come to her palace she said, sighing:

"I do not often oppose what my sister does. She is a strong and brilliant sun and I am a pale moon beside her. Yet I have always wished she did not favor the eunuchs as she does, and especially that An Teh-hai."

By this Prince Kung knew that she had heard the rumors concerning the Chief Eunuch and so he said boldly:

"Now is the time, Majesty, when the Empress Mother must learn the lesson you have tried to teach her. With your permission I will arrest this infamous An Teh-hai and have him beheaded. There is nothing more to be said when his head rolls in the dust."

The Empress Dowager made a small scream and put her clenched hands to her mouth. "I do not like to see anyone killed," she faltered.

"It is the only way to rid the Court of a favorite and so it has always been in history," Prince Kung replied. His demeanor was calm, his voice was steady. "Moreover," he went on, "this An Teh-hai has corrupted two generations of our emperors. Our late Emperor was debauched while he was yet a child by this same eunuch. And now I hear —nay, I have seen with my own eyes—that our young Emperor is led in the same evil ways. In foolish disguise he is even taken into the streets at night, to brothels and to lewd theaters."

The Empress Dowager sighed and murmured that she did not know what to do. Whereupon Prince Kung put forth a bold question. "If I prepare a decree, Majesty, will you sign it with your own imperial seal?"

She shuddered, her delicate frame aquiver. "What—and brave the Other One?" she whimpered.

"What can she do to you, Majesty?" Prince Kung urged. "The whole Court, even the nation, would condemn her if she even touched you with intent to harm you."

Thus persuaded, she did sign the decree when the Prince had prepared it, and in swift secret he despatched it by courier.

By now An Teh-hai had gone beyond Nanking and had reached the heavenly city of Hangchow. There he had seized the great house of a wealthy merchant and he began to exact tribute from the populace, demanding gifts of money and treasure and beautiful maidens. All citizens were soon in a mood of fury and revenge and yet none dared to refuse him, for he had his eunuchs and his bodyguard of six hundred armed men. Only the magistrate of that city was bold enough to complain and he, too, sent secret memorials to Prince Kung, describing the orgies and the evils of the arrogant handsome eunuch. To this magistrate, therefore, Prince Kung sent the secret decree of death. Immediately the magistrate invited An Teh-hai to a vast banquet, where, he said, the most beautiful virgins of the city could be seen, and in much joy An Teh-hai prepared for the feast. But when he entered the guest hall of the magistrate's palace he was seized and forced to his knees, while his eunuchs and guards were held in the outer court. There the magistrate showed him the decree declaring that he would obey it at this very instant. An Teh-hai screamed that the seal was only the seal of the Empress Dowager and not of the Empress Mother, who was the real ruler and his patron. But the magistrate replied:

"By law the two are one and I do not recognize one above the other."

With this he lifted his hand and thrust down his thumb from his clenched fist and at the sign his headsman stepped forward and cut off An Teh-hai's head with one blow of his broadsword, and the head fell upon the tile floor so heavily that the skull cracked and the brains spilled out.

When the Empress Mother heard that her favorite and her loyal servant was dead, she fell into such wrath that she was ill for four days. She would not eat or sleep, her rage burning hot against her sister-Regent but hottest against Prince Kung.

"He alone could have made a lioness of that mouse!" she cried, and she would have ordered Prince Kung himself beheaded, except that Li Lien-ying, in terror at such madness, went secretly to Jung Lu.

Again Jung Lu came to the palace and without delay or ceremony he stood in the doorway of the bedchamber where the Empress Mother lay restless upon her bed, and the curtain hanging between them, he said, his voice cold and quiet with sad patience:

"If you value your place, you will do nothing. You will rise from your bed and be as usual. For it is true that the Chief Eunuch was a man of surpassing evil, and you did favor him. And it is true also that you broke law and tradition when you gave permission for him to leave the capital."

She heard his voice of judgment and she said nothing for a while. Then she spoke, pleading for his mercy:

"You know why I bribe these eunuchs. I am alone in this place—a lonely woman."

To this he said but one word. "Majesty—"

She waited but there was no more. He was gone. She rose at last and let herself be bathed and attired, and she took some food. All her ladies were silent, none dared to speak, but she seemed not to notice whether they spoke or did not. She went to her library with slow and weary steps and for many hours she read the memorials laid there on the table for her. When the day was done she sent for Li Lien-ying and she said to him,

"From this day on you are Chief Eunuch. But your life depends upon your loyalty to me and to me alone."

He was overcome with joy and lifting his head from the floor, where he knelt in obeisance, he swore his loyalty.

From this day on, the Empress Mother allowed herself to hate Prince Kung. She continued to accept his service, but she hated him, and waited for the time when she could subdue his pride forever.

In all this trouble the Empress Mother had not forgotten Jung Lu's advice to betroth the young Emperor soon, and the longer she pondered the counsel which her kinsman had given to her the more she found it to her liking, and this for a certain reason that none but herself knew. Her son, so much hers in his good looks and proud heart, had one way to wound her, and so deeply that she could not speak of it openly even to him, but must prevent him in every small way that she could, lest by speaking she confirm him in what she feared to say in words. Since his childhood he had preferred the palace of Sakota, the Empress Dowager, to his mother's. Often when he was but a child and she went to find him, he was not in his own palace and when she asked where he was, a eunuch told her that he was with the Empress Dowager and now still more often when she sent for him or went to find him, he was there.

Too proud to show hurt, the Empress Mother never reproached him, but she pondered in her heart why it was that her son preferred this other to herself. She loved him with fierce possession, and she dared not put the question to him, lest she hear him say what she feared, nor would she humble herself to speak even to Prince Kung or to Jung Lu of the wound that lay so deep within her. Indeed, she needed not to ask. She knew why her son went often to the other palace and stayed long, whereas to her he came when called and left her soon. The cruelty of a child! She, his mother, must often cross his will, for she must teach and train him for his future. She must create Emperor and man from his raw youth, and he resisted shaping. But his foster mother, her co-Regent, that mild Sakota, felt no duty to reprove him or to teach him and with her he could be what he was, a merry child, a lounging boy, a teasing lad, and she only smiled. When he was willful she could always yield, for she bore no burden for him.

Here a jealous anger raged through the Empress Mother. It might even be that Sakota had bought that toy for him, the foreign train, and hid it in her rooms, where he could play with it in secret. Was it so indeed? Doubtless, for this morning after audience her son had been all eagerness to leave her, in haste to have done with his duties, but she had compelled him to be with her here a while in her own library, that she might search his mind and see if he had listened to the memorials that day presented. He had not listened and to her reproachful questions he had cried in a naughty voice:

"Must I remember every day what some old man mumbles at me through his beard?"

She had been so angered by his insolence to her, who was his mother, that, though he was Emperor, she put out her hand and slapped his cheek. He did not speak or move but fixed his great eyes on her in a rage, and she saw his cheek stained red where she had struck him. Then, still without a word, he had bowed stiffly to her and turned and left her. Doubtless he had gone straight to his foster-mother. Doubtless Sakota had soothed and comforted him and told him how she, his mother, had always a temper, and how often she, the gentler one, had been struck when they were children under one roof.

At this the proud Empress Mother sobbed suddenly. If she had not her son's heart, then she had nothing. Alas, how little comfort is a child! And she had given up all for him, had spent her life for him, had saved a nation for him, had held the Throne for him.

Thus grieving, she wept awhile, then dried her tears upon the kerchief fastened to the jeweled button of her robe and then fell to thinking how to get her way, even with her son. Sakota must be supplanted by another woman, someone young and lovely, a wife who would enchant the man already budding in him. Yes, Jung Lu's counsel was wise and good. She would betroth her son, not against the eunuchs, for they were only half-men, but against that soft silent woman who gave mild motherhood to a child not her own.

I will not have Sakota mothering my son, she told herself. Sakota, who could give birth to nothing but a feebleminded girl!

And, strengthened as always by her anger, she clapped her hands and summoned her eunuch and sent him for Li Lien-ying, the Chief Eunuch, and within an hour she had given commands for the parade of maidens, what day it was to be, where it must take place, and what the tests were for admittance. No maid outside the Imperial Manchu clans could be considered, and no plain-faced maiden and none older than the Emperor by more than two years. A year or so, yes, that was wise, for the wife then could lead and guide, but not so old that any bloom was lost.

The Chief Eunuch listened and said yes, yes, he knew what the young Emperor liked, and begged six months or so to do his best in. But the Empress Mother refused so long a time, and gave him three, and dismissed him from her presence.

When she had thus decided for her son, she set her mind again to those affairs of the realm from which she had no peace. They were both small and great, and now the most troublesome was the continuing stubbornness of the Western invaders who demanded the right to send emissaries to the Dragon Throne, yet refused to obey the laws of courtesy and submission, whereby they must prostrate themselves in the presence of the Emperor. She had lost patience again and again when such demands were presented to her as Regent.

"And how," she had inquired, "can we receive emissaries who will not kneel? Shall we degrade the Dragon Throne by allowing our inferiors to stand before us?"

As usual she had ignored what she could not solve, and when a certain member of the Board of Censors, Wu K'o-tu by name, begged to memorialize the Throne in favor of the foreign envoys, she refused to accept his memorial, saying that this matter of the foreign envoys was no new one, and could not be solved in a moment. She observed from her reading of history that two hundred years earlier an envoy from Russia had demanded the right to stand instead of kneel before the Dragon Throne and this demand had been refused and the envoy had returned to Russia without seeing, face to face, the Emperor, then ruling. True, an envoy from Holland had once submitted to the imperial custom and had knelt while he addressed the Throne, but other Western envoys did still refuse to follow this precedent. True again, the English mission under an English lord, McCartney, was allowed to come into the presence of the Ancestor Ch'ien Lung, with deep bows instead of kneeling head to earth, but this meeting had taken place in a tent in the imperial park at Jehol, and not in the palace proper. And only twenty-three years later another English lord, Amherst, failed in his mission because the Emperor Chia Ch'ing, then ruling, had insisted upon the proper obeisance to the Throne. For the same reason, the Empress Mother herself pointed out, in answer to the Censor Wu, the Emperor T'ao Kuang and the late

Emperor Hsien Feng had never received a Western emissary, and how could she, therefore, dare to do what they had not thought right to do? A bare fifteen years ago, she further reminded this Censor, who was always too ready to allow privileges to foreigners, Prince Kung's own father-in-law, the honored nobleman Kwei Liang, had argued with the American minister Ward that he himself, were he an emissary from China to the United States, would be entirely ready to burn incense before the President of the United States, since any ruler of a great people must be given the same respect that one gives to the gods themselves. But the American would not agree, and therefore was not received.

"I will allow no one to approach the Dragon Throne who will not show due respect," she steadfastly declared, "since to do so would be to encourage rebels."

In her heart she determined never to allow a foreigner to cross the threshold of the Forbidden City, for indeed these foreigners were becoming daily more troublesome in the realm. She recalled that her great general, Tseng Kuo-fan, now dead, had told her how the people of the city of Yangchow, on the Yangtse River, had risen against the foreign priests in that city, destroying their houses and temples and driving them from the city because they taught that the young should not obey their parents or the gods but should only obey the one foreign god whom they preached. And she recalled how deeply offended were the people of Tientsin when French emissaries made a temple into a consulate, removing the gods and casting them upon a dung heap as though they were refuse.

These matters, which at the time the Empress Mother had considered small affairs and scarcely worth more than a day's attention, she now knew were but a sign of the greatest danger in her realm, which was the invasion by the Christians, those men who went where they willed, teaching and preaching and proclaiming their god the one true god. And the Christian women were scarcely less dangerous than the men, for they did not stay within the gates of their homes, but walked freely abroad, even into the presence of men, and behaved as only women of ill repute behave. Never before had there been such persons as these who declared their religion the only one. For hundreds of years the followers of Confucius and Buddha and Lao Tse had lived together in peace and courtesy, each honoring the other's gods and teachings. Not so these Christians, who would cast out all gods except their own. And by now all knew that where the Christians first went, then traders and warships soon would follow.

To Prince Kung, when such rumors came to the Throne, the Empress Mother one day declared herself in these words:

"Sooner or later, we shall have to rid ourselves of foreigners, and first of all we must be rid of these Christians."

But Prince Kung, always easily alarmed when she spoke of ridding the realm of foreigners, again cautioned her, saying, "Majesty, remember, if you please, that they possess weapons of which we know nothing. Let me, with your permission, draw up a set of rules to govern the behavior of the Christians, so that our people may not be troubled."

She gave him that permission, and he presented a memorial soon after, containing eight rules. They met in her private audience hall, she upon her throne, and after receiving his obeisance and hearing what he brought, she said:

"Today my head aches. Tell me what you have written and spare my eyes."

So saying, she closed her eyes to listen, and he began:

"Majesty, since the rising of the Tientsin Chinese against the French nuns, I say that Christians may not take into their orphanages any save the children of their own converts." She nodded in approval, her eyes still closed.

"I also ask," Prince Kung went on, his head bowed before the Empress Mother, "that Chinese women shall not be allowed to sit in the foreign temples in the presence of men. This is against our custom and tradition."

"It is propriety," the Empress Mother observed.

"Moreover," Prince Kung went on, "I have asked that foreign missionaries shall not go beyond the bounds of their calling—that is, they shall not protect their converts from the laws of our land if these converts commit a crime. That is, foreign priests shall not interfere, as they do now, in the affairs of their converts when these are brought before magistrates."

"Entirely reasonable," the Empress Mother said, approving.

"I have asked," Prince Kung continued, "that missionaries do not assume the privileges of officials and emissaries from their nations."

"Certainly not," the Empress Mother agreed.

"And evil characters," Prince Kung went on, "must not be received into their churches as a means of escape from just punishment."

"Justice must be free to work," the Empress Mother declared.

"These requests I have made to the foreign emissaries resident here in our capital," Prince Kung then said.

"Surely these are mild requests," the Empress observed.

"Majesty," Prince Kung replied, his grave face more grave, "I grieve to say that the foreign envoys do not accept them. They insist that all foreigners here shall remain entirely free to roam where they wish and do what they like, without censure or arrest. Worse than this, they refuse so much as to read my document, though sent to their legation with due courtesy. There is one exception. The minister from the United States alone has replied, not with agreement but at least with courtesy."

The Empress Mother could not restrain her feelings at such monstrous offense. She opened wide her eyes, she struck her hands together, and rising from her throne she paced the floor, muttering and murmuring angry words.

Suddenly she paused and looked back at Prince Kung. "Have you told them that they build a foreign state within our state? Nay, they build many states, for each sect of their various religions makes its own laws on our land, without regard to our state and our laws."

Prince Kung said with mournful patience. "Majesty, I have so spoken to the ministers of all nations here resident."

"And have you asked them," the Empress Mother cried, "what they would do to us were we to go to their countries and so conduct ourselves, refusing to obey their laws and insisting upon our own freedom as though all belonged to us?"

"I have so asked," Prince Kung said.

"And that is their reply?" she demanded. Fire flew from her eyes, and her cheeks were scarlet.

"They say there is no comparison between their civilizations and ours, that our laws are inferior to theirs, and therefore they must protect their own citizens."

She ground her white teeth together. "Yet they live here, they insist upon staying here, they will not leave us!"

"No, Majesty," Prince Kung said.

She sank upon her throne. "I see they will not be satisfied until they possess our land as they have already possessed other lands—India and Burma, the Philippines and Java and the islands of the sea."

To this Prince Kung did not reply, for indeed he could not. He, too, feared it was true.

She lifted her head, her lovely face gone pale and stern.

"I tell you, we must rid ourselves of foreigners!"

"But how?" he asked.

"Somehow," she said, "anyhow! And to this I shall give my whole mind and heart from now until I die."

She drew herself up straight and cold, and did not speak for a matter of minutes, and he knew himself dismissed.

Thereafter in all the Empress Mother did, in work or pleasure, she kept within her mind and heart this one question—how could she rid her realm of foreigners?

In the autumn of the sixteenth year of the young Emperor T'ung Chih, the Empress Mother decided that he should take his consort, and having decided she consulted with the Grand Council and those clansmen and princes who must agree with her. Upon the day prescribed by the Board of Astrologers, therefore, six hundred beautiful maidens were called, of whom one hundred and one were chosen by the Chief Eunuch, Li Lien-ying, to pass before the young Emperor and his imperial mother.

It was autumn, a day of brilliant sunshine, and courtyards and terraces blazed with chrysanthemums. The Empress and her co-Regent sat in the Palace of Eternal Spring to view the maidens. This hall was a favorite of the Empress Mother, for the wall paintings in the verandas surrounding the courtyard were from *The Dream of the Red Chamber,* a book she loved to read, and so skillfully had the artist done his work that the paintings seemed to open the walls to scenes beyond.

In the middle of this place of beauty were set three thrones, and on the central one, higher than the rest, the Emperor sat, while his mother and his foster mother, as Regents, sat on either side. The young Emperor wore his imperial-yellow dragon robes, his round hat on his head and upon it the sacred peacock feather fastened by a button of red jade. He held his shoulders straight and his head high, but his mother knew that he was excited and pleased. His cheeks were scarlet and his great black eyes were bright. Surely he was the most beautiful young man under Heaven, she thought, and she was proud to know him hers. Yet she was divided between pride and love, jealous lest one of the maidens be too beautiful and take him from her, yet longing to make him happy by giving him the most beautiful.

A golden trumpet now blew three blasts to signify that the procession was about to begin. The Chief Eunuch prepared to read the names of the maidens as they passed, each to pause for an instant before the Throne, to bow deeply, then to lift her face. One by one they came into the far end of the hall, too distant yet to be seen beyond the bright and many-colored garments that they wore, their headdresses sparkling and twinkling in the light from the great doors thrown open to the morning sun.

Again the trumpet blew its golden notes, and listening, her head not turning, her eyes fixed upon the flowers on the wide terrace outside the hall, the Empress Mother recalled that day, a lifetime ago, it seemed, and yet less than twenty years, when she herself was one of the maidens who stood before the Emperor.

Ah, but what a difference between that Emperor and this handsome son of hers! How her heart had dropped disconsolate when she looked at the wizened figure, the pallid cheeks of that Emperor, but what maiden could fail to love her son? Her eyes slid toward him, but he was stealing looks at the far end of the hall. The maidens were coming one by one, tripping over the smooth tiles of the floor, a moving, glittering line of beauties. And here was the first one, her name—but it was impossible to remember their names. The Empress Mother looked at the record which a eunuch had placed beside her on a small table, the name, the age, the pedigree—no, not this one! The girl passed, her head drooping.

One by one they came, some tall, some small, some proud, some child-like, some dainty in prettiness, some as handsome as boys. The young Emperor stared at each one and made no sign. The morning crept past, the sun rose high and the broad beams bright upon the floor grew narrow and disappeared. A soft gray light filled the hall and the chrysanthemums, still sunlit, glowed like running flame along the terraces. The last maiden passed late in the afternoon and the trumpet blew again, three concluding notes. The Empress Mother spoke.

"Did you see one you like, my son?"

The Emperor turned the sheets of the written records he held and he put his finger on a name.

"This one," he said.

His mother read the description of the maiden.

"Alute, aged sixteen, daughter of Duke Chung Yi, who is one of the first Bannermen and a scholar of high learning. Although he is Manchu, the family being Manchu without mixture, their history recorded for three hundred and sixty years, yet this Duke studied the Chinese classics and attained the noble scholastic rank of Han Lin. The maiden herself has the pure requirements of absolute beauty. Her measurements are correct, her body is sound, her breath is sweet. Moreover, she also is learned in the books and in the arts. She is of good repute, her name being unknown outside her family. Her temper is mild and she is inclined to silence rather than to speech. This is the result of her natural modesty."

The Empress Mother read these favorable words.

"Alas, my son," she said, "I do not remember this one among the many others. Let her be brought before us again."

The Emperor turned to the Empress Dowager at his left. "Foster Mother, do you remember her?"

To the surprise of all, the Dowager replied, "I do remember her. She has a kind face, without pride."

The Empress Mother was secretly displeased to think that she had failed where the other had not, but she showed only courtesy in her reply.

"How much better are your eyes than mine, Sister! It is I then who must see the maiden again."

So saying she beckoned to a eunuch who relayed her command to the Chief Eunuch and Alute was returned to the viewing place. She entered once more, and the Imperial Three stared at her as she crossed the long distance between the door and the Throne. She walked gracefully, a slight young girl, seeming to drift toward them, her head drooping and her hands half hidden in her sleeves.

"Come nearer to me, child," the Empress Mother commanded.

Without diffidence but with exquisite modesty the young girl obeyed. The Empress Mother put out her hand then and took the maiden's hand and pressed it gently. It was soft but firm and cool without being cold. The palm was dry, the nails were smooth and clear. Still holding the narrow young hand, the Empress Mother next examined the girl's face. It was oval, smoothly rounded, the eyes large, and the black lashes long and straight. She was pale, but the pallor was not sallow and the skin was lucent with health. The mouth was not too small, the lips delicately cut and the corners deep and sweet. The brow was broad and neither too high nor too low. The head was set upon a neck somewhat long but graceful and not too slender. Proportion was the beauty here, each feature in good proportion to all, and the figure was neither tall nor short, it was slender but not thin.

"Is this a suitable choice?" the Empress Mother inquired in doubt.

She continued to stare at the girl. Was there a hint of firmness about the chin? The lips were lovely but not childish. Indeed, the face was wiser than the face of one only sixteen years of age.

"If I read this face aright," she went on, "it signifies a stubborn nature. I like to see a soft-faced maiden, not one so thin as this one. Even for a common man an obedient wife is best, and the consort of an Emperor must above all be submissive."

Alute continued to stand, her head lifted, her eyes downcast.

"She looks clever, Sister," the co-Regent ventured.

"I do not wish my son cursed with a clever wife," the Empress Mother said.

"But you are clever enough for us all, Mother," the young Emperor said, laughing.

The Empress Mother could not keep from smiling at such retort, and willing to be good-natured and even generous on such a day she said, "Well, choose this maiden, then, my son, and do not blame me if she is willful."

The maiden knelt again and put her head upon her hands folded on the floor. Three times she bowed her head to the Empress Mother, three times to the Emperor now her lord, and three times to the Empress co-Regent. Then rising, she walked away as she had come, with the same drifting, graceful gait, and so disappeared from their sight.

"'Alute,'" the Empress Mother mused. "It is a pleasant name—"

She turned to her son. "And what of concubines?" she asked. For it was customary that the four most beautiful girls after the one chosen should be set aside as imperial concubines.

"I pray you choose these for me, Mother," the Emperor said carelessly.

This pleased the Empress Mother, for if sometime she should wish to weaken the tie between her son and his Consort, she could command a concubine whom she had chosen, who, thus bound to her by favor, could step between the royal pair.

"Tomorrow," she promised. "Today I'm surfeited with girlish beauty."

So saying she rose, smiled at her son, and the day of choice was ended.

When the Empress Mother had chosen concubines the next day, it remained only for the Board of Astronomers to consult the heavens and search the stars for the lucky date of marriage. This they declared to be the sixteenth day of the tenth solar month of this same year, the hour to be exactly midnight. On the day and at the hour a member of this Board, careful that the very moment be certain, walked before the wedding sedan, wherein Alute sat behind its scarlet curtains to be carried from her father's house to the palace of the Emperor, and this Board member held in his hand a thick red candle whereon were marked the hours, so that not one moment could pass the midnight without his knowing. Exactly at the hour—nay, at the minute and the second—the Emperor, waiting with his courtiers, the Empress Mother and the Empress Dowager, accepted Alute for his bride. She stepped from the wedding chair, two matrons at her elbows, and two other matrons, the four being titled as Teachers of the Marriage Bed, came forward to receive her and present her to the Emperor.

Thirty days of feasting followed, the afternoons and nights of plays

241

and music, the people of the nation forbidden work or trouble and commanded to enjoy their ease and pleasure. When these days were ended, too, the young Emperor and his Empress were ready to be declared the heads of the nation, but first the Regents must step down from where they had ruled for twelve full years, and though the Empress Mother spoke of herself as only one of two, all knew she was the sole ruler. Again the Board of Astronomers must choose the lucky day, and after studying the stars and omens, the twenty-sixth day of the first moon month was chosen. On the twenty-third day of that same month the Empress Mother sent forth an edict, signed by the Emperor and sealed with the great seal always in her possession, which declared that the Regents now requested him to take the Throne, for they wished to end their Regency. This request the Emperor answered by his own edict saying that he in filial piety must receive it as a command from the older generation and his edict ended thus: "In respectful obedience to the commands of their Majesties, We do in person on the twenty-sixth day of the first moon of the twelfth year of the reign of T'ung Chih enter upon the important duty assigned to Us."

After this, the Empress Mother announced she would retire to enjoy the accumulating years of her life, and so she did, and she let her son rule alone, thereafter, and she declared that her goal was won, her duty done, for she gave the realm intact to her son, the Emperor.

These were her days of peace and pleasure. No longer did the Empress Mother rise in the darkness before dawn to hold audience for those who came from near and far to appeal to the Throne. No longer must she consider the affairs of the nation, make judgments and decide punishments and rewards.

She slept late, rising when she felt inclined, and when she waked she lay awhile, thinking of the day ahead, the lovely empty day in which she had no duty save to be herself. Weighted as she had been all these years with the cares of the realm, today when she woke she could think of her peony mountain. In the largest of her main courtyards she had commanded a hill to be raised and then terraced with peony beds. The young leaves were full and the early buds were swelling into great flowers, rose-colored and crimson and pure white. Each morning hundreds of new blooms waited for her coming, and more eagerly than she had ever hastened to the Throne Hall she rose and made ready for the viewing. She had slept as usual in her inner garments of long pantaloons tied at the ankle and a soft silk tunic with wide sleeves. When she was bathed she put on fresh pantaloons and tunic of pink silk and short outer robe

242

of blue brocaded silk, reaching only to her ankles, for she planned to spend the day entirely with her flowers and birds, and she could not cumber herself by a long robe. While an aged eunuch dressed her hair, she watched the Court ladies make her vast bed, for she would not allow servants or eunuchs or old women to touch her bed, saying that they were dirty, that they had foul breath or some other defect. Thus only her young and healthy ladies could attend the bed, and she watched all they did lest any detail be overlooked. First the quilts and three mattresses must be taken into the courtyard to be aired and sunned all day and she allowed the eunuchs to carry only these. While they did so, the ladies removed the felt that covered the woven bed bottom and swept the bottom with a small broom made of braided horsehair. They must sweep, too, into every corner of the heavy carving of the wooden sides of the bed and the frame that supported the satin curtains. Over the felt they must then place three mattresses which had been aired and sunned the day before, and these were covered with yellow brocaded satin. Over them were spread fresh sheets of delicately tinted silk, very smooth and soft, and over these again were placed six silken covers of pale purple, blue, green, pink, gray and ivory. To cover these the ladies spread last a yellow satin counterpane, embroidered in golden dragons and blue clouds. In the curtains of the bed were hung small bags of dried flowers mixed with musk, and as the scent faded, new bags were hung.

When the eunuch had dressed her hair, parting it in the center and braiding it and bringing the braid into a knot on top of her head, he set upon her crown the high Manchu headdress she always wore, and pinned it through the knot with two long pins. The Empress Mother herself had arranged in her headdress the fresh flowers she loved, and for today she chose small scented orchids freshly plucked. When the headdress set with orchids was in place, she washed her face again and this time herself, and she rubbed into her cream-white skin the foam of a perfumed soap. This in turn she washed away, the water very hot, and now she smoothed into her skin a lotion made of honey, asses' milk and the oil of orange peel. When this was absorbed, she dusted upon her face a pale-pink powder, very soft and fine and scented.

There remained only the choice of jewels for the day. For these she sent for her lists and read aloud the number of a jewel case. A lady whose duty it was to tend the jewels went to a room next to the bedchamber, where the jewels were kept. Here the walls were lined with shelves and upon the shelves were cases of ebony, each numbered, each with its gold lock and key, and upon each case was written what jewels were inside. There were some three thousand boxes in all, yet such jewels were only for daily use. Beyond this room was still another, strongly padlocked, where state jewels were kept, which the Empress Mother wore only upon the occasion of imperial functions. Today, since her robe was blue, she chose sapphires and seed pearls set in earrings, rings, bracelets and a long chain about her neck.

When the jewels were fastened upon her she had next to choose her kerchief. It was the last touch of her toilet, to be decided upon only when she had finished all else, and today she chose an Indian gauze, white imprinted with blue and yellow flowers, and she fastened it over the sapphire button of her robe. With this, she was ready for her morning meal, whose dishes waited for her in her pavilion. Under each dish was a small lamp to keep the food hot. From one dish to the other she drifted, choosing here and there, her ladies standing at a distance, until from twenty dishes she had eaten a light breakfast of sweetmeats, followed by a bowl of millet gruel, which she supped. Only now could the ladies come forward to choose from what she had rejected, and they came forward somewhat timidly, careful not to eat from the dishes she had chosen.

But today the Empress Mother was in pleasant mood. She reproved no one, she was amiable with her dogs, courteously waiting to feed them until her ladies had finished their meal. Not always was she so amiable, for when angry for some reason she fed her dogs first before the ladies ate, saying that only her dogs could she trust as her friends, always loving, always loyal.

When all had eaten she went into her gardens to view her peony mountain. It was the season of returning birds, and as she walked the Empress Mother listened for the wild sweet music that she loved. When a bird called she answered, pursing her lips and replying so perfectly that after a while, she standing motionless in the middle of the garden and her ladies at a distance with the dogs in leash, a bird came fluttering down from among the bamboos, a small yellow-breasted finch, which with coaxing murmuring sounds the Empress Mother persuaded to alight upon her outstretched hand. There it clung, half alarmed, half bewitched, while upon the Empress Mother's face there came a look so tender, so enchanting, that her ladies were moved to see it, marveling that this same face could sometimes be so harsh and cruel. When the bird flew away again, the Empress Mother called to her ladies to come near, and as it pleased her to do, she instructed them thus:

"You see how loving kindness conquers fear, even in animals. Let this lesson be engraved upon your hearts."

"Yes, Majesty," they murmured, and they marveled again because this imperial woman could be so varied, generous and kind, indeed, and yet as truly they knew secretly that she could be vengeful and ruthless.

But this was a good day, her pleasant mood continued, and her ladies prepared to enjoy themselves with her. In season it was the third day of the third month of the moon year, and the Empress Mother bethought herself of a play she had written, for now that the heaviest cares of state were upon her son, the Emperor, she enjoyed her leisure not only in painting and calligraphy but also in writing plays. This imperial woman, so diverse and rich in her genius, might have chosen her own greatness had she been able to single one gift above another, but she could not make her own choice of what she loved best to do, and so she did something of each and in all she excelled. As for those affairs of state which had absorbed her until her son sat upon the Dragon Throne, they seemed forgotten or ignored, yet the eunuchs were her spies, and through them she knew everything.

When she had walked about her gardens for an hour, when she had rested and eaten again, she spoke amiably to her waiting ladies. "The air of this day is fine, the wind is still, the sun is warm, and it would be a pastime to see our court actors perform my play, *The Goddess of Mercy.* What do you say?"

At this all the ladies clapped their hands but the Chief Eunuch, Li Lien-ying, made his obeisance. "Majesty," he said, "I venture to fear that the actors have not yet learned their lines. This play is very subtle, the lines must be spoken with sureness and clarity that humor and fancy be not lost."

The Empress Mother did not approve what he said. "The actors have had time, they have had plenty of time," she declared. "Go at once and tell them that I shall expect the curtain to rise before the beginning of the next period of the water clock. Meanwhile I will say my daily prayers."

So saying the Empress Mother walked with her usual grace through a pavilion to her own private temple, where a white jade Buddha sat upon a great lotus leaf of green jade, holding in his right hand an uplifted lotus flower of rose red jade. On his right stood the slender Kuan Yin, and on his left the God of Long Life. Before the Buddha the Empress Mother stood, not kneeling but with her proud head bowed as she told the beads of a sandalwood rosary she took from the altar.

"*O mi t'o fu,*" she murmured for each bead, until the one hundred and eight sacred beads were told. Then she put down the rosary and lit a stick of incense in the urn upon the altar and again she stood with bowed head while the fragrant smoke curled into the air. She was careful to pray each day, and while she prayed first to the Buddha, who was Lord of Heaven, yet she never left her temple until she had bowed too before the Goddess of Mercy. This goddess she loved extravagantly, imagining in her secret thoughts that they two were sisters, one Queen of Heaven and the other the Queen of Earth. Sometimes in the middle of the night she even so addressed the goddess, murmuring thus behind her bed curtains:

"Sister in Heaven, consider my troubles. These eunuchs—but do you have eunuchs in heaven, Sister? I doubt it, for what eunuch is fit for heaven? Yet who serves You and Your angels, Heavenly Sister? Surely no man, even in heaven, can be pure enough to be near You."

And sometimes, now that she had time to remember, she would inquire of the goddess whether in Heaven it were possible to receive at last a faithful lover. Nay, she did even mention his name.

"Sister in Heaven, you know my kinsman, Jung Lu, and how we would have been man and wife, except for my destiny. Tell me, shall we be free to wed in some other incarnation or shall I still be too great? I, sitting at Your right hand, in Heaven, Sister, I pray You raise him up to me, so that at last we may be equals even as my sister, the English queen, Victoria, once raised her Consort."

All but the truth she told the goddess, and now, gazing into that pure and pensive face, she wondered whether her Heavenly Sister did perhaps know all the truth, told or not, in such midnight thoughts.

When she came out from the temple she led her ladies and her dogs through a large courtyard, where stood two immense baskets made of cedarwood logs in which grew ancient vines of purple wisteria. The vines were in full blossom, scenting the air until the fragrance drifted through the pavilions and the corridors of palaces. It was their season and the Empress Mother came every day to see the wisteria in bloom. Through this courtyard she passed after she had admired the flowers, her entourage behind her, and next she led the way through a corridor that was built into the side of a hill, and by this means she came to her theater.

The theater was like none elsewhere in her realm, nor, she believed, even in the whole world. Around a great open courtyard was a brick building, five stories high, and open in the front toward the courtyard. The three top stories were storerooms for costumes and sceneries. The lower two stories were stages, one above the other, the upper one made like a temple for the sacred plays concerning gods and goddesses, which the Empress Mother loved best to see, for she was ever curious about the lives of Heavenly Beings. Inside the courtyard itself were two long buildings wherein were sitting rooms and pavilions, and here the Court might rest when so invited by the Empress Mother. These buildings were raised ten feet above the ground, level with the lower stage, and faced with glass, so that in wind or cold the Empress Mother still could watch the play. In summer the glass was moved away and gauze was hung, so thin that eye could see through it clearly, yet strong enough to forbid flies and mosquitoes, but especially flies, for the Empress Mother would not allow so much as one fly to come near where she was, and if a fly perched upon a bowl of food, she refused it even to her dogs. In these buildings were three rooms which she alone could use, two to sit in, one of them a library so that she could take up a book when the play was dull, and the third to sleep in when she was inclined, waking again when the play grew lively.

This day, the hour being after noon, she chose the sitting room, and there upon a cushioned throne she sat surrounded by her ladies to watch the play that she had written. It was not the first time she had seen its performance, but she had not been satisfied with the skill of the actors and she had commanded certain changes. In secret they complained that she expected magic of them, but from her was no escape, and today they did their best, achieving such wonders as a great lotus flower rising from the middle of the stage, wherein sat a living Goddess of Mercy, who was a young and delicate eunuch, his face so delicate and pretty that he made a lovely girl. As the goddess rose from the center of the lotus, a boy rose on her right, and a girl on her left, who were her attendants, the girl holding a bottle of jade in which was thrust a willow branch, for it is a legend that if the goddess dips a willow branch into the jade bottle and lifts it above a corpse, then life returns to the dead. Many pieces of magic the Empress Mother devised in her plays, for she was charmed by magic of all sorts and listened eagerly to old wives' tales and legends told by these eunuchs who were the Buddhist priests in the imperial temple. And she liked best the tales of magic which came first out of India with the Buddhist pilgrim priests, a thousand years ago, which tell of runes and sacred rhymes and talismans and secret words that, when chanted, spoken and pronounced, can make a human man safe against a spear thrust or a blow. She all but believed such tales in spite of her natural shrewdness and distrust, for she felt herself too strong to die, and she mused often upon whether there might be a magic that could prevent death and make her eternal. All this wonder and hope and longing to believe in heavenly power, half fantasy, half faith, she put into her plays, exacting a skill nearly magic to perform them, for she directed her own plays, even to the sceneries, and she devised curtains, wing slides and drop scenes which she had never heard of elsewhere but made from her own fertile fancy.

When the play ended she clapped her hands, for indeed it was well done and she was pleased with herself, as playwright. As usual when she was gay, she declared that she was hungry, and so the serving eunuchs came to lay tables for her next meal. It was the habit of the Empress Mother to take her meals wherever she happened to be, and now while she waited she talked with her ladies and asked them questions about the play and what they thought, and she encouraged them to tell her its faults, for she was too large-minded to fear their judgments and was only eager to make what she did more perfect. When the tables were laid the serving eunuchs formed two long lines from kitchens several courtyards away and they passed the covered dishes of hot food from hand to hand and with great speed to the four upper eunuchs who set them on the tables. Now the ladies stood back while the Empress Mother chose what she liked and she ate indeed with good appetite. Since she was in high spirits she pitied the ladies still hungering and she told a eunuch she would drink her tea in the library and so withdrew. Two eunuchs followed, one bearing her white jade cup set in a saucer of pure gold and covered with a lid of gold, and the other bearing a silver tray on which stood two jade bowls, one filled with dried honeysuckle flowers and the other with rose petals, and with them a pair of ivory chopsticks tipped with gold. These flowers the Empress Mother liked to mix with her tea in such delicate proportion that she must do it herself.

It was now as she sipped her tea that the present shadow of her life fell hard upon her. For as she sat upon her cushioned couch, she heard a dry cough at the door and recognized the voice of the Chief Eunuch, Li Lien-ying.

"Enter," she commanded.

He came in and made obeisance, while around her the eunuchs waited.

"Why am I disturbed?" the Empress Mother inquired.

He lifted up his head. "Majesty, I ask to speak to you alone."

She put down her tea bowl and made a gesture with her right hand. All withdrew, a eunuch closed the door.

"Get up," she said to Li Lien-ying. "Sit yonder. What has the Emperor done?"

The tall gaunt eunuch rose and sat down on the edge of a carved chair and turned his hideous wrinkled face away from his sovereign.

248

"I have stolen this memorial from the archives," he said. "I must return it within the hour."

He rose and drew from his robe a folded paper in a long narrow envelope and, kneeling before her, he presented it with both hands, remaining on his knees while she read it quickly. She knew the handwriting. It was that of Wu K'o-tu, the same member of the Board of Imperial Censors who had earlier wished to memorialize the Throne concerning the receiving of foreigners, and whom she had refused. This present memorial was addressed to the Emperor, her son.

"I, most humble slave, do now present this secret memorial beseeching the Throne to end official conflict by granting permission to ministers of foreign governments to stand instead of kneel before the Dragon Throne, and by this permission to show imperial magnanimity and the prestige of the Superior Man. Until this time nothing has been accomplished by insistence upon tradition, and the foreign ministers are only alienated."

The Empress Mother felt old fury stir in her breast. Was her will again to be disputed? Was her own son to be roused against her? If the Dragon Throne were no longer venerated, what honor was left?

Her eyes hurried down the lines and caught a quotation from the ancient sage. "As Mencius has written, 'Why should the Superior Man engage himself in quarrels with the lower order of birds and beasts?'"

She cried out passionately, "This cursed Censor twists even the ancient words of a great sage to his own ends!" Nevertheless she read on to discover what Wu K'o-tu had written.

"I hear that the rulers of foreign nations are deposed by their subjects as though they were puppets. Is this not because these rulers are merely men, and not one of them a Son of Heaven? With my own eyes I have seen foreign men walking in the streets of Peking like servants and without shame, their females walking ahead of them or even riding in sedan chairs. In all the treaties these foreigners have made with us, there is not one word concerning reverence for parents and elders or respect for the nine canons of virtues. There is no mention of the four principles, namely, the observance of ceremony, the individual's duty to other human beings, integrity of character and a sense of shame. Instead, they speak only and always of commercial profit. Such men do not know the meaning of duty and ceremony, wisdom and good faith. Yet we expect them to behave as civilized men. They do not know the meaning of the five relationships, the first of which is that between sovereign and subject, and yet we expect them to behave as though they did know. We might as well bring pigs and dogs into the Audience

Hall and expect beasts to prostrate themselves before the Dragon Throne. If we insist upon such men kneeling, how can it increase the luster of the Throne?

"Moreover, these foreigners even dare to say that their absurd rulers, whom they presume to call emperors, are to be placed on a level with His Sacred Majesty. If we can overlook such shame as this, why do we trouble ourselves about their envoys refusing to kneel? And again, two years ago, when Russian barbarians pressed upon China from Ili and all the northwest and seized vast stretches of our land, carrying on an aggression never before known in history, our statesmen showed no shame. Why then do we cry out about the humiliation of foreigners refusing to kneel before the Dragon Throne? And, as a fact, how can we force them to kneel when they will not? Have we the armies and the weapons to compel them? This, too, must be considered. The master sage, Confucius, when asked in what lay the art of government, replied that there are three requisites, plenty of food, plenty of armies, and the confidence of the people. Asked which of these could be dispensed with in time of necessity, the master replied, 'Dispense first with the troops, next with the food supply.' If therefore our imperial government is not able to compel the foreigners to its will, it is better to act the part of generosity rather than to rouse the doubts of the people.

"It seems, therefore, that the Throne should issue a decree excusing the foreign envoys from performing the ceremonies of the Court and if in the future these foreigners commit offensive acts because of their ignorance, such should be overlooked, for it is unworthy to dispute with these foreigners. At the same time, it should be explained to the foreigners, and to the people, that this decree is an act of clemency and in no wise a precedent. Let us proceed to develop our strength, biding our time.

"I, the writer of this worthless memorial, am but an ignorant inhabitant of a wild and remote district and know nothing of affairs of State. Greatly daring and of rash utterance, I present this my memorial, knowing the while that in so doing I risk the penalty of death."

In her natural anger against the audacity of the foreign envoys, to which was now added such advice as the Censor had proposed, the Empress Mother's hands itched to tear the memorial into a thousand pieces and fling them away to be lost, but she was too prudent to yield even to herself. This Wu K'o-tu was a wise man, a man of years and of high honor. He did more than preach the duties and the ceremonies. He practiced them most rigorously and without excusing himself from one ounce of burden. Thus when the Court fled to Jehol and the foreigners had seized the capital, Wu K'o-tu had remained in the city with his aged mother in her last illness. Risking his life, he had stayed at her side, meanwhile ordering as fine a coffin as could be made in such duress. When she died he closed her eyes and saw to it that she was placed comfortably into the coffin. Even then he was not willing to leave her, but hired a cart at great cost and accompanied her to a temple in another city where she could lie in peace and safety until such time as her funeral could take place.

The Empress Mother knew that such righteousness was rare indeed and she restrained her wrath and, folding the memorial, she returned it to the Chief Eunuch.

"Replace this where you found it," she said, and not deigning to reveal to him what her thoughts were, she dismissed him from her presence.

But the mood of pleasure was gone. She could take no more joy that day in the theater. She sat brooding while the actors performed their parts and she did not lift her head to see what they did or listen to their most seductive songs. In the midst of the last scene, a glorious display of the entire cast, dressed all as Heavenly Beings, singing and gathered about the Queen of Heaven, while at their feet clustered a score of small monkeys, alive but trained to play the parts of devils who had yielded to her kindly power, the Empress Mother rose without a word and walked away so swiftly that her ladies, bemused by the play, did not see her until she was all but gone. Then in haste and confusion they followed. Nevertheless, she kept them at a distance by an imperious gesture and alone she returned to her palace. Only then did she speak and it was to send a eunuch for Li Lien-ying again.

The Chief Eunuch came with gigantic strides, and he appeared before her as she sat in the great carved chair in her library, but not reading, and indeed as motionless as a goddess. Her face was pale and her great eyes bright and cold.

"Bid my son attend me," she said when she saw the eunuch. Her voice was cold, too, as cold as silver.

He made obeisance and retired and she waited. When a lady opened the door, she waved her away, and the door closed again.

The minutes passed and the Chief Eunuch did not return. The minutes crept into an hour and still he did not come, nor was there a message from the Emperor. The Empress Mother sat on while the light of afternoon faded from the courtyards and twilight crept into the vast library. Still she waited. The serving eunuchs came in on noiseless feet to light the candles in the hanging lanterns and she let them do so, not speaking until the last was lit.

Then she said in her silver-cold voice:

"Where is the Chief Eunuch?"

"Majesty," a eunuch replied, making obeisance, "he stands outside in the Waiting Pavilion."

"Why does he not enter?" she asked.

"Majesty, he is afraid." The eunuch's voice trembled.

"Send him to me," she commanded.

She waited and in a moment Li Lien-ying came stealing like a tall shadow from the darkening garden. He flung himself upon the floor before her and she looked down on his crouching shape.

"Where is my son?" she asked without anger, it seemed, except for the silvery coldness of her voice.

"Majesty, I dare not—" he stammered and paused.

"Dare not bring me his answer?" she asked.

"Majesty, he sent word that he is indisposed." His voice was muffled by his hands as big as plates over his face.

"And is he indisposed?" she inquired. The cool voice seemed careless.

"Majesty—Majesty—"

"He is not indisposed," she said.

She rose, a figure controlled and graceful. "If he will not come to me, I must go to him," she said, and walked away so swiftly that the eunuch must scramble from his knees to follow her. She paid him no heed, she did not look back, and since she had commanded her ladies to leave her, none knew that she was gone except the Chief Eunuch and the lesser serving eunuchs who stood at their posts in pavilion, corridor and gateway. Yet none of them dared to move, though each turned to look at each other after she had passed. For the Empress Mother walked as though winged, her face set straight ahead, her eyes burning black in her pale face. And behind her came Li Lien-ying, not daring to stop to explain to anyone what was amiss, for even his long strides could not keep him close to that swift imperial figure in brilliant robes of blue and gold.

Straight she went to the Emperor's palace, and when she reached the splendid courtyard she mounted the marble steps to the marble terrace. The doors were closed but light streamed through the panes of silken gauze and she looked in. There sat her son, lounging in a great cushioned chair, and leaning over him was Alute. The young Consort held a cluster of cherries to the Emperor's lips, the early cherries that come from the south, such as he loved, and he was reaching for them, his head thrown back, laughing as the Empress Mother had never seen him laugh. Around him were his eunuchs and the ladies of the young Empress, and they were all laughing like children.

She wrenched the door open and stood there, bright as a goddess against the darkness of the night. The light of a thousand candles fell upon her glittering robes and headdress and upon her beautiful furious face. Her long eyes, enormous and shining, swept looks to right and left upon them all, until she brought them upon her son and Alute.

"My son, I hear that you are ill," she said in her sweet, cruel voice. "I am come to see how you are."

He sprang to his feet while Alute stood like a statue, motionless, the cherries still hanging in her hand.

"I see you are indeed very ill," the Empress Mother said, not moving her eyes from her son's face. "I shall command the Court physicians to attend you immediately."

He could not speak. He gazed at his mother, his eyes sick indeed with fear.

"And you, Alute," the Empress Mother said, carving her every word as cold and clear as icicles, "I wonder that you do not consider your lord's health. He should not eat fresh fruit when he is ill. You are too careless of your duties to the Son of Heaven. I will have you punished."

The Emperor closed his hanging jaw and swallowed. "Mother," he stammered, "I beg you, nothing is Alute's fault. I was weary—the audience lasted all day—very nearly. I did feel ill."

She put her terrible gaze upon him again and felt the heat of her own eyes in their sockets. She took three steps forward. "Down on your knees," she cried. "Do you think because you are Emperor you are not my son?"

All this while Alute did not move. She stood straight and tall, her delicate face proud and her eyes not afraid. Now she dropped the cherries she had forgotten to put down, and she seized the Emperor's arm.

"No," she cried in a low soft voice. "No, you shall not kneel."

The Empress Mother took two more steps forward. She thrust forth her right hand, the forefinger pointed to the floor.

"Kneel!" she commanded.

For a long instant the young Emperor wavered. Then he loosed his arm from Alute's hand.

"It is my duty," he said and fell to his knees.

The Empress Mother bent her look upon him in another dreadful silence. Her right hand fell slowly to her side.

"It is well that you remember your duty to your elder. Even the Emperor is no more than a child before his mother, so long as she lives."

She raised her head then and sent her gaze searching over eunuchs and ladies.

"Away with you all," she cried. "Leave me alone with my son."

One by one they crept away until only Alute was left.

"You, also," the Empress Mother insisted, unrelenting.

Alute hesitated, then with a mournful look, she, too, went away, her feet silent in their satin shoes.

When all were gone, the Empress Mother changed as suddenly as day in spring. She smiled and went to her son and passed her smooth scented palm over his cheek.

"Get up, my son," she said gently. "Let us sit down and reason together." But she took the thronelike chair which was his, and he sat upon Alute's lower chair. He was trembling, she could see his quivering lips, his nervous hands.

"Even in a palace there must be order," she said. She made her voice calm and friendly. "It was necessary for me to establish the order of the generations before the eunuchs and in the presence of the Consort. To me she is only my son's wife."

He did not answer, but his stealthy tongue slipped out between his teeth to wet his dry lips.

"Now, my son," she went on, "I am told that you plan in secret to defy my will. Is it true that you will receive the foreign ministers without obeisance?"

He summoned all his pride. "I am so advised," he said, "and even by my uncle, Prince Kung."

"And you will do it?" she inquired. Who better than he could catch the edge of her lovely voice, silver and dangerous?

"I will do it," he said.

"I am your mother," she said. "I forbid you."

Her heart grew soft against her will while she gazed at his young, handsome face, the mouth too tender, the eyes large and liquid, and in spite of his willfulness and his stubborn ways, she discerned now, as she had when he was a child, his secret fear of her. A pang of sadness passed through her heart. She would have him so strong that even her he would not fear, for any fear is weakness. If he were afraid of her, he would also be afraid of Alute, yielding to her, so that some day she, the wife, would be the stronger. Had he not often gone for comfort to Sakota, and in secret? So now perhaps he escaped to Alute because he was afraid of her who was his mother, and who loved him better than a girl could know how to love. She had given up all her womanhood for him, she had made his destiny her own.

His eyelashes fell again before her searching gaze. Alas, those lashes were too long upon a man's cheek but she had given them to him, they were like hers, and why if a woman can bestow her beauty upon her son, can she not bestow her strength?

She sighed and bit the edge of her lip and seemed to yield. "What do I care whether the foreigners kneel to the Dragon Throne? I am thinking only of you, my son."

"I know," he said, "I know it, Mother. Whatever you do is for me. I wish I could do something for you. Not in matters of state, Mother, but something you would like. What would you like? Something to make you happy—a garden, or a mountain made into a garden. I could have a mountain moved—"

She shrugged. "I have gardens and mountains." But she was touched by his wish to please her. Then she said slowly, "What I long for cannot be restored."

"Tell me," he urged. He was eager to feel her approve him again, to know he was safe from her anger.

"What use?" she replied pensively. "Can you bring back life from ashes?"

He knew what she meant. She was thinking of the ruined Summer Palace. She had told him often of its pagodas and pavilions, its gardens and rockeries. Ah, for that destruction she would never forgive the foreigners.

"We could build a new Summer Palace, Mother," he said slowly, "one as like to the old one as you can remember. I will ask for special tribute from the provinces. We must use no monies from the Treasury."

"Ah," she said shrewdly, "you are bribing me to let you have your way—you and your advisors!"

"Perhaps," he said. He lifted his straight brows and glanced at her sidewise.

Suddenly she laughed. "Ah, well," she said. "Why do I disturb myself? A summer palace? Why not?"

She rose and he stood and reaching up her hands she smoothed his cheeks again with her soft scented palms and went away. Out of the shadows Li Lien-ying followed.

There is no end to the sorrows that children bring to their parents in palace or in hovel. The Empress Mother, waited upon often by Li Lien-ying, her chief spy, next learned as the days passed that the Emperor had lied to her when he said Prince Kung had advised him to receive the foreign ministers without demanding obeisance. Instead, Prince Kung had reminded the Emperor how his ancestors had refused to allow a privilege to foreigners which they denied to their own citizens. Thus in the time of the Venerable Ancestor Ch'ien Lung, it was required that the English lord Macartney bow to the floor before the Dragon Throne, even though in revenge a Manchu prince must bow in the same manner before a picture of the English monarch, King George. Now Prince Kung made delay after delay when the foreign envoys insisted that they be received at Court, and he pleaded the illness of the Chief Secretary of the Imperial Foreign Office, and this illness lingered through four months until the Emperor himself ended it by commanding that the envoys from the West be presented before the Dragon Throne, thus proving that he, and he alone, was too lenient and too weak.

To this report the Empress Mother listened one day in her orchid garden. The months of spring were gone, it was early summer, the loveliest season, and she had no mind to cope with affairs of state. Enticed by the clear sunlight today, she had walked into her library, and upon a vast table set up therein, she was drawing a map of the new Summer Palace before she summoned architects and builders to put her dreams into brick and marble. Hither Li Lien-ying had come.

"Fetch me Prince Kung," she commanded him when he had made his report. With impatience she put down her brushes to wait until the Prince arrived.

He found her pacing up and down before the wide doors open to the courtyard. Pomegranate trees were in full bloom, their red flowers studded among the dark green leaves of the thickset trees. The Empress Mother was fond of pomegranates, flowers and fruit. She loved the burning orange red of their flowers and the sweet acid of the juicy pulp surrounding each of the thousand seeds within the tight green skin of the fruit. Prince Kung knew her liking, and when he came and had made obeisance he spoke first of pomegranates.

"Majesty, your trees are very fine. I do not see others like them. Whatever is near you takes on new life."

He had learned by now to speak to her gracefully and with submission.

She inclined her head, always pleased by praise and ready to be newly generous to him because he did not approve the Emperor's will. "Let us talk here in the courtyard," she said. They seated themselves, she upon a porcelain garden seat and he after seeming to refuse, upon a bamboo bench.

"Why should I waste your time?" she began. "But I hear that the

Emperor, my son, wishes to receive the foreign envoys without obeisance and this troubles me much."

"Majesty, he is curious as a child," Prince Kung replied. "He cannot wait to look upon a foreign face."

"Are men always children?" she exclaimed. She reached above her head and plucked a scarlet pomegranate flower and pulled it to pieces and let it fall.

He did not reply to this and kept silence until she lost patience. "Well, well," she cried, "and did you not forbid him? You are the older generation."

Prince Kung raised his eyebrows. "Majesty, how can I refuse the Emperor when he has the power to cut off my head?"

"You know I would not allow that," she rejoined.

"Majesty, I thank you," Prince Kung replied. "Yet I think you know the Consort influences him more deeply every day—a good influence, let me say, since it keeps him from the company of eunuchs and the low flowerhouses where they used to lead him, pretending he went disguised."

"Ah, but who influences the Consort?" the Empress Mother inquired sharply. "She does not come to me except when duty demands that she pay her respects. When I see her she is silent."

"Majesty," he said, "I do not know."

She brushed the petals from her satin lap. "You do know. It is the Empress Dowager—it is my cousin Sakota."

He bowed his head and was silent for awhile. Then he said, placating, "Majesty, at least the foreign envoys should not be received in the Imperial Audience Hall."

"Most surely not," she agreed, diverted as he had meant she should be. She considered for a moment, the sunlight falling through the pomegranate tree above her head upon her hands now folded and quiet in her lap. Suddenly she smiled.

"I have it! Let them be received in the Pavilion of Purple Light. They will not know it is not the palace proper. Thus we keep to reality and give them illusion."

He could not resist her mischief, reluctant though he was to yield to it. For the Pavilion of Purple Light was on the farther side of the Middle Lake, which is part of the western boundary of the Forbidden City, and in it the Emperor, by tradition, received only the envoys of the outer tribes, and this but once upon the first day of the new year.

"Majesty," Prince Kung now said, "you are as clever as the most clever man. I do admire your skill and wit. I will so order and arrange."

She was in high humor now and, moved by his praise, she invited him to come and see her plans for the Summer Palace.

There for an hour he stood, or walked about the long wide table whereon was stretched the scroll upon which she drew her dreams. He listened to her flowing talk, he heard of rivers winding among rockeries and spreading into lakes, of mountains moved from the western provinces and set with trees and pools of gold-roofed palaces and gilded pagodas set on the mountain sides and by the shores of a vast lake. He said not a word, so great was his dismay, and he dared not open his mouth to speak lest all his anger at such wasted monies rush out of him at once and cause her to command his death. He forced himself to murmur between his teeth at last:

"Who but you, Majesty, could conceive so imperial a palace?"

Then he begged to be excused and hastened from her presence. From her he went straight to the Grand Councilor Jung Lu, a device the Empress Mother guessed at once when, on the evening of that same day, before the curfew fell, her eunuch came to say that Jung Lu waited for audience.

She was at this moment leaning over the map again, her brush pointed fine to ink in a slender high pagoda.

"Let the Grand Councilor enter," she said, not lifting up her head, and knowing that Jung Lu would not approve what she did, she let him stand awhile behind her back before she spoke.

"Who is there?" she asked after moments.

"Majesty, you know."

The sound of his deep voice went to her heart now as swiftly as it ever had but she pretended that it did not.

"Ah," she said indifferently, "and why have you come? Do you not see that I am busy?"

"It is the reason for my coming," he said. "And I beg you, Majesty, to hear me, for there is but a little while before the gates are locked for curfew."

She recognized the old power of command. This man alone in the whole world she feared because he loved her and would not yield to her. Yet she was as willful now as she had been when she was a girl betrothed to him and she took her time and let him wait on while she put the jade cover on the ink slab and washed her brush in a small bowl of water and made ado with these small tasks which at other times she left to a serving eunuch. And he waited, knowing very well what she did, and that she knew he knew.

At last she walked slowly across the vast hall to her throne chair and sat down. He came toward her there and knelt before her as custom demanded, and she let him kneel, her black eyes cruel and laughing and tender all at once.

"Are your knees aching?" she asked after a while.

"It is of no importance, Majesty," he said calmly.

"Rise," she said. "I do not enjoy your kneeling before me."

He rose with dignity and stood, and she surveyed him from foot to head. When her eyes reached his she let them rest. They were alone and she could meet his look with none to reproach. Her eunuch stood his distance in the entrance hall beyond, on guard.

"What have I done wrong?" Her voice was sweet as a child's with pleading.

"You know what you do," he answered.

She shrugged her satin shoulders. "I have not told you about the new Summer Palace, for I knew that someone would tell you—Prince Kung, doubtless. But I receive the new Summer Palace as a gift from my son. It is his wish."

To this Jung Lu replied most gravely. "You know there is no money in the treasury for a pleasure palace in these times. The people are already too much taxed. Yet new taxes must be levied on every province if this palace is to be raised."

She shrugged again. "It need not be money. It can be stone and wood and rock and jade and artisans. These are everywhere."

"Men must be paid," he said.

"They need not be," she answered carelessly. "The First Emperor did not pay the peasants who built the Great Wall. When they died he put their bones among the bricks and there was no need even for burial money."

"In those days," he said in the same grave voice, "the dynasty was strong. The people dared not rebel. The Emperor was Chinese, not Manchu, as we are, and the wall was to protect their own people against invading northern enemies. But will the people now be willing to send their goods and men only to build a Summer Palace for you? And could you find pleasure in a place where walls are filled with bones of men who died for naught? I think even you are not so hard."

He and he alone of all the world could bring the tears to her eyes. She turned her head to hide them. "I am not hard—" Her voice was a whisper. "I am—lonely."

She took the end of the kerchief of flowered gauze hanging from the jade button of her robe and she wiped her eyes. The cords between the man and the woman drew taut. She longed to hear his footstep coming toward her, his hand put out to touch her own.

He did not move. She heard his voice still grave. "You should have told your son, the Emperor, that it ill behooves him to give you a gift of palaces, while the nation is beset with threats of war, with poverty and floods in the middle provinces. It was your duty to remind him."

She turned her head at this and the tears glistened on her long black lashes and shone in her tragic eyes. "Oh, this realm," she cried, "there is always misery!" Her lips quivered and she wrung her hands together. "And why do you not tell him?" she cried. "You are a father to him—"

"Hush," he said between his teeth. "We speak of the Imperial Emperor."

She drooped her head and the tears fell upon the rose-red satin of her gown.

"What ails you?" he asked. "You have all you have ever lived for. What more do you desire? Is there a woman in the world more high than you?"

She did not answer and her tears kept dropping while he spoke on.

"The dynasty is safe while you live, at least. You have made an emperor, you have given him a consort. He loves her, and being young and loving him, she will give him an heir."

She lifted her head, her eyes startled.

"Already?"

"I do not know it," he replied, "but doubtless it will be so, for I know their mutual love."

He met her eyes, his own compassionate. "I saw them a few days ago, by accident, not knowing they were near. The hour was late and I was on my way to the great gate, before the curfew fell. They were in the Pavilion of Favorable Winds."

"Too near the palace of the Empress Dowager—" she murmured.

"The gate was open," he said, "and without thought my eyes went there, and I saw them in the twilight, walking like two children, their arms about each other."

She bit her lip, her round chin quivered and her tears welled up again. At the sight of her face, beautiful in sorrow, he could not stay himself.

He took three steps and then two more, closer to her than he had been in many years. "My heart," he said, so low that none but he could hear, "they have what you and I can never have. Help them to keep it. Guide them aright. Pour all your strength and power into this new reign, for it is based on love."

But she could bear no more. She put her hands before her face and wept aloud. "Oh, go," she sobbed. "Leave me—leave me alone as I have always been!"

So passionately and deeply did she sob that he was forced to heed her lest others hear and wonder why she wept. He hesitated, sighed, and took a step backward to leave her as she had begged him to do.

But she was watching him through her fingers as she wept, and when she saw him leaving her without comfort, she flung her hands from her face in anger so hot that instantly her tears were dried.

"I suppose—I suppose—that you do not love anyone now except your own children! How many children have you with—with—"

He stopped and folded his arms. "Majesty, I have three," he said.

"Sons?" she demanded.

"I have no true sons," he said.

For a long moment their eyes met in mutual pain and longing. Then he went away, and she was left alone.

Before the end of the sixth solar month the Emperor T'ung Chih had received the envoys of the West. The Empress Mother heard the story of it from Li Lien-ying and said nothing while he told it as his duty.

The audiences took place at six o'clock, he said, soon after sunrise, and in the Pavilion of Purple Light. There upon a raised dais the Emperor sat cross-legged behind a low table. He gazed upon the strange white faces of the tall men, the ministers from England, France, Russia, Holland and the United States. All save the Russians wore straight dark clothes of woolen stuffs, their legs encased in tight trousers and their upper parts in short coats as though they were laborers, and they wore no robes. Each walked forward from his place in line, each bowed to the Emperor but made no obeisance, neither kneeling nor knocking his head upon the tiled floor, and while he stood, each gave to Prince Kung a script to read aloud. This script was written in Chinese and the meaning of each script was always the same, a greeting from some Western nation to the Emperor upon his accession to the Throne and good wishes for his prosperous peaceful reign.

To each the Emperor must reply and in the same fashion. Prince Kung mounted the dais and then fell on his knees with utmost ceremony and bent his head to the floor and took from his imperial nephew the script already prepared. When he came down from the dais he was careful each time before these foreigners to follow every law of conduct laid down centuries earlier by the sage Confucius. He appeared in haste to do his duty, he spread his arms like wings, his robes flying, and he kept his face troubled to show himself anxious to serve his sovereign. To each foreign envoy he gave the royal script. Then the envoys placed their credentials on a waiting table, and walking backward they withdrew from the Imperial Presence, pleased, doubtless, to think they had won their way and not knowing that where they stood was no palace but a mere pavilion.

All this the Empress Mother heard, and while she said nothing, her lips curving downward and her eyes scornful, her heart hardened in her bosom. How dared her son defy her even by so much, except that he was strengthened by Alute, whom now he heeded more than he did his own mother? She thought of the two of them as Jung Lu had seen them, their arms about each other, and her heart was stabbed again, and, wounded, it grew yet more hard. Ah, and why should she, too, not have what she wanted, the Empress Mother inquired of that hardening heart. She would have her Summer Palace and make it the more magnificent because her son loved Alute.

Now like an arrow shot from the sky, a frightful thought pierced her brooding brain. If Alute bore a son, and Jung Lu had said that doubtless she would bear a son, for out of strong love sons are always born, then she, Alute, would be the Empress Mother!

"Oh, stupid I," she muttered. "How did I not think that Alute truly means to depose me? What shall I be then except an old woman in the palace?"

"Get from my sight!" she cried to her eunuch.

He obeyed instantly, the shriek of her voice piercing in his ears, and she sat like a stone image, plotting again, in all her loneliness, to hold her power.

She must destroy the love that Jung Lu had bid her save. But how?

She remembered suddenly the four concubines she had chosen for the Emperor on his marriage day. They lived together in the Palace of Accumulated Elegance, waiting to be summoned. But not one was ever summoned, nor was it likely that they would be, since Alute had won the Emperor's heart. Yet one of these concubines, the Empress Mother now remembered, was very beautiful. Three she had chosen for their birth and good sense, but the fourth had been so pretty that even she was charmed by that fresh bright youth. And why should she not gather these young concubines about her? She would so do, teach them herself, and somehow persuade them into the Emperor's presence on the pretext that he needed change and diversion, that Alute was too serious, too eager in compelling him to labor for the state, hers too strong a conscience for a man so young and pleasure-loving. This fourth concubine was not of high birth. Indeed, she came from a house too low even for a concubine, and only her great beauty had persuaded the princes and the ministers to include her name among the Manchu maidens. This loveliness could be of use. The girl could entice the Emperor back to his old haunts outside the palace walls. Alute would lose him.

And all the while that the Empress Mother busied her thoughts in such plotting she knew that she did evil, yet determined that she would do it. Was she not solitary in the whole world? No one dared to love her, fear was her only weapon, and if none feared her, she would be only that old woman in the palace, the dark veil of the years creeping over her, hiding heart and mind behind the withering flesh. Now while she was still beautiful, still strong, she must gain even the Throne, if need be, to save herself from living death.

Her memory crept back through the years. She saw herself again as a small girl child, always working beyond her strength in her uncle Muyanga's great household, where her mother was but a widowed sister-in-law, and she herself no better than a bondmaid. Wherever she went, that girl child, who was she, had carried on her back a younger sister or brother, and never had she been free to run or play until they could walk alone. And then because she was quick and clever, she had helped in the kitchen and the wardrooms, forever with a broom in her hand, or cooking and sewing, or going to market to haggle over fish and fowl. At night she fell into sleep as soon as she crept into the bed she shared with her sister. Not even Jung Lu had been able to lighten her daily burdens, for he was a boy who grew into a man, and he could do nothing for her. Had she married him, he would have stayed a guardsman, and in his house she would have worked again in kitchen and in courtyard, bearing children and quarreling with servant and slave, watchful against petty thieving. How much more had she benefited even her lover by being his sovereign instead of his wife! Yet he was not grateful to her, but used his power only to reproach her.

And her son, who ought always to love her, both by right and by debt, loved his wife better than his mother. Nay, she remembered daily that he loved even his foster mother, Sakota, more than he did her, his own mother, who had spent many weary hours with that childish Emperor who was never husband to her, and for what reason except to gain the throne for him, her son. Oh, those weary hours! She remembered the pallid yellow face and the hot sick hands always fumbling at her body and her gorge rose again.

And how firmly she had held the Throne during the twelve years of her Regency, so that when her son was Emperor he might be spared the dangers of rebellion and conquest! She, and she alone, had kept the white men at bay and had forced tribute even from the wild tribes of Mongolia. She had put down the Muslim uprisings in Yünnan and the Shen-kan provinces. In peace and in safety her son now ruled, and though he knew her wisdom, he would not come to ask her guidance, who alone could guide him.

Such thoughts forced a dark lonely strength into her mind. Her blood ran strong to her heart and her whole being rose up to battle against her present fate. So wounded was she, so hurt and beset, that she forgot all love, and set her will, sharp and narrow as a sword, to cleave her way again to power.

Yet she was too just by nature to yield only to revenge and she must find other reasons for taking back her power. When her son began his reign a year ago the Empire was at peace for the first time in a score of years. Now suddenly fresh trouble arose. Upon the distant island of Taiwan, whose people were wild tribes, a few shipwrecked sailors had been washed ashore. When the savages saw these strangers they fell upon them and killed them. But they were Japanese seamen, and when the Emperor of Japan heard of the murder of his subjects, he sent his ships of war to carry soldiers to that island. These claimed the island in his name, and also other islands nearby. When Prince Kung, who was the head of the Foreign Office in Peking, protested such invasion, the Emperor of Japan declared that he would open war on China.

Nor was this all. For fifteen centuries the Emperors of China had ruled the inner country of Annam as suzerains, and the people there were grateful for protection, since it gave freedom for their own rulers and yet saved them from marauders, and so mighty was the Chinese Empire that none had dared to attack its tributary peoples. None but the white man! For Frenchmen had crept into Annam within the last hundred years, and in the last twenty had so established themselves by trade and priesthood that France had compelled the King of Annam to sign a treaty, which took away the northeastern province of Tonkin, where Chinese bandits and outlaws daily crossed to and fro to do their work.

This much the Empress Mother knew, but she had wished such troubles no longer to be her concern so that she could busy herself with her new palace. Now suddenly she decided they were her concern. She would declare that her son did nothing, the princes were given to pleasure, and unless such apathy were ended, the Empire would fall before her own life was ended. Therefore it was her clear duty to take the reins of government again into her hands.

On a certain day, then, in early summer, at her command, the young concubines came fluttering into her palace as birds released from their cage. They had given up hope of being summoned before the Emperor, and now their hope was bright again, and in devotion they surrounded the Empress Mother as angels surround a goddess. The Empress Mother could not but smile and enjoy their worship, though she knew well enough that their love was not for her, but for themselves and what they hoped. She and she alone could bring them into the imperial bedchamber. She pitied them and beckoning them to come nearer she said,

"My birds, you know that I cannot bring you all at once before the Emperor. The Consort would be angry and he would send you away again. So let me then send you to him one at a time, and it is only sensible that the prettiest shall be the first."

She was immediately fond of these four young girls now gathering about her. Such a young girl she, too, had been when she came to live behind these palace walls. She looked from one face to the other, the bright eyes gazing at her with confidence and hope, and she had not the heart to wound any of them. "How can I choose which is the pretty one?" she inquired. "You must choose among yourselves."

They laughed, four gay young voices joining together. "Our Venerable Ancestor," the tallest one cried, the one least pretty, "how can you pretend that you do not know? Jasmine is the pretty one."

All turned to look at Jasmine, who blushed and shook her head and put her kerchief to her face to hide herself.

"Are you the prettiest?" the Empress Mother asked, smiling. She enjoyed playfulness with young creatures, human or beast.

At this Jasmine could only shake her head again and again and cover her face with her hands, too, while the others laughed aloud.

"Well, well," the Empress Mother said at last. "Take your hands down from your face, child, so that I may see you for myself."

The girls pulled Jasmine's hands away, and the Empress Mother studied the downcast and rosy face. It was not a shy face so much as mischievous, or perhaps only merry. Nor was it a gentle face. Indeed, there was boldness in the full curved lips, the large eyes, the slightly flaring nostrils of the small tilted nose. Alute was like her father, who had been assistant to the Imperial Tutor to the Emperor, a man of delicately handsome face and frame. To such a woman as Alute Jasmine was the complete foil. Instead of Alute's slender graceful body, tall for a woman, Jasmine was small and plump, and her greatest beauty was a skin without blemish or fault. It was a baby's skin, cream white except for the flushed cheeks and red mouth.

Thus satisfied, the Empress Mother's mood changed suddenly. She waved the concubines away, and yawned behind her jeweled hand.

265

"I will send for you when the day comes," she said half carelessly to Jasmine, and the concubines could only retire, their embroidered sleeves folded like bright wings.

Thereafter naught remained except for the Chief Eunuch to inquire of Alute's woman what few days in the month the Consort could not enter the royal bedchamber. These were seven days distant, and the Empress Mother sent word to Jasmine to be ready on the eighth day. Her robe, she commanded, must be peach pink, and she was to use no perfume, for she herself would provide perfume from her own bottles.

Upon the day Jasmine came so robed, and the Empress Mother received her and observed her carefully from head to foot. First she commanded the small cheap jewels she wore to be taken away.

"Bring me the case from my jewel room marked thirty-two," she said to her ladies, and when the box was brought, she lifted from it two flowers shaped like peonies, made of rubies and pearls, and these she gave to Jasmine to fasten above her ears. She gave her bracelets, too, and rings, until the girl was beside herself with delight, biting her scarlet lips and flashing her black eyes in joy.

When this was done, the Empress Mother called for a heavy musk perfume, and she bade Jasmine rub it on her palms and under her chin, behind her ears and between her breasts and loins.

"Well enough," the Empress Mother said when all was done. "Do you now come with me and my ladies. We go to my son, the Emperor."

No sooner had these words left her lips than she thought—and why should she go to the Emperor? Alute would hear of her presence, for Alute had her spies, doubtless, and she would make pretext to come to bow before the Empress Mother. But, unbidden, she could not dare to come here to the Empress Mother's own palace.

"Stay—" the Empress Mother put out her hand. "Since I know my son is alone today, I will invite him here. And I will command my cooks to prepare a feast of the Emperor's favorite dishes. My son will dine with me. The day is fair. Let the tables be set under the trees in the courtyard, and let the Court musicians attend us, and after we have dined the Court actors must give us a play."

She tossed her commands into the air left and right, and eunuchs ran to obey and her ladies hastened hither and thither.

"And you, Jasmine," she said next, "you are to stand near me and tend my tea bowl, and be silent unless I bid you speak."

"Yes, Venerable Ancestor," the girl said, her big eyes lively and her cheeks scarlet.

Thus it came about that in an hour or two the bugles announced the

266

Emperor and soon thereafter his sedan entered the vast courtyard, where the eunuchs were already busy with tables and the musicians with their instruments.

The Empress Mother was seated in her private audience hall upon her small throne, and near her stood Jasmine, who held her head down while she toyed with a fan. Behind these two the ladies stood in a half circle.

The Emperor came in wearing a robe of sky-blue satin embroidered in gold dragons, his tasseled hat upon his head, and in his hand a jade piece to cool his palms. He bowed before his mother without obeisance, since he was Emperor, and she received his greeting and did not rise. Now this was a symbol, for all must rise before the Emperor, and the ladies looked at one another to ask why the Empress Mother kept her seat. The Emperor seemed not to notice, however, and he sat down on a small throne on his mother's right, and his eunuchs and guardsmen withdrew to the outer court.

"I heard you were alone today, my son," the Empress Mother said, "and to guard against your melancholy until the Consort returns, I thought to keep you here for a while. The sun is not too hot for us to dine under the trees in the courtyard, and the musicians will beguile us while we dine. Choose a play, my son, for the actors to perform for our amusement afterwards. By then it will be sunset and so one day passed."

She said this in a sweet and loving voice, her great eyes warm upon him, and her beautiful hand outstretched to touch his hand upon his knee.

The Emperor smiled and was astonished, as anyone could see, for of late his imperial mother had not been kind. Indeed, she had reproved him much, and he would have refused to come to her this day, except he was unwilling to bear her wrath alone. When Alute was with him, she gave him strength.

"Thank you, my mother," he said, pleased to know she was not angry. "It is true I was lonely, and true, too, that I was casting here and there in my mind to know how to spend the day."

The Empress Mother spoke to Jasmine. "Pour tea, my child, for your lord."

The Emperor lifted his head at these words and stared at Jasmine, nor did he take his eyes away while with pretty grace she took the bowl of tea from a eunuch and presented it with both hands.

"Who is this lady?" the Emperor inquired as though she were not there.

"What!" the Empress Mother cried in feigned surprise. "Do you not

267

recognize your own concubine? She is one of the four I chose for you. Can it be that you do not yet know who they are?"

In some confusion the Emperor shook his head and smiled again but ruefully. "I have not summoned them. The time has not yet come—"

The Empress Mother pursed her lips. "In courtesy you should have summoned them each at least once," she said. "Alute must not be too selfish while her younger sisters waste their lives in waiting."

The Emperor did not answer. He lifted his bowl and paused for her to take drink from her own bowl and then he drank and Jasmine knelt and took the bowl again. Now as she did this she raised her eyes to his and he looked down for that instant into her face, so gay and vivid, so childlike in its hues of cream and rose beneath the soft black hair that he could not look away too quickly.

Thus began the day, and while it passed the Empress Mother summoned Jasmine again and again to wait upon the Emperor, to fan him, to keep away a vagrant fly, to serve him when they dined at noon beneath the trees, to fetch him tea and choose sweetmeats for him while the play went on, to put a footstool near his feet and cushions beneath his elbows, and so until the sunset fell. At last the Emperor smiled openly at Jasmine, and when she came near him she smiled at him, not shyly or with boldness, but as a child smiles at a playmate.

The Empress Mother was well pleased to see these smiles, and when twilight fell and the day was done, she said to the Emperor:

"Before you leave me, my son, I have a wish to tell you."

"Say on, Mother," he replied. He was in a happy mood, his belly filled with favorite foods, his heart lightened and his fancy teased by the pretty girl who belonged to him, his for the taking, if ever he so wished.

"You know how I long to leave the city when the spring comes," the Empress Mother said. "For many months I have not stirred from these walls. Now why should we not go together, you and I, and worship at the tombs of our Ancestors? The distance is but eighty miles, and I will ask our provincial Viceroy, Li Hung-chang, to send his own guard to protect us as we come and go. You and I, my son, alone may represent our two generations, since it would not be fitting for you to take the Consort with you upon so mournful a journey."

She had already set her mind secretly to take Jasmine with her as though to serve her, and it would be easy to send Jasmine to her son's tent at night.

The Emperor considered, his finger at his lower lip. "When shall we go?" he asked.

"A month from this very day," the Empress Mother said. "You will be alone then as now, and in these days when the Consort cannot come to you, we will make the journey. She will welcome you the more when you return."

Again the Emperor wondered why his imperial mother was so changed, that she should thus speak of Alute. Yet who could ever know her reasons? And it was true that though she could be cruel and hateful she could be as truly kind and loving toward him, and between these two halves of her he had gone uncertain all his life.

"We will go, my mother," he said, "and it is indeed my duty to worship at the tombs."

"Who can say otherwise?" the Empress Mother replied, and was pleased once more at her own cleverness.

So all came about as she had planned. On a certain night far outside the walls of Peking, in the shadow of the Ancestral Tombs, the Emperor sent a eunuch to bring Jasmine to him. He had spent the day in worship before the tombs, his mother always at his side, instructing him in obeisance and in prayers. The day began with sunshine, but in the afternoon there came a thunderstorm and after it a steady rain which continued into the night. Under the leathern roof of his tent the young Emperor lay wakeful and lonely. It was not seemly to bid his eunuch strum a violin or sing, for these were days of mourning and respect for the eight Ancestral Emperors who surrounded him in their tombs. He lay listening to the rain and fell to thinking of the dead and how certainly one day he would be the ninth to lie outside in the rain. And while he so thought a fearful melancholy seized him, a dread and terror lest he would not live his life out but might die young. He fell into a fit of shivering and he longed for his young wife who was so far away. He had promised her to be faithful to her, and it was this promise which had prevented his summoning until now even one concubine into the bedchamber. But he had not made fresh promise for these days at the tombs, for indeed, not he nor Alute could know that his imperial mother would bring Jasmine as her companion. Nor had his mother spoken of her. Nor had he himself made one sign throughout the solemn day that he saw Jasmine. But he had seen her as she moved here and there about his mother's tent, where he had taken his night meal after the ceremonial fast. Now he thought of her and he could not put her image away.

To his eunuch he only said that he was cold. "I am chilled to my marrow," he said. "I never felt so cold as this before, a coldness strange as death."

The Emperor's eunuchs had been well bribed by Li Lien-ying and so this eunuch said at once:

"Sire, why do you not send for the First Concubine? She will warm your bed and quickly drive the chill from your blood."

The Emperor pretended to be unwilling. "What—while I am in the shadow of the tombs of my Ancestors?"

"A concubine, merely," the eunuch urged. "A concubine is no one."

"Well—well," the Emperor agreed, still seeming to be unwilling.

He lay shivering while the eunuch ran through the wet darkness of the night, and the rain thundered on the taut leathern roof above his head. And in a very little while he saw the flash of lanterns and the tent door parted like a curtain. There Jasmine stood, wrapped in a sheet of oiled silk against the rain. But rain had caught in the blown strands of the soft hair about her face, it glistened on her cheeks and hung on the lashes of her eyes. Her lips were red and her cheeks as red.

"I sent for you because I am cold," the Emperor muttered.

"Here am I, my lord," she said. She put aside the oiled silk and then her garments one by one and she came into his bed, and her body was warm from head to foot against his chilled flesh.

In her own tent the Empress Mother lay awake in the darkness and listened to the steady beating of the rain, a peaceful sound, and all was peace within her heart and mind. The eunuch had reported what he had done, and she had given him an ounce of gold. She needed now to do no more. Jasmine and Alute would carry on the war of love, and knowing her own son, she knew that Jasmine was already the victor.

The summer passed, the Empress Mother sighed that she was growing old, that when the Summer Palace was built she would retire there for her last years. She said her bones ached and that her teeth were loose, and there were mornings when she would not rise from bed. Her ladies did not know what to make of such pretended illness and old age, for the truth was the Empress Mother seemed instead to be renewed in youth and strength. When she lay in bed, insisting on her headaches, she was so young and beautiful, her eyes so bright, her skin so clear, that lady looked at lady and wondered what went on inside that handsome skull. Never had the Empress Mother eaten so well and heartily, not only at her meals but of the sweetmeats that she enjoyed between meals. When she moved it was not slowly and with dragging footsteps, but with fresh grace and youthfulness.

Yet she insisted she was not well, and when Jung Lu came to ask for audience she refused him, and even when Prince Kung came urging audience she would not yield.

Instead, she summoned her Chief Eunuch and demanded of him, thus: "What does that tyrant of a prince want of me now?"

The Chief Eunuch grinned. He knew well that her illness was a pretense of some sort and that she waited for a purpose that even he did not yet know. "Majesty," he said, "Prince Kung is much disturbed at the present behavior of the Emperor."

"And why?" she asked, though she knew well enough.

"Majesty," the Chief Eunuch said, "all say the Emperor is changed. He spends his days in gaming and in sleep, and far in the night he roams the city streets dressed as a common man, and with him are but two eunuchs and the First Concubine."

At this the Empress Mother made great show of horror. "The First Concubine? It cannot be!"

She raised herself on her pillows and then fell back and closed her eyes and moaned.

"Oh, I am ill—very ill! Tell the Prince I am like to die because of this evil news. I can do nothing more, tell him. My son is Emperor now and only princes can advise him. He does not hear me. Where is the Board of Imperial Censors? Surely they will advise him."

And she would not allow audience to Prince Kung.

As for that Prince, he took her words as command, and he did so attack the Emperor face to face that he roused a fury in his imperial nephew, and on the tenth day of the ninth solar month of that same year, the Emperor sent forth a decree signed with his own name and the imperial seal, declaring that Prince Kung and his son, Ts'ai Ch'ing, were stripped of all their ranks, degraded thus because Prince Kung had used unbecoming language before the Dragon Throne.

At this the Empress Mother did rouse herself, and the next day she sent out another edict above her own name and Sakota's as her co-Regent, commanding all ranks and honors to be restored again to Prince Kung and his son, Ts'ai Ch'ing. This she did alone and without Sakota's knowledge, knowing that her weak sister-Empress Dowager would not dare to speak a word in protest even at this use of her name. And, such was the honor of her place as Empress Mother, none dared to dispute this edict, and by its firmness she restored herself very much toward power by this seeming favor to Prince Kung, who was of the older generation and much respected by all.

As for the Emperor, before he could decide what next to do he fell ill of black smallpox, caught somewhere in the city when in disguise he went out to amuse himself. In the tenth month, after many days of restless fever while his skin broke out in pox, he lay near to death. The

Empress Mother went often to his bedside, for long ago as a small child she had caught the smallpox and it left her immune, without one scar upon her faultless skin. Now she was all mother, and truly so, and she was wrung with strange twisted sorrow. She longed to grieve with her whole heart, as mothers should, and in this grief relieve her secret agony. But she could not be only mother even now. As she had never been mere wife, she was not mere mother. Her destiny was still her burden.

On the twenty-fourth day of that same month, however, the Emperor improved, his fever fell, his tortured skin grew cool, and the Empress Mother sent forth an edict to say the people's hope could be renewed. On the same day, too, the Emperor sent for the Consort, who till now had been forbidden in his chamber because she was with child. Now that the Emperor's skin was clear and his fever gone, the imperial physician declared it safe for her to come and she went to him with all speed, for indeed her heart was desolate at these many weeks apart. Her days she had spent in praying at the temple, and her nights were sleepless, nor could she eat. When she entered the royal bedchamber, she was pale and thin, her delicate beauty, so much dependent on her mood and health, was for the moment gone, nor had she stayed to change the gray and unbecoming robe she wore. She entered all impatience, thinking to embrace her love, but on the threshold she was stopped. There by the great bed whereon her lord lay sat the Empress Mother.

"Alas," Alute murmured, her hands fluttering to her heart.

"And why alas?" the Empress Mother answered sharply. "I do not see alas, when he is so much better. It is you who are alas, for you are as pale and yellow as an old woman. And I take this wrong of you who carry his child inside you. I swear I am angry with you."

"Mother," the Emperor pleaded weakly, "I beg you to spare her—"

But Alute could not stop the rush of her own anger. After all these days of waiting and anxiety her usual patience broke. She was not truly patient at best, for she had a strong nature, a mind clear and disciplined, a sense of truth too much for ordinary use.

"Do not spare me," she said, standing straight and slender in the doorway. "I ask no favor of the Empress Mother. Let her anger fall on me instead of you, my lord, since fall it must, for we cannot please her." These words came from her narrow lips, each word separate and distinct.

The Empress Mother rose to her feet and sped toward the luckless girl with both her hands upraised, and when she was near enough she slapped Alute's cheeks again and again until her jeweled nail protectors brought blood.

The Emperor wept aloud upon his bed, from weakness and despair. "Oh, let me die, you two," he sobbed. "Why should I live when I am caught between you like a mouse between two millstones?"

And he turned his face to the inner wall and could not stop his sobbing. No, though both women flew to his side, and the waiting eunuchs hastened into the bedchamber and though the Empress Mother sent for the Court physicians, none could heal him of his sobbing. He sobbed on and on until he lost his reason and did not know why he sobbed except he could not stop. Suddenly in extreme weakness his pulse faded and ceased to beat. Then the chief physician made obeisance to the Empress Mother, waiting by the bedside in her carved chair.

"Majesty," he said, sadly, "I fear no human skill can now avail. Evil has seized the destiny of the Son of Heaven, and it is not given to us to know the means to prevent his departure. We, the Court physicians, did fear some such fate, for on the ninth day of the tenth solar month, but two short days ago, two foreigners, Americans, came to our city. They brought with them a large instrument and setting it on the ground, they endeavored to look through its long tube into the sky. At this same moment, Majesty, the evening star was risen in clear radiance, and upon its shining surface we discerned a black spot, something heavier than a shadow. Upon this we drove the foreigners away. Alas, it was too late. Their evil magic was already set upon the star, and we, the Court physicians, looked at each other, fear in every heart. Thus was today's fate foretold."

When the Empress Mother heard this, she shrieked that she could not believe it and she summoned Li Lien-ying and screamed at him to know if the tale were true. The Chief Eunuch could but say it was, and he knocked his head upon the tiled floor.

So ended the brief life of the Emperor. When his breath ceased and his flesh grew cold, the Empress Mother sent everyone away, the princes and the ministers who had come as witnesses for death, the eunuchs and the serving men. Even Alute she sent away.

"Go," she told the young widow. "Leave me with my son." The gaze she bent upon the young widow was not cruel but desolate and cold, as though the sorrow of the mother was far beyond the sorrow of the wife.

What could Alute then do except obey? Her dead lord's mother was now her sovereign.

And when all were gone, the Empress sat beside her son and pondered on his life and death. She shed no tears, not yet, for her sorrow must be fulfilled. She thought first of herself and how once more she was supreme in power. Alone she stood above the earth, transcending womanhood, a height unknown before to any human being. In loneliness she looked down upon the face of the son she had borne, a young man's handsome face, proud in death, and calm. And while she looked the face grew young again, she fancied all the lines away, until she saw a little boy, the child she had adored. The tears welled up as hot as flame and her heart which had not moved till now, grew soft and quivering, a heart of flesh at last. She sobbed, the tears ran down her cheeks and fell upon the satin coverlet, and she took his dead hand in both her hands and fondled it and laid it against her cheek as she had used to do when he was small. Strange words came welling up like blood from her heart.

"Oh, child," she sobbed, "would that I had given you the little train— the foreign train—the toy you longed for and you never had!"

Her sorrow centered suddenly and without reason upon this toy she had refused him years ago and she wept on and on, forgetting all she was, except a mother whose only child was dead.

In the night, deep in the night, the hour forgotten, the door opened and a man came in. She leaned upon the bed, still weeping but now silently, and she did not hear the footsteps. Then she felt her shoulders seized and she was lifted strongly to her feet. She turned her head and saw his face.

"You—" she whispered.

"I," Jung Lu said. "I have waited outside the door these past three hours. Why do you delay? The clans are all astir to put an heir upon the Throne by dawn, before the people know the Emperor is dead. You must act first."

Within the instant she subdued her heart and made her mind clear to remember a plan she had long ago prepared for such an hour as this.

"My sister's eldest son is three years old," she said. "He is the heir I choose. His father is the seventh brother of my own dead lord."

He met her eyes straightly. They were deadly black against her pale face, but fearless, and her lips were firm.

"Tonight you have a fearful beauty." His voice was strange and wondering. "You grow more beautiful in danger. Some magic in you—"

She heard and lifted up her head, the sad lips parted, and the tragic eyes grew soft.

"Say on," she whispered. "Oh, love, say on!"

He shook his head, then gently took her hand. Side by side these two looked down upon the great bed whereon the dead Emperor lay, while their hands clasped. Through his hand she felt him quivering, his body trembling against his will, and she turned toward him.

"Oh, love," she whispered, "he is our—"

"Hush," he said. "We may not speak a word of what is past. The palace walls have ears—"

They must not speak, never could they speak, and after one long silent moment they loosed their hands, he stepped back and made obeisance. She was again the Empress and he her subject.

"Majesty," he said, his voice held low against the listening walls, "go at once and fetch the child. Meanwhile, foreseeing this moment, I have in your name summoned the Viceroy, Li Hung-chang. His armies are already near the city gates. None know it. The horses' feet are muffled and the men have wooden bits in their mouths to prevent a heedless word. By sunrise you will have the child here in the palace, and your loyal soldiers will crowd the city streets. Who then dares dispute your rule?"

Strong heart met strong heart. These two, in an accord made perfect by their hidden love, parted once more upon their common purpose. Jung Lu was gone, and in that instant the Empress left the bedchamber of the dead. Outside the door the Chief Eunuch waited for her, and when she came he followed, and with him those lesser eunuchs and her ladies who were faithful to her. None asked how Jung Lu had entered the gates of the Forbidden City, where after nightfall no man might enter. In this strange night of turmoil no one asked.

The Empress moved swiftly now to do her will.

"Summon me my sedan," she commanded Li Lien-ying. "Let no one speak or whisper and bid the bearers wrap their feet in cloth."

Within minutes she had fastened a cloak about her and, saying not a word to tiring woman or to her ladies, she passed them all and entered into her sedan chair and the curtains were let down. A secret gate behind the palace was opened and waiting for her, and the Chief Eunuch led the way, and thence into the dark and lonely streets. All day the snow had fallen and now it lay deep upon the cobblestones and silenced every footstep and beside the sedan the gaunt giant figure of the Chief Eunuch ran in silence, through falling snow. Thus they came to the palace of Prince Ch'un. The bearers set down the sedan, the Chief Eunuch beat upon the gate and when it opened he forced his way inside, stopping the gateman's cry with his hand upon the man's mouth. Behind him came the Empress Mother, her robes flying, and they crossed the many courtyards and entered the house. All were sleeping save the watchman, who stood awed to let the Empress Mother pass.

Ahead of her ran the Chief Eunuch, and he roused the Prince, and then his lady, and they came out, their faces frightened and their garments put on anyhow in haste, and they fell before her in obeisance.

The Empress Mother said, "Sister, I have no time to tell you anything except my son is dead—give me your son to be his heir—"

At this Prince Ch'un cried out:

"Oh, Majesty, I pray you do not take the child to such a fate—"

"How dare you speak so?" the Empress Mother cried. "Is there a greater destiny than to be Emperor?"

"Oh, wretched me," Prince Ch'un answered. "I, the father, must make obeisance every day before my own son! The generations are confused because of me, and Heaven will punish all my house."

He wept, he knocked his head upon the tiled floor so diligently that blood ran down his forehead and he fell into a faint.

Yet the Empress Mother would not wait upon him or any man. She pushed him and her sister aside and went swiftly to the child's nursery and stooped above his bed and lifted him up in her own arms, wrapped in his blankets. He was asleep, and though he whimpered he did not wake and so she bore him away.

But her sister ran after her and seized the end of her flying sleeve.

"The child will cry when he wakes in a strange place," she pleaded. "Let me come with him at least for a few days."

"Follow me," the Empress Mother said across her shoulder. "But do not stop me. I must have him safe within the palace before sunrise." This she did. The night passed. When the sun rose and the temple priests struck their brass drums for morning prayer, the Court criers went everywhere in the streets and cried the death of the Emperor Mu Tsung, which was T'ung Chih's dynastic name, and they cried in the next breath a new emperor already upon the Dragon Throne.

In his strange nursery the little Emperor wailed his fright. Not even his mother could quiet him, though she held him continually in her arms. For each time he lifted his head from her breast he saw the carved and gilded dragons crawling on the high beams above his head and he cried in fresh terror and yet he could not keep from looking. At last, when two days had past, his mother sent a eunuch to the Empress Mother to say the child had wept until he was ill.

"Let him weep," the Empress Mother made reply. She was in her library, working on her palace plans, and she did not turn her head. "Let him learn early that he will have nothing that he wants by weeping, though he be the Emperor."

Without lifting her head she worked on until the white light of the snowy day came to an end. When she could no longer see she put down her brush and for a long time she sat in meditation. Then she beckoned to a waiting eunuch.

"Fetch me the Consort," she said. "And bid her come alone."

The eunuch ran to show his zeal and within minutes Alute came with him and made obeisance. The Empress Mother waved the eunuch off and bade the young widow rise from her knees and sit on a carved stool nearby. There she stared awhile at the young figure, drooping in mourning robes of white sackcloth.

"You have not eaten," she said at last.

"Venerable Ancestor, I cannot eat," Alute said.

"There is nothing left in life for you," the Empress said.

"Nothing, Venerable Ancestor," Alute said.

"Nor will there ever be," the Empress Mother continued, "and therefore were I you, I would follow my lord to where he is."

At this Alute lifted her bowed head and gazed at the stern, beautiful woman who sat so calmly on her thronelike chair. She rose slowly and stood a moment and then sank to her knees again.

"I pray you give me leave to die," she whispered.

"You have my leave," the Empress Mother said.

One more long look passed between these two, and then Alute rose and walked toward the open door, a sad young ghost, and the eunuch closed the door behind her.

The Empress Mother sat awhile as motionless as marble, and then she clapped her hands to summon the eunuch.

"Light all the lanterns," she commanded. "I have my work to do."

And she took up her brush again. While the night drew on to deeper darkness, she dipped her brush into the colors spread before her and made complete her plan. Then she put down her brush and surveyed the great scroll. The dreaming palaces rose clustering about a wide lake, and gardens bloomed between, and marble bridges spanned the brooks that fed the lake. She smiled to see so fair a picture and after long gazing, suddenly she took up her brush again. She dipped it in her brightest color pots and against the mountain behind the palaces she set a pagoda, tall and slender, whose sides were sky-blue porcelain and whose roofs were gold.

That night at midnight the Chief Eunuch coughed at her door. She rose from her bed and walked silently to open it. He said:

"Alute is no more."

"How did she die?" the Empress Mother asked.

"She swallowed opium," he said.

Their eyes met in a long and secret look.

"I am glad there was no pain," the Empress Mother said.

IV

The Empress

In the fourth moon month the wisteria blooms. It was the duty of the Court Chief Gardener to report to the Empress the exact day upon which the vines would blossom and he had so reported. The Empress did then decree that upon this day she would not appear in the Audience Hall, nor would she hear any affairs of state. Instead, she would spend the day in the wisteria gardens and with her ladies, enjoying the color and the fragrance of the flowers and with due courtesy she also invited her cousin the Empress Dowager, since she and Sakota were co-Regents again.

On this day, then, at midmorning, she sat in the wisteria pavilion at ease in her large carved chair, set high like a small throne upon a platform. She made no pretense now that any was her equal, for she knew at last that her power depended upon herself and her own inner strength. Her ladies stood about her.

"Amuse yourselves, little ones," she said. "Walk where you will, watch the goldfish in the pools, talk as you will, in whispers or aloud. Only remember that we are here to enjoy the wisteria and do not mention sorrows."

They thanked her in murmurs, these young and beautiful ladies robed in the brightest hues of every color, the sunshine falling upon their flawless skins and pretty hands and lighting their black eyes and glittering upon their flowered headdresses.

They obeyed her but cautiously, careful that always some remained. When twenty drifted away, another twenty clustered about her. But the Empress did not seem to see them. Her eyes were always upon the little Emperor, her nephew, who played with his toys on a terrace nearby.

With him were two young eunuchs whom she ignored. Suddenly she lifted her right hand and palm downward she beckoned to the child.

"Come here, my son," she said.

He was not her son, and when she spoke the words her heart turned against him. Yet she spoke them, for she had chosen him to sit in her son's place upon the Dragon Throne.

The boy looked at her and then came slowly toward her, pushed by the elder of the two young eunuchs.

"Do not touch him," the Empress commanded sharply. "He must come to me of his own accord."

Still the child did not come willingly. He put his finger in his mouth and stared at her, and the toy he held dropped to the tiled path.

"Pick it up," she said. "Bring it to me that I may see what you have."

Her face did not change. Beautiful and calm, she neither smiled nor was angry. She waited until, compelled by her powerful stillness, the child stooped and took up the toy and came toward her. Baby though he was, he knelt before her while he held up the toy for her to see.

"What is it?" she inquired.

"An engine," he replied, his voice so small that she could scarcely hear him.

"These engines," she mused, not putting out her hand to take the toy. "And who gave you an engine?"

"No one," the child answered.

"Nonsense," she said. "Did it grow in your hand?" And she nodded to the young eunuch to speak for him.

"High Majesty," he said, "the little Emperor is always lonely. Here in the palaces are no children for him to play with. And lest he cry until he sickens, we bring him many toys. He likes best the toys from the foreign shop in the Legation Quarter."

"Foreign toys?" She put the question in the same sharp voice.

"The shop is kept by a Dane, High Majesty," the eunuch explained, "and this Dane sends everywhere in Europe for toys for our little Emperor."

"An engine," she repeated. Now she reached forward and took the toy. It was made of iron, small but heavy. Under the body were wheels, and upon the top a chimney.

"How do you play with this?" she inquired of the little Emperor.

He forgot his fear of her and scrambled to his feet.

"Ancient Mother, like this!" He seized it and opened a small door. "Inside here I can light a fire with bits of wood. And here I put water and when the water boils, steam comes out and then the wheels go round. Behind it I hook some cars, and the engine pulls them. It is called a train, Ancient Mother."

"Is it indeed," she mused.

She looked at the child thoughtfully. Too pale, too thin, the face too weak, a reed of a boy—

"What else have you?" she asked.

"More trains," the child said eagerly. "Some wind with a key, and I have a great army of soldiers."

"What soldiers?" she asked.

"Many kinds, Mother," he said. He forgot to be afraid of her and even came close enough to lean upon her knees. She felt a strange pain where his arm rested and in her heart a yearning for something lost.

"My soldiers carry guns," he was saying, "and they wear uniforms, painted, of course, because they are tin soldiers, not real ones."

"Have you Chinese soldiers?" she asked.

"No Chinese soldiers," he said, "but English and French, German and Russian and Americans. The Russians wear—"

"And can you tell them one from the other?" she asked.

He laughed aloud. "Oh easily, Mother! The Russians have beards —long—" he measured his hands against his waist. "And the French have beards only here—" he touched his forefinger across his upper lip. "And the Americans—"

"All, all have white faces," she said in the same strange voice.

"How did you know?" he asked, surprised.

"I know," she said.

She pushed him away, her hand at his elbow, and he stepped back, the light gone from his eyes. At this moment Sakota, Empress Dowager, came in with four of her own ladies, walking slowly, her figure stooping under the heavy headdress that made her face so small.

The little Emperor ran to meet her. "M-ma!" he cried. "I thought you were never coming!" His fond hands reached for hers, and he laid her palms against his cheeks. Over his dark head Sakota looked across the courtyard and met the imperial gaze fastened upon her.

"Loose me, child," she murmured.

But he would not let her go. While the Empress watched he clung to Sakota, walking beside her as she walked, holding in his hands a fold of her gray silk robe.

"Come and sit near me, Sister," the Empress said. She pointed with her jeweled thumb to a carved chair near her own, and Sakota came toward her and bowed and took her seat.

Still the little Emperor stood by her, clinging to her hand. This the

Empress saw as she saw everything, but without seeming to notice. Her long calm eyes rested upon the child and then moved to the wisteria vines. The male vines, huge and old, had been planted close to the female that the flowers might be at their best. Together they twined around the twin pagodas and foamed in a froth of white and purple over the roofs of yellow porcelain tiles. The sun was warm, and bees, made frantic by the fragrance, buzzed over the blossoms.

"Those bees," the Empress observed. "They gather here from everywhere in the city."

"Indeed, they do, Sister," Sakota replied. But she did not look at the flowers. Instead, she smoothed the childish hand she held, a thin small hand, the veins too clear under the soft skin.

"This little Son of Heaven," she murmured, "he does not eat enough."

"He eats the wrong foods," the Empress said.

It was an old quarrel between the two of them. The Empress believed that health lay in simple foods, in vegetables cooked slightly, in meats not fat, in few sweets. These foods she commanded for the little Emperor. Yet she knew very well that he refused them when her back was turned and that he ran to Sakota to be fed sweetened dough balls and rich dumplings and roasted pork, dripping with sugar. When he had pains in his belly she knew that Sakota in her fond blind love gave him whiffs of opium from her own pipe. This, too, the Empress held against her cousin, that she yielded to the foreign opium habit, smoking in secret the vile black stuff that came from India under foreign flags. Yet, Sakota, sad and foolish woman, believed that it was only she who truly loved the little Emperor!

The brightness of the morning clouded under such thoughts and Sakota, seeing the beautiful imperial face grow stern, was frightened. She beckoned to a eunuch.

"Take the little Emperor somewhere to play," she whispered.

The Empress heard as she heard every whisper. "Do not take the child away," she commanded. She turned her head. "You know, Sister, that I do not wish him to be alone with these small eunuchs. There is not one of them who is pure. The Emperor will be corrupted before he is grown. How many emperors have thus been spoiled!"

At such words the waiting eunuch, a youth of fifteen or sixteen years, crept away abashed.

"Sister," Sakota murmured. Her pale face spotted crimson.

"What now?" the Empress demanded.

"To speak so before everyone," Sakota said, faintly remonstrating.

"I speak the truth," the Empress said firmly. "I know you think that

I do not love the royal child. Yet which loves him the more, you who pander to his every peevish wish or I who would mend his health by good food and healthy play? You who give him over to these small devils who are eunuchs or I who would keep him from their foulness?"

At this Sakota began to cry quietly behind her sleeve. Her ladies ran to her but the Empress motioned them away, and she herself rose and took Sakota by the hand and led her into the hall at the right of the court. There she sat down upon a gilded couch and drew Sakota down beside her.

"Now," she said, "we are alone. Tell me why you are always angry with me."

But Sakota had a soft stubbornness of her own and would not speak. She continued to sob while the Empress waited, until she, who was never patient long, grew too impatient to listen any more to the wailing half-stifled sobs of the weak woman.

"Weep," the Empress said relentlessly. "Cry until you are happy again. I think you are never happy unless the tears are streaming from your eyes. I wonder your sight is not washed away."

With this she rose and walked out of the pavilion and away from the garden and into her library. There, forbidding anyone to enter, she spent the rest of the bright spring day, her books before her, and the fragrance of the wisteria drifting in through the wide and open doors.

But her thoughts were not with her books. Though she sat as motionless as an image of carved ivory, her thoughts were restless inside her beautiful skull. Was she never to be loved? This was the question that rose too often from the crowded days of her life. Millions of people depended upon her wisdom. Here in the palace no one could live unless she willed it. She was just, she was careful, she rewarded those who were faithful and she punished none but the evil. Yet she discerned no love for her in any face she saw, not even in the child's face, though he was her own nephew, her very blood, and now her chosen son. Even that solitary one she loved and still did love in the depths of her being, even Jung Lu, had not spoken to her now for two years, nay for three, except as a courtier speaks to his sovereign. He came no more into her presence as once he had, he made no excuse for audience, and when she summoned him he came as haughtily as any prince and kept his distance, scrupulously performing his duty and yielding nothing more. And yet he was so matchless a man that maidens in the city, gossip said, declared that they would have husbands only when they were as handsome as Prince Jung Lu. The Empress had lifted him to be a prince by now, but high as he was he came no nearer to her. Yet he was loyal to her, she knew him loyal, but it was not enough. Could her heart never be cured of longing?

She sighed and closed her books. Of all human beings herself she knew the least. Knowing herself so little, how could she know why today she had been cruel again to Sakota? She sat motionless, too honest to avoid her own question and thus relentless even with herself, she perceived that she was jealous for the child's love, a strange old jealousy reaching into the past, when her dead son had been a lad and like this living child had escaped her by loving Sakota instead of her who was his mother.

Yet it was I who loved him, she thought, and mine was the duty to teach and train him. Had he lived longer he might have known—

But he had not lived. She rose restlessly, never able to bear the thought of her son dead and in his tomb. She wandered out again into the wisteria gardens and seemed not to see her patient ladies, waiting through the hours outside her door. The air was cool with sunset and the fragrance was gone. She shivered and stood for a moment, gazing about her at the splendors of the scene, the iridescent pools, the purple-laden vines laced with white, the bright roofs of gold and the sculptured beasts upon their crests, the tiled walks and the crimson walls. All this was hers, and was it not enough? It must be enough, for what more could be hers? She had her heir, her chosen. The child Emperor was in his ninth year, tall and slender as a new bamboo. His pale skin was translucent and too delicate, but his will was strong and he made no secret that he loved Sakota better than his imperial aunt and foster mother. The only one more proud than he was the Empress herself. She would not stoop to woo the boy, nor could she even hide her deepening dislike of him because of her heart's disappointment. The rising strife between the beautiful aging Empress and the young Emperor pervaded the whole court, dividing courtiers and eunuchs, one against the other, and in this division the silly woman who was Sakota began to make faint dreams of power. She who had ever been the weakest and most timid creature in the palace had such dreams. From Li Lien-ying the Empress heard gossip that her cousin-Empress planned to take her rightful place as the Consort of the Emperor Hsien Feng, a place, she declared privately, that had been usurped by her cousin.

The Empress had laughed at such a tale. She could still laugh a hearty peal when faced with absurdity.

"Surely it is a kitten against a tiger," she said, and would not yield a moment's further heed, nor did she reprove her eunuch when he joined in her laughter.

In that same year, nevertheless, Sakota struck a feeble blow. It was upon that sacred day when the whole Court must make obeisance before the Eastern Imperial Tombs. When she arrived at noon with her cortège, the Empress was amazed to find that Sakota had set her will to be the first to offer sacrifice before the dead Emperor Hsien Feng and thus take precedence in all the ceremonies of the day. Now the Empress had come here with full preparation of mind and spirit. She had fasted the day before, taking neither food nor water, and she had risen at dawn and outside the hall where she had meditated through the long and lonely night, Jung Lu had waited with other princes and the ministers to escort her to the tombs. Through the deep vast forest which surrounds the Tombs of the Eight Emperors, the Empress was carried in her palanquin. All traveled in silence, and in the dim dawn not even a bird song fell upon her ears. In solemnity and reverence she came, pondering the weight of her position, her many peoples subject to her alone, and upon her alone the weary duty weighed to keep them safe from foreign enemies now threatening in ever-growing power. She who seldom prayed to Heaven did pray today within her heart for wisdom and strength, and she prayed to the Imperial Ancestors as gods to guide her thoughts and plans, fingering the jade beads of her Buddhist rosary, one for each prayer.

In such grave mood, what shock then to find that foolish one, Sakota, persuaded by Prince Kung, now always jealous of Jung Lu, at the Tombs before her! Indeed, Sakota stood ready before the marble altar and in the central place, and when the Empress descended from her palanquin she smiled a small evil smile and motioned to her to stand at her right, while the left place was empty.

The Empress gave one haughty stare, her black eyes wide, and then ignoring Sakota's invitation, she walked without a hint of haste into the pavilion nearby. There she seated herself and beckoned Jung Lu to her side.

"I do not deign to question anyone," she said when he knelt before her. "I do but command you to bear this message to my co-Regent. If she does not yield her place at once, I will command the Imperial Guard to lift her from her feet and put her into prison."

Jung Lu bowed to the floor. Then, his handsome aging face as cold and proud as ever nowadays, he rose and bore the message to Sakota. From her he soon returned to make obeisance before the Empress, and he said:

"The co-Regent received your message, Most High, and she replies that she is rightfully in her place, you being only the senior concubine.

The empty place at her left is for the dead Consort, her elder sister, who, after her death, was raised to the place of Senior Empress."

This the Empress heard, and she lifted up her head and gazed into the distance of dark pines and sculptured marble beasts. She said in her most calm voice,

"Go back again to the co-Regent with the same message that I sent. If she does not yield, then command the Imperial Guardsmen to seize her and Prince Kung also, with whom I have been always too lenient. Henceforth I shall be merciful no more to anyone."

Jung Lu stood up and summoning the guardsmen, who followed him in their blue coats, their spears lifted and glittering in their right hands, he approached Sakota again. In a few minutes he returned to announce that she had yielded.

"Most High," he said, his voice level and cold, "your place waits. The co-Regent has moved to the right."

The Empress came down then from her high seat and walked with great state to the Tomb, and looking neither to the left nor right she stood in the center and performed the ceremonies with grace and majesty. When these were done she returned to the palaces in silence, acknowledging no greeting and giving none.

The life in the palace closed above this quarrel and one day followed another in seeming peace. Yet all knew that there could be no peace between these two ladies, who had each her followers, Jung Lu near the Empress and beneath him the Chief Eunuch, and with Sakota, Prince Kung, an old man now, but still proud and fearless.

The end was certain, but whether it would have come as it did had Jung Lu not committed a madness, unnatural and unforeseen, who knows? For in the autumn of that same year a rumor crept up like a foul miasma that Jung Lu, the faithful, the noble-hearted, the one above all to be trusted, was yielding to the love advances of a young concubine of the dead Emperor T'ung Chih, who had remained a virgin because her lord had loved only Alute. When the Empress first heard this foul report of Jung Lu come from the thick lips of her eunuch she would not believe it.

"What—my kinsman?" she exclaimed. "I would as soon say that I myself could play the fool!"

"Venerable," Li Lien-ying muttered, grinning hideously, "I swear that it is true. The Imperial Concubine makes eyes at him when the Court meets. Do not forget that she is fair enough and still young, indeed, young enough to be his daughter, and he is at the age when a man likes his women as young as his own daughters. Remember, too, that he never did love the lady whom you gave to him, Majesty. No, three and three are still six and five and five are always ten."

But the Empress only kept on laughing and shaking her head, while she chose a sweetmeat from the porcelain tray upon the table at her elbow. Yet when the eunuch brought her proof a few moons later, she could not laugh. His own serving eunuch, Li Lien-ying now told her, had waylaid a woman servant as she took a folded paper to a certain altar in the inner room of the imperial Buddhist temple. There a priest received it and for pay he thrust it into an incense urn, where a little eunuch found it and again for pay took it to the gate where Jung Lu's manservant received it, all bribed by the concubine who thus made herself a fool for love.

"Majesty, pray read for yourself," the eunuch begged.

The Empress took the perfumed sheet. It was indeed a note letter of assignation.

"Come to me at one hour after midnight. The watchman is bribed and he will open the third moon gate. There my woman will hide behind the cassia tree and she will lead you to me. I am a flower awaiting rain."

The Empress read and folded the letter again and put it in her sleeve, and Li Lien-ying waited on his knees before her while she mused. And why delay, she asked herself, when proof was in her hands? She was so close in heart and flesh to the man Jung Lu that a word that either spoke went straight to the other as arrow sent from bow. Whatever intervened of time or circumstance had always crumbled when her heart spoke to his. She could not forgive him now.

"Bring me here the Grand Councilor," she commanded the waiting eunuch. "And when he comes then close the doors and draw the curtains and forbid entrance to everyone until you hear me strike this bronze drum."

He rose, and always ready to make mischief, he went in such haste that his robes flew behind him like wings. In less time than she needed to subdue her rage Jung Lu came in, wearing his long robes of blue, upon his breast a square of golden embroidery, upon his head a high cap of the same gold and in his hands a length of carved jade which he held before his face as he approached the Empress. But she would not see his splendid beauty. She sat upon her private throne in her great library, her robes of crimson satin sewn with gilt dragons falling to her feet and her headdress set with fresh white jasmine flowers so that about her clung their matchless scent, and saw him as an enemy. Even he!

Jung Lu prepared to kneel as her courtier but the Empress forbade it.

"Sit down, Prince," she said in her most silvery voice, "and pray put down the jade. This is no formal summons. I speak to you in private to inquire of this letter placed in my hand an hour ago by my palace spies, who, you know, are everywhere."

He would not sit, not even at her command, but he did not kneel. He stood before her and when she plucked from her sleeve the perfumed letter he did not put out his hand to take it.

"Do you know what this is?" she asked.

"I see what it is," he said, and his face did not change.

"You feel no shame?" she asked.

"None," he said.

She let the letter flutter to the floor and folded her two hands together upon her satin lap. "You feel no disloyalty to me?" she asked.

"No, for I am not disloyal," he replied. And then he said, "What you ask of me, I give. What you do not ask or need remains my own."

These words so confounded the Empress that she could not answer. In silence Jung Lu waited and then he bowed and went away, not asking for her permission, nor did she call out his name to stay him. Thus left alone, she sat immobile as any image, while she pondered what he had said. So used was she to doing justly that even now her mind weighed his words against her heart. Had he not spoken truly? She should not have listened so quickly to a eunuch. There was not a woman in the realm whose heart did not answer to Jung Lu's name. Was this his fault? No, surely he was above the petty loves and hates of lesser persons in the palaces. Then she had done him much injustice when she could believe him easily disloyal to her, his sovereign. And should she in justice blame him for being a man? And she sat thinking how she would reward him with some new honor and oblige him to be faithful.

For a day or so, nevertheless, she was unkind to Li Lien-ying and short in what she said to him, and he was prudent and withdrew and planned another way to gain her ear. Thus some weeks later, one day after the Empress had given her usual audience to her princes and her ministers, a eunuch, not Li Lien-ying, brought to her a private memorial from the Emperor's tutor, Weng T'ung-ho, who said therein that he had a duty to report to her a secret matter. Immediately she suspected that again it had to do with the young concubine, for this tutor hated Jung Lu, who had once been scornful of him in an archery tournament when the tutor had pretended prowess and had failed miserably, for he was a scholar and had a scholar's reedy frame and was no archer.

Nevertheless, the Empress received the memorial which the tutor had sent her thus secretly. It said simply that if she would go at a certain hour to the private chamber of a certain concubine, she would see a sight to surprise her eyes. He, Weng T'ung-ho, would not risk his head to reveal a secret, except that he did so from duty, since if scandal went unnoticed in the imperial palaces, what then would take place in the nation and among the people, to whom the Empress was a goddess?

When the Empress had read this memorial she dismissed the petty eunuch by her lifted hand, and with her serving women she went swiftly to the Palace of Forgotten Concubines, and to the room where the lady lived, a concubine whom she had once chosen for her own son and whom he had never summoned.

Softly she opened the door with her own hands, while around her servants and eunuchs, stricken by her unexpected presence, could only fall upon their knees and hide their faces in their sleeves. She flung the door wide and suddenly and saw the horrid sight she feared. Jung Lu was there, seated in a great chair beside a table upon which were set trays of sweetmeats and a jug of steaming wine. At his side knelt the concubine, her hands folded on his knees, while he gazed smiling down into her loving face.

This was the sight the Empress saw. She felt within her breast such pain and heat of outraged blood that she put her hands against her heart to save it. And Jung Lu looked up and saw her. He sat an instant gazing at her and then he put the girl's hands from his knees and rose and waited, his arms folded on his breast, for the imperial wrath to fall upon him.

The Empress could not speak. She stood there and they gazed at each other, man and woman, and in that moment knew that each loved the other with a love so hopeless, so eternal and so strong that nothing could destroy what was between them. She saw his proud spirit unchanged, his love still immaculate, and what he did here in this room was meaningless between them. She closed the door as softly as she had opened it and returned to her own palace.

"Leave me alone awhile," she bade the eunuchs and the serving women, and alone she mused upon the scene she has discovered. No, she did not doubt his love or loyalty, but here was the wound—he was in some measure a common man, flesh as well as spirit. Flesh made its demands even upon him, and he had yielded. Even he, she murmured, even he is not great enough for such loneliness as I must bear.

Her temples ached. She felt her headdress heavy on her head and she lifted it from her and set it upon the table and smoothed her forehead with her hands.

Sweet it might have been to know that for her sake he could and did deny the common flesh of common man! So might her own loneliness be lightened to know that though he stood below her he was equal to her greatness.

Here her thoughts ran around the world to find Victoria, the English Queen, whom never having seen she thought of as her sister ruler, and she addressed her thus in secret communication. Even as widow, Sister Empress, you are more lucky than I have been. Death took your love away unsullied. You were not cheated for a silly woman.

Yet Victoria could not hear. The Empress sighed, tears rolled down her cheeks and fell like jewels on her bosom, and love ebbed from her heart.

I thought I was alone before, she told herself most somberly. But now I do accept the full depth of loneliness.

Time passed while she sat musing and with each moment the dark knowledge of her utter loneliness steeped through her soul until she was drenched with bitterness fulfilled. She sighed again and wiped away her tears, and as though she came out from a trance she rose from her throne and walked here and there about the great stately hall. She could now think of her duty and the punishment which Jung Lu must accept, if she were just. And just she was and always would be, and to all alike.

The next day, at the hour of early audience, before sunrise, she announced, and by imperial edict, that the Grand Councilor, Jung Lu, was from this moment relieved of all his posts and hereby she declared his full retirement from the Imperial Court. No charge was made against him, nor needed to be made, for already rumor had carried the news of her discovery far beyond the palaces.

At dawn she sat upon the Dragon Throne, which she had taken for her own when her son died, and her ministers and princes stood before her, each in his place, and they heard their fellow thus condemned and none spoke a word. Their looks were grave, for if one so high as Jung Lu could fall so low, then none was safe.

And the Empress saw their looks and made no sign. If love were not her guard, then fear must be her weapon. In loneliness she reigned and no one was near her and all were afraid.

Yet fear was still not enough. In the second moon of the next year Prince Kung took upon himself a task which was hateful, but to which he said he was compelled. One cool spring day, after audience, Prince Kung petitioned to be heard privately, a favor which for long he had not asked. Now the Empress was eager to leave the Audience Hall and return to her own palaces, for she had planned to spend the day in her gardens, where the plum blossoms were beginning to swell with spring warmth. Nevertheless, she was constrained to yield to this Prince, for he was her chief advisor and her intermediary with the ever more demanding white men. These foreigners liked Prince Kung and trusted him, and in commonsense the Empress took advantage of their trust in her Prince. Therefore she stayed, and when the other princes and ministers were gone, Prince Kung came forward and making his usual brief obeisance he presented himself thus:

"Majesty, I am not come to you on my own behalf, for I am rewarded enough by your past generosity. It is your greatness now that I invoke and on behalf of the Empress Dowager and your co-Regent."

"Is she ill?" the Empress asked with mild interest.

"Indeed, Majesty, it may be said that she is ill from much distress of mind," Prince Kung replied.

"And what distress has she?" the Empress, still distant.

"Majesty, I do not know whether it has come to your ears that the eunuch Li Lien-ying has grown arrogant beyond all bearing. He even calls himself Lord of Nine Thousand Years, a title which was first given to that most evil eunuch of the Emperor Chu Yu-chiao, in the Ming Dynasty. Majesty, you know that such a title means the eunuch Li Lien-ying holds himself second only to the Emperor, who alone is Lord of Ten Thousand Years."

The Empress smiled her cool smile. "Am I to be blamed for what the lesser folk of the palaces call one who is their master? This eunuch rules them for me. It is his duty, for how can I busy myself with the small affairs of my royal household when I bear the burdens of my nation and my people? Who rules well is always hated."

Prince Kung folded his arms and kept his eyes no higher than the imperial footstool but his mouth was grim. "Majesty," he said, "if it were the lesser folk who rebel, I would not stand here before the Dragon Throne. But the one with whom this eunuch is most rude, most cruel, and indeed most arrogant is the co-Regent herself, the Empress Dowager."

"Indeed," the Empress observed. "And why does not my sister-Regent herself complain to me? Am I not generous to her in all ways, have I ever failed in duty to her? I think not! If she cannot perform the ceremonies and the rites it is because her health is frail, her body weak, her mind depressed. It has been necessary for me to do what she could not. If she complains, let it be to me."

Upon this she dismissed the prince with her right hand uplifted, and he could only go, aware of her displeasure.

For the Empress, nevertheless, the day was spoiled. She had no heart to walk about the gardens, though the air was freshened by the recent dust storms, and the sun shone down without a cloud between heaven and earth. No, she went into a distant palace and there she secluded herself, wrapped about with the cloak of her great loneliness. Of love she dreamed no more, and she had only fear. Yet fear must be absolute or it too was not enough. No one must dare to complain of her or of those who served her. She would silence every tongue that did not praise her. Yet still she preferred mercy, if mercy were enough.

Upon this, she went with her ladies to the Buddhist temple within the palace walls and she burned incense before her favorite Kuan Yin. There in the silence of her own heart, she prayed the goddess to enlighten her and teach her mercy, and she prayed that Sakota might awaken to the grace of mercy shown her so that life could be saved.

Strengthened by her prayers, the Empress then sent messengers to the Eastern Palace and announced her coming. There she went in the twilight of the day and she found Sakota lying in her bed beneath a quilt of amber satin.

"I would rise, Sister," Sakota said in her high complaining voice, "except that today my legs gave way beneath me. I have such pains in my joints that I dare not move."

The Empress sat down in a great chair that had been placed for her, and she sent away her ladies so that she could be alone with this weak woman. When they were alone she spoke bluntly, as she had used to do when they were children under the same roof.

"Sakota," she said, "I will not accept complaints made to others. If you are not pleased, then tell me yourself what you would have. I will yield you what I can, but you are not to destroy my palace from within."

Now whether Prince Kung had fed some sort of alien strength into this foolish lady or whether she was goaded by her own despair, who can tell? For when she heard these words she raised herself on her elbow and she looked at the Empress with sullen eyes and she said:

"You forget that I am above you, Orchid, and by every right and law. You are the usurper and there are those who tell me so. I have my friends and followers, though you think I have not!"

Had a kitten sprung into a tigress, the Empress could not have been more surprised than she was now. She rose up from her chair and ran at Sakota and seized her by the ears and shook her.

"Why, you—you weak worm!" she cried between her grinding teeth. "You ungrateful worthless fool, to whom I am too kind—"

But Sakota, thus goaded, reached out her neck and bit the Empress on the fleshy part of her lower thumb and her teeth clung there until the Empress was compelled to loose her jaws by force while the blood streamed down her wrist and dripped upon her imperial-yellow robe.

"I am not sorry," Sakota babbled. "I am only glad. Now you know I am not helpless."

The Empress answered not a word. She drew her silk kerchief from its jade button at her shoulder and she wrapped it about her wounded hand. Then still without a word she turned and walked in her most stately fashion from the room. Outside, the eunuchs and the serving women were clustered, their ears pressed against the doors. Now all fell back, and her ladies, standing near, their faces grave, their eyes startled, could only bow in silence as she passed and then fall in behind her, for who dares irreverence when a royal tigress goes to battle?

As for the Empress, she returned to her own palace. In the dead of that night, after long and lonely thought, her aching hand against her bosom, she struck the silver gong that summoned Li Lien-ying. He came in alone and stood before her. So close these two were that he was always somewhere near her, and he knew through listening ears what had befallen.

"Majesty, your hand pains you," he said.

"Yes," she said. "That female's teeth hold the poison of a viper."

"Let me dress the wound for you," he said. "I have a skill from an old uncle, now dead, who was a physician."

She let him take the silk handkerchief away, and he did it tenderly, pouring hot water from the kettle on her brazier into a basin and adding cold enough to make the water no more than flesh warm. Then while the water soaked the hardened blood away he washed her hand clean and dried it on a towel.

"Can you bear more pain, Majesty?" he asked.

"Have you need to ask?" she answered.

"No," he said. And with that he took a coal from the brazier between his thick thumb and finger and he pressed it into her wound to cleanse it. She did not shrink and made no moan. Then he threw down the coal, and he opened a box to which she pointed and chose from it a clean white silk kerchief and he bound her hand again.

"A little opium tonight, Majesty," he said, "and by tomorrow the pain will be gone."

"Yes," she said carelessly.

He stood waiting then, while she seemed to muse as though she had forgot her burning hand. At last she spoke.

"When there is a noxious weed within a garden, what is there to do but pluck it out and by the root?"

"Indeed, what else?" he agreed.

"Alas," she said, "I can but depend on one who is most loyal."

"That am I, your servant," he said.

They exchanged one look, a long look, and he bowed and went away.

She called her serving woman then, who made ready an opium pipe and helped her to bed, and sucking in the sweetish smoke, the Empress gave herself to dreamless sleep.

On the tenth day of this same month Sakota, Empress Dowager, fell ill of a strange and sudden illness, which could not be cured by all the zeal of the Court physicians. Before their remedies could reach her vital organs, she died, convulsed by inner agonies. An hour before her death when already she knew her fate, she roused herself and asked for a scribe, and to him she spoke this edict, to be sent forth when she was gone. These were her dying words:

"Though I am of good frame and had imagined that I would surely live to a ripe old age, yesterday I was stricken with an unknown illness, exceedingly painful, and now it appears that I must depart this world. The night draws near, all hope is gone. I am forty-five years of age. For twenty years I have held the high position of the Regent of the Empire. Many titles have been given me, and rewards accorded me for virtue and for grace. Why should I therefore fear to die? I do but ask that the twenty-seven months of usual mourning be reduced to twenty-seven days, in order that the thrift and sobriety in which I have lived may also mark my end. I have not desired pomp or vain display in all my life, nor do I wish them for my funeral."

This edict was sent forth by Prince Kung in the name of the dead, and the Empress said nothing, though she knew that such last words reproached her for her own extravagance and love of beauty. Nevertheless she kept the added bitterness within her heart and when, in yet another year, a new disaster fell upon the nation, she took the chance once more to blame Prince Kung. Here was the circumstance. Frenchmen had claimed the province of Tongking as booty, and when the Empress sent a fleet of Chinese junks into the river Min to expel them, the Frenchmen were victorious and the fleet was destroyed. Upon this the Empress fell into a mighty rage and she wrote an edict with her own hands, accusing Prince Kung of incompetence, if not of treason, and though she made her words mild and full of mercy, she made the blow severe. Thus she wrote:

"We recognize the past merits of Prince Kung and therefore we will, in clemency, allow this prince to retain his hereditary princedom, and all the emoluments thereby, but he is hereby deprived of all his offices and also of his double salary."

And with Prince Kung the Empress dismissed also his several colleagues. In his place she put Prince Ch'un, the husband of her sister and the father of the little Emperor, and with him such princes as she chose. Her clansmen were angry, for Prince Ch'un was thus made chief of state and at her command, and they feared he would set up a dynasty of his own, usurping that of T'ung Chih. But the Empress feared no one on earth or in the heavens. Her enemies were gone and in her lonely pride she silenced all who opposed her. Yet she was too prudent to appear a tyrant without reason and when the Censor Erh-hsün sent his memorial before her, declaring that if Prince Ch'un were given so much power then was the Grand Council useless, she remembered that this censor was a good and upright man, experienced as the one-time Viceroy of Manchuria and again as her Viceroy in the province of Szechuen, and she answered him with care. In an edict which she commanded sent to all parts of the realm, she observed that by law and custom a prince of the blood should never have held such power as she had given to Prince Kung. Yet she had been compelled to summon what aid she could in her task of rebuilding the nation to its former strength and glory. Moreover, she said, Prince Ch'un's present appointment was only temporary. And she closed her edict thus:

"You, Princes and Ministers, do not realize how great and numerous are the problems with which We must deal alone. As to the Grand Council, let the Councilors beware of making Prince Ch'un's position an excuse for shirking their responsibilities. In conclusion, We desire that in the future Our Ministers pay more respect to the motives behind their Sovereign's actions, and abstain from troubling Us with their querulous complaints. The Memorialist's requests are hereby refused."

It was ever her habit to write in plain firm language, without wasteful ceremonial words, and when her ministers and princes received this edict they were speechless. In such silence the Empress ruled for seven years and as a tyrant absolute and gracious.

They were good years. The Empress, surrounded by the silence of her princes and her ministers, gave few audiences. She observed the ceremonies carefully nevertheless, and considered the wishes of her people. She proclaimed all festivals and allowed many holidays and Heaven approved her reign, for in all these years there was neither flood nor drought and harvests were plenteous. Nor was there war anywhere throughout her realm. In distant places her foreign foes maintained themselves but they did not come out for battle. Moreover, since she ruled by fear, her subjects carried no rumors to her ears and her councilors hid their doubts inside their minds.

In such tranquillity the Empress could devote herself to the fulfillment of her dream. It was to complete the building of the new Summer Palace. She let her wish be known and when the people heard it, they sent gifts of gold and silver, and provinces doubled their tribute. Nor would she allow anyone to think her dream was only for herself. In edicts, which she wrote as letters to her subjects, she gave thanks to them and declared that the Summer Palace would be her retreat when she had given the Throne to its rightful heir, Kwang Hsü, the young Emperor, her nephew and adopted son, which she would do, she promised, as soon as he had completed his seventeenth year.

Thus the Empress made even her dream seem righteous before the people, and so it seemed also to her. As pleasant duty, then, she spent her time in designing and causing to be built vast halls of magnificence and beauty to satisfy her soul, and for this she chose to return to the ancient site of the Emperor Ch'ien Lung. This Emperor, who had been strong son of a strong mother, had built his pleasure palace to his mother's wish. The lady had once visited Hangchow, a city of pure beauty, and had admired the great pleasure houses there, until her son, Ch'ien Lung, declared that he would build a like one for her outside the walls of Peking. This was his Summer Palace, and he built it with every grace and convenience and in it gathered treasures from the whole world. All had been destroyed, however, by the command of the Englishman Lord Elgin, and only the invincible ruins now remained.

This was the site the Empress chose, fulfilling thus not only her own dream but rebuilding those dreams of the Imperial Ancestors. With matchless taste she included in her plans the Temple of Ten Thousand Buddhas, which Ch'ien Lung had made and the foreigners had not destroyed, and the bronze pavilions which their fires had not burned, and the fair placid lake. But other ruins she would not rebuild or have removed. Let them stand, she said, for memory's sake, to lead the minds of men to ponder on the end of life and how all palaces may be destroyed by time and enemies.

Near the southeastern region of the lake, she planned and caused to be built her own palaces where she and the Emperor could live apart and yet not too far. There, too, she placed a vast theater where in her old age she could enjoy her favorite pastime, and near the marble gates, roofed with blue tiles, she set the Audience Hall, for even on holidays, she said, the ruler must be ready to hear the voices of the ministers and princes. This Audience Hall was stately and very large, decorated with carved woods and precious ancient lacquered furniture and ornaments, and upon its glass doors were painted huge the character for longevity. Before the hall there stretched a marble terrace, whence wide marble steps led to the lake. On the terrace itself were placed bronze birds and beasts and in summer awnings of silk shaded the deep verandas.

Westward the imperial woman built her home, one hall after another surrounded by the deep pillared verandas where in meditation she loved to walk. When rain fell she paced back and forth to gaze over the misted waters and the dripping cypress trees. In summer she ordered fragrant matting of sweet grass to be stretched over her courtyards, and these were outdoor rooms, filled with rockeries and flowers; and among all her flowers she still loved best the small green orchids for which she had been named as a child. Along the lake she built a marble-pillared corridor, a mile long, and here, too, she walked, to gaze upon a peony mountain, crabapple trees and oleanders, and pomegranates. With increasing passion she loved beauty, for beauty, she told herself, and only beauty, was pure and good and worthy of her love.

Encouraged by her people's willingness, the Empress grew reckless with magnificence. Her royal bed was hung with imperial-yellow satin whereon she caused to be embroidered, by the finest craftswomen, a cloud of flying phoenixes. From everywhere in the Western world she gathered clocks for her amusement, clocks of gold set with jewels. Some were made with cunning decorations of birds that sang, some with cocks that crowed, some centered upon streams of running water that turned the inner wheels. Yet, in spite of such toys, she made a library for herself that the greatest scholars envied and she never ceased to read her books.

And always, everywhere she looked, she saw in vistas the blue waters of the lake. In its center was the island upon which stood a temple to the Dragon King to which led a marble bridge with seventeen arches. Upon that island, too, was a small sandy beach, and half buried in its sand the bronze cow, placed by Ch'ien Lung, stood stalwart through the centuries to ward off floods. Many bridges the Empress caused to be built so that wherever she might wish to go she went, but one bridge she loved above all others, a hunchbacked bridge that curved into the air for thirty feet. There, so high, she loved to stand and gaze across the water upon the roofs, the pagodas and the terraces of her vast possession.

Lulled by beauty, she let the years slip by, until one day her eunuch, whose duty it was to remind her of what she forgot, begged her to remember that the young Emperor, Kwang Hsü, her nephew, was now near the end of his seventeenth year and therefore she should choose a consort for him. On this day the Empress was watching the completion of a new pagoda which she had designed to carry further the pointed height of a mountain behind the Summer Palace. Nevertheless she perceived at once that Li Lien-ying was right and she must no longer delay the marriage of the Heir. What care she had spent upon the choice of Consort for her true son! She felt no such care now except that she would choose a woman always loyal to herself as Empress, and above all not one like Alute, who had loved her lord too well.

"I desire only peace," the Empress said to Li Lien-ying. "Name me some maidens you know who will not love my nephew as Alute loved my son. Strife I can no longer bear. I will not be disturbed by love or hate."

Then seeing that Li Lien-ying, now growing fat, looked ill at ease as he knelt before her, she bade him sit and rest himself while he thought what names to suggest. The huge eunuch gladly obeyed, puffing and sighing and fanning himself, for the season was too warm for spring, and everywhere the trees and shrubs were bursting into early bloom.

"Majesty," he said after thought, "why not that good plain maiden who is the daughter of your brother, Duke Kwei Hsiang?"

The Empress clapped her hands softly in approval, casting upon the ugly face of her slave a look of affection. "Why did I not think of her?" she replied. "She is the best among my younger ladies of the Court, silent and ready, modest and always devoted to me. She is my favorite—I daresay because I can forget she lives!"

"And for the imperial concubines?" Li Lien-ying inquired.

"Name me some pretty girls," she said carelessly, her eyes already lifted to the tall spire of the pagoda rising above the pine trees. "Only let them be stupid," she added.

To which the Eunuch said, "The Viceroy of Canton deserves reward, Majesty, for holding down the rebels always restless in the southern provinces. He has two daughters, one pretty and one fat, both stupid."

"I will name them," the Empress said, still carelessly. "Do you prepare the decree," she added.

Thus directed, Li Lien-ying rose with great heaves and sighs, while she laughed at him, which pleased him, and he mumbled that his Old Buddha must not disturb herself, for he would arrange everything and she need only appear on the day of the wedding.

"You!" she scolded, pointing at him with her outthrust little finger, wearing its ruby-jeweled nail shield. "You dare to call me Old Buddha!"

"Majesty," he said, puffing and panting, "it is what the people call you everywhere, since you prayed down the rains last summer."

It was true that in the last winter no snow fell and the skies continued hard as blue sapphire through the spring and even in the summer no rains came down. The Empress then decreed prayers and fasting and she herself prayed and fasted and commanded the whole Court so to do. On the third day Buddha yielded, the skies melted and the rains rushed out. The happy people ran into the streets and drank the blessed rain and bathed their hands and faces and praised their Empress for her power even with the gods and cried out:

"She is our own Old Buddha!"

Since then the Chief Eunuch had always called her Old Buddha. It was gross flattery and she knew it was and yet she liked it. Old Buddha! It was the highest name a people could bestow upon a ruler, for it meant they beheld in him a god. And by now she had forgot that she was ever a woman. At the age af fifty-five, she was a being apart from men and women and beyond them all, as Buddha was.

"Get away with you," she said, laughing. "What will you be saying next, you monstrous fellow!"

But when he had gone she wandered here and there, lonely among the fabulous gardens she had made, the sun falling on her handsome aging face and on the glittering robes she loved to wear. At the distance which she now demanded, her ladies followed as usual like a flock of hovering butterflies.

The wedding day drew near, an ill-fated day, not blessed by Heaven. The omens were not good. The night before a mighty wind blew down from the north and tore away the matting roofs the eunuchs had built to cover the great entrance courtyard of the Forbidden City, the place the Empress had decreed for the wedding ceremonies. The dawn opened gray and dark, rain fell early and the skies were relentless. The red wedding candles would not light, and the sweetmeats were soft with damp. When the bride entered the vast courtyard and took her place beside the bridegroom he turned his head away to show his dislike and the Empress, seeing him thus offend the one she had chosen, could not hide her rage except by such effort that anger turned inward and boiled through her veins and settled in her heart to a bitter deathless hatred for her nephew because he could defy her. There he sat, a tall, pale reedy boy, a weakling, his face not bearded, his hands too delicate and always trembling, and yet he was stubborn! This was the heir she had chosen for the Throne! His weakness was rebuke to her, his stubborn will an enemy. Thus she raged in secret while tears ran down the young bride's sallow cheeks.

The rites proceeded, the Empress seemed indifferent, and when the day was ended she left the Forbidden City and returned to her Summer Palace, henceforth to be her home.

From there in the first month of her fifty-sixth year she declared by edict to the nation that once more she had retired from the Regency and that the Emperor now sat alone upon the Dragon Throne. As for herself, she said, she withdrew from the Forbidden City. And so she did, within that same month, moving all her treasures to the Summer Palace, with the intent to live and die there, against the wish of her many princes and her ministers. These besought her to keep one hand at least upon the reins of empire, for the Emperor, they declared, was headstrong and weak-willed, a dangerous combination of waywardness and yielding.

"Too much under the sway of his tutors, K'ang Yu-wei and Liang Ch'i-Ch'ao," they said.

"And Majesty, he loves too well those foreign toys," her Chief Censor said. "To this day the young Emperor, though he is a man now and wed, will sit before his toy trains and wind a key or light a small fire to see them run along toy tracks. We doubt that this is only play. We fear he has his plans to build these foreign railroads upon our own ancient soil."

She laughed at them, very gay to think that she had shaken off her cares and duties. "It is your business now, my lords and princes," she declared. "Do what you will with your young sovereign, and let me rest."

They were troubled to a man, the more because Prince Kung and Jung Lu were banished from the Court. "But may we come to you if our young Emperor will not heed us?" they inquired. "Remember, Majesty, that he fears only you."

"I am not in another country," she said, still waggish. "I am but nine miles away. I have my eunuchs, my spies and courtiers. I shall not let the Emperor take away your heads, I daresay, so long as I know you are loyal to me."

Her great eyes shone and sparkled as she spoke and her lips, still red as youth itself, curved and smiled and teased, and seeing her high humor they were assured again and went away.

She let the years glide by once more, though keeping secret hold upon her power through spies in every palace. Thus she learned that the young Emperor did not love his plain Consort, that they quarreled, and that he turned to his two concubines, the Pearl and the Lustrous.

"But they are stupid," Li Lien-ying in his daily gossip told her. "We need not fear them."

"They will debauch him," she said indifferently. "I have no hope of him or any man." She seemed not to care, but for a moment her great eyes were bleak and lightless. "Ah well," she said, and roused herself and turned her head away.

Yet she could be as sharp in her command as any ruler is. When the princes of her own Yehonala Clan desired by memorial to raise the title of Prince Ch'un, the Emperor's father, and thus give the Emperor the opportunity to show filial piety by placing his father higher than himself in the law of generations, she would not allow it. No, the imperial line was still to be through her, and not through any other. Kwang Hsü was her son by adoption, and she was the Imperial Ancestor. Yet with her old grace, she refused gently so that she did not wound Prince Ch'un, whom she had chosen for her sister's husband now many years ago. She praised the Prince, she spoke of his unchanging loyalty and then said that he himself would not accept the honor, so modest was he.

"Whenever I have wished to bestow a special honor on this Prince," she said by royal edict, "he has refused it with tears in his eyes. I have long since granted him My leave to ride in a sedan chair with curtains of apricot yellow silk of the imperial rank, but not once has he ventured so to do. Thus does he prove his loyalty and unselfish modesty, to My people as well as to Myself."

Alas, in a few short years after this edict was sent forth the worthy prince fell mortally ill. The Empress had grown so deeply into peace and rest that she showed herself indifferent and did not so much as visit him, although he was her imperial brother-in-law. Censors then reminded her of her duty, which angered her so that she bade them to mind their own affairs, for she knew what she would do and would not. Nevertheless, roused by her anger, she did visit Prince Ch'un and often until in the next summer he died. In her *Decree Upon the Death of Prince Ch'un* she praised him for the perfect performance of his duties as the Chamberlain of the Palace, the Head of the Navy and the Commander of the Manchu Field Forces, all duties which she had given him. And she herself examined details for the funeral and she presented the corpse with a sacred coverlet to wear inside the coffin, and upon the coverlet she bade her woman embroider many Buddhist prayers for his soul. When he was in his grave she made one more command concerning this dead Prince. His palace she ordered to be divided into two parts, one to be the ancestral hall for his family clan and the other, where the young emperor had been born and whence she had taken him in secret haste so many years ago, she declared now would be an imperial shrine.

Thus the lingering years drew on to that most honorable dawn when the Empress would celebrate her sixtieth birthday. With matchless vigor she had now completed the Summer Palace, her abode of beauty and of peace for her old age. Under her command, which even the young Emperor dared not refuse, she had taken treasure from all the Government Boards, and at the very last, when all was done, she had the final whim to build a vast white marble boat to stand in the midst of the lake, connected by a marble bridge to the land. Where were the monies to come from for this? The Emperor sighed and shook his troubled head when he received her messages.

This time he dared to send his doubt back to her, couched in most delicate and filial words. But she flew into one of her mighty rages and tore the sheets of silken paper and threw them into the air above her head and when they came fluttering down upon the floor, she bade a eunuch sweep them up and cast them into a kitchen fire.

"My idle nephew knows where the money is," she shouted, for now in her old age when she was denied or that which she ordered was delayed, she indulged in those shouts and shrieks and tantrums which before she had enjoyed only in her childhood. All were astonished to see her thus, and in such moods only Li Lien-ying could calm her.

"Say where the money is, Majesty," he said, breathing hard in asthma. "Say where it is, and you shall have it."

"Why, you big bag of wind," she cried. "There is all that unspent money in the Navy Treasury funds."

It was true that millions of dollars in silver bullion lay in the Navy Treasury and here was the reason. In those years the dwarf men from the islands in the Eastern Seas also threatened the Chinese shores. These islanders were men used to ships and waters, whereas the people of China were landsmen and had few ships except the old heavy junks upon which fishing families or water merchants lived, and junks could only creep up and down the coasts. But the dwarf men, as Chinese called the Japanese, had learned how to make Western steamships of iron, upon whose decks they fastened cannon as the white men did. In much alarm worthy Chinese citizens throughout the nations had gathered monies together and given the sums to their ruler, first to the Empress when she was Regent and now to the Emperor, saying that these monies were for the building of a new navy, whose ships were to be all of iron and upon whose decks were to be fastened foreign cannon, so that when the islanders attacked, they could be repulsed.

"And why do we need fear those dwarfs?" the Empress had said with rich contempt. "They can do no more than harass our shores, for our people will never let them march inland. It is folly to spend good gold upon foreign ships which would be no better than those toys my nephew loved to play with when he was a child—and still plays with, I hear."

When she had read the Emperor's message and had torn it into flying pieces, she said, "I daresay my nephew wants those ships for toys again, but this time to sail seas upon. Thus he wishes to waste the imperial treasures."

So persistent was she that at last the Emperor did yield, against the advice of his tutors, and so she had her marble boat. Upon this boat she now planned the ceremonies of her sixtieth birthday. In the tenth moon month of that year all was arranged, the thirty days of feasting, a holiday for the whole nation, and many prizes and honors to be awarded to her loyal subjects. To pay for such vast celebration, officials were invited to give the Empress one fourth of their annual salaries, and she declared also that she was ready to receive money gifts before her birthday, in order that all might enjoy the feasts and plays.

And in her heart the Empress planned a private pleasure for herself. In these years while Jung Lu had been banished because he had once accepted the love of a lonely concubine, she had not seen his face. Now the concubine was dead, and the Empress found her anger dead, too, and buried with that woman, and there was no further reason why she should punish herself by punishing the one she still loved above all. She was past the age of lovers and she and Jung Lu could be friends again, kinsman and kinswoman. She allowed feeling to pervade her shrewd brain at last. A faint echoing warmth stirred even in the ashes of her heart, and it was sweet to think that she would see his face, that they could sit down, forgetting each the follies of the other, and speak of what they were now, she soon to fulfill her sixtieth year, and he already beyond it. She sent him her letter and not as a decree.

"I do not say this is a decree," she wrote, her beautiful writing brushing the page with firm yet delicate strokes. "Let it be greeting and invitation, a hope that we may meet again with quiet hearts and wise minds. Come, then, before the ceremonies for my sixtieth birthday. Let us spend an hour together before we mingle with the Court."

She set the day before her birthday, the hour, midafternoon; the place, her own library. And because she knew that Jung Lu despised eunuchs, she sent even Li Lien-ying away upon an errand in the city, bidding him examine some new jades that had come in from Turkestan. The afternoon was fair, the season late autumn, a warm day without wind. The sun poured down into the palace courtyards and shone upon the thousands of chrysanthemums in the late bloom. It was already the tenth month of the year, but the court gardeners held back the buds so that upon the imperial birthday the flowers might be at their height. In her library the Empress sat at ease, in robes of yellow satin embroidered in blue phoenixes, and her hands were folded and quiet upon her knees.

At the third hour she heard the tread of footsteps. Her ladies opened the doors wide and looking down the corridors beyond she saw the tall figure of Jung Lu. To her dismay her old heart sprang to life again.

"Oh, be still, heart," she murmured while she watched him come. Still the most beautiful of all men, her heart cried! But he was grave, she saw that, and he had put on somber garments, a long blue robe of dark satin, and a winged black satin hat. Upon his breast he wore an ornament of crimson jade and in his hands a prince's scepter proclaimed a wall between himself and her. She sat motionless until he stood before her. Their eyes met, and then he made effort to kneel in old obeisance. But she put out her right hand to prevent him and motioning to two chairs nearby, she came down from her throne and holding his sleeve lightly between thumb and forefinger, she led him there and they sat down.

"Put down your jade piece," she said imperiously.

He put it down upon the small table between them, as though it were a sword, and waited for her to speak again.

"How have you been?" she asked, and she looked at him sweetly, her too brilliant eyes grown soft and tender of a sudden.

"Majesty," he began.

"Do not call me Majesty," she said.

He bowed his head and began once more. "It is for me to ask how you are," he said. "But I see with my own eyes. You are not changed. Your face is the face I have carried all these years inside my heart."

Neither of them spoke of the years. There was no need now to speak of what was past. No other soul could stay love between their two souls. No other creature lived when they were alone together, except themselves. Yes, she thought, gazing at him frankly with her young-old eyes, he was still her own, her love, the only human whose flesh was of her flesh and hers of his. It was strange to love him so well again but now without longing, a comforting and comfortable love. She sighed and felt a gentle happiness pervade her.

"Why do you sigh?" he asked.

"I thought I had much to tell you," she replied. "But now, face to face as we are, I feel you know all of me."

"And you know all there is of me to know," he said. "I have not changed—not since the first day we knew what we were, I to you, and you to me, have I changed."

304

She made no answer. Enough, enough was said. The years in the listening palace walls had set the habit of silence upon their lips, and they sat quietly for a space, not moving, and felt their inner souls renewed by such communion. When she spoke to put a question, her voice was sweet and humbled.

"Have you advice to give me? These many years I have listened to no prince's counsel, lacking yours."

He shook his head. "You have done well."

Yet she discerned something held back, words he would not say.

"Come," she said, "you and I—have we not always spoken truthfully, you to me, and I to you? What have I done that you do not approve?"

"Nothing," he said, "nothing! I will not spoil your birthday. The least of your subjects is allowed the privilege of his sixtieth birthday, and shall you not enjoy yours?"

She paid heed to this. Her birthday? "Come," she urged. "The truth, the truth!"

"I trust your own sense of wisdom," he replied unwillingly. "If, perchance, our forces are defeated by the Japanese enemy entrenched now in the weak state of Korea after the invasion last summer, then it may be that in the midst of sorrow for the nation, you will not wish to allow rejoicing for yourself."

She considered this awhile. She sighed, sat motionless and thoughtful, her eyes downcast. Then slowly she rose and slowly walked across the tiled floor to her throne again and there sat down. And he rose, too, and waited until she was on her throne and he came toward her and knelt in the old obeisance and this time she did not forbid him. She looked down upon his broad bowed back and said: "Sometimes I do foresee such trouble ahead that I know not where to turn for help. In the darkness of my nights I wake and stare into the future, and there, as close to me as my own hand, I see the looming clouds. What will befall my realm? I have thought that, once my birthday is past, I ought to summon soothsayers and know the evil, however monstrous, that I feel approaching."

He said in his strong deep voice, "Better than soothsayers, Majesty, is to be prepared."

"Then yourself take command of my forces here in the capital," she urged. "Be near me and protect me as you used to do. I will not forget the night you came to my tent when we were in the wild mountains near Jehol. Your sword saved my life that night—and my son's."

Cold and bitter longing clutched her heart to speak aloud the words she thought. It was our son you saved. But she would not speak them.

He was dead, that son, and buried as Emperor and son of Emperor before him, and so let him rest in his imperial grave.

"I accept the charge," Jung Lu said, and rising, he grasped his prince's scepter firmly in both hands and left her presence.

Alas that her birthday was never to be celebrated! The people gave much money for triumphal arches to be raised above the roadways from the imperial city to the Summer Palace, high altars were built, whereon the abbots of the Buddhist temples were to have recited sutras. The whole nation, peoples of all the provinces and outlying territories, prepared for a month of rejoicing for the most honorable day of their sovereign. But suddenly, before these enjoyments could come to pass, the enemy from the islands of Japan fell upon the Chinese fleet of junks and utterly destroyed them, and the people of Korea, under suzerainty of the Dragon Throne, sent out loud cries for help, for now the Japanese warriors overran their land too, and unless they were aided, they could be no more a nation.

The Empress, receiving such messages of disaster by hourly couriers, and but a few days before her birthday, was distracted into rage. In her secret and relentless mind she knew her own guilt, that she had spent upon the Summer Palace the monies from the Imperial Navy Treasury which might have built ships able to overcome the ships of the enemy. But it was her nature that though she knew her fault, she would not allow the knowledge to influence her before the eyes of others, if so to do would weaken her imperial power. The Throne must be maintained inviolable, supreme. She prepared herself therefore for a mighty rage against her enemies. First, she refused to eat for a whole day. Next, she would not sleep or take rest. Instead, she spent the entire day of fasting in pacing up and down inside her palace. Nor would she allow herself to be diverted by her favorite pets, nor by flowers nor by the songs of caged birds. She would not open a book or unroll a scroll or accept any of her usual pastimes. She paced up and down, first in her vast library and then in her corridors until word spread over the Forbidden City like an evil wind that the Empress was in fury and none knew where her wrath would break, but break it must.

In the ferment of her mind, her thoughts whirling about the clear cold center of her own knowledge of where the chief fault lay, she chose two to blame, and she was not one of them. First, she would summon the lesser of the two, that general whom she had most trusted, Li Hung-chang, and upon him she would pour her anger. This decided, she sent the Chief Eunuch for him, and she waited at the appointed hour in her private audience hall, but she commanded all the doors to be left open so that listening ears could hear the tumult of her wrath and spread the news throughout the palace, whence it would penetrate the city and the nation.

"You!" she cried at the stout tall general when he stood before her. She would not deign to use her forefingers to point at him but only her two little fingers, her hands outstretched. "You dare to lose our boats, even that good chartered troopship, the *Kowshing!* It lies at the bottom of the sea. Where shall we find the money to pay for it? See what your stupidity has done for our realm!"

The general knew better than to utter a word. He remained kneeling in obeisance, his splendid robes spread out upon the floor. And she knew that he would not dare to reply and so she rushed on to fresh wrath.

"You!" she cried again, and she hurled the word at him like a curse, and she pointed her two little fingers at him as though to stab him through. "Where has your mind been all these years and upon what has your heart dwelled? You have forgot the welfare of the nation! Your concern has been only for those merchant steamboats you have made to sail upon our rivers, and for the foreign railroads you built, though you know very well how I hate such foreign objects, and I hear that you have even built a foreign weaving mill in Shanghai, whose profits you pocket! Do you not know that proper devotion to the Dragon Throne requires your entire time and thought? How dare you think only of yourself?"

Still he would not answer, though the Empress waited with both little fingers outstretched toward him. So she began again, stabbing the air above his head with her two fingers.

"During these ten years, how much has been lost because of your greed and your selfishness! France has seized Annam and attacked Taiwan, and only with difficulty were we able to free ourselves from a foreign war with that nation, and this at the same time that we have been distressed by the war in Korea with Japan. And how is it that all these foreign peoples dare to threaten us and attack us? It is because our armies and navies are weak, and whose fault is this weakness but yours? You shall stay by your post, you recreant and traitor, for what you have not been able to do you must now do, and you shall be stripped of all honors. Like a slave you may not rest, and like a slave you shall be punished."

She put down her hands and drew her breath in and out loudly several times and then she ordered him to leave her.

"Get up," she said. "Go to your duty. By any means you can, undo

307

what you have done. Peace we must have, with whatever honor you can save for your Sovereign."

He rose and dusted off his knees and walked backward from her presence, bowing as he went, and on his full square face she saw a look of patience which somehow struck her to the heart. For this man had saved her more than once and he had been obedient to her command, and she knew that he was still loyal. Some day she would be lenient toward him again but not today. She would not let her heart soften to anyone and her greatest wrath was yet to fall. For next she summoned the Emperor by her own handwriting and to her name she set the imperial seal.

But on that day when she had despatched the command, a strange mad turmoil upset the whole Summer Palace. Near evening, when the Empress rested in the Pavilion of Orchids, one of her ladies came running through the round marble gate, her robes flying and her hair disordered. The serving woman, who knelt beside the Empress to fan the small insects away, put up her hand for silence, for the Empress slept. But the lady was too frightened to heed and she cried out in a shrill high voice,

"Majesty, Majesty—I saw—I saw—"

The Empress woke at once and fully, as she always did. She sat up on her couch and looked at the lady with a piercing stare.

"Saw what?" she asked.

"A man shaved like a priest," the lady gasped. She clutched her bosom and began to weep with fright.

"Well, well," the Empress rejoined, "a priest, I suppose—"

"No priest, Majesty," the lady insisted, "but only bald like a priest. Perhaps he was a Thibetan monk—ah, but he wore no yellow robes! No, he was black from neck to feet and taller than any man I ever saw, and he had such great hands! Yet, Majesty, the gates are locked, and none save eunuchs are here inside the walls!"

The Empress turned her eyes toward the sky. The sun had set, and the soft red light of afterglow poured into the courtyard of the pavilion. Indeed, no man should be here now.

"You are dreaming," she said to the foolish lady. "The eunuchs are on guard. No man can enter."

"I saw him, Majesty, I saw him," the lady insisted.

"Then I myself will find him," the Empress declared firmly. So saying she sent the serving woman to bring the Chief Eunuch to her, and when he heard the tale he called twenty lesser eunuchs and they lit lanterns and held swords, and encircling the intrepid Empress, they searched long and found no one.

"We are fools," the Empress cried at last. "That lady had a nightmare or she was drunk. So you, Li Lien-ying, bid the eunuchs carry on the search while you hold the lantern for me."

So they two walked back, he ahead to light the way, until she returned to her library room. She had but crossed the threshold when lifting her head she saw upon the writing table a long sheet of red paper whereon were brushed in huge bold strokes these words, "I hold your life inside the hollow of my hand."

She seized the paper and read it twice and threw it at the waiting eunuch.

"See this!" she shouted. "He hides here—an assassin! Get back to the search."

By now her ladies flocked about her, and while Li Lien-ying made haste away, they consoled the Empress with many words and sighs.

"Be sure, Majesty, the eunuchs will find him," they said, and they declared that now since all knew the hairless man was real and not a dream, he could be quickly found.

They lit candles, a score or so, and led the Empress to her sleeping chambers, saying that she must not fall ill with weariness, and they would stay with her all night. But as they entered into the chamber they saw a sheet of red paper pinned on her yellow satin pillow and upon it with the same bold strokes were brushed these words:

"When the hour comes, I bring my sword. Asleep or waking, you must die."

The ladies shrieked but the Empress was only angry. Then suddenly she seized the red paper and crumpled it into a ball and threw it across the floor. She laughed, her black eyes aglitter. "Now come," she commanded, "be silent, my children. The fellow is some clown who loves to tease. Go to bed and sleep and so will I."

They made a chorus against her. "No, Majesty, no—no, Majesty, we will not leave you."

Still smiling, she yielded, and with her usual grace she let them undress her and put her to bed. And six ladies lay on mattresses the serving women brought and put upon the floor, while others went to their rooms to sleep until midnight and then another six would take their place until dawn. Meanwhile Li Lien-ying had summoned the eunuchs and they surrounded the sleeping chamber, standing with their swords drawn, until the night was spent.

At dawn the Empress woke, she yawned pleasantly behind her outspread hand. She smiled and said she felt the better for the commotion

of the hairless man. "I am lively," she declared. "We have been too in-
dolent in all this beauty of our palace."

She went out from her chamber that morning, bathed and dressed, her
hair set with fresh flowers, to eat her early meal, her eyes looking everywhere to see that all was in usual order. Suddenly she saw, laid upon
the dishes, the red sheet of paper, and the same strong strokes of black.

"While you slept, I waited," the black words declared.

The ladies screamed again, some wept aloud, and the serving women
ran in and struck their cheeks with their palms. "But we put out the
dishes only now and we saw no man come in!"

"He will be found," the Empress said lightly, and again she crumpled
the paper and threw it to the floor. Nor would she allow the dishes to be
removed, although the ladies shuddered and implored, saying that the
meats might be poisoned. No, she ate as usual and felt no pains, and
during that whole day the search went on. None saw the man, but four
more red sheets of threats were found here and there.

So went this search for two full months, by day and night, a zealous
search, for now and again a lady or a eunuch saw a glimpse of the hairless man, in black from neck to feet, and his pale face and head all of a
color. One lady indeed fell into sickness and her mind went weak because she said when she had opened her eyes one morning from her
sleep she saw the man's face staring at her, but upside down as though
he hung from the roof, and when she screamed the head went upwards.

Nevertheless the Empress would not be afraid, although day and
night the eunuchs stood on guard. No one outside the walls knew the
story, for the Empress had forbidden one word to be told lest the city
be disturbed and rascals come out from among them to seize the chance
of some confusion.

One night, while the Empress lay sleeping in her chamber, the wakeful
eunuchs stood on guard as usual in the halls outside and in the courtyards about. In the still hours between midnight and the dawn they
heard a door creak open slowly and against the faint moonlight a black
foot appeared, a leg, a thigh thrust in the narrow space. The eunuchs
sprang together to lay hold upon that secret being. He fled, but eunuchs
everywhere were waiting, and in a garden behind a great rock the Empress had ordered from a distant province they caught the hairless man
between their hands.

The Empress was awakened by the eunuchs' shouts and cries. She
rose swiftly from her bed, for she had commanded that whatever hour
the man was caught, he must be brought before her. Her women
wrapped her in her robes and set her headdress on her head, and in a

moment she sat upon her throne in her Audience Hall. Here the eunuchs brought the man with ropes wound about his body.

He stood before the Empress and he would not bow, though eunuchs seized him by the neck to force him down.

"Let him stand," the Empress said, and her voice was mild and cool.

She stared down upon the tall bold figure, a young man, his head shaven, and she saw his strange tiger face, the sloping forehead, the tight-drawn mouth, the slanting eyes. A black garment, cut to his shape, fitted his thin body like a skin.

"Who are you?" she demanded.

"I am no one," the man said, "nameless, of no significance."

"Who sent you here?" she asked.

"Kill me," the man said carelessly, "for I will tell you nothing."

At such impudence the eunuchs shouted and would have fallen on him with their swords but the Empress put up her hand.

"See what he has on his person," she commanded.

They searched the man while he stood carelessly at ease, indifferent to them, and they found nothing.

"Majesty," Li Lien-ying now said, "I pray you give this fellow to me. Under torture he will speak. And I will see that he is beaten slowly with bamboos split thin and sharp. He shall not move, for he shall be laid upon the ground, his arms and legs outspread and fastened down with wire tied to stakes. Leave him to me, Majesty."

All knew how Li Lien-ying dealt torture, and all approved with groans and cries.

"Take him and do what you will," the Empress said. As she spoke she met the man's eyes full, and she saw that they were not black like other human eyes but yellow, and as impudent as are the eyes of wild beasts which fear no human. She could not turn her own gaze away, so loathsome and yet strangely beautiful were those yellow eyes.

"Do your work well," she bade the eunuchs.

Two days later Li Lien-ying returned to make report.

"What names did he speak?" the Empress asked.

"None, Majesty," he said.

"Then continue torture but make it twice as slow."

This was her command but Li Lien-ying shook his head.

"Majesty," he said, "it is too late. He died as though he willed it, and he did not speak."

For the first time in her life the Empress felt afraid. The strange yellow eyes seemed still to watch her. Yet when had she allowed herself to fear? She put out her right hand and plucked a jasmine flower from a blooming tree set in a porcelain pot nearby, and held the fragrance to her nostrils and breathed it in for comfort.

"Now let him be forgot," she said.

Yet she it was who could not forget the hairless man. He left behind him the shadow of darkness and suspicious doubt. The beauty of her palace was dimmed, and though she walked in her gardens every day and showed her old zeal for each flower and fruit in season, and though daily she commanded the Court actors to present some merry play, her easy joy was gone. She had no fear of death, but what she felt was a heavy sadness, since somewhere there were those who wished her dead. Could she have found those enemies, she would have killed them, but where were they to be found? None knew and all were troubled.

One day in late afternoon she sat among her ladies on the great marble boat and she saw Li Lien-ying come near. She had played gambling games all day and still she played, her tea bowl in one hand while with the other she moved her pieces here and there to win the game.

"Majesty, your tea is cold," the eunuch said. He took her bowl and let a serving eunuch fill it. When he put it down upon the table near her he whispered that he had news.

She seemed not to hear, she played her game out and then she rose, and with a look she summoned him to follow her.

When they were alone in her own palace, her ladies standing at a distance since they knew the eunuch had some business to report, she waved her fan to signify he should not kneel and nodded to him to begin what he had to say.

"Majesty," he said, his hissing whisper near her ear.

She struck him slowly with her fan. "Stand back," she cried imperiously. "Your breath is foul as rotting carrion."

He put up his hand then to hold back his breath and began his tale. "Majesty, there is a plot."

She turned her face away and held her fan before her nose. Oh, cursed delicacy, she thought, that made her smell twice as keenly as another might all stinks and odors! Did not this eunuch serve her with his whole heart, she would not keep him near her.

"Majesty," he began again, and thus he unrolled the plot. The young Emperor now listened to his tutor Weng T'ung-ho, who urged him that the nation must be made strong, or it would surely fall at last into the hands of waiting enemies, their jaws open and their saliva dripping, to eat up the Chinese people. The Emperor, Li Lien-ying went on, had asked what should be done, to which the tutor had replied that the great scholar, whose name was K'ang Yu-wei, must give advice, for this scholar was wise not only in history but in the new Western ways. He alone could advise how to build the ships and railroads and the schools for young men who could renew the nation. The Emperor had then sent for K'ang Yu-wei.

The Empress turned her head somewhat, her fan still between her and the eunuch. "And is this K'ang already in the Forbidden City?" she inquired.

"Majesty," the eunuch said, "he is daily with the Emperor. They spend hours together and I hear that he declares the Chinese men must cut their queues off as the first reform."

At this the Empress dropped her fan. "But their queues are the sign of subjection these two hundred years to our Manchu dynasty!"

Li Lien-ying nodded his heavy head up and down three times. "Majesty, K'ang Yu-wei is a Chinese revolutionist, a Cantonese. He plots against Your Majesty! Yet I have worse to tell. He bade our Emperor send for Yuan Shih-k'ai, the general who commands our armies under Li Hung-chang, as you know, Majesty. This Yuan has imperial orders now to seize you by force, Majesty, and keep you imprisoned."

The eunuch gave a mighty sigh, so foul a blast that the Empress put up her fan again in haste to shield herself. "Doubtless my nephew plots to have me killed," she said too mildly.

"No, no," the eunuch said. "Our Emperor is not so evil. It may be that K'ang Yu-wei has so advised, but my spies tell me that the Emperor has forbidden harm to your sacred person, Majesty. No, he says you shall only be imprisoned here in your Summer Palace. You are allowed your pleasures but all your power shall be stripped away."

"Indeed," she said. She felt a strange sweet strength invade her blood. To do battle was still delight and she would have the victory yet again.

"Well, well," she said, and laughed. Then Li Lien-ying, at first astonished at her high humor, laughed with her silently, his ugly face made more hideous by his mirth.

"There is none like you under Heaven," he said tenderly. "You are not male or female, Majesty, but more than either, greater than both."

They exchanged look for look in mutual mischief, and she struck him gaily on the face with her folded fan and bade him be off.

"And close your mouth and keep it closed," she said, "for I swear that vile gusty breath of yours surrounds you as you go."

"Yes, Majesty," he said gaily, and put up his hand, thick as a bear's paw, against his smiling mouth.

It was not her imperial way to make haste in any cause. She meditated much on what her spy had told her. While she let days pass in idle pleasure she showed no fear. The summer passed, one long lovely day upon another, and she pursued her habits, taking pleasure in a large northern dog, his coat as white as snow and he snarling at all except her, his mistress. To her only he showed devotion, and he slept beside her bed at night. Her small cinnamon-colored sleeve dogs were jealous and she laughed much to see them circling the great dog like angry imps. But while she walked in gardens, or picnicked on the lake, or sat in her theater to watch the plays she loved, she was thinking deeply always of the world beyond and what price she must pay to keep peace and beauty living. Twice those island enemies, the men of Japan, had been bought off from war, once by gold and again by yielding to them rights over her tribute people of Korea. Ah that, she now felt, was the weakness of her faithful Viceroy Li Hung-chang, and had he not persuaded her twice to yield, these small brown island dwarfs would not now dream of swallowing her whole vast realm. War, open war against the enemy, brave attack if not on sea then on land, must be her defense at last. And Yuan Shih-k'ai must begin the war, not on Chinese soil but in Korea and from there drive the Japanese into the sea and so to their own bitter rock-ribbed islands. Let them starve there!

On the loveliest afternoon in summer she so shaped her mind and will, and at the same moment she was listening to a love song chanted by a young eunuch dressed as a girl, in that ancient play *The Tale of the Western Pavilion*. The Empress smiled and listened, and she hummed the tune of the love song and all the while within her heart and mind she planned war. That night she summoned Li Hung-chang and laid down her commands, and would not heed his moans and sighs that his armies were too weak, his ships too few.

"You need no great armies or vast fleets," she said, "even if at worst the enemy attack Chinese soil, why, then, the people will rise up and drive them into the sea, and the waves will drown them."

"Ah, Majesty," he groaned, "you do not know the evil times! Here in your palaces you live apart and dreaming."

And he went out sighing loudly and shaking his troubled head.

Alas, the year was not spent before war was made and victory lost. The enemy came quickly and inside a handful of brief days their ships had crossed the seas. That general, Yuan Shih-K'ai, was driven from Korea and the enemy was next on Chinese soil. The Empress for once was wrong. Her people yielded. Her villagers stood silent when the short strong men of Japan marched up their streets and toward the capital itself. They carried guns, these men, and villagers have no guns and being prudent they did not show knives and scythes which are no more than toys. When the enemy demanded food and drink the villagers, still mute, set forth wine and tea and bowls of meats.

At this evil news the Empress moved quickly. She was a good gamester who played to win but well she knew when she could not. She sent word to Li Hung-chang to surrender before the realm was lost and to accept what terms he must. A bitter treaty then was forged, the terms of which shook even the haughty heart of the Empress so that she retired for three days and nights and would not eat and sleep, and Li Hung-chang himself went to the Summer Palace to comfort her. He told her that the treaty was indeed bitter but the throne had a new friend to the north, the Czar of Russia, who for his own sake would not have Japan grow strong.

The Empress listened and took heart. "Then let us get these yellow foreigners from our shores," she said. "At any price they must be got away. And from now on I shall spend my whole strength until I devise some plan to rid myself of every foreigner, white or yellow, and none shall be allowed to set foot upon our soil. No, not until the end of time! As for the Chinese whom we Manchus rule, I will win them back again, save for those young men who have breathed in foreign winds and drunk down foreign waters. My Grand Councilor Kang Yi said but the other day to me that we should never have allowed the Christians to set up schools and colleges, for they have encouraged Chinese to be ambitious to rule themselves and the young Chinese now are wily and rebellious and puffed up with false foreign knowledge."

She struck her palms together and stamped her right foot. "I swear I will not die or let myself grow old until I have destroyed every foreign power upon our soil and have restored the realm to its own history!"

The General could not but admire the woman and his sovereign. The Empress was still beautiful, still strong, her hair as black, her long eyes as great and sparkling as ever they had been in youth. Her will, too, had not abated.

"If anyone can do this, it is only you, Majesty," he said, and then he swore a simple oath to serve her always.

So time passed. Again the Empress seemed to play the idle days and months away, now painting her dream landscapes, now writing poetry, now toying with her jewels and designing new settings for her emeralds and pearls and buying diamonds from Arab merchants. Yet behind all such employments she wove her plans. She seemed indifferent to the Emperor and his tutors. But at night when all the palaces were still and dark, she listened to the stories that her spies brought to her lonely chamber and thus she knew from day to day the plots of the Emperor and his advisors. Against their plots she thus prepared herself. First she lifted Jung Lu up again, this time to be the Viceroy of the province, and it was made easy by the death of Prince Kung who, if not her enemy, had long not been her friend. On the tenth day of the fourth moon of this severe year he died of lung and heart diseases.

Then she waited, learning meanwhile that the Emperor had summoned Yuan Shih-kai to be his general. She was in several minds when she heard this news. Should she wait still longer to seize back the throne or should she move at once? To wait was her decision, for she liked best to appear upon a scene like Buddha, and when all was manifest to bring down judgment. Meanwhile her spies told her that Yuan Shih-kai had left the city by a secret way and none knew his direction.

I will wait, she thought. I have found my wisdom always in waiting. I know my own genius and my mind tells me that the hour is not yet here.

And again she let the days slip past. The summer heat subdued itself to early autumn. Days were warm but nights were chill. The autumn flowers budded late, the last lotus lilies bloomed upon the lake, the birds lingered day by day before they flew southward, and autumn crickets piped their fragile music in the pines.

On a certain day after Prince Kung had died and had been buried with due honor, the Empress sat in her library to compose a poem. The air was mild, and as she mixed her inks she chanced to look toward the sunlit court, and in the bright square of sunlight by the open doors she saw a blue dragonfly floating on the air, its wings outspread. How strange, she thought, for she had never seen a dragonfly so blue, nor seen one with its gossamer wings so still. It was an omen, surely, but of what? She wished the color were not blue, a royal blue, for this was the hue of death. She rose in haste and went toward the door to frighten off the creature. But it was not afraid. Evading her hands, it moved higher above her head. When her ladies, waiting in the far corners of her library, saw this they came forward and they too reached up their hands and waved their fans and cried out, but still the creature floated far above them. The Empress then bade them summon a eunuch who was to fetch a long bamboo, but before they could obey her, they heard commotion at the gate and suddenly the Chief Eunuch appeared, unbidden, to say that a messenger had come to announce the arrival of the Viceroy Jung Lu, from Tientsin.

Not often in the years since the Empress had commanded Jung Lu to take Lady Mei to wife had he come near her throne of his free will. He waited to be summoned, and once she had reproached him for this. To which he had replied that she must know that he was always her loyal servant, and she had but to put her jade sign into a eunuch's hand and send him forth and he, Jung Lu, would come, whatever the hour and wherever he was.

The Empress bade the serving eunuchs to prepare for his coming, and she returned to her seat. But she could not finish the poem, for when she looked up to find the dragonfly, it was still gone. Its coming, then, was portent, an omen which she could not disclose even to the Court soothsayers, for Jung Lu would not come except for gravest cause, and she would not disturb the Court until she knew what the cause was. With fierce impatience covered by her calm bearing she put down her brushes and strolled out about her gardens until noon, and would not rest or touch food before she knew what Jung Lu came to tell her.

Toward evening he came, and his palanquin was set down in the great outer courtyards and eunuchs carried the news. The Empress waited for him in her central courtyard, in these summer months a vast outdoor living space, for mattings, woven of sweet straw and the color of honey, were spread over bamboo framework to make roofs. In the soft cool shade tables were spread and chairs set out, and around the many verandas that walled the courtyards were pots of flowering trees. The Empress seated herself upon a carved chair set between her two favorite ancient cypress trees, which the imperial gardeners kept closely trimmed into the lean shapes of wise old men, and this because the Empress wished to be reminded always of the true ways of the ancestors, shaped to staid beauty and simple dignity.

A summer warmth had returned that day and now a southern wind wafted the fragrance of the late lotus flowers from the lake where they closed slowly for the night. The scent pervaded the air and the Empress breathed it in and she felt the old sharp pain of contrast between the calm of everlasting beauty and the turmoil of human conflict. Ah, if Jung Lu had been coming to her now as her old and well-loved husband, and if she could but wait for him as his old and loving wife! They were young no more, their passion spent unused, but the memory of love remained eternal. Indeed, her mellowed heart was more tender now than ever toward him and there was nothing left that she could not forgive him.

Through the dusk, lit by great flickering candles set in stands of bronze, she saw him coming. He walked alone and she sat motionless and watching. When he reached her he prepared to fall upon one knee but she put out her hand upon his forearm.

"Here is your chair," she said, and motioned with her other hand toward the empty chair at her left.

He rose then and sat beside her in the sweet twilight, and through the gate they watched the torches flare upon the lake for the night's illumination.

"I wish," he said at last, "that you could live your life here undisturbed. Your home is beauty and here you do belong. Yet I must tell you all the truth. The plot against you, Majesty, now nears its crisis."

He clenched his hands upon the knees of his gold-encrusted robe, and her eyes moved to those hands, large and strong. They were still the hands of a young man. Would he never be old?

"Impossible to believe," she murmured, "and yet I know I must believe, because you tell me."

He spoke on. "Yuan Shih-kai himself came to me four nights ago in secret, and I left my post in haste to tell you. The Emperor sent for him twelve days ago. At midnight in the small hall to the right of the Imperial Audience Hall they met."

"Who else was there?" she asked.

"The imperial tutor, Weng T'ung-ho."

"Your enemy," she murmured, "but why do you recall another woman to me now? I have forgot her."

"How well you love cruelty," Jung Lu retorted. "I forgive him, Majesty, and you do not. The pale small love that sprang up in a woman's lonely heart is nothing to me. I learned a lesson from it, nevertheless."

"And what lesson needed you to learn?" she asked.

"That you and I stand somewhere far from other humans, and though we are lonely as two stars in Heaven we must bear our loneliness, for it cannot be assuaged. Sometimes I feel our very loneliness has kept us one."

She moved restlessly. "I wonder that you speak so when you came to tell me of a plot!"

"I speak so because I take this moment to pledge myself again to you," he said.

She put her fan against her cheek, a screen between them.

"And was no one else in the small hall?" she asked.

"The Pearl Concubine, the Emperor's Favorite. You know, for you know every wind of gossip, that the Emperor will not receive his Consort, whom you chose. She is still a virgin. Therefore all her heart has turned to hate. She is your ally."

"I know," she said.

"We must count every ally," he went on, "for the Court is divided. Even the people on the streets know that it is so. One party is called Venerable Mother and the other is called Small Boy."

"Disgraceful," she muttered. "We should keep our family secrets private."

"We cannot," he replied. "The Chinese are like cats. They creep through every crevice in silence, smelling out their way. The country is in turmoil and Chinese rebels who are ever waiting to destroy our Manchu dynasty are again ready to seize power. You must come forth once more."

"I know my nephew is a fool," she said sadly.

"But those about him are not fools," he said. "These edicts that he sends forth like pigeons every day, a hundred edicts in less than a hundred days—have you read them?"

"I let him have his way," she said.

"When he comes here to call upon you each seven days or so, do you ask him nothing?"

"Nothing," she said. "I have my spies."

"One reason that he hates you," he said bluntly, "is that your eunuch keeps him waiting on his knees outside your doors. And did you bid the Emperor kneel?"

"He kneels," she said indifferently. "It is his duty to his Elder."

But she knew that it was true that Li Lien-ying in his impudent self-confidence did keep the Emperor kneeling. And she was guilty, too, for she pretended that she did not know it. Her greatness was penetrated with such small mischiefs, and she knew her smallness as well as her greatness, and did not change herself, accepting what she was.

Jung Lu spoke on. "I know, too, that your eunuchs have compelled the Son of Heaven to pay them bribes to bring him to you, as though he were but a palace official. This is not fitting and well you know it."

"I know it," she said, half laughing, "but he is so meek, so frightened of me, that he tempts me to torture."

"Not so frightened as you think," Jung Lu retorted. "The hundred edicts are not the work of a weak man. Remember that he is your nephew, his blood of the clan blood of Yehonala."

His grave eyes, his solemn voice, compelled her to her greater self. She turned her head away and would not look at him. This, this was the man she feared. Her heart trembled at the knowledge, and the strange impulse of lost youth rushed into her blood. Her mouth went dry, her eyelids burned. Had she missed life itself? And now she was

319

too old, even for the memory of love. What she had lost was lost without recall.

"The plot," she murmured, "you said the plot—"

"It is to surround this palace," he said, "and force you to immolate yourself, promise never to decree again, promise to put away your spies, to yield the great imperial seal, and employ yourself henceforth with flowers, caged singing birds, your favorite dogs—"

"But why?" she cried. Her fan dropped, her hands fell helpless on her knees.

"You are the obstacle," he told her. "But for you they could bring a new nation into being, a nation shaped and modeled on the West—"

"Railroads, I suppose," she cried, "guns, navies, wars, armies, attacks on other peoples, the seizure of lands and goods—" She leaped from her carved chair and flung up her hands and tore at her headdress. "No, no—I will not see our realm destroyed! It is the heritage of glory from our Ancestors. I love these people whom I rule. They are my subjects, and I am not foreign to them. Two hundred years the Dragon Throne was ours and now is mine. My nephew has betrayed me and in me all our ancestors."

Jung Lu rose beside her. "Command me, Majesty—"

His words restored her. "Hear me, then. Summon to me at once my Grand Council. All must be secret. Let the leaders of our imperial clan come also. They will beseech me to depose my nephew, they will implore me to return to the Dragon Throne. They will say my nephew has betrayed the country to our enemies. This time I will hear them and make ready to do what they ask. Your own armies must replace the Imperial Guardsmen at the Forbidden Palace. When the Emperor enters Chung Ho Hall tomorrow at dawn for the autumnal sacrifices to our tutelary gods let him be seized and brought here and placed upon that small island in the middle of the lake, which is called Ocean Terrace. There let him wait, imprisoned, for my coming."

She was herself again, her vigorous mind at work, imagination seeing all the scenes ahead as though she planned a play. Jung Lu spoke behind his hand, his eyes glittering upon her.

"You wonder," he murmured, "you Empress of the Universe! What man's mind can run like yours from yesterday beyond tomorrow? I need not ask a question. The plan is perfect."

They faced each other full, he stood a long moment and then he left her.

In two hours the Grand Councilors arrived, their bearers running through the night to bring them to the Empress. She sat upon her throne robed in imperial garments, her phoenix-gilded satins, her jeweled head-dress set as a crown upon her head. Two tall torches flamed beside her and blazed upon the gold threads of her robes, and glittered on her jewels and in her eyes. Each prince stood within the circle of his men and at a sign from the eunuchs all fell to their knees before her. She told them why she summoned them.

"Great princes, kinsmen, ministers and councilors," she said, "there is a plot against me in the imperial city. My nephew, whom I made Emperor, designs to put me into prison and kill me. When I am dead he plans to rout you all and set up new men who will obey his will. Our old ancient habits are to end, our wisdom flouted, our schools destroyed. New schools, new ways, new thoughts are now to be put in their place. Our enemies, the foreigners, are to be our guides. Is this not treason?"

"Treason, treason!" they shouted one and all.

She put out her hands with her old coaxing grace. "Rise, I pray you," she said. "Sit down as though you were my brothers, and let us reason together how to foil this hideous plot. I do not fear my death but the death of our nation, the enslavement of our people. Who will protect them when I am gone?"

At this Jung Lu stood up to speak. "Majesty," he said, "your general, Yuan Shih-k'ai, is here. I thought it well to summon him and now I beg that he himself may tell the plot."

The Empress inclined her head to signify permission and Yuan Shih-k'ai came forward, wearing his warrior robes, his broad sword hanging from his girdle, and he made obeisance.

"On the morning of the fifth day of this moon," he said in a high level voice, "I was summoned for the last time before the Son of Heaven. I had been summoned thrice before to hear the plot, but this was the last audience until the deed was done. The hour was early. The Emperor sat upon the Dragon Throne in all but darkness, for the light of morning had not yet reached the Throne Hall. He beckoned me to come near and hear him whisper his commands and I did so. He bade me make all haste to Tientsin. There I was to put to death the Viceroy Jung Lu. When this was done I was to hasten homeward again to Peking and, bringing all my soldiers with me, I was to seize you, Majesty and Sacred Mother, and lock you in your palace. Then I was to find the imperial seal and myself take it to the Son of Heaven. The seal, he said, should have been his when he ascended to the Throne, and he could not forgive you, Majesty, he said, because you have kept it for yourself, compelling him, he said, to send his edicts forth signed only by his own private seal, and thereby proving to all the people that you did not trust him.

For sign that his command was absolute he gave me a small gold arrow for my authority."

And Yuan Shih-k'ai drew from his girdle a gold arrow and held it up for all to see, and they groaned.

"And what reward did he promise?" the Empress next inquired, her voice too mild, her eyes too bright.

"I was to be the Viceroy of this province, Majesty," Yuan replied.

"A small reward for so much done," she said. "Be sure that mine will be much greater."

While the General was speaking the Grand Councilors had listened, groaning to hear such perfidy. When he had finished they fell upon their knees and begged the Empress to take back the Dragon Throne and save the nation from the barbarians of the western seas.

"I swear I will grant your request," she said graciously.

They rose again and took counsel and decided together under her royal approval that Jung Lu must return secretly to his post as soon as he had replaced the guards at the Forbidden City with his own men. When the Emperor came at dawn to receive the litany which the Board of Rites had prepared for the sacrifice to the tutelary deities, the guards and the eunuchs were to seize him and bring him to put him on the Ocean Terrace Island and there bid him wait his venerable mother's arrival.

The hour was midnight when all was approved. The Councilors returned to the city and Jung Lu without further farewell went to his post. The Empress then descended from the throne and, leaning on her eunuch's arm, she went to her sleeping chamber, and there, as though it were any usual night, she let herself be bathed, perfumed, her hair brushed and braided, and in her scented silken night garments she went to her bed. The hour was dawn, the very hour the Emperor was to be seized, but she closed her eyes and slept most peacefully.

She woke to silence in the palaces. The sun was high, the air was sweet and chill. In spite of fears and cautions of the Court physicians who declared the winds of night were evil, the Empress always slept with windows open and not even her bed curtains drawn. Two ladies sat near to watch her and outside her door a score of eunuchs stood on guard, not more, nor fewer, than were usual. She woke, she rose as usual, and as usual let her woman make her toilet, lingering somewhat longer, perhaps, upon her choice of jewels and choosing amethysts at last, a dark and gloomy gem that she did not often wear. Her robes, too, were dark, a heavy gray brocaded satin, and when her women brought her orchids for her headdress she forbade their use, for on this day she would be stately.

Yet she ate her usual hearty breakfast and she played with her small dogs and teased a bird by singing his own song until he sang himself half mad to drown her mocking music. Meanwhile Li Lien-ying waited in the outer hall until at last she summoned him.

"Is all well?" she asked when he appeared.

"Majesty, your command has been obeyed," he said.

"Is our guest on the Ocean Terrace Island?" she inquired. Her red lips quivered as though with secret laughter.

"Majesty, two guests," he said. "The Pearl Concubine ran after us and clung to her lord's waist with both her arms and locked her hands so fast that we dared not delay to part them, nor could we take the liberty of killing her, without your order."

"Shame on you," she said, "when did I ever order—ah, well, if he is there, she matters nothing. I go to face him with his treason. You will accompany me and only you. I need no guard—he's helpless."

She snapped her thumb and forefinger toward her favorite dog, and the great creature, huge and white as a northern bear, loped to her side and slowed his pace to hers. Behind them followed Li Lien-ying. In silence they walked toward the lake and crossed the marble bridge, but as she went she looked at all the beauty she had made, the fiery maples on the hillside, the late rosy lotus lilies upon the lake, the golden roofs and the soaring slender pagodas, the terraced gardens and the clustering pine trees. All, all were hers, created by her mind and heart. Yet all would lose meaning were she a prisoner here. Yes, even beauty could not be enough, were she to lose her power and freedom. Alas, she wished she need not hold another prisoner, yet she must and not for her own sake alone but for a people's. Her wisdom, she did in truth believe, must now save the nation from her nephew's folly.

Thus affirming her own will she reached the island, and her great dog at her side and the tall dark eunuch following, she entered the pavilion.

The Emperor was there already in his priestly robes of worship and he rose to receive her. His narrow face was pale, his large eyes sad, his mouth, a woman's mouth for delicacy, the lips gently carved and always parted, was trembling.

"Down on your knees," she said, and sat herself upon the central seat. In every hall, pavilion, chamber or resting place, this central seat was hers.

He fell on his knees before her, and put his forehead to the floor. The great dog smelled him carefully from head to foot and then lay down across her feet to guard her.

"You!" the Empress said most bitterly, and gazed down upon the kneeling man. "You who should be strangled, sliced and thrown to wild beasts!"

He did not speak or move.

"Who put you on the Dragon Throne?" she asked. She did not raise her voice, she needed not, it fell as cold as steel upon his ears. "Who went at night and took you from your bed, a whining child, and made you Emperor?"

He murmured something—words she could not hear. She pushed him with her foot.

"What do you say? Lift up your head, if you dare to let me hear you."

He lifted up his head. "I said—I wish you had not taken that child from his bed."

"You weakling," she retorted, "to whom I gave the highest place in all the world! How much a strong man would rejoice, how grateful he would be to me, his foster mother, how worthy of my pride! But you, with your foreign toys, your playthings, corrupted by your eunuchs, fearful of your Consort, choosing petty concubines above her who is your Empress—I tell you, there is not a Manchu prince or commoner who does not pray that I take back the throne! By day and night I am besought. And who supports you? Fool, who but Chinese rebels? It is their plot to coax and flatter and persuade you to listen to them, and when they have you in their power, they will depose you and end our dynasty. You have betrayed not only me but all our Sacred Ancestors. The mighty who have ruled before us, these you would sacrifice. Reforms! I spit upon reforms! The rebels shall be killed—and you, and you—"

Her breath came suddenly too tight. She stopped and put her hand upon her heart and felt it beat as though it must break. Her dog looked up and growled and she tried to smile.

"A beast is faithful but a man is not," she said. "Yet I will not kill you, nephew. You shall even keep the name of Emperor. But you shall be a prisoner, guarded, wretched. You shall implore me to sit in your place and rule. And I will yield, though unwilling and truly so, for how proud I might have been if you were strong and ruled as a ruler should. Yet since you are weak, not fit to rule, I am compelled to take your place. And from now on until you die—"

At this moment curtains parted in a doorway and the Pearl Concubine ran in and threw herself upon the floor beside him and sobbing loudly she besought the Empress to blame him no more.

"I do assure you, Holy Mother," so she sobbed. "He is sorry that he has disturbed your mind. He wishes only what is good, I do assure you, for a man more kind and gentle never lived. He cannot hurt a mouse. Why, I do assure you, Imperial Mother, my cat caught a mouse the other day and he with his own hands pried her mouth open and took the mouse and tried to coax it back to life!"

"Be silent, silly girl," the Empress said.

But the Pearl Concubine would not be silent. She lifted up her head and sat back on her heels and while the tears ran down her pretty cheeks she shrieked at the haughty woman who was Empress.

"I will not be silent, and you may kill me if you like! You have no right to take him from the Throne. He is the Emperor by will of Heaven and you were but a tool of destiny."

"Enough," the Empress said. Her handsome face was stern as any man's. "You have passed beyond the boundaries. From now on you shall never see your lord again."

The Emperor leaped to his feet. "Oh, Sacred Mother," he shouted. "You shall not kill this innocent one, the only creature who loves me, in whom there is no flattery or pretense, who has no guile—"

The concubine rose to her feet and clung to his arm and laid her face against him. "Who will make your supper as you like?" she sobbed. "And who will warm you when your bed is cold—"

"My niece, his Consort, will come here to live," the Empress said. "You are not needed."

She turned imperiously to Li Lien-ying and he came forward for her command. "Remove the Pearl Concubine. Take her to the most distant part of the palace. In the Palace of Forgotten Concubines there are two small inner rooms. These shall be her prison until she dies. She shall have no change of clothing until the garments that she wears fall from her in rags. Her food shall be coarse rice and beggar's cabbage. Her name must not be mentioned in my presence. When she dies, do not inform me."

"Yes, Majesty," he said. But by his pale face and smothered voice he showed that even he could not approve the harshness of the task, except he must. He took the woman by the wrist and dragged her away. When she was gone the Emperor slipped to the floor, crumpling senseless at his sovereign's feet. Above him the white dog stood and growled, and the Empress sat motionless, in silence, her eyes fixed upon the vista of the open doors.

V

Old Buddha

ONCE more the Empress ruled, and now because she was old, she said, and because no sign of womanhood was left to one so old she put aside all feint of screen and fan to shield her from the eyes of men. She sat upon the Dragon Throne as though she were a man, in the full light of torch or sun, clothed in magnificence and pride. Since she had accomplished what she had planned, she could be merciful and in mercy she allowed her nephew sometimes the appearance of his place. Thus when the autumn festival approached, she let him make the imperial sacrifices at the Altar of the Moon. Thus on the eighth day of the eighth moon month, at the Festival of Autumn, she received him in the Audience Hall under guard appointed by Jung Lu and there before the assembled Council and the Imperial Boards, she accepted from him the nine obeisances that signified her rule over him. Later in that day by her permission and under the same guard he made the imperial sacrifices under the Altar of the Moon, and he thanked Heaven for the harvests and for peace. Let him deal with gods, she said, while she dealt with men.

And she had much to do with men. First she put to death the six Chinese rebels whose advice had led the Emperor astray, and much she raged and grieved because the chief rebel of them all, that K'ang Yu-wei, escaped her with the help of Englishmen and on a foreign ship was taken to an English port and there lived safe in exile. Nor did she let her family clansmen go free. Prince Ts'ai, friend and ally of the Emperor, she cast into the prison chamber of the clan, and this man's treachery she knew because his wife was another of her nieces, and he hated this wife and in her anger the woman had borne tales to her royal aunt. But when all had died who should be dead and the Empress had no enemies left alive inside her Court, she set herself to still another task, and this was to make what she had done seem right to all the people. For she knew the people were divided, that some took the Emperor's part and said that the nation should be shaped to new times and have ships and guns and railroads and learn even from their enemies, the Western men, while others declared themselves for the sage Confucius and all the ancient ways and wisdom and these longed to free themselves of new men and new times and return to old ways.

Both must be persuaded, and to the task the Empress now set herself. By edicts and by skillful gossip leaking from the Court through eunuchs and ministers, the people were informed of the grave sins of the Emperor, and his chief sins were two, first, that he had plotted against his ancient aunt, had even planned her death so that he might be free to obey his new advisors and, next, that he was supported and upheld by foreigners, and was too simple in his mind to see that they hoped to make him their puppet and so seize the whole country for themselves. These two sins convinced all that the Empress did well to resume the imperial seat, for while those who revered Confucius and tradition could not condone a youth who plotted to destroy his elder, yet none could forgive a ruler who made friends of white men or Chinese rebels. Before many months had passed, the people approved the Empress as their sovereign and even foreigners said that it was better to deal with a strong female than a weak male ruler, for strength could be trusted but weakness was always doubtful.

And here was the wile and wit of this Old Buddha. She knew the power of woman, and so that men could be persuaded, she made a feast and invited as her guests the wives of all white men who were ambassadors and ministers from Western lands and lived in the capital to represent their governments. Never in all her many years had the Empress looked upon a white face but now she prepared to do so, although the very thought revolted her. But if she won the women, she said, the men would follow. She chose her birthday for the meeting, not a great birthday but a small one, her sixty-fourth, and she invited seven ladies, wives of seven foreign envoys, to appear at audience.

The whole court was stirred, the ladies curious, the serving women busy, the eunuchs running here and there, for none had seen a foreigner. Only the Empress was calm. She it was who thought to order foods the guests might like, and she sent eunuchs to inquire if they could eat meat or did their gods forbid, and whether they liked mild Chinese green teas or black Indian teas, and would they have their sweetmeats made with pig's fat or with vegetable oils. True, she was indifferent to their answers, and she ordered what she wished, but courtesy was done.

Thus she planned every courtesy. At midmorning she sent Chinese guards in full uniform of scarlet and yellow and on horseback to announce the sedan chairs. An hour later these sedans, each with five bearers and two mounted horsemen, waited at the gates of the British Legation, and when the foreign ladies came out, the chairs were lowered and their curtains drawn, for the ladies to enter. As though this were not courtesy enough, the Empress commanded the chief of her Board of Diplomatic Service to take with him four interpreters, all in sedans and accompanied by eighteen horsemen and sixty mounted guards to receive the ladies. Each man was dressed in his official robe and each held himself in high dignity and gave every courtesy to the foreign guests.

At the first gate to the Winter Palace the procession stopped and the ladies were invited to enter on foot. Inside the gate seven court sedans waited, all cushioned in red satin, and each borne by six eunuchs, garbed in bright yellow satin girdled with crimson sashes. With escorts following, the ladies were now carried to the second gate, there to dismount again.

The Empress had commanded that they be ushered into a small foreign train of cars, drawn by a steam engine, which the Emperor had bought some years before for his amusement and his information. The train carried them through the Forbidden City to the entrance hall of the main palace. Here the guests came down from the train and sat upon seven chairs and drank tea and rested. The highest princes then invited them to the great Audience Hall, where the Emperor and his Consort sat upon their thrones. The Empress, that arch diplomat, had willed her nephew to sit at her right hand this day, so that in the eyes of all they might appear united.

According to the length of their stay in Peking, the guests now stood in rank before the thrones, and an interpreter presented each in turn to Prince Ch'ing, who then presented her to the Empress.

The Empress gazed at each face, and however much she was amazed by what she saw, she leaned down from her throne and put out her two hands and clasped the right hand of each lady in her own jeweled hands, and upon the forefingers of their hands she placed a ring of pure and heavy Chinese gold, set with a large round pearl.

They gave their thanks, and to each the Empress inclined her head. Then, followed by her nephew, she rose and left the room, her eunuchs flocking behind to screen her as she went.

Outside the doors she turned left toward her own palace, and without speaking to him, waved the Emperor toward the right. The four eunuchs who were his guard by day and night led him again to his prison.

In her own dining hall the Empress ate her usual noon meal, surrounded by her favorite ladies, while her foreign guests dined in the banquet hall with her lesser ladies, eunuchs and interpreters remaining to do them courtesy. The Empress, while she ate heartily as usual, was in good spirits, laughing much at the strange faces of the foreigners. Their eyes, she said, were most strange of all, some pale gray, others light yellow, or blue like the eyes of wild cats. She declared the foreigners coarse in bone, but she granted that their skins were excellent, white and pink, except for the Japanese, whose skin was coarse and brown. The English lady was the handsomest, the Empress said, but the dress of the German lady was the most beautiful, a short jacket worn over lace and a full long skirt of rich brocaded satin. She laughed at the high cockade the Russian lady wore upon her head, and the American lady, she said, looked like a hard-faced nun. Her ladies laughed and applauded all she said, and they declared they had never seen her in better wit, and so in pleasant humor the meal was finished and the Empress changed her robes and returned to the banquet hall. There the guests had been escorted to another hall while tables were cleared, and when they returned the Empress already sat upon her throne chair to receive them. She had meanwhile sent for her niece, the young Empress, who now stood beside her. As the guests came in, the Empress presented her niece to each in turn, and she was much pleased to see the looks of praise they gave the niece, admiring her rich crimson robes and her decorations and her jewels. Until now the Empress had not put on her finest robes or jewels, but seeing the looks of the foreign ladies, she perceived that they, in spite of being only foreigners, discerned the quality of satins and jewels, and she decided privately that when she received them for the third and last time at the end of the day she would astonish them with her own beauties of apparel. She felt pleased by her guests and she rose and held out her hands to them as they came near, one by one, and put her hands on her own breast and then on theirs and repeated again and again the words of the ancient sage, "All under Heaven are one family," and she bade the interpreters to explain what she said in English and in French. When this was done, she dismissed the guests, sending them to her theater and saying that she had chosen her favorite play for their amusement and that the interpreters would explain it to them as the actors played.

Again she withdrew, and now she went to her chambers and, being somewhat weary, she allowed herself to be first bathed in warm scented waters before she was clothed in fresh garments. This time she chose her costliest robe of gold-encrusted satin embroidered in phoenixes of every shade and hue, and she wore her famous great collar of matched pearls and she even changed the shields upon her fingernails from gold set with pearls and jade to gold set with Burmese rubies and Indian sapphires. Upon her head she wore a high headdress of pearls and rubies interset with diamonds from Africa. Never, so her ladies said, had they seen her more beautiful. Indeed, the freshness of her ivory skin, the red of her unwrinkled lips, the blackness of her fabulous eyes and clear brows, were those of a woman in her youth.

Once more the Empress returned to the banquet hall, where her guests were now drinking tea and eating sweetmeats, and she came in state, not walking but borne in her palace chair, and eunuchs lifted her to her throne. The foreign ladies rose, their admiration bright upon their faces, and she smiled at all, and lifted up her bowl of tea and drank from one side, and summoning each lady to her she put the other side of the bowl to the lady's lips, and again she said, "All one family—under Heaven, all are one." And feeling bold and free and much in triumph, she commanded gifts to be brought and given to the ladies, a fan, a scroll of her own painting, and a piece of jade, to each alike. When this was done and the ladies were overcome with gratitude, she bade them all farewell and so the day was over.

Within the next few days her spies reported that the foreign ladies had praised her much to their lords, saying that no one so gentle and beautiful and generous with gifts as she had shown herself to be could also be evil or cruel. She was well pleased and she felt that she was indeed what they had said she was. Now, having won the favor of all, she set herself to clean away rebels and reformers from among the Chinese whom she ruled, and to bring the whole people under the power of her own hand and heart again. The more she pondered this task the more she perceived that it could not be done so long as the Emperor, her nephew, lived. His melancholy, his pensive ways, his very submission, had won those who surrounded him, even while they obeyed her. And once again she compelled herself to do what must be done, while Li Lien-ying whispered in her ear.

"So long as he lives, Majesty," the gaunt eunuch insisted, "the nation will remain divided. They will seek the excuse for division between you, Sacred Mother, and him. They are born for division, these Chinese. They love dissent and never are they happier than when they plot and plan against their rulers. The rebel leaders foment eternally beneath the

331

waters. They remind the people day and night that a Manchu and not a Chinese sits above them. Only you can keep the peace, because the people know you and trust your wit and wisdom, though you are Manchu."

"If only my nephew were a strong man," she sighed. "How gladly then would I entrust the people's destiny to him!"

"But he is not a strong man, Majesty," the eunuch whispered. "He is weak and willful. He listens to the arch rebels among the Chinese and refuses to recognize their plots. He destroys the dynasty without knowing what he does."

She could but agree that this was true, yet she could not give the secret command for which the greedy eunuch waited.

That day she paced the terrace of the palace and she gazed across the lotus-filled waters to the island upon which her nephew was imprisoned. Yet how could a palace be called a prison, for though it had only four rooms, they were large and comfortably furnished and the surrounding air was calm and pleasant. She could see her nephew even now as he wandered about the narrow island, and with him, though at a distance, were the ever-watchful eunuchs who guarded him.

It was time to change those eunuchs and put others in their place lest if any stayed more than a month or two, their sympathies might be stirred toward the young man whom they guarded. Thus far they had been faithful to her, and each night one or the other copied the diary which her nephew wrote every day. Into the night she read what he wrote and knew to the last beat of his heart, the last thought of his mind, what he felt. Only one eunuch did she doubt somewhat and he was surnamed Huang, for he gave always too good a report of his charge. "The Emperor spends his time reading the good books," Huang always said. "When he is tired he paints or he writes poetry."

While she paced to and fro upon her terrace, she considered what Li Lien-ying had said this day. Then abruptly she rejected it. No, it was not time yet for her nephew to die. The blame for his death must not lie upon her who had chosen him. It was true that she wished him dead but it was not crime only to wish. Let his death wait upon Heaven.

When next Li Lien-ying came into her presence she was cold to him and coldly she said, "Do not speak to me again of the Emperor's journey to the Yellow Springs. What Heaven wills Heaven itself will do."

These words she said in so stern a voice that he bowed in obeisance to show that he would be obedient.

Yet who could have dreamed that the Chinese rebels would somehow contrive to find their secret way to the ear of the lonely young Emperor?

Through the eunuch Huang they did so. One morning in the tenth moon month of that year the young Emperor escaped from his eunuch guards and fled through the pine woods on the north side of the island to a small inlet where a boat waited. But a eunuch saw his flying robes through the trees and cried out and all the eunuchs ran fast as feet could hasten and they caught the Emperor as he was about to step into the boat and they held his robes and besought him not to escape.

"For if you escape, Son of Heaven," they pleaded, "Old Buddha will have us all beheaded."

No other plea could serve so well. The Emperor had a tender heart and he hesitated while the boatman, who was a rebel in disguise, shouted to him that he must not delay, that the lives of the eunuchs were of no worth. But the Emperor looked down into the faces of the imploring eunuchs and among these was one young eunuch, a lad scarcely more than a child, gentle and kind, who had always stayed near his royal master night and day to serve him. And looking down upon this weeping lad the Emperor could not step into the boat. He shook his head and the boatman, not daring to delay longer, rowed his boat into the silent mists of dawn.

The sad tale was carried to the ears of the Empress, and she listened and did nothing, seemed to do nothing, but she put the story into her heart to remember against the Emperor. And meanwhile she allowed to be put to death every rebel and prince and minister who had supported the Emperor. But him she let live, for she had her weapon. So deeply did her subjects revere the ancient wisdom of Confucius, that she needed only to remind them that the Emperor had plotted to kill her and they would cry him a traitor. And she knew that the young Emperor knew this was her weapon, and indeed, she could twist it in his own heart, for he had a tender conscience, and he too still reverenced the Sage.

For her mercy Jung Lu commended her. Again he asked for private audience and he said: "While it is true, Majesty, that the people would never condone a plot against you, yet they would not revere you were you to allow the life of the Emperor to be taken, even by accident. He must be imprisoned, I acknowledge, for he will be the tool of your enemies, but grant him every courtesy. Let him appear at your side when you receive the envoy from Japan, ten days hence, and let him appear when envoys come from the outer territories. You, Most High, can afford every act of grace and kindness. Let me even suggest that the Pearl Concubine—"

But here she put up her two hands to signify silence. The very words

"Pearl Concubine" were not to be spoken in her presence. She gazed at him in cold stillness and he said no more. She was sometimes Empress and sometimes woman, and this day he saw only the Empress.

"I will speak of other matters," he said. And he spoke on thus: "While there is peace now in the realm, yet the people are restless. They show angers here and there and against the white men first of all. An English priest has been murdered by mobs in Kweichow province. This will bring the English hornets again about the Throne. They will demand indemnities and concessions."

The Empress flew into lively rage. She clenched her hands and struck her knees three times. "Again these foreign priests!" she cried. "How is it they will not stay at home? Do we send our priests wandering over the earth to destroy the gods of other peoples?"

"They are the fruit of the defeats we have suffered in battle with the Western men," Jung Lu reminded her. "We have been forced to allow their priests and traders to enter our ports together."

"I swear I will have no more of these persons," the Empress declared. And she sat brooding, her beautiful eyes darkened by frowns and her red mouth sullen. She forgot that Jung Lu stood before her or pretended that she did, and seeing her mood he made obeisance and went away and she did not so much as lift her head.

In the last month of that year still another foreign priest was murdered, this time in the western province of Hupeh, and he was not killed cleanly and swiftly but with beatings and bone-twistings and skin-slicing. In the same month mobs of villagers and city dwellers rose against foreign priests in the province of Szechuen, and this was because of old rumors creeping over the nation that the priests were also sorcerers, that they stole children and made medicine from their eyes, and ground their bones to make magic brews.

The Empress was beside herself, for when their citizens were killed, the foreign envoys became arrogant and threatening and declared that their governments would make war unless there were full retribution. Indeed, the whole world seemed to stir against her. Russia, England, France and Germany were muttering and dissatisfied. France, whose priests had been several times killed, now sent word through her envoys that she would attack with her ships of war unless she were granted a piece of land as a concession in Shanghai. Portugal, too, demanded more land surrounding Macao, and Belgium insisted that the price of two Belgium priests murdered must be a concession of land at Hankow, that great port upon the Yangtse River. Japan meanwhile was plotting for the rich and fruitful province of Fukien and Spain grumbled thunder upon the horizon, for a Spanish priest had been among those dead. Italy was angriest of all and her envoys demanded the concession of Samoon Bay in the province of Chekiang, the finest Chinese territory.

Upon such disaster, the Empress summoned her ministers and princes for special audience, and she sent for her general Li Hung-chang to come from the Yellow River, where she had ordered him to rebuild the dikes against a flood.

The day of audience was hot, and a sandstorm blew from the north-west. The air was stifled with fine sand, and while the princes and ministers waited for the Empress they held their kerchiefs to their faces and closed their eyes against the sand. But when the Empress appeared, she seemed not to know the presence of the storm. She was in her most regal robes, and when she descended from her imperial sedan and walked to the Dragon Throne, leaning upon the arm of Li Lien-ying, she compelled all by her proud indifference to take the kerchiefs from their faces and fall in obeisance before her. Only Jung Lu was not present and she marked his absence in an instant.

"Where is the Grand Councilor, my kinsman?" she demanded of Li Lien-ying.

"Majesty, he sent word that he was ill. I think he is ill because you have sent for Li Hung-chang."

This dart of malice implanted in her mind, he stepped back and she proceeded with stately grace to open audience. One by one she called upon prince and minister to give his opinion upon the crisis, and to each she lent her courteous attention. Last of all she called upon the aged general Li Hung-chang, who came forward with unsteady steps and with difficulty knelt to make obeisance. She watched him as two eunuchs lowered him to his knees but she did not give permission for him to sit instead of kneel. Today she demanded every sign of submission and what she did not grant none could take.

"And what have you to say, most honored protector of our Throne?" she inquired in a pleasant voice.

To which Li Hung-chang replied, not lifting his forehead from the floor: "Most High, it is a matter I have considered for many months. We are surrounded with angry enemies, men alien to us and to our ways. Yet we must avoid war at all costs, for to engage in war against so many would be indeed to mount the tiger. It is prudent therefore to entice one enemy to become our ally. Let this one be the northern enemy, Russia. Among them all, Russia is most Asian, like ourselves, a people alien it is true, but Asian."

"And what is the price to make an enemy our friend?" she asked.

The old man trembled under the sweet coldness of her voice. She saw his shoulders shiver and his clasped hands quivered. He could not speak.

"No," she said strongly. "I will answer my own question. The price is too great. What boots it if we conquer our other enemies only to become the vassal of the one? Does any nation give something, anything, for nothing? Alas, I have not found one man who will do such a thing. We will repel all enemies. Indeed, I will not rest until every white man and woman and child is driven from our shores. I will not yield. We take back our own."

She rose from the throne as she spoke, and the ministers and princes stared to see her seem to grow tall while they watched. Her eyes blazed black light, her cheeks flushed, she spread out her hands, her ten fingers outstretched, and the jeweled shields upon her nails were golden talons. Power streamed from her, the very air grew sharp and needled through with angry heat. They fell upon their faces, one and all, and she looked down upon the bent bodies of these men and felt ecstasy flow through her veins a creeping fire.

And at this same instant she thought of Jung Lu and how he had not come to support her. She let her eyes roam over the bent figures of the men, their brilliant robes outspread upon the tiled floor in every hue and color and her eyes chose the form of the Grand Councilor Kang Yi, a man no longer young, but who through all his years had spent his strength in preserving what was ancient, ever against the new and for the old.

"You, my Grand Councilor Kang Yi," she said in loud clear tones, "you shall remain for private audience. You, my lords and princes, are dismissed."

So saying she stepped down from her throne and Li Lien-ying came forward and with her hand upon his forearm, she walked in stateliness between the bowed assembly and to her sedan. Her will was set, her mind was firm. She would not yield again to white men.

An hour later the Grand Councilor Kang Yi stood to hear her commands. It was midafternoon, the Hour of the Monkey, the place her private audience hall. The Chief Eunuch was near, seeming not to hear but hearing all, the bribe which Kang Yi had given him warm in the inner pocket of his robe. While the Empress spoke she gazed across the wide hall toward the doors opened on her gardens. The night wind had died and the air was freshly cleansed by the sandstorm.

"I vacillate no more," the Empress said. "I am relentless toward all enemies. I shall reclaim our land. I shall take it back, foot by foot, counting no cost."

"Majesty," Kang Yi said, "for the first time I feel hope." He was a tall man and in his prime, a scholar and a Confucian.

"What is your advice?" the Empress asked.

"Majesty," he said, "Prince Tuan and I have often spoken of what we would advise if our advice were asked. We agree, he and I, that we should use the anger of the Chinese against the Western men. The Chinese are sick with fury for their stolen land, for all the wars against them, for gold they pay in indemnity because of priests the mobs have killed. They have made secret bands among themselves, sworn to destroy these enemies. Here is my counsel, humbly offered, Majesty. I do not claim wisdom. But since these roving bands exist, why not use them, Majesty? Let your approval be made known to them secretly. When all these bands are added to the five-pronged armies that Jung Lu has built, who can resist us? And will not the Chinese be most fervent in loyalty to you, Holy Mother, when they know you are with them against the aliens?"

The Empress heard and pondered, and the plan seemed good. She asked a few questions more, she praised him once or twice, and then she dismissed him. So high was her mood at this fresh hope that when Li Lien-ying came forward to put in his advice, she did not reprove him.

"What better plan?" he asked. "This Grand Councilor is a sage and prudent man."

"He is, indeed," she agreed.

She caught him looking at her sidewise, his eyes narrowed and sly in his harsh face. "Well?" she asked. They knew each other deeply, these two.

"I warn you, Majesty," he said. "I think Jung Lu will not approve the plan." He put out his tongue and touched his upper lip and drew down the corners of his mouth.

She smiled at the wryness of his face. "Even I will not heed him, then," she said.

Nevertheless, in a few days she sent for Jung Lu, ready to reprove him for what her spies said he had done.

"How now?" she asked when he appeared before her. The hour was late and she had not let him take his evening meal. No, she said, he could eat later.

"What have I done, Majesty?" he inquired.

For the first time she thought he looked old and tired. "I hear you have allowed the foreign ministers to augment their guard."

"I was compelled," he said. "It seems that they also have their spies

337

who brought them word somehow that you, Majesty, have listened to Kang Yi, and do intend to approve the bands of secret Chinese rebels whose purpose, as all know, is to destroy the foreigners among us down to the last child. Majesty, I said I would not believe that you could approve such folly. Indeed, do you think that even you can fight against the whole world? We must negotiate, propitiate, until we make our forces strong enough for victory."

"I hear the people muttered curses when the foreign troops came in," she said. "And Kang Yi has been to Chu-chou and he says the province now is organized to fight the enemy. He says that at Chu-chou he found the magistrate had arrested some of the secret rebels, who belong to the order of the Boxers, but he, Kang Yi, commanded them to be released and brought before me to show their powers. He says that they have magic which prevents their death. Even when guns are fired against their bodies they are not wounded."

Jung Lu cried out in anguish. "Oh, Majesty, can you believe such nonsense?"

"It is you who are foolish," she retorted. "Do you forget that at the end of the Han dynasty, more than a thousand years ago, Chang Chou led the Yellow Turban Rebels against the Throne and took many cities, though he had less than half a million men? They, too, knew magic against wound and death. And Kang Yi says that he has friends who many years ago saw this same magic in Shensi province. I tell you, there are spirits who aid the righteous."

Jung Lu was beside himself by now. He wrenched his hat from his head and threw it on the floor before her and he seized his hair in both hands and tore out two handfuls.

"I will not forget your place," he said between set teeth. "But still you are my kinswoman, that one to whom I long ago gave up my life. Surely, I deserve the right to say you are a fool. For all your beauty and your power, you, even you, can be a fool. I warn you, if you listen to that stone-head, Kang Yi, who has no knowledge of the present but lives in centuries now dead, and if you listen to your Chief Eunuch and his kind or even to Prince Tuan, who dreams of folly, too, then I say you do destroy yourself and with you the whole dynasty. Oh hear me—hear me—"

He put his hands together to beeseech her and gazed into the face he still adored. Their eyes met and clung, he saw her will waver and dared not speak lest he undo what he had done.

She spoke in a small voice. "I asked Prince Ch'ing what he thought and he said doubtless the Boxer bands might be useful."

"It is only I who dare to speak the truth to you," he said. He took one step forward and thrust his hands into his girdle lest he put them out toward her. "In your presence Prince Ch'ing dares not say what he says to me in private—that these Boxers are imposters and pretenders, ignorant robbers who seek to rise to power through your approval. But what man worships you as I do?" His voice sank and his words came out a dry reluctant whisper.

She dropped her head. The old power still held. All through their lives his love had stayed her.

"Promise me at least that you will do nothing without telling me," he said. "It is a small promise." He urged her when still she did not speak. "A reward—the only one I ask."

He waited for a time and all the while he waited he kept his eyes fixed upon her drooping head. And she kept her head down, and saw his two feet planted on the floor before her, strong feet in velvet boots half hidden by his long blue satin robe. Faithful in her service, those two feet—stubborn, brave and strong.

She lifted up her head. "I promise."

"Majesty," Kang Yi said, "you do wrong. Your heart grows soft with age. You do not allow even foreigners to be done away with. Yet one word from you and they would be gone, even to their dogs and fowls, and of their dwellings not one brick would be left to stand upon another."

His spies had told him how Jung Lu was his enemy and he had made haste to audience.

She turned away her head. "I am weary of you all," she said.

"But, Majesty," he urged, "now is not the time for weariness. It is the hour of victory. And need you lift a hand? No, only speak, and others do your work. My son attended Chi Shou-cheng's theatricals yesterday and he said everyone was talking of Jung Lu's folly in allowing the foreign troops to enter the city. And Chi's father-in-law, Yu Hsien, wrote last month from Shansi saying that while there are not many Boxers in his provinces he is encouraging men to join them, so that his province may unite with all the others when the time comes to strike the blow against the Western enemy. We wait your word—only your word, Majesty."

She shook her head. "I cannot speak it," she said.

"Majesty," Tung Fu-hsiang said, "give me your leave and I will demolish the foreign buildings in our city in five days."

The Empress sat at audience in the Winter Palace. She had returned to the Forbidden City the day before, leaving the autumn beauty of the Summer Palace behind her. The Boxers, without permission, had burned the railway to Tientsin.

Alas, were they invulnerable? Who could know? In the heat of mid-summer she had sent for her bearers to bring her here, fanning herself all the way.

"Majesty," Kang Yi said, "I beg that you will excuse Tung. He has the coarse ways of a soldier, but he is on our side, though he is Chinese."

"This right arm," Tung boasted, and held out his thick right arm.

The Empress turned away her head. She glanced toward the assembled council. Jung Lu was not there. He had asked for leave two days ago but she had not replied. Nevertheless he was gone.

"Majesty," the Grand Councilor Ch'i Hsiu said, "let me prepare a decree for your signature. At least let us break off relations with these foreigners. This will frighten them, if no more."

"You may prepare it," the Empress said, "but I will make no promise to sign it."

"Majesty," Kang Yi said again, "yesterday I went to the birthday celebration of the first lady in the household of Duke Lan. More than a hundred Boxers live in his outer courtyard, under their own com-mander. They have the gift of calling upon magic spirits to enter their bodies. I saw youths no more than fourteen or fifteen years old, who went into trances and spoke strange languages. Duke Lan says that when the time comes these spirits will lead the Boxers to the houses of Christians to destroy them."

"I have not seen it with my own eyes," the Empress declared. She raised her hand to end the audience.

"Majesty," Li Lien-ying said in the twilight, "many citizens are shel-tering the Boxers." He hesitated and then whispered, "If you will not be angry, Majesty—your own adopted daughter, the Princess Imperial, is paying for two hundred and fifty Boxers to be quartered outside the back gate of the city, and her brother, Prince Ts'ai Ying, is learning their magic. The Boxers from Kansu are preparing to enter the city. Many people are leaving, fearing a war. All await your word, Majesty."

"I cannot give it," the Empress said.

On the sixteenth day of that fifth moon she sent Li Lien-ying to find Jung Lu and bring him to her. She must take back her promise. This morning her spies had brought her news that still more foreign soldiers were marching overland from the coast. This was to avenge the death of yet another foreigner, killed by angry Chinese in the province of Kansu.

It was noon before Jung Lu came, dressed in his outdoor garments as though he came from garden or hillside. But she paid no heed to his looks.

"Am I still to be silent while the city fills with foreign soldiers?" she demanded. "The people will rise against the throne and the dynasty be lost."

"Majesty, I agree that we must not allow more foreign soldiers to enter the city," Jung Lu replied. "Nevertheless I say that it will disgrace us if we attack the envoys of foreign nations. They will think us savage and ignorant of the laws of hospitality. One does not poison the guest inside the house."

"What would you have me do?" she inquired with bitter looks.

"Invite the foreign ministers to leave the city, with their families and their friends," Jung Lu said. "When they are gone their troops will go with them."

"And if they will not go?"

"Perhaps they will go," he said calmly. "If they do not, then you cannot be blamed."

"Do you release me from my promise?" she demanded.

"Tomorrow," he said, "tomorrow—tomorrow."

In the night, in the deepest darkness, she was suddenly awakened by bright light. As always she slept with her bed curtains drawn back and now the light shone through the windows. It fell not from a lantern or the moon but from the sky itself, crimson and on fire. She sat up and called to her women who slept on pallets on the floor about her bed. They woke, one and then the other three, and they ran to the window.

"Aie," they cried, "aie-aie-aie—"

The door burst open and from behind it, his face carefully turned away, Li Lien-ying shouted that a foreign temple was in flames, the fire lit by unknown hands.

The Empress rose from her bed and cried out that she must be dressed at once. Quickly the women put on her robes and then with her eunuchs she went outside into her most distant courtyard and there climbed her peony mountain, from whence she could look over the walls and down into the city. Smoke mingled with flames hid the scene but soon a fearful stench of roasting flesh spread into the air. Behind her handkerchief the Empress inquired what this stench was and Li Lien-ying told her.

The Boxers were burning the French church near by, and inside were hundreds of Christian Chinese, men, women and children.

"What horror," the Empress moaned. "Oh, that I had forbidden the foreigners from the very beginning! Years ago I should have forbidden them, and the people could not have strayed to foreign gods!"

"Majesty," Li Lien-ying said, "be comforted. It was the foreigners who fired first upon a crowd at the gate of the church and brave Boxers took revenge."

"Alas," she mourned, "the Canon of History tells us that when fires rage in the imperial city common pebbles and precious jade alike are consumed."

She turned away and refused to look any more and brooding that whole day upon what she had seen, while the air reeked with the scent of death, she commanded the eunuch to move her goods and her books to the Palace of Peaceful Longevity, where she could not see or hear what went on in the city and where the air was purified by distance.

"Majesty," they urged, "unless you would see all lost, you must use the magic of Boxers. The foreign soldiers are filling the streets like flood waters flowing through the city gates."

"Now, now, Majesty, without delay—"

"Majesty, Majesty—"

They clamored before her. She gazed at one face and another in the small throne room, Kang Yi, Prince Tuan, Yuan Shih-K'ai, and her highest princes and ministers. They had come in haste at her summons for meeting before audience, and they stood in disarray. This was no time for obeisance or ceremony.

At her right the Emperor sat upon a low carved chair, his head bowed, his face pale, his long thin hands folded in listlessness upon his knees.

"Son of Heaven," she said to him, "shall we use the Boxer horde against our enemies?"

If he said yes, was not his the blame?

"Whatever you will, Holy Mother," he said and did not lift his head.

She looked at Jung Lu. He stood apart, his head bowed, his arms folded.

"Majesty, Majesty!" the voices cried about her, the voices of men, roaring and echoing into the high painted beams of the lofty roof.

She rose to her feet and raised her arms for silence in the twilight of this early morning hour. She had eaten nothing and she had not slept while the fires burned on and foreign soldiers marched through the

342

gate—nay, not one gate but through four, converging from the four corners of the earth upon this, her city. What remained except war?

"The hour has come," she cried. "We must destroy the foreigners in their legations!" she cried aloud in the sudden silence. "One brick must not be left upon another nor one human being allowed to live!"

Silence followed again. She had broken her promise to Jung Lu. He strode forward and fell before her in obeisance.

"Majesty," he cried, and the tears ran down his cheeks, "Majesty, though these foreigners are indeed our enemies, though they have only themselves to blame for their own destruction, yet I beseech you to consider what you do. If we destroy these few buildings, this handful of foreigners, their governments will denounce us in wrath, their armies, their navies, will fly across land and sea to attack us. Our ancestral shrines will be crushed into dust, even the tutelary gods and the people's altars will be razed to the ground!"

In her bosom her heart trembled and the blood turned cold in her veins. Yet she hid her terror. She had never shown herself afraid and the old strong habit held, though her fear was monstrous and near despair. Her beautiful face did not change nor her eyelids quiver.

"I cannot restrain the people," she declared. "They are mad with vengeance. If they do not rend our enemies, they will rend even me. I have no choice. As for you, Grand Councilor, if you have no better advice than this to bestow upon the Throne, then leave us. You are excused from further attendance."

Immediately Jung Lu rose up, his tears dried on his cheeks, and without word or gesture, he left her presence.

When he was gone the Councilor Ch'i Hsiu drew from his high velvet boot a folded paper. This he opened slowly and with great dignity he approached the throne and in obeisance he presented the folded paper. "Majesty," he said, "I have presumed to suggest a decree. If I am permitted, I will read it aloud."

"Do so," the Empress commanded. Her lips were stiff and cold, but she sat motionless and in state.

He began to read, and all could hear what he had written. It was a decree of war against the foreigners, to be signed, if she approved, by the Empress and sealed with the imperial seal. He read to the end, while all listened, the silence so deep that his one voice echoed to the roof. When he had finished he waited for her will and all waited with him.

"It is excellent," the Empress said in a calm cold voice. "Let it be sent forth as a decree from the Throne."

All cried approval, not loudly but in low solemn tones, and Ch'i Hsiu folded the paper and put it again in his velvet boot and making obeisance he stepped back to his place.

It was now dawn, the usual hour appointed for general audience, to which this was preliminary, and Li Lien-ying came forward and held out his arm and the Empress put her right hand upon his forearm and stepped down from the throne and into her sedan which waited on the terrace. From here she was carried to her own palace to drink tea and eat a few sweetmeats, but without long delay she entered her sedan again and was borne this time to the Hall of Diligent Government. There the Emperor waited for her in his own palanquin, and when she arrived he came down first to receive her, kneeling as she stepped from her sedan.

He gave greeting. "Benevolent Mother!"

She nodded slightly but did not answer him and at the entrance to the Hall she walked slowly, supported on her right by Li Lien-ying and on her left by a second eunuch, her hands resting on their forearms. At this entrance knelt the chiefs of her clan, the princes, the Grand Councilors except Jung Lu, the Presidents of the Six Boards and the Nine Ministries, the twenty-four Lieutenant-generals of the twenty-four Banner Divisions, and the Comptrollers of the Household.

Behind the Empress the young Emperor followed slowly, his face was wax pale, his large eyes downcast and his pallid hands folded on his belt. The Empress sat upon the Dragon Throne and he took the lower throne at her right.

When all courtesies and dignities had been performed, and each group of officials stood in proper place, the Empress began to speak. At first her voice was weaker than she wished, but as she considered what her enemies had done, anger lent strength to her voice and brilliance to her sleepless eyes.

"Our will is set," she declared, "our mind is firm. We can no longer tolerate, in decency and pride, the outrageous demands of the foreigners. It was our intention indeed to suppress if possible the Chinese Boxers. Now it is no longer possible. They have heard the threats of our enemies, which extend even to my own person, for yesterday they sent their envoys to declare that I must withdraw from the Throne and allow my nephew to rule—and this, though all know how lamentably he has failed as a ruler! And why do they wish me to withdraw? It is because they fear me. They know I am not to be changed, whereas if my nephew sat in my place they could shape him like wax to their fingers. The insolence of these foreigners is exemplified in the French Consul at Tientsin who demanded the Taku forts as part of the price for the death of a mere priest."

She paused and looked regally about the great Hall. The light of flaring torches fell upon the grave and troubled faces turned toward her and upon the drooping head of the Emperor at her side.

"Will you not speak?" she demanded of him.

The Emperor did not lift his head. He wet his lips and clasped and unclasped again his long thin hands. For a time it seemed he could not speak. She waited, her great eyes unwavering upon him, and at last she heard his mild trembling voice.

"Holy Mother," he said, wetting his lips between every two words. "I can only say—perhaps it is not for me to say, but since you ask me—it seems to me that what Jung Lu said is wise. That is to say—in order to avoid bloodshed—that is, and since it is impossible for us to fight the world—we having no ships of war or Western weapons—it is better to allow the foreign ministers and their families to leave the city peacefully. But it is not I—of course not I—who can make such decision. It must be as my Benign Mother wills."

Immediately a member of the Council spoke to the Empress. "I beg you, Majesty, proceed with your own plan," he said loudly. "Let every foreigner be killed and their kind exterminated. When this is done the Throne will have time and strength next to crush the Chinese rebels who foment the south again."

The Empress welcomed this approval and she said, "I have heard Jung Lu's advice and it need not be repeated to me. Let the edict be prepared declaring war."

She rose as though to end the audience but immediately there was an outcry of dissension. While some upheld and approved what she had decreed, others besought her to hear them and she could only sit down again and hear one after the other, this one declaring that a war would be the end of the dynasty, for China would certainly be defeated, in which case the Chinese would seize the throne. The Minister of the Foreign Office even said that he had found the foreigners entirely reasonable in their dealings and for his part he did not believe that they had sent a document demanding her withdrawal from the Throne. Had not the foreign ladies praised her? Indeed, he had himself noticed that the foreign ministers were milder and more courteous since she had received their ladies.

At this Prince Tuan rose up in anger, and the Empress bade the minister withdraw in order to avoid a quarrel. Then Duke Lan, protector of the Boxers, rose up in his turn to say that he had had a dream

345

the night before, wherein he had seen Yü Huang, the Jade Emperor god, surrounded by a vast horde of Boxers in their patriotic exercises and the god approved.

To this dream the Empress listened with all her heart and she smiled her lovely smile and said mildly that she remembered from her books that so the Jade Emperor had appeared to an Empress in ancient times. "It is a good omen," she concluded, "and it means that the gods are for us and against the barbarian enemies." But still she did not promise to use the magic of the Boxers. Who knew it to be true or false?

She dismissed them then and returned to her own palace and not once did she speak to the Emperor again or seem to see him present. Now that her will was done her fears lessened and she was weary and longed for sleep.

"I will sleep this whole day," she told her ladies while they prepared her for bed. "Let no one wake me."

It was an hour after noon, at the Hour of Sheep, when she was waked suddenly by the voice of Li Lien-ying outside her door.

"Majesty," he called, "Prince Ch'ing waits and with him is Kang Yi."

The Empress could not evade such summons and so, once more robed and in her proper headdress, she went out and there in her antechamber she found the two in much impatience.

"Majesty," Kang Yi exclaimed when he had made obeisance, "war has begun already. En Hai, a Manchu sergeant, this morning killed two foreigners, one the German minister who rode through the city in his sedan—coming, it was said, to beg you for a special audience. En Hai killed them both, and hastened to Prince Ch'ing to get reward."

The Empress felt fear clutch her heart dry.

"But how could our edict reach the people so quickly?" she demanded. "Be sure the sergeant should not be rewarded if he killed without command."

Prince Ch'ing hesitated and cleared his throat. "Majesty," he said, "since this is crisis, Prince Tuan and Ch'i Hsui issued orders immediately after audience today that all foreigners were to be killed wherever seen."

The two men looked at each other.

"Majesty," Kang Yi urged, "indeed, our enemies have wrought their own destruction. The sergeant says that the white guards fired first and killed three Chinese."

"Oh, horror!" the Empress cried. Her fear became distress and she wrung her hands together. "Where is Jung Lu?" she cried, distracted. "Make haste—fetch him here—the war begins too soon—we are not ready." So saying she turned and fled into her own chamber again.

There refusing food or comfort she waited for Jung Lu and in two hours he came, looking gloomy and too grave for her beseeching eyes.

"Leave me," she told her ladies. "And do not let another enter," she told her eunuch.

When all were gone, she looked up at Jung Lu and he looked down at her.

"Speak," she said faintly. "Tell me what to do."

"I had the guards ready to escort the foreigners to the coast," he said in his deep sad voice. "Why did you not obey me?"

She turned away her head and wiped the corners of her eyes with the kerchief hanging on her jade button.

"Now having disobeyed me," he went on, "you ask me what to do."

She sobbed softly.

"Where will you find the monies to pay these Boxers?" he demanded. "Do you think they work for nothing?"

She turned her head again to look up at him to beg him to advise her, help her, save her once more, and lifting up her eyes to his face she saw him suddenly turn ashen gray and clutch his left side and then before her eyes sink to the floor.

She ran to him and lifted his hands but they were listless and cold. The lids of his eyes fell halfway down, the pupils of his eyes were fixed and staring, and he drew his breath in great gasps.

"Oh alas, alas!" she cried in a loud voice, and at the cry her ladies came running into the hall and seeing the Empress kneeling beside the tall form of the Grand Councilor they screamed in turn so that eunuchs hastened in.

"Lift him up," the Empress commanded. "Put him upon the opium couch."

They lifted Jung Lu up and laid him upon a double opium couch at the far end of the hall, and they put a hard pillow under his head, and while they did this the Empress sent a small eunuch flying for the Court physicians, who came instantly when they heard the news. And in all this Jung Lu did not move or cease his labored breathing.

"Majesty," the chief physician said. "The Grand Councilor rose from a sickbed to come to you."

The Empress turned on Li Lien-ying with terrible eyes. "Why was I not told?"

"Most High," Li Lien-ying said, "the Grand Councilor forbade it."

What could she say? She was confounded by the steadfast love of this man, who had given up all he was or could be for her sake. She controlled the turmoil of her heart, her love and fear equally to be hidden,

347

and she made her voice calm. "Let him be carried to his own palace, and do you, imperial physicians, stay by him night and day. And send me news of his health every hour, day and night. As for me, I shall go to the temple to pray."

The eunuchs stepped forward to obey and the physicians after obeisance followed, and when all were gone the Empress rose and without speaking to her ladies, who circled behind her, she walked to her private temple. It was now the Hour of the Dog, after day and before night, and twilight filled the courts. The air was sad and still, the sun's heat still lingering and the night winds delayed. She walked slowly as though she bore an infinite burden and when she came to the temple she went to her beloved goddess, the Kuan Yin. Lifting three sticks of sandalwood incense, she lit them at the flickering candle and thrust them into the ashes of the jade urn upon the altar. Then she took up the rosary of jade beads which lay upon the altar waiting always for her hand and as she counted the beads she prayed in her heart the prayer of a lonely woman.

"You who are also lonely," she prayed silently to the goddess, "hear the prayer of Your younger sister. Deliver me from my enemies, who would take this glorious land which is my inheritance, and cut it into pieces like a melon to be eaten. Deliver me—deliver me of my enemies! This is still my first prayer. And next I pray for the nameless one whom I love. He fell before me today. It may be this is his hour to die. Sustain me! But intercede, I pray You, Elder Sister, before the Old Man in Heaven and let the hour be postponed. I am Your younger sister! If the hour cannot be postponed, then dwell in me that I may in every circumstance, even in loneliness and in defeat, bear myself proudly. You, Elder Sister, look down upon all mankind with unchanging face, Your beauty untouched, Your grace unmoved. Give me the strength so to do."

She told the beads one after the other until her very prayers were drained away and only the last bead remained. And now she felt her last prayer was answered. Though her enemies prevail, though her love die, she would not let her face be changed nor her beauty fade nor her grace be moved. She would be strong.

Alone now the Empress lived through the days, while war raged about her, each day a month in length and weight, and into her awful loneliness few voices penetrated. She heard the voice of Prince Tuan.

"Majesty," he implored her, "these Boxers have a secret talisman, a circle of yellow paper which each carries on his person when he goes to battle. On this paper there is a creature painted in red, a creature not man nor devil. It has feet but no head, and its face is pointed and surrounded by four halos. The eyes and eyebrows are exceedingly black and burning. Up and down its strange body are written these magic words, 'I am Buddha of the Cold Cloud. Before me the black God of Fire leads my way. Behind me Lao Tzu himself supports me.' In the upper left hand corner of this paper are these words: 'Invoke first the Guardian of Heaven' and on the lower right hand corner are written these words: 'Invoke secondly the Black Gods of Pestilence.' Whoever learns these mystic words destroys by each incantation a foreign life somewhere in our country. Surely, Majesty, it does no harm to learn the magic words."

"It does no harm," the Empress agreed, and she learned the mystic words and repeated them seventy times a day and Li Lien-ying praised her for each time, while he counted how many foreign devils were gone. And he told her that wherever the sword of a Boxer touched, whether on flesh or on wood, flame burst out, and he told her that whenever an enemy was captured alive the Boxers sought the will of Heaven by this means, that they rolled a ball of yellow paper and set it afire, and if the ashes went upward, the enemy was to be killed but if the ash fell to the earth, he was not killed. Many such stories this eunuch told the Empress and she doubted them yet was so hard pressed that she half believed them, too, wanting much to believe that somewhere help could be found.

Yet what help was there? As if the angry foreigners were not woe enough, there came up from over the whole country murmurings and complaints of great floods and starving villages, of harvests not reaped and seed not sown. The people in despair rose up throughout the realm, they plundered the rich and robbed those who had a little food and among those who were so attacked there were also foreign priests who had always food and money. Among thousands who were plundered a few white priests were also found, but the foreign ministers protested the death of even one such priest and they declared that unless the people were put down their governments would send still more armies and warships. In all the world there was not one nation nor even one man to whom the Empress could turn for help while Jung Lu lay helpless upon his bed, speechless and deaf. When she inquired of her General Yuan Shih-K'ai what she should do, he replied only that the Boxers were fools, that he had ordered twenty of them stood up in a court before him to be shot and he himself had seen them fall and die like common men. And he begged the Empress not to put her faith in these charlatans, but he did not tell her in whom to put her faith and she found no help.

Meanwhile, Prince Tuan was always beside her throne and he boasted that he could drive the barbarians into the sea and he begged for the word of her command. Still she delayed and hoped for peace and while she delayed Prince Tuan began to force her secretly by allowing angry men, here one and there one, to attack the foreigners in their legations. Her old and loyal Viceroy in the southern city of Nanking sent a memorial and he wrote beseeching her not to allow such attacks, and he begged her to protect the foreign ministers and their families and followers and the priests who lived in the outer provinces.

"The present war," he wrote, "is due to bandits spreading slaughter and arson on the pretext of paying off a grudge against Christianity. We are face to face with a serious crisis. The foreign governments are already uniting to send troops and squadrons to attack China on the pretense of protecting their subjects and suppressing the rising rebellion. Our position is critical and I have made necessary preparations in my province so as to resist them with all my might.

"Nevertheless, Majesty, let benevolence and power move together. Respectfully I suggest that you inflict stern and exemplary punishment on all those rebels who attack officials and missionaries, who are innocent. Thus let benevolence and righteous wrath be displayed together, manifest and bright as the sun and the moon."

When the Empress received this memorial she considered its writer, the Viceroy, and how good a man he was and faithful to her as sovereign and she replied to him by special couriers who ran in relays more than two hundred miles a day, and thus she said, brushing the characters with her own skillful hand:

"We would not willingly be aggressors. You are to inform the various legations abroad that We have only calm and kindly feelings toward them and urge them to devise some plan whereby We may make a peaceful settlement, to the interest of all."

When she had sent this despatch, she pondered and wrote a public edict, an edict in which she spoke thus to the whole world:

"We have endured a succession of unfortunate circumstances following one upon another in rapid confusion, and We are at a loss to account for the situation which has brought about hostilities between China and the Western powers. Our envoys abroad are separated from Us by the wide seas, and they are not able therefore to explain to the Western powers the real state of Our feelings."

She then described the present war, how Chinese rebels and disorderly persons in every province had combined to create disturbance and how, had she not intervened for mercy and put down such persons, every foreign missionary would have been killed in every province. The further misfortune of the German minister had then occurred, and the insistence of the foreign warriors to take the Tientsin forts, which the Chinese Commandant could not accept, whereupon the foreign warriors had bombarded the forts.

She concluded thus:

"A state of war has thus been created, but it is none of Our doing. How could China be so foolish, conscious as she is of her weakness, as to declare war on the whole world at once? How can she hope to succeed by using untrained bandits for such a purpose? It must be obvious to all. This is a true statement of Our situation, explaining the measures forced upon Us to meet it. Our envoys abroad must explain the meaning of this edict to those governments to whom they are accredited. We will and do instruct our military commanders to protect the legations meanwhile. We can only do Our best. In the meantime, you, Our Ministers, must carry on your duties with renewed care. None can be disinterested spectators at such an hour."

Yet the Empress was not satisfied that she had done all she could and under her own hand she sent telegrams to the most powerful sovereigns of the outer world. To the Emperor of Russia she sent greetings and then she said:

"For more than two and a half centuries Our neighboring empires have maintained unbroken friendship, more cordial than those existing between any other powers. Nevertheless recent ill feeling between converts to Christianity and the rest of Our people have given opportunity to evil persons to foment rebellion until the foreign powers themselves have been persuaded that the Throne opposes Christianity." She then described how this had been done and she ended with these words:

"And now that China has incurred the enmity of the Western world by circumstances beyond Our control, We can only rely upon Your country to act as intermediary and peacemaker on Our behalf. I make this earnest and sincere appeal to Your Majesty to come forward as arbitrator and save us all. We wait Your gracious reply."

And to the Queen of England, the Empress gave a sister's greeting and she reminded this Queen that most of China's trade was done with England, and concluded thus:

"We therefore ask You to consider that if by some circumstance the independence of Our Empire should be lost the interests of Your country would suffer. We are striving in anxiety and haste to raise an army for Our own defense and in the meantime We rely upon You as Our mediator, and will await hourly Your decision."

And using the name of the Emperor with her own she wrote last to the Emperor of Japan, sending her letter through her minister in Tokio, and she wrote:

"To Your Majesty, greeting! The Empires of China and Japan hang together, like lips and teeth. Therefore as Europe and Asia face each other for war, Our two Asian nations must stand together. The earth-hungry nations of the West, whose tigerish eyes are now fixed in greed upon Us, will certainly one day glare also at You. We must forget discord and think of Ourselves only as comrade peoples. We look to You as Our arbitrator with the enemies that surround Us."

To all these messages the Empress received no reply. She waited day and night, unbelieving, and day and night Prince Tuan and his followers pressed about her. "Friend or enemy to the Throne, minister or rebel," Prince Tuan said, "all are united in this one hatred against these foreign Christians who have come here against our will to trade and preach."

How monstrous now was her loneliness, encompassing the earth and high as Heaven! No human voice could reach her and no god spoke. The Empress sat in her Throne Hall day after day. The ministers and princes were silent when Prince Tuan and his followers spoke. Silent were the majesties abroad and silent Jung Lu lay upon his bed. The summer days passed by, one after the other, equal in brilliance, and no rain fell. While the people surged and strove and complained, the skies stretched over all without cloud or shadow. Last year there were floods and now came drought and the people cried out that the times were too evil and that Heaven was wroth. And while she meditated, outwardly as calm and still as the goddess Kuan Yin, within she was numb with confusion and despair. The city filled with rebels and Boxers, and all good people hid inside their houses. The foreign legations were preparing for attack, their gates were locked, and guards waited with their guns ready.

On the twentieth day of the fifth moon month the Empress knew that waiting was useless. Nothing now could stay destruction. At dawn the city blazed into fire. More than a thousand shops were set on fire by rebels and Boxers and rich merchants fled the city with their families. Now the war was not only against the foreigners but also against the Throne and against her.

On this day she received two memorials from the ministers Yuan and Hsü, both in her Foreign Office. They reported that they had themselves seen the bodies of dead Boxers in Legation Street, where they had been killed by foreign guards. Yet, they said, these guards were not to be blamed for what they had done, for the Western envoys had promised the Throne previously that their guards were summoned in larger numbers than usual only for defense, and when the storm was over they would be detached again from the city. The Emperor had inquired of the minister Hsü after audience only a few days before whether China could resist attack from abroad, he had caught hold of the minister's sleeve in his anxiety, and he had wept when Hsü replied that China must expect defeat. And the minister Yuan said when he heard the legations had been attacked, that it could only be called a grave breach of international law.

Still the Empress could not move. Where, she inquired of silent Heaven, could she turn? The insolent memorials heaped reproach upon her.

Again days passed. Within the legations the foreigners locked themselves as into a fortress. She heard that the foreigners starved and in her anxiety for them she sent them food, but it was returned, for they feared it was poisoned. She heard that their children were ill and fevered with lack of water, but when she sent kegs of clean water these, too, were returned.

On the fifteenth day of the sixth moon month the last blow fell from the hand of Heaven. Hundreds of Chinese Christians were murdered by the Boxers outside the gates of a prince's palace and the Empress, when she heard of the innocent dying with the guilty, put her hands to her ears and trembled. "Oh, if the Christians would but recant," she moaned. "Then I would not be compelled to this evil war."

But they did not recant and this angered the Boxers still more. One morning the Empress was drinking her morning tea. The sun was not yet shining over the wall and the dew was cool upon the lilies outside the door of her palace. In the midst of the turmoil and the battle in the city she was grateful for such a moment as this. Suddenly she heard loud shouts and the beat of tramping feet upon the stones of the outer terraces. She rose and hastened to the gate of her own palace, and there she saw a horde of noisy drunken men, their faces crimson, their broadswords drawn. At their front, half frightened, half boastful, she saw the tall thick form of Prince Tuan himself.

He clapped his hands when he saw her and motioned to his followers to be silent and arrogantly he addressed her.

"Majesty! I cannot hold back these true patriots. They hear that you are sheltering those devils' pupils, the Christian converts. More than that, they are told that the Emperor himself is a Christian. I cannot be responsible, Majesty—I will not be responsible—"

Her jade tea bowl was still in her hands and she lifted it high above her head and crashed it to the stone upon which she stood. Her huge eyes glowed and shone with cold fire.

"You traitor! Stand forth!" Thus she commanded Prince Tuan. "How dare you come here in the early morning when I am drinking tea and make a commotion? Do you dream yourself the Emperor? How dare you behave in this reckless and insolent fashion? Your head sits no more tightly on your shoulders than the head of any commoner! It is I and I alone who rule! Do you think that you can approach the Dragon Throne unless I speak?"

"Majesty—Majesty," Prince Tuan stammered.

But she would not stop the fountain of her anger. "Do you think because the times are confused that you can come here and create a riot? Get back to your place! For a year you will receive no salary. As for these vagabonds, these scavengers who follow you, I will have them beheaded!"

Such was the power of her presence, the hard clarity of her ringing voice, the beauty she still possessed, that even they were subdued and one by one they went away. Then she sent word to the Imperial Guards that indeed these men were to be beheaded and their heads hung on the city gates because they had dared to come into her presence when she had not commanded them.

On this same day came evil news from Tientsin that the foreign soldiery had captured that city and were marching now in full force to the capital to rescue their beleaguered countrymen inside the fortress of the legations. As for the Imperial Army, it was in retreat. What could she do but wait and pray?

On the tenth day of the seventh month of the moon year, in answer to her daily prayers to her goddess, the Empress received word that Jung Lu had awaked from his stupor. She returned to the temple to give thanks and then sent baskets of special foods to nourish him quickly to strength again. Nevertheless it was four more days before he could be carried into her presence in a palanquin and when she saw his pallor and the weakness of his limbs, she cried out that he was not to rise. Instead, she came down the two steps from her throne and sat down beside him in a chair.

"Where have you been, kinsman?" she inquired in her most tender voice. "Your body has lain inert on your bed, while your soul and mind have wandered far away."

"Wherever I have been I cannot remember now." His voice was high and weak. "But I am returned, by whose will I do not know, unless it was your prayers that brought me back."

"It was my prayers," she said, "for I have been alone indeed. Tell me what I must do. Do you know that a war rages in the city and that Tientsin has fallen? The enemy approaches the city—"

"I know all," he said. "There is no time. You must heed my words well. You must seize Prince Tuan, whom the foreigners blame for everything and you must order him beheaded. This will prove your innocence and your will for peace."

"What—and yield to the enemy?" she cried in outrage. "To behead Prince Tuan is a small matter but to yield to the foreign enemy—no, that is too much, that I cannot do! The meaning of my whole life crumbles into dust."

He groaned to hear her. "Oh, stubborn woman," he sighed. "When will you learn that you cannot stay the tides of the future?" And he motioned to the bearers of his palanquin to carry him away again, and torn in heart and mind the Empress did not bid him stay.

Day pressed upon day, and she clung to each day, trying to believe that the magic of the Boxer band still held. The city lay half in ashes and the foreigners in the legations still would not surrender. What, then, could this mean except that they had hope of their relieving armies now approaching? Five times on the third day she summoned her princes and ministers to audience in the Hall of Peaceful Longevity. To these audiences Jung Lu also came, and desperately forcing himself he rose from his palanquin and took his place. But he had no other advice to give than that which he had given and which she would not receive. As for the ministers and princes, they remained silent, their faces pale and lined with fear and weariness.

In this silence Prince Tuan again spoke loudly and boasted much, declaring that the Boxers had prepared their secret incantations and when the foreign troops reached the moat outside the city wall they would not be able to cross. Instead, they would fall in the water and be drowned.

To this Jung Lu shouted in a voice suddenly strong, "The Boxers are no more than thistledown, and when the enemy foreigners approach they will fly away like thistledown!"

His words were fulfilled. At the Hour of the Monkey on the fifth day, it being midafternoon, Duke Lan rushed into the library where the Empress perused the wise books where alone now she could find comfort, and he cried out without greeting or obeisance, "Old Buddha, they are here—the foreign devils have broken through the gates as fire through wax!"

She looked up and the blood drained from her heart.

"Then my kinsman was right," she said in a small, wondering voice.

355

She closed the book and rose, and standing there she meditated, pinching her full lower lip between her thumb and finger.

"You must flee, Majesty," the old duke cried. "You and the Son of Heaven together! You must flee northward."

She shook her head, still pondering, and seeing that she could not be moved he made haste away to find Jung Lu who alone could persuade her. In less than an hour Jung Lu was there and he came in, walking now with a cane and still uncertainly, but strengthened to do what he could for her.

She had sat down again, but the book was not opened and she clasped her hands on her knees so tightly that her knuckles and her fingers were white. She looked up when he came in, her great eyes opaque, the pupils lost in the darkness.

He came close to her and spoke in low and tender tones:

"My love, you must hear me. You cannot stay here. You are still the symbol of the Throne. Where you are is the heart of the nation. Tonight, after midnight, at the Hour of the Tiger when the moon is down and the stars not yet bright, you must escape."

"Again," she whispered. "Again, again—"

"Again," he agreed. "You know the way, and you shall not go alone."

"You—"

"No, not I. I must stay to rally our forces. For you will come back, as you did before, and I must save the Throne for you."

"How can you, without armies?" she murmured. Her head drooped and he saw great tears hanging on the long straight lashes. They fell one by one and rolled down the smooth heavy satin of her silver-gray robe.

"What I cannot do by force I shall do by wisdom," he said. "The throne will be here for you. That I promise."

She lifted up her face and he looked down and saw that she had yielded. To terror she had yielded, to fear, if not to him, and in pitying love he took her hand and held it for a moment. He put her hand to his cheek and pressed it there and then he loosed it gently and stepped back.

"Majesty," he said, "there is no time to lose. I must prepare your disguise and select those who shall take my place as guard for you. Your women must stain your skin and dress your hair as a Chinese peasant woman's and you must leave the palace by the hidden gate. Two ladies only—more will seem too many. The Emperor must go with you dressed as a peasant, too. The concubines you must leave behind—"

She listened, saying not a word. When he was gone she sat down and opened her book and her eyes fell upon strange words written centuries

before by the sage Confucius. "For lack of a broad mind and true understanding, a great purpose has been lost."

She stared at the words and heard them as though a voice had spoken
them. Out of the past they came direct into her heart and mind, and
she received them humbly. Her mind was not broad enough, she had
not understood the times, and her purpose was lost—her purpose to save
the country. The enemy had won. She closed the book slowly and she
surrendered her spirit. From now on she would not shape the times but
be shaped by them.

They marveled at her proud calm, not knowing. She gave commands
to everyone concerning the safe disposal of her books, her paintings, her
scrolls, her jewels. For the hiding of her treasure, her ingots of silver
and gold, she commanded Li Lien-ying to build a false wall in a certain
chamber and behind this wall the treasure was concealed. When all was
done, in haste but order, at the Hour of the Tiger she summoned first
the Emperor, and then the concubines and told the concubines why she
could not take them with her.

"I must preserve the Emperor and myself," she said, "not for our
worth, for, indeed, we have none of ourselves, but because we must protect the Throne. I carry the imperial seal with me, and where I am the
state is. Here you will remain and you need not fear, for the Grand
Councilor Jung Lu himself, miraculously recovered for this hour, will
rally all our armies. Moreover, I do not believe that the enemy will
penetrate these palaces. Continue then as though I were here. The eunuchs will be with you to serve, except for Li Lien-ying who goes with
me."

The concubines wept softly and wiped their eyes with their sleeves.
None spoke except the Pearl Concubine, whom the eunuchs had dared
to bring from her prison. There she stood, her cheeks pale and loose,
her beauty gone, her body clad in faded rags. But still she was rebellious.
Her onyx eyes, set like jewels under moth brows, still flamed. She cried
out to the Empress:

"I will not stay, Imperial Mother! I claim my right to go with my
lord to serve him."

The Empress rose up like an angry phoenix. "You!" she called and
she stabbed the air with her two little fingers. "You dare to speak, who
brought down half this trouble on his head! Could he have thought of
so much evil had you not whispered in his ears?"

She turned to Li Lien-ying and, borne up on the power of her wrath,
she gave command.

"Take this woman and cast her into the well by the Eastern Gate!"

The Emperor fell on his knees as she uttered this command but the Empress would not allow him to speak. This imperial woman, who could be all softness and charm when she was in the peaceful presence of beauty, in time of danger was ruthless.

"Not a word," she cried, stabbing her fingers into the air above the Emperor's head. "This concubine was hatched from the egg of an owl. I brought her here to nourish and to uphold me and she has rebelled against me."

She looked at Li Lien-ying and immediately he beckoned to a eunuch and the two of them laid hold upon the concubine and carried her away, she silent and pale as stone.

"Get you into your cart," the Empress said to the kneeling Emperor, "and drop the curtain lest you be seen. Prince P'u Lun is to ride on your shaft, and I will lead in my own cart. The mule is for Li Lien-ying. He must follow as best he can, though he is the worst of riders. And if anyone stops us, say that we are poor country folk fleeing into the mountains. Ah, but go first by the Summer Palace!"

So said, so done. Behind her curtains the Empress sat upon the cushion in her cart, straight as a Buddha, her face fixed, her ears alert, her eyes resolute. Only when, hours later, the carts passed by the Summer Palace did she issue command again. "Stay," she said when the beloved towers of the pagodas came into view. "We will remain here a little while."

She descended from her cart though she would allow no other to descend, and alone, except for one eunuch, she wandered the marble corridors, the empty palaces, and beside the lake. Here was the core of her heart. Here she had dreamed of living out her quiet old age among people peaceful and prosperous. Here it might be she could never return. What if the foreign enemy again destroyed this place, as long ago they had done? Ah, but she had come back, she had rebuilt, and in rebuilding she had strengthened and glorified the past. But then she had been young and now she was old. Age, too, had defeated her.

In quiet she stood for the last long gaze, and then she turned, a figure slender and elegant in the coarse blue cotton garments of a Chinese peasant, and she stepped into her cart.

"Westward," she commanded, "westward to the city of Sian."

The journey proceeded day by day for ninety days and the Empress kept her face resolute and calm whatever her heart was. Never did she forget that the Court looked to her as to the sun, although she was in flight. When they had left one province and had entered into the next, it was no longer necessary to maintain disguise, and the Empress, after bath, could put on her royal garments again. With this she felt renewed spirits, and her courage rose. In this province of Shansi the people were not afraid of war but they were bitter with a fearful famine. Nevertheless on the very first evening her favorite general, who had come north with his troops, gave to the Empress a basket of fresh eggs, a jeweled girdle, and a satin pouch for her pipe and tobacco. This cheered her, too, and was a good omen of the love which her subjects still felt for her. Indeed, as the days passed, starving though they were, the people brought baskets of wheat and millet and thin fowls to the Empress and she was ever more comforted by such love, and she began to take pleasure in the surrounding beauty.

At a pass between the hills, named the Pass of Flying Geese, she commanded all to halt, in order that she could enjoy the spectacle. As far as eyes could reach the bare-flanked mountains rose against a sky of royal purple. In the valleys the shadows were black. Her favorite general, now traveling with her as guard, wandered away for a short distance and found a steep meadow upon whose grasses grew a mass of yellow flowers. He plucked an armful of them and brought them to the Empress saying that the gods had spread them there as an imperial welcome. The Empress was touched by such a pretty compliment, and she told a eunuch to pour the general a bowl of buttermilk tea to restore his strength. By such small pleasant means the weight was lifted somewhat from her heart. She slept well at night and she ate heartily even of the poor fare.

On the eighth day of the ninth month she reached the capital of the province and there the Viceroy Yü Hsien awaited her with every show of reverence. This Viceroy was he who, believing in their show of magic, had upheld the Boxers, and he had caused every foreign man, woman and child in his province to be killed. The Empress accepted his obeisances and his gifts when he met her at the city gates for welcome and she praised him saying that he had done well to clean his province of the enemy and that she knew that he was honest and loyal.

"Nevertheless," she said, "we are defeated and it may be that the foreign enemy, when they are victorious, will demand your punishment, and if this is so, then I must seem to punish you, but I shall reward you in secret. We must hope for future victory yet to come, in spite of present defeat."

At this Yü Hsien made obeisances nine times in the dust before her. "Majesty," he said, "I am ready to accept dismissal and punishment at your hands."

But she wagged her forefinger at him. "You were wrong, though, in promising me that the Boxers could not be killed because of their magic. They are dead in large numbers. The foreign bullets went through their bodies as though their flesh were wax."

"Majesty," Yü Hsien said in all earnestness, "their magic failed because they did not abide by the rules of their order. For robbery, they killed innocent persons who were not Christians and thus allowed themselves to be overcome by their own greed. Only the pure can use magic."

She nodded her head to this and so proceeded to the viceregal palace which was prepared for her. And she was pleased when upon her arrival she found certain gold and silver vessels taken from a storeroom and cleaned and polished for her use now. These vessels had been made two hundred years before for the Imperial Ancestor Ch'ien Lung, when he came to this city on his way to worship at the Five-Crested Mountain.

Never was autumn more glorious than now. Day after day the sun shone down upon land and people. Harvests were once more plentiful and farmhouses were full of food and fuel. The war was far away and the citizens seemed scarcely to have heard of it. In peace and plenty they gave her homage and declared that indeed she was their Old Buddha and to her they gave thanks. Again her spirits rose and her heart was robust with courage and pleasure, and the more because many of her princes and ministers now followed her and slowly the Court assembled itself.

Her mood was dimmed suddenly by a letter, written as a memorial from Jung Lu, and he told her therein that their cause was lost and that his good aide, Chung Chi, had hanged himself in despair. To this the Empress replied, first bestowing honors upon the dead man for his loyalty and bravery and then commanding Jung Lu to come to her to make full report. She was prepared then for no better news when he arrived, for while he journeyed to her, his wife was taken suddenly ill and died in a strange city. This news the Empress heard by courier, and she was determined to comfort him and rouse his spirits by her own renewed health.

When Jung Lu was announced upon the day after her own arrival at the city of T'ai Yuan she sent word that he rest only an hour and then appear before her.

She received him in a small ancient hall. There she sat with folded hands upon a great carved chair of southern blackwood set on a low platform to resemble a throne. She allowed none to be near when she and Jung Lu met. Her ladies she dismissed, saying that they must go into the fresh air and the sunshine and Li Lien-ying she commanded to wait in the anteroom.

The door opened and Jung Lu came in, tall and gaunt from sorrow and fatigue, but always fastidious in her presence, he had used his hour to bathe and put on fresh robes. As usual he made a feint of obeisance and as usual she put out her right hand to prevent him. He stood before her and she rose, the platform lending her height, and they exchanged a long lingering look.

"I grieve that your wife has left you for the Yellow Springs," she said in a low voice.

He acknowledged this by a slight bow. "Majesty, she was a good woman," he said, "and she served me faithfully."

They waited, one for the other, but what could be said between them now?

"I shall lift up another to her place," the Empress said at last.

"As you will, Majesty," he said.

"You are tired," she observed. "Do not act with ceremony. Let us sit down together. I have need of your wisdom." She descended from the platform and crossed the room with her old controlled grace, a slender figure regal and upright as she had ever been, and she sat down in one of two straight wooden chairs between which was a small two-tiered table. At her gesture he sat down in the other chair and waited for her to speak.

She waved a silk fan upon which once, in a moment of idleness, she had painted a landscape of this province. "Is all lost?" she asked at last, and looked sidewise at him from her long eyes.

"All is lost," he said firmly. He sat with his large beautiful hands planted upon his satin-covered knees and upon these hands she now fixed her eyes. They were fleshless hands, but exceedingly strong, and well did she know their strength.

"What is your counsel?" she asked.

"Majesty," he said, "there is only one course for you to follow. You must return to your capital and yield to the demands of the enemy and so again save the Throne. I have left Li Hung-chang behind to nego-tiate the peace. But before you return you must order Prince Tuan to be beheaded, as an earnest of your repentance."

"Never!" she exclaimed and she folded her fan with a sharp crack of ivory sticks.

"Then you can never return," he replied. "So great is the hatred of the foreigners against Prince Tuan, whom they consider the instigator of their persecution, that they will destroy the imperial city rather than let you come back to it."

She felt the blood chill in her veins. The fan dropped from her hand. She thought of all her treasure hidden in that city, and more than such treasure the inheritance of the imperial ancestors, the glory and the power. Could these be lost and if they were, what was left?

"You are always too abrupt," she observed. She pointed with her little finger to her fan and he stooped and picked it up and put it on the table, and she knew that he did not give it to her lest their hands touch.

"Majesty," he said in his deep patient voice, "the foreigners will pursue you even here if you do not show submission."

"I can move westward again," she insisted, "and where I stay, there I declare my capital. Our Imperial Ancestors did so before me. I am but following their footsteps."

"As your Majesty wills," he said. "Yet you know, and I know, and, alas, the whole world will know, that unless and until you return to our ancient imperial city, you are in flight."

But she would not yield, not instantly, even to him, and rising she bade him leave her and go to rest and she ordered special delicacies for him to eat, and so they parted. No, not instantly would she yield and therefore the next day she commanded the Court to be ready to move westward to the distant city of Sian in the province of Shensi, and there she said she would declare her capital, not, she maintained, in flight, but because there had been a recent famine in this province and the needs of the Court could not be met. Though the famine was past, yet all accepted her decree and as soon as a place was prepared for her, the Court set out for the west.

By her command Jung Lu rode beside her palanquin, and he said no more of her return to Peking and she asked no counsel. Instead, she spoke of the desert beauty of the landscape and she concerned herself with passing scenes and she quoted poetry and all this she did to cover her secret despair. For in the end she did not doubt that he was right. Somehow, some day, she must return to the imperial city at whatever cost. Yet she hid this inner certainty and she cheerfully and steadfastly continued westward, each day adding miles to the distance between herself and the Dragon Throne. When they came to the city of Sian, she took residence with the Court in the Viceroy's palace which had been cleaned and furnished for her anew, the walls painted red, the outer courtyards surrounded by palisades, and in the main hall a throne had been built and cushioned with yellow silk. Her own chambers were behind the throne room and on the west side were rooms for the Emperor and his Consort and to the east was a room for Li Lien-ying, near his royal mistress and ready for her summons.

Here established, the Empress now insisted upon simple food to save expense. Though a hundred dishes of the finest dainties from the south were daily declared ready for preparation she chose only six for each meal. She commanded that only six cows be kept for the milk which she enjoyed drinking when she rose in the morning and at night before she slept. In spite of her long journey the Empress declared herself in good health, except for sleeplessness, and when she was restless at night, a eunuch, trained to the task, massaged her until she slept.

Now that she had settled in her exile capital, she again gave audience and daily couriers came from the distant imperial city bringing news. She bore all until they told her that the Summer Palace was desecrated once more. Soldiers of several Western nations had made merry in her sacred palaces, she heard. Her throne, she heard, they had carried to the lake and cast into the deepest waters, and they had stolen her personal robes and paintings and upon the walls of the halls and the chambers, even in her own bedchamber they had drawn lewd and ribald pictures and made coarse writings. When she heard this she fell ill with rage and vomited her food. In weakness during the next few days she knew that she must return to the capital, and that before she could return, she must yield to the demands of the enemy that all who had aided the Boxer band must die. This her General Li Hung-chang made clear to her in his daily memorials sent by courier. Yet how could she yield at such a price? And through all this Jung Lu was daily at her side, impassive, silent, pale, while he waited for the inevitable end.

Often she turned to him, her great eyes black in her pale and beautiful face and sometimes she spoke and sometimes was silent.

"Is there no other escape from my enemies except to yield?" she asked one day.

"Majesty, none," he said.

She asked no more. Speechless, she lifted her eyes to his and he smiled sadly and made no answer. One night when she sat in her courtyard alone in the twilight, he stood before her unannounced and he said,

"I come as your kinsman. Why do you not yield to your destiny? Will you live your life here in eternal exile?"

She had upon her knees a small cinnamon dog, born in exile, and she played with its long ears while she spoke slowly and with long pauses.

"I am unwilling to kill those who have been loyal to me. Of the lesser ones I will not speak . . . But consider, I pray, how I can kill my good minister, Chao Shu-ch'iao? I do not think that he believed in the magic of the Boxers. His fault was in hoping for their strength at arms. Yet the foreigners insist that he is to be beheaded . . . And consider also that I am told to order the death of Prince Chia and how shall I mention the names of Ying Nien and Yu Hsien? There remains also Ch'i Hsiu. And I refuse to command execution for Prince Tuan . . . Eh, alas—I can speak no more names. All are loyal to me and many have followed me in exile. Am I now to turn on them and destroy them?"

Jung Lu was all tenderness and patience. His face, thin with withering age and sorrow, was gentle beyond the face of any man. "You know that you cannot be happy here," he said.

"Long ago I cast my happiness away," she said.

"Then think of your realm," he argued with unending patience. "How can the realm be saved and the people united again if you remain in exile? The rebels will seize the city if the foreigners do not hold it. The country will be divided as thieves divide their booty. The people will live in terror and danger and they will curse you ten thousand times because for a few lives you were not willing to return to the Throne and gather together the broken threads of their life and weave them whole again."

He spoke grave words and she could not but heed them. As ever, when she was reminded of greatness, she became great. While the little dog whined upon her knees to feel the touch of her hand, she meditated, stroking his tawny head and smoothing its ears. Then she put the small beast down and rose to meet Jung Lu's waiting gaze.

"I have been thinking only of myself," she said. "Now I will think only of my people. I return again to my Throne."

On the twenty-fourth day of the eighth moon month, which is the tenth month of the sun year, the roads were dried after the summer rains, and the earth was firm. The Empress began the long journey home, and in imperial state. She would return, she said, not with humility but with oblivious pride. At the gate of the city where there was a temple she paused with her court to make sacrifice to the God of War. From there she commanded steady marching, at the pace of twenty-five miles a day, for she was ever merciful to the bearers of palanquins and sedans and to the mules and Mongol horses which carried the gifts and tributes she had received while in exile.

Day after day the fine weather of autumn held, and there was neither wind nor rain. One sadness marked the return and this was that she received before her departure the news of the death, in weakness of old age, of her faithful General Li Hung-chang. She had been sometimes displeased with this General, for he alone among all her generals had dared to speak the truth to her. While he was Viceroy in Chihli he had remained above corruption and he had built an army incorruptible. In his old age, against his own heart, she had sent him to the distant south to control the Cantonese rebels and thither he had gone, again to serve with patience and skill. When she summoned him northward once more he was already of great age, and he had delayed his coming until she was willing at last to renounce the Boxer horde. Then he had come to the imperial city and there, with Prince Ch'ing, he had made peace with the foreign enemies, a sad peace, but one which could save the country if she yielded. Now that he was dead the Empress Mother gave him his due, and she announced that she would cause a shrine to be built within the imperial city itself, beside other shrines already dedicated in the provinces where he had served her. Fickle she often was in her favor, and she had made willful excuses when she was displeased with Li Hung-chang, saying that she could not understand his dialect and that he did not speak a pure Chinese. But willfulness was cleansed at last from her whole being and she was chastened by terror and loss.

It was soon to be seen that Jung Lu was correct in his counsel. The return to the capital was a royal return. Everywhere the people welcomed the Empress with praises and with feasts, believing, now that the exile was over, their country was safe and all would be as it had been before. At K'ai-feng, the capital of the province of Honan, most splendid theatricals awaited her, and she commanded the Court to rest, so that she might enjoy her favorite pastime which she had denied herself while the country was at war. At this time she publicly, though gently, reproached the Viceroy because he had before advised her not to return to the capital, but to live in exile. When the Viceroy, Wen T'i by name, offered to swallow gold as expiation, she was merciful and refused his request and for this, too, the people praised her.

When she reached the Yellow River, again she paused. The autumn skies were violet blue, cloudless and clear, and the dry air was warm by day and cool by night.

"I shall offer sacrifices to the River God," she declared, "and I shall make absolution and give thanks."

This she did with much pomp and magnificence, and the brilliant noonday sun glittered on the splendid colors of her robe and upon those robes which the Court displayed. And while she worshipped, the Empress was pleased to see among the crowds that lined the river banks a few white-skinned persons, of what country she did not know, but now that she had decided to be merciful and courteous to her enemies she

365

sent two eunuchs to take wine, dried fruits and watermelon as gifts to the white persons, and she commanded her ministers and princes that foreigners were to be allowed to watch her enter the capital city itself. After this, she stepped upon a great barge which the loyal magistrates had built for her and for her Court to cross the river, and this barge was made like a mighty dragon, its scales of gold, and its eyes rubies, burning red.

But proof of her resolution to be courteous now to those who had been her enemies was that at a certain place she came down from her palanquin and entered into a train of iron cars. This train ran on iron rails, and the railway was a toy of the Emperor's, which she had always forbidden to be used. Now, however, she would use it to show the foreigners how changed she was, how made anew, how modern, how able to understand their ways. Nevertheless she would not, she declared, enter the sacred walls of the city in the bowels of this iron monster. In respect for the Imperial Ancestors, she commanded that the train stop outside the city that she might be carried through the imperial gate in her royal palanquin. A temporary station was therefore built outside the city and vast pavilions were built near this station for her use and as resting places for the Court. Here they were to be welcomed by officials and by foreigners, and these pavilions were furnished with fine carpets, with delicate porcelain vases, with potted trees and late blooming chrysanthemums and orchids. In the central pavilion thrones were set up, one for the Empress, made of gold lacquer, and a smaller one for the Emperor, made of hardwood painted red and gold.

Thirty iron cars were needed for the Court and their possessions and this long train wound its way among the bare hills and drew up at the station. From a window the Empress looked out and she was heartened to see a great crowd of her subjects who waited for her, princes and generals and the officials of the city standing in front, wearing official robes. To one side she saw foreign envoys in their strange dark coats and trousers, and she stared at their grim faces, repelled by their pallor and their large features, and then she forced a courteous smile.

All was performed in honor and in order. When the princes and generals and other Manchu and Chinese saw the face of the Empress at the window, they fell upon their knees, and the chief officer of the imperial household shouted to the foreigners to remove their hats, although this they had already done. First to come down from the train in much pride and state was the Chief Eunuch, Li Lien-ying. He paid no heed to anyone but immediately made himself busy in checking and examining the number of boxes of tribute and treasure that bearers carried from the boxcars. Next, the Emperor came down from the train but the Empress made a sign and he hastened to a sedan chair that was waiting and to him no greeting was given. Only when all was ready did the Empress herself descend from the train. Supported by her princes, she came down the steps and stood in the brilliant sunshine to view the scene and to be viewed, while her subjects bowed in obeisance, their foreheads on the clean-swept earth.

The foreigners stood together at the left, their heads bared but not bowed, and she was amazed at their number.

"How many of these foreigners are here?" she said in a clear voice which carried through the windless air to the very ears of the foreigners themselves. When they appeared to understand what she had said, she smiled graciously in their direction and then stood talking with her usual liveliness to several of the managers of her imperial household. All praised her, saying that she looked in health and youthful for her many years, and indeed, her skin was flawless even under the relentless sun, and her hair still abundant and black. When Li Lien-ying had finished his task he brought her the list of treasures, each chest checked and counter-checked, and the Empress took the scroll and examined it closely and gave it back to him, while she nodded approval.

When this was done, the Viceroy, Yuan Shih-K'ai, asked permission to present to her the foreign manager and engineer of the train, and she with perfect grace agreed to receive them. When the two tall white men stood before her, bareheaded, she thanked them for their courtesy in obeying her command whereby the train was not to travel beyond fifteen miles an hour, that she might arrive in safety. This done, she entered her gold palanquin and was lifted up by the bearers and carried to the city. She had decreed that her entrance was to be by the South Gate of the Chinese city, and thence she went to the great entrance gate of the imperial inner city. Here she paused again to worship at the shrine to the God of War, and she came down from her palanquin and knelt before the god to burn incense and give thanks, while the priests chanted their rituals. She rose from her knees when the service was finished and chancing to lift her eyes upward as she came from the shrine, she saw on the walls a hundred or more foreigners, men and women, who had come to gaze at her. At first she was angry and she was about to call out that they should be scattered by the eunuchs. Then she remembered. She was indeed the ruler, but by the mercy of this same enemy. She subdued her anger and forcing herself, yet so gracefully that all seemed natural to her and only courtesy and pleasure, she bowed to the foreigners, now to the right, now to the left, and smiled here and there toward them. This done, she went into her sedan again and so was carried once more into her own palace.

How beautiful was this ancestral palace to her now, undefiled by the enemy, saved by her surrender! She went from room to room, and into the great Throne Hall which Ch'ien Lung had built.

And I shall use this Throne Hall now for my own, she thought, and I shall rule from here—

And behind this Throne Hall were her courtyards, all as they had been, the gardens safe, the pools calm and clear. And beyond them was her small private throne room, and beyond it her sleeping chamber. All, all was as she had left it, the splendid doors untouched, their vermilion hues unmarred, the gold rooflets above them safe. And safe, too, was her Golden Buddha in his shrine.

Here, as did my Sacred Ancestor, I live and die in peace, she thought—

But it was too soon to think of peaceful death. Her first care when she had rested and had eaten her meal, was to know if her treasure was still safe. To that inner place she went, accompanied by her eunuch, and she stood before the wall, examining every crack and ledge of bricks.

"Not one brick has been moved," she said, much pleased. Then she laughed, her laughter as gay and mischievous as ever it had been. "I daresay," she said, "that foreign devils passed this place again and again, but they had no wit or magic to know what lies here."

She commanded then that Li Lien-ying should have the wall torn down and he must examine and check every parcel of her treasure and report to her.

"You must watch sharply," she admonished. "I will not lose to thievish eunuchs what I have not lost to foreign devils."

"Am I not to be trusted, Majesty?" the eunuch asked and rolled his eyes and pretended to be wounded.

"Well, well," she said and went away again to her own chamber. Ah, the peace here, the joy of return! The price was high and it was not yet all paid, nor ever could be paid in full nor the debt ended, for so long as she lived she must be gracious to her enemies and pretend to love them. To this task she set herself this same day before the sun was set, and she announced that she would invite the wives of foreign envoys to visit her again, and she herself wrote the invitation, saying that in pleasant memory she renewed acquaintance. Then, that every stain might be removed from her, she commanded honors for the Pearl Concubine, and she decreed an edict saying that this lady had delayed too long before joining the Emperor in his exile, and because she was unwilling to watch the desecration of the imperial shrines and the pollution of the palaces by foreign enemies, she had leaped into a deep well.

This done, the night fell, and the Empress inquired of Li Lien-ying whether Jung Lu had yet arrived. If so, she would summon him to make report.

"I go, Majesty," the eunuch said, and soon returned to say that Jung Lu had reached the imperial city a short time ago and even now approached.

In her private throne room she waited, and soon the curtains were put aside by Li Lien-ying and Jung Lu was there. He leaned heavily upon two tall young eunuchs, and between these youths he looked so aged, so infirm, that the joy of her return drained from the heart of the Empress.

"Enter, kinsman," she said, and to the eunuchs she said, "Lead him here to this cushioned seat. He is not to make obeisance or tire himself. And you, Li Lien-ying, bring a bowl of strong hot broth and a jug of hot wine and some steamed bread. My kinsman is too weary in my service."

The eunuchs ran to obey and when they were alone the Empress rose and went to Jung Lu and stood at his side, and seeing no one near she felt his brow and smoothed his hands. Oh, how thin his hands were, and his cheeks how fleshless, and the skin hot to her touch!

"I pray you," he whispered, "I pray you stand away from me. The curtains have eyes, the walls have ears."

"Shall I never be able to minister to you?" she pleaded.

But he was so uneasy, that she saw, and so troubled lest her honor be soiled, that she sighed and went back to her throne and sat there. Then he drew from his bosom a scroll and reading from it slowly and with difficulty, for his eyes seemed dim, he gave report that after she had gone from the train, he had supervised the ladies of the Court as they came down from the train. First of these were the Consort and the Princess Imperial, and these he had escorted to two yellow-curtained sedans. Next had come the four imperial concubines and these he had led to four sedans, whose curtains were green and only bordered with yellow satin. These were borne away by their bearers to the imperial city. After them the ladies of the Court descended and he led them to the official carts, each cart for two ladies.

"As usual," he said, looking up from the scroll, "the elder ladies made much complaint and talk, each had to tell the other of the fearful journey on the train, the filth of smoke, and how they vomited. But talk was ended at last and I myself supervised the removal of the boxes of bullion, each marked with the name of the province and the city that had sent tribute—no small task, Majesty, since you will remember that before we entrained the baggage alone filled three thousand carts. Yet this is all nothing. I fear the anger of the people when they learn the cost of this long journey home. The Imperial Highway, Majesty, and the splendid resthouses, every ten miles, will make many taxes—"

Here the Empress stopped him with tender kindness. "You are too weary. Rest yourself now. We are home again."

"Alas, a thousand burdens remain to be carried," he murmured.

"But not by you," she declared. "Others must bear them."

She scanned his aging handsome face with careful love and he submitted to her searching eyes. They were closer now, these two, than marriage itself could have made them. Flesh denied, their minds had interwoven in every thought, their hearts had mingled in every mood, and knowledge was complete. She put out her right hand and stroked his right hand gently, and felt it cool beneath her palm. In such communion a moment passed. Then, speechless, they interchanged a long deep look and he left her.

How could she know that it was the last time that she was to touch his living flesh? He fell ill in that same night of his old illness. Again he lay upon his bed unconscious for many days. The Empress sent her Court physicians to him and when none could heal she sent a physician, partly soothsayer, whom her brother Kuei Hsiang proclaimed magic in his cures. But fate forbade, and Jung Lu's life was come to its end. He died, still silent and unknowing, before dawn in the third moon month, the fourth sun month, of the next new year. The Empress decreed full mourning for the Court and she herself wore no bright colors for a year, and she put aside her jewels for that time.

But none could light the inner darkness of her heart. Had she been only woman, she could have stood beside his coffin and herself laid the purple satin coverlet upon his shoulders. She could have sat the night out in his dead presence and worn white mourning to signify her loss. She could have wept and wailed aloud to ease her heart. But she was imperial woman, and she could not leave her palace nor weep aloud nor show herself moved beyond the point of lofty grief for a dead loyal servant of the Throne. Her one comfort was to be alone, and she coveted such hours as she could steal from her heavy daily tasks of new government of a troubled land.

One night when she had bade her women draw the curtains so that she could weep unseen, she lay sleepless, the silent tears draining from her heart, until the watchman beat his midnight drum. And still she lay sleepless, and was so desperate with the weary weight of sorrow that she fell into a dream, a trance, and felt her soul taken from her body. She dreamed she saw Jung Lu somewhere, but young again, except that he spoke with old wisdom. She dreamed he took her in his arms and held her and for so long that her sorrow lifted and she felt light and free, her burden gone. And then she seemed to hear him speak.

"I am with you always." This was his voice. "And when you are most gentle and most wise, I am with you, my mind in yours, my being in your being."

Memory—memory! Yet was it not more than memory? The warmth of certainty welled through her soul and into her body. When she awoke, the weariness was gone from limbs and flesh. She who had been loved could never be alone. This was the meaning of the dream.

There came such a change in the life of the Empress thereafter that none could comprehend it, and only she knew and she kept it secret. She was possessed by ancient wisdom and she made defeat a victory. She fought no more but yielded, with grace, her lively mind. Thus, to the amazement of all, she even encouraged young Chinese men to go abroad and learn the skills and knowledge of the West.

"Those who are between fifteen and twenty-five," she decreed, "those who have good intelligence and good health may cross the Four Seas, if they wish. We will defray the cost."

And she summoned to her the minister Yuan Shih-K'ai and the rebel Chinese scholar Chang Chih-tung and after many days of hearing them face to face, she decreed that the old imperial examinations belonged to the past, and she sent out an edict saying that two thousand five hundred years ago, in the time of that good and enlightened ruler the Regent Duke Chou, doubtless universities were not unlike the present seats of learning in the West, and she proved by history books that the eight-legged classical essay was not sent down from ancient times, but was a device of Ming scholars only some five hundred years ago, and therefore that present youth should go not only to Japan, but also to Europe and America, since under Heaven and around the Four Seas, all peoples were one family.

This she did one year after the death of Jung Lu, in body.

Before another year had passed, she decreed against the use of opium, not suddenly, for she was tenderly mindful of the aged men and women who were used to a pipe or two at night to waft them to sleep. No, she said, within ten years, year by year, the importation and the manufacture of opium must be stopped.

And in that same year, while she meditated much, she saw that the foreigners, whom she would not call enemies and yet could not call friends, for they were still strange to her, would never agree to yield those evil special rights and privileges which gave to all white men, good and evil alike, the same protection, unless she decreed that tortures must end for any crimes committed, and she decreed that law and not force and agony must judge the crime. Dismemberment and slicing, she commanded, must be no more, and branding and flogging and the punishment of innocent relatives must cease. Once, long ago, Jung Lu had so adjured her, but she had not heeded him then. Now she remembered.

And who, she asked herself, would take her place when she died? Never would she leave the realm to the weak young Emperor who was her eternal prisoner. No, strong young hands must be raised up, but where was the child? And who, indeed, was strong enough for the centuries ahead? She felt the magic of the future. Mankind, she told her princes, might yet increase to the stature of the gods. And she grew curious about the West whence new power streamed and she said often that, were she younger, she might herself travel westward and see the sights beyond.

"Alas," she said with plaintive grace, "I am very old. My end is near."

When she spoke thus her ladies protested much, saying that she was more beautiful than any woman, her skin still fresh and fair, her long eyes black and bright, her lips unwithered. All this was true, she granted with a modesty enlivened by the ghost of her old gaiety, and yet she, even she, could not live forever.

"Ten thousand thousand years, Old Buddha," they replied. "Ten thousand thousand years!"

But she was not deceived and her next decree was to send the best of her ministers, in imperial commission, led by the Duke Tsai Tse, to the countries of the West and this was her instruction.

"Go to all countries and see which are the most fortunate, the most prosperous, the people most happy and at peace and content with their rulers. Sift them down to the four best, and stay a year in each. In each study how their rulers govern and what is meant by constitutions and people's rule, and bring back to Us a full understanding of these matters."

She had her enemies and they were among her own subjects. They said that she was bowing down before the foreign conquerors, that she had lost her pride, that the nation was humiliated by her humility.

"We Chinese," a certain Chinese scholar thus memorialized, "are despised like rustics when we are servile to foreigners, but what shall we say when our Empress Herself demeans Herself by Her too-open friendship with the wives of foreign ministers. Her smiles, the waves of Her kerchief when She sees a foreign woman on the street while riding in Her palanquin to worship at the Altar of Heaven? We hear there is even foreign food in the palaces and dining halls furnished with foreign chairs and tables. And this goes on while the Legations rage against us at the Foreign Office!"

And yet another wrote, "At Her age, the Empress cannot change Her habits or Her hatreds. Doubtless the foreigners themselves are asking what deep plans She has against them."

And still another said, "Doubtless in this strange new mood the Empress seeks only peace for Her old age."

To all her judges the Empress smiled.

"I know what I do," she said from her heart possessed. "I know well what I do, and nothing now is strange to me. I heard of such things long ago but only now I heed them. I was told—but only now I believe."

Those who listened to her did not understand but this, too, she knew, and she did not change.

When the days of mourning for Jung Lu were finished, the Empress sent out edicts of invitation to all foreign envoys and their ladies and their children for a great feast on the first day of the New Year. The envoys themselves were to feast in the great banquet hall, the ladies in her own private banquet hall, and the imperial concubines were to receive the children in their apartments, with such serving women and eunuchs as were needed to care for them.

Never before had the Empress prepared so vast a feast. The Emperor was to remain with the envoys and she would appear after the feast. The dishes were to be both Eastern and Western. Three hundred cooks were employed, the Court musicians were instructed and the Imperial Players prepared a program of four plays, each three hours long.

The Empress herself planned an effort. She commanded the daughter of her plenipotentiary to Europe, a lady both young and beautiful, whose attendance at the Court was compulsory for two years, to teach her to give greetings in English to the foreign envoys. France, the Empress declared after studying maps, was too small a country for her to heed its language. America was too new and uncouth. But England, she declared, was ruled also by a great woman, for whom she had always a fondness. Therefore she chose the language of the English Queen. Indeed, she had commanded a portrait of Queen Victoria to be hung in her own chamber and she studied it and declared that upon the face she discerned the same lines of longevity that were carved upon her own.

How astonished, then, were the foreign envoys when the Empress welcomed them in the English tongue! She was borne into the great hall in her imperial sedan, carried by twelve bearers in yellow uniform, and the Emperor stepped forward to assist her. She came down, her jeweled hand upon his forearm, and, glittering from head to foot in a robe of gold, embroidered with bright blue dragons and wearing her great collar of matched pearls, her headdress set with flowers of rubies and jade, she inclined her head to right and to left as she walked to the Throne with her old youthful grace. What was she saying? One envoy after another, bowing before her but never to the floor, heard words which his ear could not at first recognize, but which repeated again and again became clear.

"Hao ti diu—" she said, "Ha-p'i niu yerh! Te'-rin-ko t'i!"

They comprehended, one after the other, that the Empress asked how they did, she wished them happy new year, she invited them to drink tea. These foreign envoys, tall stiff men in stiff garments, were now so moved that they burst into applause, which at first surprised and even bewildered the Empress, who had not in her life before seen men clapping their hands palm to palm. But gazing at the angular foreign faces, she saw only approval of her effort and she laughed gently, much pleased, and when she had sat on her throne, she remarked left and right to her ministers and princes, in her own tongue:

"You see how easy it is to be friends even with barbarians! It requires only a little effort on the part of civilized persons."

In such mood the feast day ended, and when gifts had been bestowed upon the foreign ladies and upon their children and money wrapped in red paper distributed to their servants, the Empress retired to her own chamber. As was her habit now, she reviewed her days and years, thinking over her long life and planning for the future of her people. She had done well this day, she mused. She had laid foundations of accord and friendship with foreign powers who could be friends or enemies. And she thought of Victoria, the Western Queen, and she wished that they two could meet and talk together of how to shape their two worlds to one.

All under Heaven are one family, she would tell Victoria—

Alas, before such dreams could grow the news was cried across the seas that Victoria was dead. The Empress was aghast.

"How did my sister die?" she cried.

When she heard that Victoria, though beloved of her own people, had died of old age as any common mortal does, the knowledge struck like a sword into the imperial heart.

"Die we all must," the Empress murmured, and looked from one face to another.

But they saw that she had not until now felt death near her. And to herself she murmured that she must find an heir, a true heir, for if Victoria was dead, then anyone could die, though she herself was strong, and still able to live for another brace of years, long enough to see a child grow to a youth, or if Heaven's will was good, to manhood itself, before she descended into her imperial coffin. It was indeed her duty once again to find an heir, a child, for whom she must rule while she trained him to be Emperor. But this time she would let the Heir be taught what the world was. She would summon teachers from the West to teach him. Yes, she would let him have iron trains and ships of war and guns and cannon. He must learn to make Western war and then in his time, when she was gone, even as Victoria was gone, he in his age would do what she had failed to do. He would drive the enemy into the sea.

What child, what child? The question was a torment until suddenly, an hour later, she remembered that a child had been born in Jung Lu's palace. His daughter, wed to Prince Ch'un, had given birth to a son but a few days before. This child, this boy, was Jung Lu's grandson. She bent her head to hide her smile from Heaven. This would lift her beloved even to the Dragon Throne! It was her will and Heaven must approve.

Yet she would not announce her choice too soon. She would placate the gods and preserve the child's life by keeping her plan secret until the Emperor lay upon his deathbed—not far off, surely, for pains and ills consumed his flesh. He had not been well enough to offer the autumn sacrifices in person, complaining that the many times he must kneel, the genuflections he must make, were far beyond his strength, and she had made them in his place. It was an ancient law that the Heir must not be proclaimed until the Emperor's face was turned toward the Yellow Springs and death near. Or, if not near enough, her eunuch could most delicately poison—

She heard a sound of rushing wind and lifted up her head.

"Hark," she cried to her ladies, standing at their usual distance from her throne. "Does the wind bring rain?"

For in the last two months the country had been cursed by a dry cold that reached the very roots of trees and winter wheat. No snow fell, and in the last seventeen days a most unseasonable warmth had crept up from the south. Even the peonies, bewildered, had sent up shoots. The people had flocked to temples to reproach the gods, and seven days ago she had commanded the Buddhist priests to take the gods out daily in procession and compel those gods to see for themselves what damage was abroad.

"What wind is this," she now inquired, "and from what corner of the earth does it arise?"

Her ladies asked the eunuchs who ran into the courts and held up their hands and turned their faces this way and that and they came back crying that the wind was from the eastern seas and that it was full of moisture. Even as they spoke all heard a clap of thunder, unseasonable and unexpected, yet clear enough. A roar came from the streets, the people running out from every house to look at the skies.

The wind rose higher. It shrieked through the palaces, and great gusts tore at the doors and windows. But this wind was clean, a clean wind from the sea, dustless and pure. The Empress rose from her throne and she walked into the court beyond and she too lifted up her face toward the swirling sky and she smelled in the wind. At this same instant the skies opened and rain came down, a cool strong rain, strange in winter but how welcome!

"A good omen," she murmured.

Her ladies ran out to escort her in but she put them aside for one more moment while the rain fell on her. And while she stood a great voice rose from far beyond the walls, the sound of many people crying out together—

"Old Buddha—Old Buddha—sends the rain!"

Old Buddha—that was she, and her people called her goddess.

She turned and walked the few steps to her private throne room again and stood there inside the doorway, her satin garments dripping rain upon the tiled floor, and while her ladies made themselves busy with their silk kerchiefs to wipe her dry she laughed at their sweet reproaches.

"I have not been so happy since I was a child," she told them. "I remember now that when I was a child I loved to run into the rain—"

"Old Buddha," her ladies murmured fondly.

The Empress turned to reprove her ladies with all grace and gentleness.

"Heaven sends the rain," she said. "How can I, a mortal, command the clouds?"

But they insisted, and she could see that they desired eagerly to praise her.

"It is for your sake, Old Buddha, that the rain comes down, the fortunate rain, blessing us all because of you."

"Well, well," she said, and laughed to indulge them. "Perhaps," she said, "perhaps—"